S A C R E D
TECHNOLOGIES

Cover and layout design by Lance Buckley

ISBN: 979-8-9946798-0-7 (paperback)

Published by Nicholas Hersey
www.tyherseybooks.com

THE NEW DAWN

BOOK ONE

SACRED TECHNOLOGIES

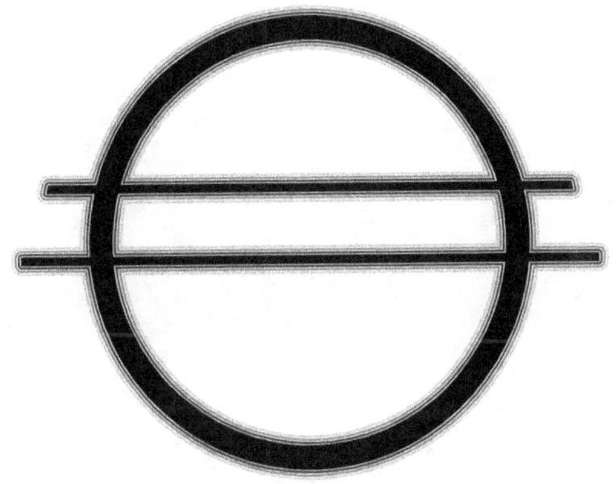

TY HERSEY

For Josephine
AML

PART I

THE CALL

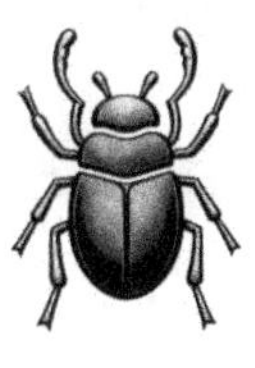

1

WILLOW WAS SO ABSORBED IN the operation that she hadn't heard the evening bells of the Citadel, nor had she noticed that mid-morning had slipped into twilight in a matter of minutes. On the desk in front of her was the engine of a glider bike detached from the rest of its body, which was likely being stored somewhere in the Academy's training repository. The blinding silvers that once reflected off the metal plating had softened into daylight's final ambers. She threaded a pair of pliers through a narrow gap in its casing, her concentration fogging both her glasses and the goggles strapped over them.

There, clinging to one of the valve caps, was the rogue strand of hair that she was certain had infiltrated her pristine creation at some point earlier that day. Careful not to move the air in the slightest, she closed in on the valve. Once the hair sat within the jaws of her pliers, she clamped them shut and plucked the intruder from the cap.

With the extraction complete, the walls of her focus finally dropped, and she looked around the workshop. The number of hours that had passed came as no surprise, as the distortion of time was always the most prevalent when she entered the Academy's sciences lab. Here she could satisfy the urge, the primitive impulse to do the thing that all humans were meant to do—*to create*. Her textbooks left her ravenous mind yearning for more, but within the walls of the Academy they would have to do.

Around her were the workstations of the other students, cluttered with the less sophisticated relatives of the devices on her desk. They all met the same requirements, solved the same problems, and to the untrained eye looked entirely identical. But Willow knew that hers were different. She took pride in her creations, even if they were not allowed to be hers. No instruction was ever skipped and no detail overlooked, no matter how small. Testing was routine, executed with the same precision she brought to every step. Any flaw was addressed immediately, never shrugged off. Her workstation itself was a beacon of order among the others. The stack of blueprints at the corner of the desk sat in crisp formation. Each device was equally spaced and perfectly aligned. An entire academic career's worth of work sat in front of her, a potent reminder that the next phase of life was quickly approaching.

"He's coming! He's coming!"

A boy's voice rang triumphantly down the hallway outside the lab. Willow brightened at Noah's squeaky excitement and pulled herself away from the workbench. Sounds of scurrying tumbled into a graceless *thud* outside the door. Willow stashed the pliers inside the front pocket of her coveralls and started for the doorway, where Noah had just made his recovery.

"Willow! We… we gotta…"

He dropped his hands to his knees. His cheeks, splashed with a hundred beautiful freckles, sucked in air with hungry breaths.

"I told you last week that you shouldn't be skipping physical training," Willow said, her voice edged with smug amusement. "And the week before that I said the same thing. And guess what?"

Noah peeled one hand off his knee in a half-hearted wave. "Yeah… yeah… we get it. You were right, again." He lifted himself up as his breaths began to lose their desperation. "I probably should have listened to you and not ducked out for a midday stop at the bakery, but if we start reviewing my life choices now, we'll be here all night, and there just isn't time for that." He pointed out the window. "The grand priest returns!"

She ripped off her goggles, nearly taking the glasses underneath with them. The strap caught the bun of tightly curled hair atop her head, but she wiggled free and dashed to the window.

"Come on, if you turn that crank, we can get the emergency window open and sit out on the ledge!" she said.

She grabbed one of the handles on either side of the window and pushed until the wheel began to turn. Noah took the other handle, color returning to his cheeks. The tall panes of glass slowly receded into the wall and the warm evening air of summer's end spilled into the room.

"How did you know that I would still be here?" Willow asked, cranking the wheel.

Noah laughed. "Are you kidding me? It's the week of graduation. Where else would Willow Dinn be? There are mere hours left to make sure the angles on your renderings are straight and every last bolt is tightened on your gadgets, all of which no doubt reached perfection long ago, but you're too stubborn to see it for yourself!"

After one more rotation, her lever found its stopping point. She reached across the opening and pulled Noah by the arm to the ledge outside. The stone beneath them had begun to cool as the sun kissed the horizon, but the warmth of his company never seemed to fade.

Every time she sat out here, she always hoped that the city would seem less claustrophobic, but somehow the rows of uniform streets and clustered buildings felt even more cramped from this height. The houses and shops were all the same. Their individual characteristics were just strong enough to differentiate them from one another, but that was where the distinctions ended. They had all been designed from the same schematics and under the same set of restrictions, with the same set of eyes ensuring their compliance.

The back of Noah's round head popped into her line of sight, searching the ground far beneath her feet. "They were at the southern gates when I came running up here. They should be passing by any second now!"

Willow shoved his head out of the way and examined the street below for herself. "What do you think it's like in the other capital cities?" she asked. "Do you think the kids in Laurelmist are watching their grand priestess return?"

Noah chuckled and Willow shot him a look.

"What's so funny? Don't think a girl can be the head of a city?"

"No, no! Willow, you're so smart you could start running this place the day after we graduate. I was laughing because… all I can picture is our grand priest in a dress."

Willow snorted and fell into Noah's shoulder. She felt him bouncing along with her, and the more he laughed, the harder she found it to stop, powerless against the sounds of his joy.

Noah flung his arm toward the street. "Here come the bikes!"

Far below, a line of single-rider vehicles zipped around the corner of the block, gliding over the cobblestone. The pilots angled forward, their grips steady on the throttles. They wore the same dark red that patrolled the streets, guarded the Citadel, and waged war outside the city walls. Today though, their responsibility was securing the return of the grand priest.

As the glider bikes raced underneath Willow's dangling feet into the heart of the city, sharp orange flares caught the glints of chrome on the back fins of each vehicle.

"Ow," said Noah, pinching one eye shut. "Sometimes I think Roh put those good-for-nothing restraining bolts on the rear thrusters just to give me headaches."

Willow smiled, because in his world there was always space for the things that mattered in hers—even if he never got the names right.

"Those restraining *clasps* are what keep His children safe," she said, but the words were not hers. "They limit the output of the thrusters to eighty percent, therefore reducing the risk of accident to the pilot and allowing His children to safely fulfill their sacred obligations."

Noah rolled his eyes and leaned closer. "I bet yours can hit a hundred perc—"

"Shush!" She flipped around, her heart in her throat as she scanned the workshop behind them. "You know what would happen if anyone found out, Noah."

"I know, I know, I'm sorry…" He lowered his voice but couldn't hide his zeal. "I just get so excited thinking about it! No instructions. No teachers. Just you, the real you, using that big old brain of yours." He poked a finger into the side of her forehead. "At least tell me this—do you think it'll be done anytime soon? What's left?"

Willow brought his finger down slowly but didn't let go.

"You know what's left." She looked out at the plaza in the city center. "It's the one thing that turns an already suspicious after-school project into an outright crime. It's too dangerous."

"So, you're just going to bail on it? You can't just give up."

Willow shrank into herself. "I don't know. After everything… it's all just so confusing."

A breeze swept between the buildings below, and she felt his thumb graze hers.

"Are you going to be alright tomorrow?" he asked. "I can tell Madame Rex you got sick or something."

"You don't lie, Noah."

"I would for you."

Willow's smile was weak, but it was the best she could muster. "No, it's okay."

Doubt pushed down on Noah's brow.

"Really," she said. "I'm trying my best to just move on. If I keep making a big deal out of it, then it keeps being a big deal, you know?"

"I guess. But you better believe that I'll be right there beside you the whole time."

Willow looked down at their knotted hands and her smile steadied. "I'm counting on it."

At first, she thought the moment had gotten the best of them, their joined hands trembling. But then the ledge shuddered beneath them as the sky rumbled and people spilled into the streets below. Windows flung open. Rooftops were claimed. Eager faces looked up to the heavens. Hands that were not clasped tightly in prayer pointed to the sky. The sounds of celebration were drowned by the roar from above as a dark shadow swam over the street.

Willow's curls broke loose as the wind picked up. Squinting, she watched the belly of the transport skim the rooftops, blotting out the sun in sudden midnight. Its wings stretched the width of two city blocks, cutting through the air on a direct course for the Citadel. The ratio of cabin size to wingspan would have allowed for optimal lift efficiency if the thrusters hadn't been misaligned by a few degrees. But there would be time after graduation to notice such mundane flaws in the Sacred Technologies. An entire lifetime.

"Now, maybe if he let us take a ride in that thing once in a while, it would be easier to stay awake during the sermons!" Noah yelled in her ear.

As the booming engines simmered into a distant hum, the noise of the street rang uninhibited. Spirits soared in the excitement that the flying behemoth had left behind, though it was only a taste of the celebration to come tomorrow. As it was at the turn of every season, life was about to change for the citizens of Midbell.

The dancing bodies and outstretched arms melted into Willow's periphery. Sounds smoothed into nothingness, and suddenly the protection of her high-altitude perch crumbled. The rest of the crowd slipped away, and all that remained was the woman with the red hair.

"Noah, look!"

"Hm?" Noah grunted, his eyes still following the transport.

She tugged on his sleeve and pointed down to the street. "There! Right next to the—"

Her head whipped from one end of the street to the other. She picked through what felt like a thousand faces, but the moving limbs and shifting bodies made her search nearly impossible. The woman was gone.

"Gah!" Her fists curled in frustration. "It was that woman with the bright red hair again. She's following me, I know it!"

"Hmm… Maybe she just came out to see the grand priest's ship come back in? I mean half the city must be out there right now."

"She was looking right at me. This is the fourth time I've seen her this week alone. Twice last week. The week before that, when my class went to the water purification plant, I saw her near the entrance before we went in and again afterwards on the way home. It's like she's everywhere!"

"Have you tried saying anything to her?"

"I can't. It's like she's there one second and then—" Willow snapped her fingers. "—she's gone."

Noah rustled his eyebrows. "Well, if she's looking for trouble…" He smacked his fist into his palm. "… she'll have to go through me first."

"Woah! Easy now, Lomp!"

They both jumped to their feet.

"You can't just be swinging those fists around. You might hurt yourself, little buddy!"

Willow's chest sank as the voice that had just entered the room registered: Kurt Avis, the top student on the Academy's military track and Haven's most detestable lowlife. A predator in training pads, his boots clomped against the lab floor as he approached his prey. The boy and girl that came in behind him fanned to either side, all three sniffing out reasons for being where they didn't belong.

Noah stepped back into the workshop in front of Willow. "What are you doing here, Kurt?"

The brute feigned interest in the contents of one of the desks. "We were just doing some rounds… Wanted to stop by and admire all the hard work of our colleagues." He snatched a metal sphere off the desk and tossed it up to himself.

Willow's blood reached a boil before the orb made it back down. "Put that back! It's not a toy!"

"Oh relax! We're not hurting anything." Kurt tossed the orb to the other boy, who discarded it on a different desk.

"You shouldn't even be here," Willow said. "The lab is only for the students in the sciences only."

"What about Lomp? He ain't exactly built for the sciences if you know what I mean," Kurt snickered. "Actually… maybe if he spent a little more time reading and a little less time stuffing his face…" He threw the back of his hand at Noah's stomach.

"Don't touch me," Noah said, shoving the meaty paw away.

The contact of their hands sucked the air out of the room. Something flickered in Kurt's eyes, and even his cronies held still. He dropped his head and laughed.

"Take it easy, Lomp! I'm just kidding around."

Willow knew it was a fragile respite.

"Say, what were you two doing up here all alone?"

He wasn't owed a response but the opportunity to give one never came. The other girl started smacking her lips together and the boy gave a repulsive imitation of what he thought kissing sounded like.

Kurt slapped his hand over his heart. "Aw, that's so sweet. Come up here for a little privacy before the First of Season tomorrow?" He whistled around the room. "I'll give it to you, Lomp, this is quite the date spot. Nothing more romantic than the smell of chemicals and burning metal."

Noah's face flushed a ripe shade of vermillion.

"We were watching the grand priest return from the Council of Four," Willow said. "Thought you'd be there to kiss his feet when he landed."

Kurt chewed on his vile response. "I bow before Grand Priest Talon just like my father, and his father before him, because our family has walked His righteous path for generations."

Willow glared at Kurt, who flashed a horrible grin.

"Better to be born on your knees in faith than at the end of a rope in sin," he said.

She shuddered as his words crawled down her spine, and she popped her knuckles one by one.

"Knock it off!" Noah barked, then charged at Kurt with all his might.

Still savoring Willow's reaction, Kurt was caught off guard and crashed to the ground between the rows of desks. When he lifted his head, his enraged eyes locked on Noah.

"You're dead," Kurt said, and lunged forward.

In a flash Kurt had Noah pinned to the ground, squirming by the throat. Willow tried to pull him off, but he knocked her to the floor with ease. His fist rose to the ceiling, but before it could come hurtling down, a hand wrapped around his wrist.

"Mr. Avis!"

A second hand grabbed the back of his collar and yanked him off Noah. Above them stood a woman dressed in the fine emerald robes of a Midbell educator whose presence flattened any antics, just as it had in the halls of the Academy for decades. Her hair was pulled back as tightly as her face, and the eyes behind her glasses were knives, pointed at the pair of boys on the floor.

"The youngest member of the High Army's most celebrated family assaulting another student? After hours in an area of the Academy in which you have no business being? Need I explain the optics to you?"

"I..." Kurt stammered.

"Get up and go home," she said. "I hope you can manage a few more hours without finding any more trouble. Commander Logan is expecting all the military-track students in the plaza at daybreak—and his patience for such behavior is far less forgiving than my own."

The many years' worth of never hearing the word "no" stained Kurt's face with a pathetic pout. He climbed off the floor, and without his entourage, which had conveniently disappeared, he marched to the door alone. As he stood in the entrance, his devilish eyes shot a look over his shoulder, and he flashed that horrible grin one last time.

Willow grabbed Noah's hand and hoisted him up. "Are you okay?"

He stared back at her, concerned. "Are you?"

Madame Rex jumped in. "Mr. Lomp, I am not sure whether to lecture you on the stupidity of your actions or commend you for the sheer bravery required to attack someone who has more muscle mass in one arm than you do in your entire body."

Noah lowered his head, smirking.

"Regardless, I must issue the same warning to you as I did to him. This laboratory is for the use of students within the sciences designation only. I'm sure Miss Dinn would be happy to recount her accomplishments to you somewhere off school grounds."

"Yes ma'am," Noah said.

"Furthermore, you should be preparing for your tour of the mines later this week. You must have the operating procedures memorized by heart if you hope to step foot down there. The foremen do not budge when it comes to protocol. One step out of line can have severe consequences."

"I understand."

"Good." Madame Rex switched to Willow. "Any doubt that your work does not exceed the caliber of the city's finest engineers is assuredly the result of exhaustion, Miss Dinn. Now, get that emergency window shut, and then I want you both to go home."

They nodded and went to the levers. As the panels slid shut, Willow stole one last peek at the street below. Among the hundreds of people still on the streets, she found only one, and the rest of the world softened into a blur. There, right where she had left her, was the woman with the red hair.

She blinked and the woman was gone.

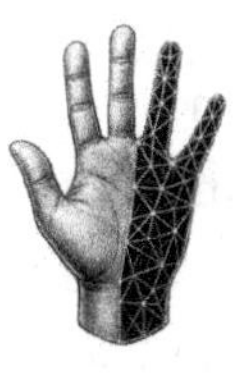

2

TWO VERSIONS OF THE SAME world had been created from a single point of intervention. Both existed without ever touching, connected only by their shared origin. The reflection in the storefront window placed Annika in a world identical to the one she knew, but one she would never be able to access. Here, she could only be an observer, watching her own image. She looked the same: a capable build, viridian eyes that were keenly alert to the activity in the plaza behind her, and bright red hair that held the early-afternoon sunlight. People around her moved as echoes of themselves, and the buildings she saw were mirrored translations of Midbell's architecture. They were all one half of a whole, forever forbidden from coalescence.

A tap on the other side of the glass broke her trance. Her focus adjusted to the inside of the store, where a bald, thick-necked man with rogue whiskers was staring back at her, arms folded atop his protruding belly.

"If you're going to buy anything, get in here and make it fast!" shouted the muffled voice behind the window. "The First of Season is about to start!"

She blinked at him emptily and then walked away. The utility of the vantage point would expire soon anyway. On this day of celebration, as it was in all four capital cities of Haven at the beginning of each season, the people of Midbell assembled to witness the miracles that their creator had sent them.

From the back of the forming crowd, Annika could see all corners of the plaza equally. Hordes of rapturous citizens were accumulating fast, covering the marble groundwork and forcing conversations into full-breath exclamations.

"Praise the Sacred Technologies!"

"May he offer Roh's blessings!"

"Shine upon us His light!"

"Will he tell of more attacks from the constructs?"

Above them all loomed the Citadel, a towering black cathedral at the heart of Midbell. Its midnight hues came from the volume of Torridium required to build such an extravagant structure, which could have powered the city for a decade. The tallest spire pierced the cloudless sky, dyeing a sliver of the atmosphere in perpetual night. At the top was a large golden ring, intersected by two horizontal lines—the same insignia the soldiers wore on their chests into battle, and that stamped the bottom corner of every blueprint worthy of the Church's approval.

Two soldiers ascended the steps on either side of a platform at the base of the Citadel. Their maroon armaments clanked with each movement, and the black spears in their hands weaved in and out of visibility against the Citadel's exterior. They stopped at the top of the stage, facing one another, and then pivoted to the audience. The volume of the plaza swelled—soon the First of Season would begin.

And soon the target would arrive.

There were shopkeepers, engineers, miners, artisans, clergy—but aside from the coddled infants and toddlers hoisted onto shoulders, there were no children. The Academy had yet to release its students, so Annika would wait.

She allowed the constraints on her focus to loosen, because tracking the target was not her only reason for being here—with an entire city in one place, the availability of data was plenteous.

The plaza rippled across a spectrum of emotions: timid glances to unrestrained outbursts of joy; friends embracing and strangers meeting for the first time; individual citizens amalgamating in the acts of a shared ritual. Their bodies spoke as loud as their words. Eyes flashed, stances shifted, pitches rose, and colors fluctuated. It was an algorithm with too many moving variables to be measured—it could only be experienced.

Her attention closed in on the hands of two women just a few rows ahead. Their interlaced fingers evoked a warm, deep sensation inside her. It began between her shoulder blades and melted into her chest, leaving her both full and hollow. Her heart rate increased, and a faint response rose to the surface of her skin. The feeling was nameless, but not unfamiliar.

One of the women leaned into the other's ear. Annika narrowed her eyes and let the woman's lips fill the gaps that the noise from the rest of the plaza prevented her from hearing.

"Of all His blessings, I am most grateful to have received you."

A group of broad-shouldered agricultural workers cut into her line of sight and then the women were lost to the crowd. Annika let several breaths pass, lingering in the warmth that the interaction had kindled.

Footsteps scurried behind her and someone knocked into the back of her arm. She turned just as a pair of children ran past her, giggling as they squirmed their way through the audience.

The students had arrived.

She panned over the crowd, sorting through thousands of faces until she found the one she was looking for.

On the heels of a woman adorned in emerald robes came a group of teenagers struggling to keep pace. Unlike the others, the girl at the rear of the pack followed out of obligation, not enthusiasm. Undoubtedly trying to ward off the memories of last autumn's First of Season, she kept her eyes on the ground. She wore ill-fitting coveralls, frayed at the ankles. Even with the additional height granted by a bun of dark, tight curls, she barely reached the noses of her peers.

Clearly seeing the details of her appearance did not hold as much necessity as it once did. A year had been spent learning the patterns of her movements, and her identity became easier to detect through her innate physical qualities—the length of her strides, the distribution of weight, the cadence of her breathing—involuntary subtleties that were unique to Willow Dinn. Mental models were trained on walks to school, a strict schedule of classes that was never deviated from, early-morning trips to the bakery and lazy afternoons at the fountains, moments with the boy that turned into hours, and all the secret outings to the lake when no one was supposed to be watching. Her life ran in parallel to Annika's, but the task was to observe, not to engage. Like opposite poles of a magnet, contact was not in their nature.

The emerald robes came to a halt. While the other students turned to the stage, Willow curled inward, folding her arms across her chest as one might do in the final winds of autumn, not at its beginning. She popped her knuckles one by one, her default response to any sort of distress. Her eyes retreated into the endless sea of bodies behind her, searching for escape, and for a fraction of a second fell upon the only pair staring back at her. She continued her pass, but when she switched back, Annika was gone.

Alternating between the girl and the people in her path, Annika secured a new vantage point. Her watch had been compromised before, and it would be again. The girl was too perceptive, and their confrontation would be inevitable.

But until that day, her direction was to observe, not engage.

The overlapping chatter of the crowd solidified into a vigorous surge of cheering, and the doors of the Citadel opened. Out of the blackness, the svelte figure of a man appeared. Shadows peeled off his face as he stepped onto the stage. The sharp angles of his jaw supported a pair of high cheekbones and converged at the gray goatee on his chin. His eyes were dyed a frigid blue—as cold as the sky would be by the next First of Season. He was dressed in crimson and black robes that grazed the ground with each step. His dignified, somehow lifeless strides were backed by roaring thunder from the audience. Disengaged from the zeal that his presence incited, he wore an expression void of spirit and continued toward the edge of the stage.

Annika exchanged her empty disposition for wide eyes and a smile, flattening her identity into the multitude. Every day was an act, but the First of Season required a performance of a higher caliber. To feign such emotion when she could not define the logic of its purpose was a challenge, but her ability to do so convincingly was critical. So, she cheered, prayed, and shouted hollow words to the heavens.

At the front of the stage, the man woke from his slumber and snapped an electric focus to the crowd. His eyes flashed with vigor and the corners of his mouth stretched to his ears as the soulless disposition with which he had arrived was animated. He threw his hands out to the audience and the plaza shook.

"Bring us His blessings, your holiness!"

"Praise Roh!"

"Smite the constructs!"

The two soldiers slammed their spears in a synchronized *CLANG* that reverberated into the streets. Be it by the wordless command or the raw anticipation of what was to come, the audience stood in silence. Grand Priest Talon was about to speak.

"My fellow children of Roh! Let us rejoice on this holy day! It is a privilege to welcome you all to this autumn's First of Season. Words cannot capture the joy that fills me as I look out upon your faces. You have waited patiently for months to see what new Sacred Technologies the Creator would bring us, and it is my privilege to deliver these blessings to you."

Applause erupted, and Talon stretched out his hands.

"Roh has graced us with yet another marvelous summer. We were introduced to some of the most innovative Sacred Technologies we have ever seen! His brilliance knows no bounds!"

Another cascade of ovation fell over the plaza.

"But with autumn also comes great promise. Our farms are flour-ishing and our mines have never seen such high production of His holy mineral! We must be grateful to the Creator, who has allowed us to keep our families fed, our city powered, and our soldiers armed. To bring His ideas to life is the ultimate honor. We are but an extension of His grace—forging Haven's prosperity through His will. And soon we welcome the next generation of disciples on this holy quest."

The younger faces in the crowd lit up.

"This is one of the brightest cohorts of young minds to ever walk the halls of the Academy. Remember this as you carry His wisdom into the world: Roh has given you the talents and tools to fulfill your duties. All you need to do is listen for His call. Come! Hear Him and join us!"

Youthful squeals rose to the top of the noise.

"And we must not forget about the valiant efforts of our military, whose selflessness keeps our families safe and our faith strong. We cannot ignore the reality that there are those out there beyond our walls who refuse the truths of Roh and celebrate the dark arts. If left unchecked, they threaten to disrupt the peace we have worked so hard to achieve. But worry not! As I stand before you, the honorable General Kodo is leading our brave brothers and sisters to purge Haven from the heathens that roam the Wilds. Join me now as we pay respect to those who have sacrificed themselves for the security of our society."

As Talon bowed his head, Annika and the rest of the city followed his lead. The calm that came next found its volume in the absence of noise, but the silence was broken by a lone voice from the back of the crowd.

"Why would Roh allow the constructs?"

The two soldiers on stage snapped toward the source of the question. Talon gently raised a hand to each guard and nodded. He returned his hands behind his back and took a sweeping breath as he looked out grimly over his people.

"I will speak candidly with you, my brothers and sisters. His kingdom is under attack. The danger I speak of is not from the tribes of occultists, nor is it from the many dissenters who roam the Radials, banished from our society. It is a much more sinister evil… one conceived by some unholy deviant whose sole purpose is to bring torment and discord to the lives of His children. The Council of Four considers these artificial beings to be the greatest threat that we have ever faced. These monstrosities have infiltrated our home and will stop at nothing to dismantle the order He has built. They are faceless and nameless. What motivates them, we do not know. They look just like you and me. They will speak to you just like your neighbor. They may even work beside you or shop at your stores! But I can assure you that these abominations are not the children of Roh. No, their origins are from the deepest wells of impiety."

Gripped with horror, the faces of the crowd clung to his words.

"It is now more than ever that we must understand the importance of accepting that the Sacred Technologies are the *only* technologies. We see the danger that results from unchecked development. There is only one Creator, and it is He. Only by your adherence to His code can we maintain a beautiful and harmonious society. It is your unwavering loyalty to Him that will rid our world of this malevolence. I promise you that through allegiance to our way of life—the way He has intended it to be—we shall have peace."

"The nonbelievers will suffer!"

"Supreme is Roh's word!"

Talon basked in the fervor of the crowd and then threw his arms to the sky. Behind him, the top of a giant screen rose out of the stone, its inner mechanisms buzzing with the effort required to raise the colossus. The passion of the audience followed the upward crawl with glimmering eyes and craned necks. Their captivation turned to hushed reverence when a definitive hiss locked the screen into place.

Among the enraptured anticipation was one outlier. Unlike the others, it was not wide-eyed eagerness that shook Willow's body, but the unforgiving conditions of wherever she had been transported to. She was lost deep in the ground at her feet, and when the pressure that creased her brow looked as if it could tear through her skin, she clamped her eyes shut.

Another wave of cresting hysteria pulled Annika back to her immediate surroundings. Awoken from its suspenseful dormancy, the energy of the crowd rose to new levels. She renewed her camouflage, and, just like the screen, her face illuminated with an artificial light.

Cast over the plaza was the giant glowing insignia of the Church. The pixels stung the corner of Annika's temple like a frequency out of pitch. Wisps of a sensation whose origin she could not pinpoint drifted into her awareness, and she could only receive the image with an indirect focus.

"It is time, brothers and sisters!" Talon exclaimed. "Let us rejoice in His brilliance!"

A rendering of a pickaxe appeared on the top half of the screen, while the lower half was filled with dense blocks of text. Annika scanned through the content in a single blink: a vague description, job function codes, and promising yet inaccurate statistics.

"The first Sacred Technology that our great Creator has bestowed upon us this season is a tool for our hardy mine workers. He has optimized our alloy refinement process, leading to the improvement of the metals in the tools that we produce. These new axes will allow our miners to extract up to eighteen percent more of His holy mineral before needing replacement. They are lighter and stronger than ever before!"

The pickaxe scaled down and images of a tunic and pants joined it.

"Along with new fire-resistant fibers woven into suits of our workers, He has set us on a course for the most fruitful yield ever! Praise Roh!"

"Praise Roh!"

Next came a small rectangular box with a grated circle and two small knobs on its face and a thin metal appendage protruding from the back. The blocks of text responded to the change in subject matter, as did the description underneath the rendering:

Voice and Sound Emitter

Captivated whispers danced through the crowd.

"We bear witness to the Creator's brilliance once again! Our society, glorious and magnificent, is built upon the earnest contributions that you all make each day. The citizens of Midbell have shown their devotion to His way of life for generations. All your efforts and toil must be rewarded! He presents a new form of entertainment to relax your weary souls after a long day of service to His kingdom."

Talon gestured offstage. A figure dressed in all red robes ran up the steps and knelt at his side. They extended their hands out to the grand priest, offering one of the boxes seen on the screen. He clicked one of the knobs into a new position. A fuzzy garble came from the box, and looks of confusion were exchanged throughout the crowd. Talon raised an assuring hand and returned to the device. Distortion wavered in and out as he rotated the second knob until a voice suddenly solidified.

"—incivility and avarice that led humanity to the brink of extinction. Roh, our guardian! Roh, our savior! Praise be to Him! By His might, civilization found order. In the light of the New Dawn, life was purified. The damage thought to be irreparable was repaired, and our people were brought to salvation. From the ashes of corruption and villainy, a new world was forged. Loyal to His word, Roh thrust his children into an age of prosperity and holy renewal. And now, if we hope to avoid the mistakes of the Old World and resist the falsehoods propagated by the nonbelievers, we must follow His will until our dying breaths. For through His eternal and benevolent omniscience, He will guide us down the path of the righteous. When we hear His call, we shall follow!"

Talon stopped the voice with a turn of the first knob. Around the plaza, faces twinkled in awe.

"With this new device, households all over Midbell can listen to sermons at any hour of the day! Blessed are we to have such dedicated bishops, who are working day and night to provide these discourses to you. Let these be the light to guide your busy days! Praise Roh!"

"Praise Roh!"

As the sun made its descent, the screen cycled through a multitude of objects, tools, and schematics. Attention phased in and out depending on the relevance that the selected technology might have for the individual. Some were tangible new additions to their everyday lives, such as a new cooking appliance or workplace device, while others, like the update to the city's power grid, were mere background improvements that most citizens would not have ever been aware of had it not been for the First of Season.

Annika received them all. Each mental snapshot was logged into the repository of information collected from the First of Seasons. Different inventions but the same tactic as always—cultivating compliance behind the mask of wonder, presenting the mundane to the people of Midbell as miracles that could only be delivered by the herald of their god. But they learned not to question, only to receive, and they would continue to laud the artifice with praise and gratitude.

Eventually, the plaza's only light was from the glow of the screen.

"My brothers and sisters, what a glorious day this has been! The technologies you have seen today will be implemented into your daily lives with haste! Roh has blessed us with His generosity and wisdom once again. By His will, and His will alone, our society will prosper, for there is only one Creator, and it is He!" Talon bellowed into the night. "Praise Roh!"

"Praise Roh!"

The screen went black and the lamps along the perimeter of the plaza ignited. Hidden mechanisms hissed, and the screen began to recede back into the stage. After one final gesture to the audience, Grand Priest Talon walked to the back of the platform and disappeared into the darkness of the Citadel from which he came. The two maroon guards followed in unison, heaving the massive doors shut, and autumn's First of Season was over.

Some of the crowd dispersed, likely eager to get home and recount all the happenings of the day with their families and friends. Those who remained were quick to rekindle the energy of the day, and ceremony gave way to celebration.

Through the tangle of moving bodies, Annika watched Willow bid farewell to the freckled boy and head for the southern corridor.

Her focus switched from far to near as a pair of footsteps approached from behind. Through the cacophony of other noises, she heard them clearly. Their pace, their weight, their sureness—details she knew as well as her own. In that moment, they were the only sound.

The warmth she felt earlier returned, and when she looked behind her, he was waiting for her.

Cassian.

He had a frame to match her own, but a gentleness in the way he carried himself that made her question how the Guild's greatest warrior could also bring such stillness to every interaction she had with him. The day had left its mark on his face, dusting his jaw with stubble. His eyes, deep and brown, found hers.

"Are you staying here?" he asked.

"Yes."

"Good. Take as much time as you need. I'll make sure she gets home safely and then take the tunnels the rest of the way. Come find me when you get back?"

She nodded and he started to walk away. By no doing of her own, her hand reached out and grabbed his as he passed by.

He spun back around. "What is it?"

All she could do was stare at her hand, interlaced with his, as warmth swirled inside her. She pulled herself free and released her hold.

"Nothing," she said. "Be safe."

As she watched him dissolve into the crowd, she knew there were words left unsaid. She was hesitant to believe that any divine being was responsible for shaping the course of her life, but of all the blessings she had received, she was most grateful for Cassian.

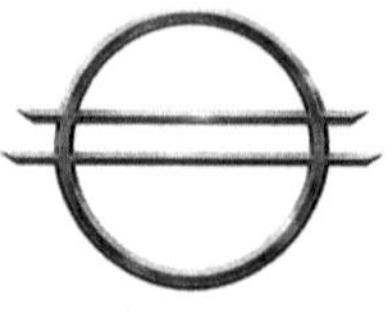

3

HEAT. UNNATURAL HEAT. HEAT FROM the flames of sin.

The ring of gray fire spun behind General Kodo, thrashing its unholy tendrils to the starry sky. Sitting across the eye of the vicious cyclone, Samuel found his form in the grizzled man's mirrored image: back straight, legs folded, sword resting on his lap. With each breath their chests rose and sank in an identical cadence. The air burned his throat and sweat stung his eyes, but not even the roar of the inferno could break Samuel's faith in the Creator's will.

Samuel watched the pernicious flames spin in the golden ring between Kodo's nostrils. The shimmering reflection danced atop a nest of bushy white bristles. Underneath the beard was a face weathered by years spent on the fields of war, but the tiny lines that stretched from the corners of his eyes were carved from experience, not decay. The accolades earned by the champion of Midbell's High Army outnumbered the wrinkles on his face a hundred to one, which was why the Creator had chosen him to lead the most important mission in their crusade's history—an assault on the Dusudé temple.

For generations, the Church of Midbell had searched for the stronghold of the Dusudé people. The sacrilegious necromancers were elusive, no more than whispers across Haven. They had never been spotted inside any of the capital cities, only by the soldiers sent into the Radials who turned their existence into folklore. Kodo had dispatched his most skilled agents to hunt down the smaller tribes and find their origins. By His gentle guidance, fragments of intel had led him to the spot where they now sat as prisoners.

Deep within the forests to the west of Midbell—the Wilds as they were known within the city—the temple hid under layers of overgrowth. A formidable foe in and of itself, the thick vegetation and sprawling treetops had prevented their transports from landing anywhere close to the temple. Forced to make the final leg of the journey on foot, the company trudged from daybreak to sundown before finally breaching the gates of the temple courtyard. It was there that their assault came to a halt before it even began. What was meant to be the glorious conclusion of this chapter of their crusade immediately spiraled into disaster.

The enemy had been dangerously underestimated. Conflicting accounts of their actual numbers, combined with far-reaching claims of mystical powers, had made them an unpredictable adversary. No amount of training could have prepared Samuel or the other good soldiers of Midbell for the myths of the Dusudé erupting into a violent reality. In a matter of seconds after their arrival, they witnessed firsthand the atrocities of which these diabolical pagans were capable. The enemy hadn't so much as drawn a sword. There hadn't been a need.

To conceive of such perverse abilities felt like an impious transgression, and to see them in the real world was to witness a violation of the Creator's natural order. Samuel watched in horror as his brothers and sisters were lifted into the air and tossed around like the toys of a child. Attacks were deflected with the move of a hand, and the weapons they used did not spawn from the mind of Roh. All around him, bodies were bound by gray clouds and twisted into irreversible contortions. But worst of all were the flames. The strongest of Dusudé were able to summon fire from within themselves and weaponize the unnatural force against His children. Blades and shields were powerless against the blistering assaults.

Yet somehow Samuel had survived. Why he had been spared a death in the blaze, he did not know, but he was not meant to question His wisdom, only to receive it.

A third man cut between Samuel and Kodo, pacing from one side of the cyclone to the other. His fingers squeezed through fistfuls of his hair as he crossed Samuel's line of vision again. He muttered something to himself and threw his hands down.

"They've had us trapped here all night. We cannot just sit around any longer. Something must be done!"

Samuel inhaled deeply. As the sweat continued to pour down the back of his neck, he let several breaths come and go. "We must have faith in the Creator, brother. When it is time to escape, He will show us the way." He did not stray from General Kodo. "We must be patient and trust in His will."

Kodo lowered his head in approval. Behind him, there was a glimpse of movement between the whipping tufts of smoke. The blur appeared again at the edge of Samuel's periphery and then disappeared.

"So that's your plan?!" exclaimed the other soldier. "To just wait for them to finish us off?!"

"If it is His will, yes." Samuel waited for another breath to pass. "But I do not believe that it is His plan for us to perish here tonight. I have faith that He will bring us back to Midbell."

"You've got to be kidding me." The man walked up and stood over Samuel. "When I saw that you had somehow survived too, I thought maybe, just maybe, we might actually have a chance of getting out of here alive." His eyes were full of loathing. "I remember you from the Academy. I was in my final year when they brought you in. The best of my class couldn't even hold their own against you in sparring practice. They even let you lead a squadron in one of the simulation tests before you completed your first field evaluation." He leaned down into Samuel's line of sight. "Where's that guy now?"

Samuel left the soldier's words untouched.

"Do you know what sets us apart from these savages?" General Kodo interjected, his tone level.

The soldier straightened his stance and faced Kodo. "Our... our weapons, sir. The Dusudé are not nearly as developed as we are."

"You will end up like our fallen comrades if you believe it is the swords we carry and the metal on our backs that separates us from them," Kodo said. "It is our *faith* that gives us the strength to rise to victory. It is our divine responsibility that we bring this land to salvation. We must trust His judgment without question. The nonbelievers may have broken our bodies here today, but when Roh wills it, we will emerge victorious."

The soldier's shoulders fell in exhaustion. "General Kodo, sir. With all due respect, we cannot remain prisoners here forever."

There was a pause before the general responded. "You misunderstand. We are not the prisoners here." Kodo's eyes broke from their connection with Samuel and found the other soldier. "They can detain us for as long as they want, but we are the ones who decide when our captivity begins. You see, it is only when we abandon our faith that we lose our freedom."

The blur reappeared on the other side of Samuel's periphery, circling toward Kodo.

"Slaughter our brothers and sisters, destroy our transports, it matters not. What remains strong is our faith in the Creator. They will never be able to take that from us." Kodo didn't blink. "You speak of them as our captors, but without belief in Roh, it is *they* who are doomed to a life of imprisonment."

The blur on the other side of the fiery curtain came to a halt behind Kodo, and its shapelessness gained form: the silhouette of a woman.

The soldier walked to the opposite edge of the cyclone and squinted into the flames.

Kodo's eyes followed the movement. "It's a bad idea, soldier. Only the patient mind will be open to see His guidance."

The soldier spun around, gripped by desperation, and spewed words as hot as the cyclone. "Your time has come and gone. Once a great warrior, now you are just an old fool. You mistake your passivity for trust in the Creator. I'd rather try my luck out there than await certain death here."

With a sharp pivot the soldier wrapped his arms around his face and dove through the fire. Over the roar of the whirling flames, Samuel heard metal rolling through the dirt, followed by a fit of cathartic laughter.

"Ha! Waste away here for all I care!" the soldier shouted from the other side. "I will return to Midbell and tell Grand Priest Talon of your demise. He will hear the tale of your failed assault on the temple and know that it was not the wicked magic of the nonbelievers that defeated the great General Kodo. No, it was his own cowardice."

The silhouette behind Kodo raised one arm in the direction of the soldier's voice.

"You are wrong, General," the soldier said. "We do not choose when our captivity begins. We choose when it ends. I choose now. The Creator—no! *No!*"

His words collapsed into a bloodcurdling scream. The shadow drove her other arm forward and the soldier's shrieks choked on themselves—silenced by a *snap*. Metal hit the dirt with a definitive and lifeless *thud*.

In the haunting stillness that followed, the woman's voice pierced the hollowness of the night like a disembodied apparition.

"Tell me, foolish knights—can your god protect you against the heat of a thousand suns?"

Kodo's eyes tightened with contempt. "Your feeble and unholy attempts at intimidation are powerless against faith in His will."

"We shall see."

The ring of flames swelled to the heavens and then flattened into the smoke. In mirrored movements, Samuel and Kodo sprung to their feet and backpedaled until the backs of their shoulders clanked against one another. They held their swords out in front of them as a single unit of two blades and one mind.

Samuel hurried to reorient himself to the surroundings that had disappeared behind the burning wall several hours ago. As his vision began to adjust to the night, the lifeless heaps of dark red scattered around the courtyard regained their form. The moonlight caught the edges of the armor, twinkling in somber glints of maroon. His brothers and sisters had fallen bravely, resting in the solace that they had carried out their sacred duties with honor, all following the path that He had preordained for them long ago.

Beyond the sea of his perished allies, shadowy figures began to take shape. Their distinct forms were lost to the night, slithering through the darkness as one godless abomination. Samuel's grip tightened around the hilt of his sword while the charred and brittle terrain crunched beneath the shapeless motions.

Suddenly a flare of light illuminated the battlefield, revealing the waves of pale gray bodies that surrounded the two remaining defenders of His word. In the light of the shimmering silver flame floating above her palm, the silhouette of the woman was brought to life. Her command had outgrown her youth, and waiting for their next wicked direction, the rest of the courtyard bent to her presence. The cuff of her robe rested at the crease of her arm, exposing the vibrant purple patterns etched into her ashen skin. A mark of sin, the purple disappeared into her sleeve, crawling out of her collar and up her neck. Across her eyes, the streak connected the tattoo from one side of her body to the other. Trapped under the ink was a beauty wasted on such an ungodly creature. The curves of her face were arranged in perfect symmetry like the panels of stained glass at the Citadel. Her eyes, rotted with yellow, still found glints of the light burning in her hand. Dancing on her cheeks were strands of sugary white hair, fallen from the braid that swayed at her waist with each step.

The elegance with which she moved was striking and in direct opposition to the repulsion that her existence instinctively demanded of Samuel. When their eyes connected, his contempt was met with reciprocal disdain.

"How powerful can your creator truly be if your words of worship are only spoken behind a blade?"

Samuel's knuckles pressed through his skin. "His light is stronger than any sorcery you can conjure. We do not fear your wicked spells, heathen."

Her mocking tone curdled into something sinister. "Then you will die braver than the rest."

She swept one arm in front of her body and closed her fist. Gray sparks flew up from the ground at Samuel's feet, igniting another spinning wall of flames. He pulled the tip of his sword back and his toes curled inward as the scorching ring began to tighten. Sweat raced down his forehead, and he felt Kodo's back press into his. Each breath was more of a struggle than the last. But just when the air that he so desperately gasped for began to sear his throat, he heard a voice from beyond the inferno.

"Enough!"

The flames cowered back into the ground and the night's cool air flooded Samuel's lungs. His heart was pounding in his ears as he watched the attention of the courtyard abandon its prisoners. One by one, torches along the top of the courtyard wall ignited with gray flames, lighting the path back to the temple. The swarm of heathens dropped to their knees, except for the woman, who folded her arms across her chest.

Samuel followed the collective gaze to the temple's entrance, where a small figure materialized out of the lingering shadows. The spectral light revealed an older, shriveled version of the woman walking toward them. Her decrepit movements relied almost entirely on the scepter in her hand, but her magisterial demeanor needed no bolstering. Heads bowed as she passed until she finally arrived at her younger counterpart.

"I told you they must be kept alive, daughter." The old woman's voice was more breath than substance. "I need to see him for myself."

Despite her uneven tread, her gaze was steady on Samuel. Her eyes had their own purple markings, but the vibrancy of the color had succumbed to the creased landscape of her face. The hair on her head had lost its luster long ago and was now no brighter than the pallid hues of her skin. Less than an arm's length away, she stopped in front of him. His teeth drew blood from the flesh of his cheek, filling his mouth with metallic acrimony. The older woman was not like the others. She bowed to no one. All the sin and vile corruption that the nonbelievers had brought to His kingdom was by her hand. The faithless found their voice in her. She was the force of depravity acting in opposition to Roh's vision of the world, and her existence in it was the highest sacrilege.

For moments there was nothing, just the godless yellowing eyes of the witch scouring the deepest parts of him. He stared back at her unblinkingly. Deception and perverse sorcery could not bend his imperishable devotion to Roh.

"The Fates have shown me his face before." The old woman drew a long inhalation, not breaking from Samuel. "It is him. He is the borrowed soul."

Murmurs scampered around the courtyard like the winds of the night. With a jerk of her wrist the daughter spun another ball of fire in her hand.

"Then let us kill him now, Mother. We can put an end to all of this tonight."

"No. I believe he still has a role to play in the salvation of our world." The mother waited for the flame behind her to calm itself into smoke and then spoke directly to Samuel. "My name is Ursa. I have been trusted to listen to the Fates and serve my people as their Elder Mother."

"You are a plague in His domain," Samuel hissed. "A blight that must be expunged."

The sword weighed heavily in his hands. In one move, His land could be purified of her wickedness.

But before the thought could translate into action, a spring of flames burst up from the ground in front of his feet. He threw a hand up and pulled his head into the nook of his arm. The heat lashed against his skin and then simmered into nothing. His hand lowered to the daughter's outstretched arm behind the Elder Mother.

"Kyra, enough!" The Elder Mother waved through the smoke. "This violence need not continue. The schism that divides us is an illusion, manufactured to keep conflict alive. You come to us seeking peace for your people, but you fight a misguided crusade."

"Misguided crusade?!" Samuel barked.

"Do not listen to her, Samuel," Kodo said from over his shoulder. "Roh has set us on the divine path. She only seeks to poison your mind."

"Your faith is the foundation of your reality, but I fear it is misplaced," the Elder Mother continued. "This perpetual state of conflict is dependent on your willingness to accept the world as it has been presented to you. Conflict will not bring peace, just as truth cannot rise from deceit. You were born in his shadow, but you are entitled to a life that is your own. Any fate that has been written for you has yet to be sealed."

A gnarl of loathing festered in the back of his throat—a fury hotter than any flame she could conjure. The role of the mortal was not to question, only to receive. To claim knowledge of His sacred plan was as arrogant as it was delusional. The heat filled him, pulsing, as he found his words from the truths that had been carved into the innermost part of his being.

"There is only one Creator, and it is He. Roh has chosen a path for all of us, and from that path, the righteous will not stray. His will materializes through our loyalty to our brothers and sisters, to this world, and to Him. The fate that has been written for me was shaped by His unceasing wisdom. I listen for His call, ready to answer."

Samuel's thoughts quietly settled back into equilibrium. "Your premonitions are nothing more than dreams. Roh's judgment is absolute, and His providence is inevitable."

The Elder Mother's wretched gaze held firm, steeping in her own deceit. "I have searched the cosmos for your god, but all I see is—"

Her attention dropped to the ground in front of her, and through the composure of her wrinkled face, alarm flickered between the cracks.

"What is it, Mother?" asked the daughter.

The noise made its way to Samuel's ears just seconds later, and he turned to the far wall of the courtyard. Leaves rustled in between measured plods, and branches snapped underneath each step. Their rapid and repetitive rhythm was not that of any child of Roh, but one he knew all too well.

"They return…" the Elder Mother said distantly. "More this time."

She lifted herself back up and mustered a volume that rang into the depths of the Wilds. "Protect the sanctum at all costs. They must not get inside!"

The courtyard jumped to its feet. Bodies split in either direction. Some sprinted to the far wall while others rushed back inside the temple. The daughter shot a glare at Samuel and then faced her mother.

"What about the borrowed soul?"

"Let him go."

"Let him go?!"

The Elder Mother brought her second hand to the scepter.

"Keeping him here as our prisoner will only prolong this suffering. If the balance of our world is to be restored, he must be free to find the truth on his own. The Fates demand it."

"But Mother—"

The remainder of the daughter's rebuttal evaporated in the screech of an explosion. Samuel tucked his face in as the courtyard erupted in a blinding flash of light. The ground beneath him shook and tiny pangs of rubble struck his armor. He opened his eyes, but the ringing in his ears slowed his entrance back into the night. Dust filled the courtyard, and through the clouds, he saw a hole blown through the far wall. At the foot of the opening, gray bodies covered the scalded earth. Those who had been farther away peeled themselves off the ground and scampered back into formation. Their recovery was not fast enough, because in a fraction of a second, a man had dashed through the hole into the courtyard.

He looked like any other human, but the precise, measured strides that propelled him forward at unfathomable speeds were anything but. Dodging rogue balls of fire with calculated grace, he weaved through the heathens' attacks.

With the futility of their individual assaults evident, the front line of Dusudé brought their movements into accordance with one another and unleashed a silver blaze. Their vile outpouring flooded the area in front of the wall, counteracting the force that the man's acceleration had accumulated. The onslaught launched him backward, and he slammed into the wall. As his flaming body dropped to the ground, the Dusudé withdrew their blistering assault, and the only sound was the man's skin crackling under the fire.

But any notion that the battle was won was quickly smothered under the man's palms as he pushed himself up from the ground. A series of rigid movements set him on his feet. Flames drenched his body and pieces of his seared flesh dangled by threads of fabricated tissue, revealing the layers of white fibers wound together to mimic the divine form He had used to create His children. Tiny beads of unholy light raced along each thread, granting life to the being by abhorrent and unnatural means.

White light pulsed from his irises, and in the opening behind him, two pairs of glowing eyes flashed in response. Two women entered the courtyard on either side of him. They shared no common trait and not a word was spoken between them. The transgression that was their creation was the only thing that connected them. After one more synchronized pulse across their eyes, the three lunged forward.

"Lay fire to the constructs!" shouted one of the Dusudé.

Kyra whirled back to Samuel, her fingers tightening into a fist. She swung her arm down, releasing an infuriated scream and a well of gray fire at his feet before tearing off toward the others.

Samuel shielded his face from the flames as Kodo seized the opening.

"His timing must not be questioned! We may not get another chance!" the general shouted, breaking into a sprint for the courtyard gates.

Samuel started after him but was brought to a complete stop by a tiny squeeze of his hand. He spun back around to find the Elder Mother's hand latched onto his. The sting of her touch coursed through his veins, bringing his blood to a boil.

"If peace is truly what you seek, then you must be willing to abandon what you believe to be real. The forces that contrived your existence do not have to define it. You are entitled to your own future. The fate of the borrowed soul is not his to decide."

Samuel tore his hand away and thrust his sword at her. The blade sliced through the air but stopped just before her throat. Control over his own movements was suddenly impossible. Agency over his body had been stolen, and the muscles inside his arms felt like they were going to rupture from the unanswered force with which he pushed.

There was no attempt to evade his strike. The Elder Mother's eyes were locked on his, and not even a sword quivering beneath her chin would divert them.

His awareness widened and he noticed a shimmering gray outline around the blade. He traced it down to the hilt, over his hands, and up his arms. Far behind the Elder Mother, he saw the daughter with one arm extended out to him. Her fingers curled, squeezing the air from the night, and he felt his bones collapsing in on themselves. There was no room left for his breath, and his periphery was slowly succumbing to the encroaching blackness.

Then the pressure released and the ground dropped from beneath Samuel's feet. He was launched backward through the air and sent tumbling toward the gates. The impact of his landing knocked his hands open and the sword that had served him since the Academy bid him a clumsy, unceremonious farewell.

Mobility slowly returned to his limbs as he tried to recapture the breath that had been ripped out of him.

"Get up, my boy!"

Kodo yanked him up by the elbow and dashed through the gates. Samuel ran after him but stopped when he reached the forest's edge. The general's form melted away into the dark thicket ahead. Instinct urged him to follow, but some inexplicable force pulled him back around for one last look at the courtyard. The Elder Mother hadn't moved, and her attention remained solely with him. He could barely see the movements of her lips, but her voice found perfect clarity in his ear, and as he disappeared into the forest, there was no escape from her final words.

"Conflict. Life. Calamity. It will be yours to decide."

4

THE NIGHT EDGED CLOSER TO daybreak by the time Annika finally left the plaza, her mind buzzing with the details of a thousand observations. She headed north out of Midbell to Power Plant 3-10, an industrial building on the outskirts of the city. The single, dimly lit screen on the high metal wall surrounding the facility was her beacon. She found the keypad underneath and entered this week's code:

487923

Next to the screen, a panel in the wall slid up, and she walked through the opening. A forest of poles and crisscrossing cables separated the facility from the outer wall. Machines covered in arrays and dials hummed as she passed, electrifying the landscape with their steady currents. Ahead, a wide beam of fluorescent light spilled out from the building's dual glass doors. She strode toward the light, her eyes quickly adjusting from the black of night.

Inside, rapidly changing numbers and graphs filled the screens that lined the walls. More of an extension of their station than waking individuals, the technicians standing at the controls underneath each screen ignored Annika as she slipped between them, and the only movement aside from their eyes was the occasional press of a button or twist of a knob.

Annika brought as little disruption as possible as she continued to the back of the room and through a narrow hallway to the lift. She pressed the call button and entrance was granted. The doors shut and she faced the buttons on the navigation panel, one for each of the three known floors of the plant. She recalled the second code:

221312

The mechanisms inside the walls hissed, and the lift began to move. Downward.

When the doors opened, she stepped out onto a long catwalk that formed a cross-shaped overlook above the cavernous room below. Hulking metal beams extended up from the lower level on either side of the walkway, supporting the towering ceilings. The space stretched far past the footprint of the structure above, its scale suited to the kind of thinking that could not be done on the surface.

She rested on the railing. Even at this hour, the hidden ecosystem was bustling with life. Clouds of smoke and sparks rose to greet her. Movement, significant and small alike, rippled across the grid of workbenches below. The depth of focus ranged from impenetrable concentration on the circuits of a motherboard to collaborative speculation over a sheet of blueprints. Every inch of tabletop found purpose: devices at various stages of assembly, piles of tools in need of repair, miscellaneous components, and stacks of books higher than anyone could reach. Cables snaked around the table legs and fed into the consoles along the walls. The screens above showed renderings of objects that no law-abiding citizen of Midbell could have identified.

It may not have always been her home, but it was the only home she had ever known.

Annika released the rail and started toward the intersection of the walkway. To her surprise, the doors opposite the lift were shut. She paused, then continued down the stairs to the lower level. Moving mindfully through the cluttered landscape of innovation, she did not let her presence interrupt the work of the others. She approached the table in the far corner of the room, littered with broken tools and rusted parts. Hunched over the table was a short, middle-aged woman with a bush of gray curls popping out of a head wrap. The original color of her overalls was long lost, hidden beneath layers of grime. Every fiber of her body was visibly strained as she tried to detach a corroded bolt from a metal rod.

"May I offer some assistance, Toni?" Annika asked.

Toni perked up, shedding the tension as she abandoned her task and spun around. She plucked the goggles off her face and pulled them down around her neck. Two rings of clean skin encircled her eyes, spared from the grease that coated the rest of her face.

"About time you got back. I was starting to think I'd have to come up there and teach those guards a lesson." Toni smacked the rod into her open palm.

"Blending in is easiest at the First of Season. My presence went unnoticed—by the city guards at least." Annika extended her hand to Toni, who reluctantly ceded the rod. With an effortless turn, she broke the bolt out of its sticking point.

"That Willow is too clever. She's going to catch on eventually," Toni said.

"If she hasn't already," Annika added, handing the rod back to her.

Toni unscrewed the bolt all the way off the rod, then added them to the collection of parts on the table. "So, any big news today?" she asked as she inspected the pile for her next venture. "Or just a repackaging of the same old stuff?"

"Nothing too remarkable. Talon introduced a commercial sound emitter that broadcasts sermons at every hour of the day."

Toni rolled her eyes. "Just what the people of Midbell were missing!"

"There was also some new kind of fire-resistant fabric for the workers at the Forge."

Toni paused. "Or for the trouble out west."

"Should we send a transmission?"

"No need. If there's trouble coming, Ursa has already seen it."

Annika nodded and peered up to the doors at the end of the catwalk.

"The five of them have been in there since Cassian got back," Toni said.

"Do you think they will finally reach a decision?"

"Listen, I just fix the junk that needs fixing. But if someone did ask me, I would say that we can't wait around for something to happen to that girl before we step in. It gets worse out there each day. The Church, the constructs. We lost three more field agents this week alone. More than that, she's one of us. She's family.

If there was a response to be given, Annika did not know what it was supposed to be. They both just stared at the heap on the tabletop.

"I need to see Isaac. Do you know if he's awake?" Annika finally asked.

"You never know with him. He gets an idea in his head and he'll be up for days on end… and then sleep through the next two. That being said, I did see the light on in his workshop not too long ago."

"I'll go see. Thank you, Toni. Please let me know if you need any more help with your…" Annika gestured at the table. "…junk."

Toni snickered and shook her head. "Will do. You tell Isaac I'll be over later."

Annika pressed deeper into the sprawl of the lower level. Rows of doorways followed her down a corridor off the main area, open just as often as they were closed, providing intermittent glimpses into the private dwelling units of the other Guild members. A couple was reading in bed with their backs against the wall. Leaning over a small table, a woman fiddled with some gadget by lamplight. Two doors down, a man was asleep at his desk with his head buried in his arms. She collected the portraits of the others like she had the Sacred Technologies, cataloging more data points until she eventually reached the door at the end of the hallway. The transom flickered, and she could hear muffled obscenities between the distant clanking.

Before she could press the access button, the noises stopped. The flickering lights went dark, and she leaned her ear to the door.

Silence.

She hesitated, then pressed the button.

Inside was pitch-black, and after several steps, the door latched shut behind her. She advanced cautiously, squinting deeper into the darkness and reaching out for points of reference. Where she anticipated the corner of a worktable, she found emptiness, and where there once had been a shelf, there was nothing. The layout she knew had been altered, compromising her ability to navigate the space.

A flash of blinding white light engulfed the room. Annika winced, raising one hand in front of her face. Out of the light, a cable spun through the air and wrapped around her forearm. The magnetic ends snapped together and the coil squeezed into her flesh. A shooting pain ran through her nerves, then her arm fell limp at her side, void of any feeling.

Out of the light, a man lunged toward her, wielding a pipe wrench above his head. She ducked out of the way as he brought the wrench swooping down, her arm dangling at her side. His eyes found her through the visor of a welding mask, and he took another swing. The wrench came crashing down on one of the tables as she slipped out of its path, sending a cloud of paper into the air.

He readied another strike, but as he brought the wrench down, Annika shot her good arm up and caught the assailant's wrist. In one swift move she pivoted around the man and twisted his arm behind his head, forcing the wrench from his grasp. She kicked the back of his knee and he dropped to the floor.

Annika knocked the wrench out of his reach as he fumbled around to face her. He got to his elbows and she watched him for any sign of movement, just as she knew he was doing to her. Seconds passed, and when no advance was made, she reached down and grabbed his arm.

"The most talented inventor in the Guild," she said as she yanked him to his feet, "but you are no warrior, Isaac."

Isaac removed the face shield and set it on the nearest worktable, adjusting the tip of his mustache that had fallen out of place during the confrontation. The mask was exchanged for a pair of glasses, smudged and crooked, and above them, one of his eyebrows was partially singed off. He tilted his head to the side until his jaw let out a *crack*.

"I really thought I had you this time," he chuckled.

"Clever tricks alone cannot win fights."

Isaac rubbed the shoulder of the arm that had just been twisted behind his back. "Eh, this was just what I needed!" He winked and tapped his knuckles against the side of his head. "A little sparring match always gets the creative juices flowing."

His long arms—charmingly lanky, as she often heard Toni describe them—stretched down to the ankles of his jumpsuit, which sat partway up his shins, and dusted off his legs. He straightened out and looked at her arm.

"What is this?" Annika asked, trying to pry her fingertips underneath the coil.

"Incredible, isn't it?" Isaac said as he sifted through the papers, tools, and wires on the workbench. "Tell me, how does your arm feel?"

"It doesn't."

"Right, right," Isaac said, nodding as he uncovered a small rectangular device with two buttons and a single glowing light. "Complete paralysis of a limb," he said proudly. "Now don't worry, it's only temporary. Ready? And... just like that—good as new!"

He pressed one of the buttons and the light on the device went out. The magnetic ends disconnected and the coil fell to the floor in a springy mess. Feeling coursed from her shoulder down into her fingertips, which she collected with a closed fist.

She picked up the coil and handed it to Isaac. "You should aim for the legs next time. A stationary target is easier to hit. Even for you."

Laughing, he tucked the coil into the pocket of his jumpsuit. "I think the only way I'd have a chance is if I aimed for the head."

He moved a crate of half-stripped circuit boards and other gutted electronics from a chair onto the floor. As Annika took its place, he settled into the chair across the desk and retrieved a notebook and pen from one of the drawers.

"Alright," he said, and clicked the pen. "Tell me everything you saw at the ceremony today."

Isaac shed his jovial demeanor, replacing it with rigid attentiveness. He followed her every word, reading the subtle movements of her face as she recounted her experience at the First of Season. His eyes did not add assessments of their own. They just received. He diverted his attention just long enough to scribble notes in his journal, written in a scrawl indecipherable to anyone else. Only when her silence told him she was finished did he relax into the back of his chair. His fingers flipped through his notes, and after he found what he was looking for, he smoothed out a new page and pushed his glasses up the bridge of his nose.

"Before Talon took the stage, you said you were drawn to a couple in front of you."

She nodded.

"What was your experience like as you watched them?" he asked, the tip of his pen hovering over the page. "Were there any physical sensations that you can remember feeling?"

She hesitated, struggling to define a logical reason for her fixation on the couple. To parse the sensations in the moment had been a challenge. To understand them well enough to articulate her experience to someone else seemed impossible.

"I… I do not know how to describe them," she finally managed.

"Okay. It's okay." He held steady with her, his face light. "We can start big. Good or bad?"

"Good."

His pen found the page, writing without his eyes ever leaving her. "Shallow or deep?"

"Deep."

"Isolated or widespread?"

"Isolated, and then widespread."

"Short or lasting?"

"Lasting."

"Cool or warm?"

Annika paused, and the image of the women's hands returned to her, as did the warmth it brought. The delay in her response must have held significance to Isaac, whose heed to every nuance of her behavior sharpened.

"Warm," she said. "It was warm."

"Can you remember a time when you felt this before?"

"Yes."

"When?"

The many times that she had felt the sensation played over in her mind, the settings were different, but one factor remained consistent.

"When I am with Cassian."

For the first time, Isaac let a reaction slip through the objectivity required of the task—a smile. He added his final note, then slid the notebook back into the drawer.

"It can be difficult to make sense of these sorts of things," he said. "I appreciate your willingness to share."

She was not sure what to say, so she just nodded.

He drummed his hands on the tabletop. "Now! Speaking of my dear brother, did you see Cassian when you got back?"

"No. The committee is still convening."

Isaac whistled. "I do not envy having to sit through that."

"A longer deliberation could signify that a decision has been reached."

"I like the way you think!" He slapped his thighs and pushed himself up from the chair. "Let's go find out for ourselves, shall we?"

AS THE SUN BEGAN ITS ascent somewhere outside, a new cohort of bodies had assembled in the lower level. Annika followed Isaac as he meandered from station to station, admiring the work of his colleagues. He inserted himself often—sometimes to contribute, but mostly to learn—and his presence was never unwelcome. Between his charisma and intelligence, he was well-liked among the other members of the Guild, and his contributions to the technical advancement of the organization made him an invaluable asset. He bounced from one table to the next, collecting more energy as he went and giving back just as much.

They paused at a table where someone was blowing into the blades of a miniature turbine positioned above a rendering of the Eastern

Radial's charted regions. Wires fed into a small battery, glowing with the charge the spinning blades generated. Isaac explained that the idea of harnessing wind power had come from one of their contacts in the Radial. It was a promising alternative to their society's dependence on Torridium—though one that the people of Midbell would likely never see.

Isaac's attention left the demonstration, not to another table, but to the foot of the stairs where a pair of women had just touched down. Several decades separated them, but they shared the same petite stature, long brown hair, and pointed facial features. Their jumpsuits resembled Isaac's, only much heavier. The weighted fabric looked like it could withstand an explosion, and Annika knew that on many occasions, it had. Hazel, the older of the two, was the head of the Guild's weapons division. Once an officer of the High Army's demolitions subsection, she abandoned her position after an episode of internal sabotage, bringing her talents and infant daughter to the Guild. That daughter, Lin, now stood next to her and served as her partner in overseeing the development of new arms. Together, they also formed two-fifths of the Guild's elected decision-making body.

"Hazel!" Isaac said as they met the pair at the bottom of the stairs. "I finished repairing those battery cells. You said you were going to stop by and pick them up, but you never showed. What in the world could have been so important that you stood me up?"

Hazel's smile stretched from ear to ear, and Lin rolled her eyes in disgust.

"Any other night you know I would have picked them up and talked your ear off, handsome," Hazel said, "but we've been at it for hours. Go talk to your brother. He's still up there with Leon and Jasper."

"Alright, alright," Isaac said. "But you better stop by tomorrow, or later today, I guess. I also cooked up some prototypes for that new insulated coolant you were asking about."

Hazel shook her head, chuckling. "The Guild would be lost without you, Isaac."

They bid farewell to the mother-daughter duo and continued up the stairs. The doors across from the lift were open, and inside, Cassian stood behind a chair at the circular table, looking as though the last several hours had stolen the next few nights from him. The conversation had left his dark hair pushed back, as it always was during discussions about the girl, when stress compelled him to do something with his hands. His arms were folded now, and he alternated between the two remaining committee members seated at the table.

On the side opposite Cassian was Leon, who had joined the Guild shortly following its inception and had been serving on the committee since the body was formed. He sought family after his own was imprisoned by the Church and quickly found an affinity with the city's other radicals. His tenure at the organization had earned him a position of authority, elected or not. Much of the Guild turned to him for leadership after the execution of its founder, despite his agreed-upon role as one-fifth of the ruling voice. Such responsibility weighed heavily upon him, his worn features and sunken eyes a product of not one sleepless night but many. His sandy, disheveled hair fell to his shoulders, and streaks of gray had begun to imbue his beard. He stared at the tabletop, avoiding Cassian's gaze.

Sitting silently between them was Jasper, a small, vicious man with beady eyes and a bald head who Annika had a preference against interacting with. Every word of his was pointed, as if he were always speaking to an adversary. He was unpleasant to everyone, but especially to her. In this moment however, with his feet on the table and the bottom of his face resting in a twisted grin, he looked pleased.

"So, that's it?" Annika heard Cassian ask from partway down the catwalk. "A full year has passed and we're just going to keep waiting?"

"I know it is not the decision you wanted," Leon said, "but it is the one that has been made."

The room shifted to Annika and Isaac as they walked through the doorway, and she could more clearly see the distress that gripped Cassian. It was becoming common to see him in this state: distracted, uncomfortable, and with his mild-mannered composure increasingly susceptible to falling apart. His connection to the Dinn family made the unceasing debate of whether or not to engage the girl more of a personal matter than organizational duty. The source of his determination and torment were one. In the brief second when their eyes belonged only to each other, she felt a flash of discomfort, as if the pain that held him was also hers.

"Phew!" Isaac let out, rubbing his hands together. "I can sense some gears turning in here! The greatest minds in the Guild battling it out, ideas sparking, decisions being made—the energy is electrifying!"

His remark fell flat upon a stiff room.

"Hello, Isaac," Leon eventually said. "Annika."

She nodded.

"I am sure Cassian will fill you in, but the committee has decided to maintain the Guild's current approach regarding the girl. No further action will be taken."

"I see..." Isaac said.

Jasper rocked in his chair. "Listen, we all want what is best for her. It's just not the right time."

"Don't pretend like this has anything to do with Willow's well-being," Cassian snapped. "You only care about what she can do for us."

"Oh, here we go again," Jasper said, rolling his eyes.

"No." Cassian took a step forward. "I'm tired of you all acting like you have any concern whatsoever for her happiness, or even her safety. She is all alone out there in a world that has already taken so much from her, and soon enough it will take what's left. We're waiting for a sign that will never come. She's too smart and too scared to show her true self. The second we know, the Church will too—and once they have her, there will be nothing we can do."

Leon pressed his hands together in front of his face and spoke with a fragile tranquility. "There is no evidence to suggest that she is anything like her father. The idea is based on an assumption, and any amount of uncertainty in this matter is too much. Premature contact would not only put her in danger, but jeopardize the safety of the entire Guild. Kip didn't want to implicate her in any of this unless he knew she wanted to be. Don't confuse the person she is with the person *you* want her to be."

Cassian was breathing heavily.

"Furthermore," Leon continued, "she may have information we need. You know what is at stake—*who* is at stake."

Jasper swung his feet off the table. "Should we really be discussing committee matters with non-committee members? Especially, you know…" He shot a barbed look at Annika. "I mean, we were nominated for a reason, right? We asked the Guild who they thought would be fit to lead and they chose us. Now, I just feel like it would be an insult to everyone else if we start blabbing about vital information with anyone who walks through that door. And besides, if their input truly mattered, wouldn't they have been here with us in the first place?"

"Annika is part of this mission," Cassian said firmly. "She deserves to know everything the rest of us do."

"Pfft, of course you would say that," Jasper spat.

"Both of you, please!" Leon squeezed his eyes shut and brought his fingers to his temples. The sounds from the lower level percolated into the room, and after several coursing breaths passed, his weary eyes opened back up.

"We have said all that needs to be said." He looked at Cassian. "You and Annika will continue to monitor Willow, but the decision to intervene will be made by this group. I must reiterate that any amount of uncertainty is too much uncertainty. When and if the time is right, there won't be any doubts—there can't be."

Cassian folded his arms again.

Leon flipped over a small circular mechanism from the center of the table and sighed. "This assembly took far longer than any of us wanted it to. I thank you both for your deliberation, but it is best that we all retire for now and get some rest."

Without any room for rebuttal, Leon rose from his chair and started for the door. Jasper was on his heels, following eagerly down the stairs, and the pair disappeared into the entrails of the lower level.

Cassian was leaning over the table, his hands pressed flat against the surface. He stared into the tabletop, untethered from the present.

As quietly as Annika had ever seen him move, Isaac slipped into one of the chairs. He tilted his head back and let his attention drift up into the ceiling. His presence added nothing and took nothing away. It simply coexisted alongside Cassian's. For several minutes, the brothers sat in mutual silence, and although nothing was happening, she sensed a need to avoid interrupting.

"I can't wait for her to see this place," Isaac finally said.

Cassian looked up, confused, but Isaac did not meet his eyes, still gazing somewhere beyond the ceiling.

"She'll get to meet everyone and see what real science looks like. Maybe she'll even get her own room. I can show her all the things that Kip showed me… show her what a mess I've made of his lab."

Cassian smirked and then dropped his head. It was quiet for a few seconds before he looked back up. "How can you be so sure?"

"Because you were right before. When we know what Willow wants from her life, so will the Church. In that moment, it's going to come down to what's more powerful—the force determined to stop her, or the one that wants to see her set free. I've imagined that scene playing out a thousand times in my head." Isaac faced Cassian. "And every time, I'd bet on you."

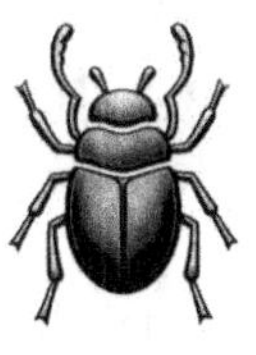

5

THE ACADEMY'S ASSEMBLY HALL WAS teeming with anticipation, a sputtering teakettle about to spill over. Every seat risked toppling over from the excitement, and chatter buzzed through the mass of first-year students as visions of their futures spun in their minds. Willow stood at the front of the hall, an unnoticed feature of the backdrop unable to compete with their gilded fantasies. She remembered sitting where they sat, a cloud of despair among the rippling waves of sunlight.

The screen beside her powered on and the emblem of the Church appeared. Some said it was the circular and infinite faith that bound His children together, but to her, it was the symbol of the toxic obedience required of anyone who dared to be born into a system to which they could not consent. The insignia was on the corner of every blueprint she received, permanently stamped onto her creative process. It marked the covers of all her textbooks, infecting the pages inside with the curse of monotony. On the sign of every storefront, engraved into the chests of the guards that passed her by, and mounted atop the Citadel, the watchful eye of the Creator never seemed to blink.

With the screen on, the noise from the other students had been unplugged, and Willow's invisible presence became the focal point of the entire room.

"I see the anticipation of the designation assignments has spared me the trouble of wrangling your attention." Madame Rex perched behind a podium to Willow's left, her voice finding every corner of the hall.

"With your core studies complete, your education at the Academy will continue for the next four years within one of the three designations, decided by your performance on the aptitude assessment."

On the other side of the podium, Kurt rocked in his chair with an apathy that only someone of his entitlement could embody. Nobody was looking at him, so he gave himself permission to vacate the situation entirely. He was the closest person to Madame Rex in the hall, yet it was unlikely that her words had permeated the endless churn of self-absorbed thought happening inside his head.

Willow despised the oaf.

"The assessment was created to evaluate your unique skills and find the correct designation for you," Madame Rex continued. "Roh guided the architects long ago to design a system that balances our citizens' lifelong happiness with a maximum output of productivity for the city. His wisdom can tell us where you will be most fulfilled with a greater degree of certainty than you ever could."

Willow traced Kurt's sleazy gaze to a pair of girls in the front row, giggling and flushed with infatuation. Despicable.

"Before receiving the results of the assessment, you will hear from members of the graduating class who have generously agreed to share their experiences in the designations."

Text replaced the emblem on the screen:

SCIENCES

"Our first speaker is the top student in the sciences designation with an impressive portfolio of Sacred Technology recreation. Her assembly error rate is less than a thousandth of a percent, matched only by the city's most experienced technicians. Based on her academic performance, she will become an indispensable asset to our society. Please welcome Willow Dinn."

Willow watched her last name darken the room. A few students clapped. Most just stared.

"Thank you, Madame Rex," she said, steadying herself. "Students in the sciences designation engage in a wide range of tasks, but at the core of all our work is the integration of the Sacred Technologies, bringing the Creator's will to life. It is our job to make sure they are built, implemented, and operated as He intended."

"Indeed." Madame Rex faced the room. "Who would like to explain where the Sacred Technologies come from? Yes—Newt Lomp." She gestured to the hand that had just shot up.

Willow smiled as the youngest Lomp, a familiar freckled face, popped up. For two brothers that apparently only shared half of their gene pool, they looked an awful lot alike. The time had never felt right to ask, but she suspected that Noah, Newt, and their sister Nina all shared a donor.

"Grand Priest Talon," Newt said assuredly.

"Yes, but where does His Holiness acquire these plans?"

His voice cracked. "Um… well… he tells us all about the new stuff at the First of Season…"

Willow stifled her amusement at the familial tendency for confidence to spurt out only to lose its grounding just as fast as it came. The week before, she had been venting to Noah about a faulty battery hookup in a quarter-scale transport that her class was working on. He listened carefully as she explained what she thought might be causing the problem, but before she could reveal the culprit, he blurted out the only term he could remember from a previous story. "The torque converter?!" She laughed because he was utterly wrong, but his enthusiasm was endearing. He didn't know the first thing about the circuitry of the battery hookups. He had just been so excited to be with her and have anything to contribute to the conversation.

"Sit." Madame Rex turned to Willow. "Would you care to pick up where Mr. Lomp left off?"

She nodded, preparing a delicate recitation in her head of the words she had heard a thousand times. "There is only one Creator, and it is He. Since the New Dawn, Roh has guided us with His boundless wisdom. He conceives new ideas for the sciences and imparts them onto the Council of Four. The grand priests and priestesses then transcribe these ideas into blueprints and share them across Haven, stoking awe, cultivating fulfillment, and improving our lives."

"Brilliantly said," Madame Rex affirmed. "Now, how will you be serving our Creator after graduation?"

Willow braced herself. "I am to become an engineer, working in vehicle development for the High Army. I will help build any relevant new Sacred Technologies that arrive each season and oversee any existing production."

A hand went up in the audience. "Will you get to build transports?"

"I've been trained to help with engine assembly and diagnostics, when the need arises, but my specialization is in single-rider vehicles."

"Glider bikes?!"

Willow nodded and the room began to stir.

"Woah!"

"I want to build a glider bike!"

"Nyoom!"

"Do you ever get to build something that you made up?"

The hair on Willow's neck turned to pins. If there had ever been air in the hall, she couldn't remember what it felt like. The front feet of Kurt's chair came creaking down to the ground, and every face in the room waited for her response.

"No," she said, avoiding eye contact with any of them. "Only the Sacred Technologies, delivered by a grand priest or priestess, are permitted to be built. The introduction of any other technology into our society is an act of treason."

Her stomach tightened into a cold knot.

"Treason, in its highest form," Madame Rex said, stepping out from behind the podium. "There is only one Creator, and it is He. Roh is the only one with the brilliance to provide us with new technology that will fit seamlessly into the harmony of our world. Anyone who believes otherwise is a danger to us all. He has given us everything we need to live beautiful and prosperous lives. Anything else would throw our world out of balance and send us back into an age of savagery."

A heavy stillness swept the hall, until the same voice that had started the digression piped up again.

"What about the Underground? Don't they invent things like the Creator?"

Willow emptied her knuckles of air. If anyone was suited to speak about insurgency hiding in the shadows of Midbell, it certainly wasn't her—a fact that everyone in the room was aware of. She prayed to Roh or anyone who was listening that whatever was about to come would pass quickly.

Madame Rex drew a fierce and mighty breath, but her lips froze in the beginning curves of a searing admonishment. Her eyes slid to Willow. She straightened, burying the fury under a revived poise.

"There is only one Creator, and it is He," she said evenly. "As for the terrorist organization known as the Underground, they shall be the subject of this warning, and then it is never to be spoken of in these halls again." Her voice sharpened. "These degenerates have chosen to disregard the delicate balance of advancement and order upon which the cohesion of our society hinges, undermining the peace of our city with their unsanctioned creations. Unrestrained innovation will inevitably lead to chaos. Only He has the wisdom to prevent our world from descending back into the madness from which it was born. He alone knows the path to salvation. Praise Roh!"

"Praise Roh!"

"Now," Madame Rex said, settling back into her post, "before we deviate for too much longer, we must continue our tour of the designations." She faced Willow. "Thank you, Miss Dinn."

The text on the screen changed.

MINISTRY

Madame Rex looked at Kurt and flicked her head begrudgingly toward the center of the room. He slapped his hands on his knees and pushed himself off the chair. His boots clomped through any etiquette, and his foul gaze found Willow.

He wanted her to take the bait—she knew that—but she refused to give him the acknowledgement of eye contact. His boyish odors of adolescence curled her nose as she headed for the empty chair, and just as their shoulders brushed, he leaned in and spat out a venomous whisper.

"Daddy would be so proud."

Willow winced but stayed true to her commitment. She got to the chair as fast as she could, and the second she sat down, her eyes clamped shut. Tears threatened to break through, but she wouldn't give him the satisfaction of seeing her cry.

A murmur turned into a rumble and suddenly the hall was chanting Kurt's name. He waved and pointed to the group of boys in the back row who had started the whole thing. An introduction was completely unnecessary, but the poster child for the graduating military cohort wasn't about to pass up an opportunity to hear his name aloud.

"How we doing, everyone? Kurt Avis, ministry designation." He licked the rancid thrill of the moment from his lips. "Top student in the military track."

The chanting abandoned any coherent pronunciation and gave way to a wave of cheering. His admirers in the front row chirped and the back corner whistled. He savored every last drop of attention, until Madame Rex cleared her throat.

"Alright, alright," he said, waving both of his hands. "You want to hear about the ministry designation and I'm your guy!"

"I thought it was the military designation!" someone shouted.

Kurt snorted. "Well, it probably seems like that—"

He dared a glance at Madame Rex, who waited for him with a piercing glare. "But... that would be greatly undervaluing the rest of the ministry and the indispensable work they do to ensure that we can serve the Creator! Where would Midbell be without its educators, bishops, and all the other clergy? Surely I can't imagine—"

"Come on! Tell us about being a soldier!"

"Yeah!"

That horrible grin reappeared. He folded his hands behind his back and started to pace in front of the screen.

"Well, my loyal comrades, let me tell you this: there are some of us who have heard His call—a call for a higher purpose. He has reached down to us, and we, His chosen few who are not satisfied with the necessary but meager contributions that other careers bring to our society, have taken His hand! We devote ourselves entirely and selflessly to the betterment of our fellow citizens as shepherds of His vision for our world!"

The faces of the students radiated adventure. Life as a soldier in the High Army was said to be one of valor and nobility. They dreamt of their futures as crusaders, traveling to the far corners of Haven to protect the holy creed of the Creator. Triumphant battles were fought. The wretched nonbelievers were slayed. They returned home to Midbell as heroes, parading through the streets with swords held high.

Willow's stomach knotted in disgust as she watched Kurt bask in the wonder of the others, standing at the gates to the deceptive path to glory that he had just opened to the impressionable minds before him. She wondered if he had ever once had a thought that was his own. Not one that he had heard at a First of Season, or in the sparring room, or delivered by his older brothers from the barracks. One that was entirely his own.

"Our first assignments will depend on the needs of the commanding officers. Some might be stationed here inside the city as patrolmen, prison guards, or protectors of the Citadel. Others will venture away from their homes and go where He leads. We trust the purpose He has given our lives. We are not meant to question, only to receive."

"Will we ever be free of the nonbelievers?"

"Yes," Kurt said with conviction. "Out there beyond the walls it's even worse than you think. The legends you've heard are true. Infidels roam the Radials and are plotting against our capital cities. Banished from our society, they will stop at nothing to ensure our demise." His eyes narrowed into slits. "But there is something else lurking outside of our borders… a horrid villainy that is colluding to destroy us, and whose crimes put these gangs of misfits and marauders to shame—the Dusudé."

The students reflected his contempt as he edged closer to the front row.

"They hail a godless creed, and their commitment to the dark arts has pledged their souls to the greatest evil. Their faithlessness will spread like a disease to the far corners of Haven unless we wipe them out first!" His words came faster, hotter. "They are not children of Roh! They are the agents of our destruction! These heathens are responsible for the insurrection and have plagued His kingdom with the constructs!"

"That is quite enough!" snapped Madame Rex, springing from her podium and shooing Kurt away from the screen.

The hall had gone cold. Any delusions of adventure and valor cowered behind the fear stoked by a single word—the same fear that held the entire city in its frigid clutches.

Madame Rex took a measured breath. "We do not know the origins of these abominations, nor can we understand the unholy motivations that brought them into being, but let me assure you that with faith in Roh and an unwavering allegiance to His way of life, His children will always be safe."

The screen behind her changed.

INDUSTRY

"Time is running short, and we must not omit the final designation from our discussion. With the students in industry designation on field tours this afternoon, we will have to utilize the resources we have available to us here."

She gestured to Newt, who shot back up.

"The Lomp family has a long lineage of dedicated workers in the industry sector. In fact, your brother is one of those lucky students out touring the mines as we speak."

"He was so excited this morning he almost left without his lunch!" Newt chuckled. "Almost."

Some of the other students laughed and even Madame Rex conceded a quarter smirk.

"Well, sometimes the excitement that comes from serving our magnificent city is so strong that we can forget about our individual needs." She straightened herself out. "And what about the other members of your family?"

"My older sister Nina works with the animals at Farm 321-C. One of my moms works in the Forge, and the other runs the fabric store right across from the fountains."

"And with your brother heading off to the mines after graduation, your family is a shining example of why the industry sector is so vital to Midbell's prosperity." Madame Rex bowed her head. "Please take your seat."

Newt sat back down, beaming.

"Those who graduate from the industry designation are the backbone of our society, tasked with the widest range of duties by our Creator. We have them to thank for the food on our tables, the power in our streets, the beautiful wares of the commercial district, and most importantly—the production of our most precious resource."

INDUSTRY disappeared, replaced by the structural formula of a chemical compound—a diagram Willow could have drawn in her sleep. Whether soldered into the exterior paneling of a transport or liquified inside the engine, it was the crux of the Church's technologies and the most regulated substance in Midbell. She stared at the rendering of black ore next to the diagram—rich, seductive midnight. Even on a screen, the glossy darkness was infinite, pulling her into the unknown.

"Torridium," Madame Rex said. "His holy mineral is the singular resource upon which all of Haven depends."

Willow drifted farther into the black infinitude. She felt the weight of the ore in her hand—not the physical mass, but the energy stored inside. It was the missing ingredient that could turn her nothing into something.

"The far-reaching applications of Roh's mineral are interwoven with the functions of our society. It is used to forge the weapons our soldiers carry and the armor on their backs, protecting us from the threats of incivility. As the primary fuel source for all homes, military vehicles, and power grids in the capital cities, it is His most precious gift to Haven, aside from life itself."

Outside the confines of the Church's rule, Willow knew that someone could use it for much, much more.

"We must praise Roh for His generosity, for no other element in existence has proven as powerful or versatile."

Someone.

"But we mustn't take this privilege lightly. Contained within is the potential for sanctified and glorious development, but also the most dangerous form of sin. Wielded by a corrupted mind, it will bring catastrophe!"

Her.

A loud *GONG* tore Willow out of her trance. The sound from the Citadel's bells roused a flurry of screeching chairs and footsteps rushing toward the entrance of the hall.

"Return to your homerooms and you will find the results of your aptitude tests uploaded on your individual terminals." Madame Rex's voice found no difficulty rising above the movement. "Today is your first step on a lifelong journey of service, fulfillment, and devotion! Praise Roh!"

As the other students pushed through the bottleneck at the doors, somewhere in the edges of her awareness, Willow succumbed to the gravitation of the rendering on the screen once again. She fell deeper into a world of possibilities. A world of unbridled creativity and imagination. Of wonder.

A world without Roh.

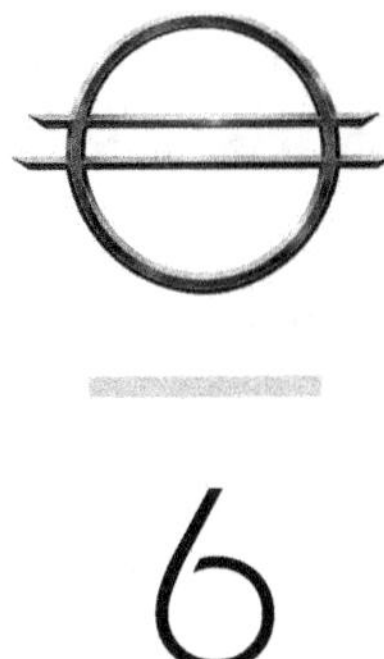

6

DEEP WITHIN THE WILDS, IN the parts of His kingdom where civilization had no claim, Samuel stood at the shore of a river. The water lapped at his boots as he detached a metal tube from his belt and submerged the canister into the river. He collected the currents, screwed the lid back on, and let the Creator's miracles do their work purifying the water.

The morning sun found the strands of blonde that fell in his face. He brushed them back as he stepped onto the shore and grabbed his charred helmet from the rocks. The metal was warm with the energy that the Creator had laid upon the day, and it was up to His children to make use of it.

From the riverbank, he climbed the nearest peak. Wisps of smoke floated above the canopy in the distance—the remains of the carnage from the night before still trapped among the clouds. Flashes of the temple poured into his mind, the Elder Mother's face filling the spaces between each blink. His palm still burned from her touch, and her vile incantations echoed inside his skull. *Life. Conflict. Calamity.* He closed his eyes and tried to squeeze his thoughts clean, but her words were louder in the void.

The borrowed soul.

His eyes flared back open and he shook himself from her hold. Only Roh knew the fates that had been written. The role of His children was not to question, only to receive.

Reclaiming his breath, he traced the smoke to its origin and then looked down at the river. Out of the side pocket of his greaves, he produced a tattered fold of paper and a chunk of ashy tree bark. He added several bends to the collection of lines on the paper and then started in the opposite direction of the smoke.

His feet moved cautiously over the forest floor. The Creator had allowed him and General Kodo to escape the temple with their lives, but witnessing the unholy atrocities of the Dusudé and fleeing in such haste had left them disoriented in the depths of the Wilds. Every rustle was a potential threat, and he would not let his guard down until they were back inside Midbell's walls.

The trees around him grew familiar, and between the staggered trunks, he could make out the small clearing where he had left Kodo. Sitting atop the pair of boulders on the far side were two unopened ration containers, but the general, who was known as much for never missing a meal as he was for his triumphant victories on the fields of war, was nowhere to be found.

Samuel reached for the sword on his back. The air that slipped through his fingers was a bitter reminder of the many things lost on the battlefield. He scanned the area at his feet and found a stick among the debris of the forest floor. It was as tall as he was, and to make use of it in any sort of defensive manner would require both hands. Back in the Academy, he had proven more than proficient with every instrument of His peace, though he always favored the two-handed fighting styles. He moved the weight of the branch between his hands. It had a decent amount of pliability—and it was certainly far from the High Army standard issue—but the true power of a weapon came from the hands that wielded it.

He edged forward slowly, mindful to stay within the shroud of the thicket. A twig snapped and his head shot to a larger tree several paces away. He crept closer, maneuvering around the litter of the forest to keep his approach concealed, and stopped once the folds of bark on the tree gained clarity. From the other side he heard breathing—measured, calculating breathing.

Suddenly a blade came whizzing over his head, and instinct pulled him to one knee, preventing a fast and certain decapitation. The blur had just missed the top of his helmet and lodged itself into the tree. He sprang up and rammed one side of the stick under the elbows above him. His hit broke the grip on the sword and sent the arms into the air. He spun around and drove the opposite end of the branch into the assailant's chest, sending them onto their back. Taking a defensive stance over the body, he angled the stick downward in preparation for a low counter, but one never came. In its absence, the reflexive rhythms of combat came to a halt, and his awareness finally caught up with his body.

Samuel stared at his general on the ground.

"Sir!" He tossed the stick aside and reached for Kodo.

"Ha!" Kodo bellowed as Samuel helped him to his feet. "Look at us. Those godless savages have us jumping at our own shadows."

"I'm so sorry, sir. Why were you hiding?"

Kodo gripped the handle of his sword. "Two of them passed through here just moments ago—hmph!" He yanked the blade free.

"Were they looking for us?"

"I don't think so," Kodo said as he sheathed the sword on his back. "A destination was guiding them, not the hunt. What soulless rituals they were off to partake in, Roh will not allow my mind to fathom."

"Here." Samuel handed Kodo the tube of water from his belt. "We should keep moving."

"Agreed." Kodo took a swig and wiped his beard dry. "How far was the river?"

Samuel accepted the canister back from the general but wasted no water on his own thirst. "Less than two clicks," he said.

"Where does that put us now?"

He pulled the map from his gauntlet and leaned in toward Kodo. "Considering the transport's coordinates when we first landed, it will take us another full day to reach Midbell, at least."

A weighted exhalation blew past the golden ring between Kodo's nostrils.

"We must not mistake adversity for opportunity, sir," said Samuel. "He has a plan for us all. Trust in His judgment and He will guide us down our rightful paths."

Kodo bowed his head. "Let us meet the fates He has written."

THEIR PACE SLOWED ONLY WHEN Samuel stopped to check the map and adjust their course. Even when orienting themselves felt impossible, despair never found him. By Roh's will, they were exactly where they were meant to be, and so long as they trusted in Him, they would never be lost. More important than any physical training or survival skill a soldier could learn was the resilience of the soul. With faith in the Creator, they could endure anything.

The sun was well past its peak when they finally stopped again, this time in a ravine at the foot of a hill whose slope was near vertical. Air flew through the bushel of white bristles on Kodo's face. Samuel looked up at the steep incline in front of them and then offered the water canister in front of the general's heaving chest.

"You must hydrate, sir. Roh has given me the strength to carry you up this hill—but I admit I would rather it not come to that."

Kodo threw his head back with a hearty, breathy laugh and accepted the water. "It will take more than this tiny hill to make me yield."

As he returned the canister, his attention settled on Samuel. "But I wouldn't have made it half this far on my own. You have shown the marks of a model soldier throughout this whole ordeal and proven yourself an exemplary devotee of Roh. It is a disservice to bury your potential so deep within the ranks. A soldier like yourself ought to be on the front line, leading and inspiring. When we get back to Midbell, you will come to the Citadel, and we shall kneel before Grand Priest Talon—together."

The words steeped Samuel in a divine warmth. He could not remember a life before he fell into the care of the Church. Midbell's Sanctuary was his first home, and the abbesses were the only parents he ever knew. The memories of his real parents were faceless shards—broken images that were more fabrication than substance. But Roh had not abandoned him, for he had a place for all His children.

As a boy, the abbesses recounted the stories of Midbell's greatest warriors to him. His youth was filled with heroic tales of honor, sacrifice, and faith, and he learned that true devotion was not a mighty blade or endless rows of cavalry but selfless action for the betterment of his brothers and sisters. The characters became his lifelong companions, and their holy examples led him down His righteous path. They had heard the call of Roh and so had he. From the Sanctuary windows, he would watch the transports come and go, and dream of a day where he too could serve the city that had taken him in.

At the Academy, most of his peers were drawn to glory, not service, and misunderstood the true significance of His call. But Samuel remained grounded in the virtues learned from the stories at the Sanctuary, because there was no higher duty, and to be chosen for such a role was a privilege. When he received his first assignment under General Kodo, one of the heroes whose footsteps brought him to the sacred path, he made a vow to Roh that His trust had not been misplaced.

"It would be my honor, sir," Samuel said.

Kodo placed his hands on his hips and looked up the incline. "This is all dependent, of course, on whether my old legs can make it up this hill!"

Samuel considered their options. "Our best approach might be to work our way up the smaller slants. We should preserve our strength for what may come."

The general nodded and looked up at the sky. "Still plenty of daylight left. No harm in taking the route of extra caution. By Roh's will, we may even be able to see Midbell from—"

Their heads snapped to a small alcove down the ravine where a groan, faint but potent, trickled out from behind the mossy overgrowth. The sound quickly lost its vigor, and Kodo motioned toward the alcove. They navigated several steps ahead of their bodies, weaving silently through the leaves, twigs, and uneven stone. Glistening beads of blood decorated their path among the decay of the forest floor. As drops turned to puddles, the cries from inside the cave weakened into whimpers.

They pressed their backs against the embankment wall next to the opening as the cries swelled into wailing.

"Gahhh…"

Samuel drew the sword sheathed on Kodo's back.

"What do you think you are doing?" Kodo mouthed.

"My life is one of many," Samuel whispered, running his sight up the blade. "Thousands are prepared to take my place should they hear His call." He faced Kodo. "But Midbell needs its champion."

He waited for no countercharge and spun into the opening. The end of the blade guided him through the entrance, stiff with vigilance. His pupils widened to accept the dim hues of the cave's interior, pulling back the shadowy curtain to the gruesome scene inside. Each step stuck to the ground as he followed the crimson trail to a woman's body, mangled and frozen in a perpetual state of deformity, with its sinful gray face to the cavern ceiling. His eyes narrowed in contempt and then spotted a second body just steps ahead. Underneath the tones of dirt and death were the holy dark reds of the High Army—a child of Roh. A scout, judging by the lightweight armor and cartographic tablet clipped to his waist, who had been ambushed while surveying the Wilds. Alone, his brother had managed to carry forward in their crusade and serve Roh until his final breath. His face, at peace inside the helmet, rested in the knowledge that a sacred duty had been fulfilled.

Below the cheek cover was the only wound: a deep laceration carved into the side of the neck. Samuel exhaled sorrow, feeling the pain himself. The lesion was the barbaric work that only the godless were capable of—savage, agonizing, and… clean. He leaned in, brow knit, to find not a single drop of blood. The shadows continued their tricks, and for a brief instant he was certain that he saw a tiny pulse of light from inside the wound.

From the other side of the cave came a soaked gargle of laughter and coughing. Leading with the sword, Samuel pivoted to face the sound. Propped up against the far wall was another Dusudé woman— alive, but barely. The pool of red beneath her grew thicker with each second that passed. Like her fallen partner, she had contributed far more than her physical being should have been able to part with, only her suffering had yet to end.

"What happened here?" Samuel demanded.

The woman spat a mouthful of blood at him.

"Speak, heathen!" he barked.

Just below her rib cage, the handle of a knife stuck out from the layers of soggy fabric, the blade itself submerged deeply into her abdomen. Through the immense pain on her face, she managed a bitter grin.

"Only after the abomination has guaranteed your safety... do you dare to show yourselves. Your people are cowards."

His eyes were slits. "Abomination? What are you talking about?"

"You zealots profess your hatred for them..." she forced out, her resentment the only thing sustaining what little life she had left. "Yet you wear the same crest."

"Lies. Your infidelity has scrambled your mind."

The woman's eyes hungered for one last strike. "The Elder Mother insisted there was value in preserving your life... but Kyra thought otherwise. She said that we should have killed you when we had the chance... and I think she was right. Death... destruction... what else is the borrowed soul capable of?"

Samuel threw the sword to the ground and lunged at her, seizing the dagger and twisting it further into her ribs. Her face twisted in pain, her mouth shaping a scream already stolen by death. He watched the life drain from her eyes while fury throbbed in his, and for several breaths, the blood rushing behind his ears was all he could hear.

"Well done, my boy." Kodo's voice echoed in the emptiness of the cavern.

"She had but one breath left. I only hastened her departure," Samuel said, still clutching the dagger.

"Even so, His precious air is best not wasted on such a vile creature," Kodo said, then shifted to the fallen soldier. "Remarkable. Two of them and hardly anything to defend himself with. A true testament to the power of Roh's—"

Kodo dropped to one knee beside the body. He studied the wound on the soldier's neck, his expression darkening.

"Bring me the knife," he said without looking up.

Samuel wrested the dagger out of the woman's torso. He wiped the blade clean on a dry patch of the woman's robes and knelt beside Kodo. The general rolled the soldier's head to the opposite side, spreading the wound and revealing what Samuel had prayed was just a distortion of the cave's unholy gloom. No blood had left the body because it had no blood to begin with. Underneath the artificial facade, there were no sliced arteries or damaged nerves. The technology inside was so sophisticated that it almost resembled a living being, but Roh's hallowed hands had played no part in the creation of this monstrosity. Where there should have been tender pinks and reds, there was only white. Millions of little fibers connected inside the throat, wrapped together to form a synthetic substitute for human tissue. What lay before them was a grotesque deviation from the natural form—a profane reinterpretation of something He had perfected long ago.

Life, but not as Roh had intended.

Samuel, fighting his own body's instinct to pull away, tightened his focus on a twist of fibers that were still intact, where a faint bead of light swam down one of the threads. Kodo took the dagger and angled the tip of the blade inside the neck. The tip touched the luminous vein, and the soldier's body convulsed.

There was no thinking, only instinct. Samuel pinned the nearest arm to the ground as the general sliced the blade across the construct's throat, irreparably uncoupling the source of the lights from its tendrils.

A breath passed, then two. Seconds stretched as they knelt over the construct in brooding silence. Kodo moved first, discarding the knife onto the cavern floor before removing the cartographic tablet from the construct's belt. The device powered on without hesitation, designed to hold a charge for weeks as all scouting equipment was. A small geographic rendering appeared. Topographic lines rippled out of Midbell to a blinking dot far to the west of the city. Beneath the map were two numbers as recognizable to Samuel as his own name—his and General Kodo's soldier identification numbers.

Samuel reached for the dial on the side of the tablet and changed the scope of the map. The area around the blinking dot gained detail, eventually revealing a pair of coordinates beside the mark—the same coordinates he had memorized before their mission, and the last known location for anyone, or anything, that might be searching for the survivors of the failed assault on the temple.

"Those were our landing coordinates," Samuel said. "Sir, do you think—"

"I don't know." Kodo's response was sealed from further questions. His gaze deepened on the crest on the construct's chest.

Samuel switched back to the body on the ground, his own thoughts twisting into knots. Like the torn fibers of the construct's throat, the threads of his reality felt frayed.

But he was not meant to question, only to receive.

The world around him was vibrating, and as he tried to center himself on the breath, the tremors only grew stronger. Dust fell from the cavern ceiling, and the walls started to shake. A hum swelled into a rumble, and the ground lost its solidity.

Kodo flashed to him, eyes wide. "Get to the top of the hill! Now!"

The two dashed out of the alcove and sprinted up the incline. Tree branches thrashed around them, flecks of debris pinging against their armor. Samuel's thighs burned as the thundering grew louder overhead. They burst from the knot of trees into the clearing at the top of the hill just as a black aircraft swept the ridge. The rumbling peaked as the transport's shadow rolled over the clearing. They threw their arms into the air, but they were too late. The transport soared past them and continued into the Wilds.

Samuel slowed to a stop, Kodo not far behind. Around them, the shaking trees came to rest, and the airborne dirt settled to the ground. The engine noise faded into a hum as the details of the transport began to lose definition.

He was not meant to question, only to receive.

"We must trust in His will," Samuel said to himself between breaths. "We must always trust in His will."

And, as He always did, Roh vindicated his faith. With a sudden change in the hum's pitch, the transport dropped its left wing and swung a wide turn. The wings leveled out, putting the transport on a direct course for the clearing.

Samuel took a step forward, fortified by the Creator's benevolence. Kodo's hand landed on his shoulder.

"The Creator has a plan for us yet, my boy."

Rustling leaves gave way to flailing branches as the craft's shadow engulfed the top of the hill once more. The transport touched down and the cabin door slid open. Two-by-two, six soldiers in shining maroon unloaded onto the grass and split to either side, straightening in unison as the final figure emerged from inside.

Commander Logan, a man of rigid poise, stepped off the transport with his hands behind his back, carrying himself with a dignity rivaled only by Grand Priest Talon. His strawberry hair, which would have otherwise never had a lock out of place, lost all sense of tidiness in the winds of the transport's rotors. A swirl of dust in the air tightened his sharp features and further narrowed the most inquisitive pair of eyes in the High Army. The details of his armor resembled those of General Kodo's—the ornamentation and angular shoulder plates of an officer. On his hip was a rapier, whose gilded handle and slender shape made it more art than weaponry, but the lethality of the blade had proven unquestionable to any who threatened to disrupt the internal order of the city.

"We pray to Roh for rescue, and in our hour of need, He sends the finest commander in the High Army," Kodo said over the drone of the engine. "Logan, brother, we rejoice at your arrival."

Logan bowed his head at Kodo. "It is a relief to see you alive, General." He offered Samuel only a glance and then looked behind them. "And the rest of your battalion?"

Kodo shook his head.

Logan's calculating expression didn't shift. "Let us not waste any more time. We need to inform the grand priest of what has happened at once."

They followed Logan into the cabin of the transport and the other soldiers folded in uniformly behind them. Logan whispered an order to the pilot as Samuel buckled himself into one of the seats along the cabin's narrow walls.

Hours—days even—of travel by foot passed beneath them. The words between Kodo and Logan slowly muffled into oblivion. Samuel was on the transport one second, then back in the alcove. He saw the construct on the ground, taunting him with the symbol of his faith embossed on its chest. Beads of unholy light dripped down the fibers of its throat and shimmered in the darkness behind his eyelids. There had barely been enough time to experience the scene in the alcove, let alone understand it.

But he was not meant to question, only to receive.

7

BLADES OF GRASS FLUTTERED IN front of Annika's face. Over the edge of the cliff, she watched the same current ripple along the surface of the lake below. The sunlight pooled on her back as she lay prone, watching—waiting. Her surroundings came gently, and nothing was missed: the leaves of the trees rustling across the basin, the tiny insects scampering along the rocky shore below, the water cascading down from the lip of the cliff and into the lake. Of all the places their task required them to go, she had a preference for this location. While they waited for the girl to appear, she always found herself listening to the falling water. She received the sound at varying degrees. Sometimes it was latent and other times it was at the forefront of her attention. On its own the sound was objective, but it evoked a sensation, steady and soothing, that she welcomed into her experience.

The reservoir was nestled in a basin to the west of the city, on the threshold of the Wilds. Past the boundaries of civilization, it was protected by the propaganda spread by the Church, whose tales of the savage necromancers living in the Wilds deterred most citizens from venturing too far outside the city limits. Discretion would not have been as important if the one person they needed to conceal their presence from had not been immune to the Church's deceptive warnings. The girl's indifference to their narratives made Annika wonder if such prudence was still even necessary, but the decision to engage was not hers to make.

Cassian lay next to her, his face behind a scope. The device was a descendant of the equipment used by the scouts in the High Army, but the modifications from the Guild gave it an identity all its own. Annika followed the direction of his gaze to the small fissure in the cliffside next to the waterfall. The passageway was too narrow for either of them to fit through, and where it led was knowledge exclusive to the lake's only other regular visitor. His fingertip adjusted one of the three dials between the eyepieces, adding a layer of thermal imaging to the extended vision.

"There's a heat signature inside." Cassian slid the second dial and squeezed his eyes. "It's faint, but there's definitely something in there."

"And strong enough to be detected through the walls," Annika added.

The distant sound of the Citadel's bells rang over the falling water, and he lowered the scope from his face.

"Her friend is touring the mines today," she said. "She will be here soon."

"Maybe then she'll give us a clue as to what she's been doing inside."

Cassian set the device on the ground next to his backpack. Having accompanied them on hundreds of field missions, she was familiar with all its folds, lumps, holes, and tears, but the contours of the canvas looked different lying in the grass next to him.

"What did you bring?" she asked, gesturing to the bag.

"Oh… right." He reached inside and pulled out a variant of the emitter that Talon had debuted at the First of Season. "A gift from Isaac."

"Why would Isaac want us to listen to Church sermons?"

"I guess he used the Church's schematics to isolate the frequencies for any military and operational transmissions." Cassian shook the box and held it up to his ear. "He claims it's portable, but I haven't been able to get it to turn on." After another fruitless twist of the knobs, he returned the emitter to the bag.

Annika rested her chin on her crossed arms and watched him peer absently down at the lake. The sheen of his black hair caught the afternoon light as his shoulders rose and fell with a deep sigh. His eyelids pleaded for respite from the growing weight hanging beneath them. The gathering of the committee had consumed most of the night, and she suspected that his mental distress had stolen the remaining hours before they needed to leave the power plant again.

"Were you able to sleep at all?" she asked.

He switched to the grass in front of him and shook his head. "It's my own fault. I thought last night would be the night, but it was foolish to think that the committee had changed their mind."

"Perhaps the heat signature will provide sufficient reason to act," she said. "Such an anomaly does not seem insignificant."

He sighed. "It's not insignificant. But it won't be enough to get them to act."

"Because there is another motive for following the girl."

Of that, Annika was certain.

Pieces of logic were missing from the committee's unwillingness to yield in their judgments if the girl's safety was the only consideration. Allusions had been made in Annika's presence, but an explanation always went unsaid. From the fragility of their eye contact, she knew the others were withholding information, but so far, the lack of knowledge had not impeded her ability to fulfill her assignment.

As she watched Cassian begin to unravel more each day, she recognized the need to understand the situation in its entirety. It was her responsibility as his partner in this endeavor to help him.

But more than that, she *wanted* to.

Cassian's mouth opened to no sound, and she realized that her statement may have sounded more like an accusation.

"I did not mean to imply any wrongdoing," she said.

"No, *I'm* sorry. You deserve to know. It's just… complicated." He exhaled. "There is something that the committee is looking for—or *someone* rather."

"And they think that Willow knows where to find this individual?"

"She might, but we don't know for sure. It was Kip who first learned of their existence… the same day that you came into our lives.

He believed that this person might have knowledge of the constructs—where they come from, what they want—more than we would ever be able to piece together on our own. But before he could learn anything of actual substance, the source of information was destroyed. He blamed himself and was determined to find them somehow."

"But he never did."

Cassian paused, as discussing Kip often required him to, then shook his head. "Leon thinks Kip might have uncovered something in his final days but never got the chance to tell the rest of us."

"To ensure the information's survival, perhaps he entrusted the location with Willow," Annika finished.

"Exactly. Direct contact could open the Guild up to discovery, and until they know for sure, the committee doesn't think it's worth the risk."

Worth the risk. An enigmatic promise of knowledge outweighed the girl's life. The examples set by Willow's father seemed to have been forgotten. In measuring potential damages and benefits, he always chose selflessness, even with clear incentive to do otherwise. Annika wondered where she would be—where any of them would be—had Kip Dinn not thought that seeking truth was worth the risk. She wondered if he had thought it was worth the risk when he assembled Midbell's most brilliant and daring minds in defiance of the Church's authority or when he commandeered a city utility station to give the Guild a home.

She wondered if he had thought it was worth the risk when he reset the rogue construct who came to their doors seeking a new life.

"Who is this person?" she asked.

Cassian's gaze retreated to the grass between them, his breath deepening. He looked back, his eyes uneasy. "All we have is a name. Jonas Adler."

He said the name once, but she heard it again.

And then again.

A searing sensation unlike anything she could remember drove into her chest. She looked down to see her body unharmed, leaving her powerless to respond. The vicious, boiling ooze poured into her lungs, clogging her throat as it crawled up to her cheeks. Her face was burning, and she forced air in and out through shallow, trembling breaths.

"Are you alright?" Cassian asked from somewhere far away.

She heard the name again. The falling water faded into the outskirts of her awareness. Darkness enclosed her periphery, and the bright blue sky above condensed into pinholes. She closed her eyes and fell into a torrent of incomprehensible thoughts. There were no images or sounds, just formless shapes racing through her head. Her ability to navigate her own mind was gone, and she was left adrift in the unrelenting obscurity.

Then came something she knew to be real—Cassian's touch. She felt the gentle caress of his hand on her cheek, guiding her face back toward him, and back toward reality.

"I'm here."

The shifting objects of her mind slowed at the sound of his voice and then dissolved completely. Gradually, the pressure that filled her released, and her breath approached its regular cadence. The falling water returned, spreading evenly throughout her awareness. She opened her eyes, not to encroaching darkness, but to the vibrant hues of life. In front of a cloudless cerulean sky, Cassian's deep brown eyes waited for her.

"I'm sorry, I shouldn't have said anything."

"I asked," Annika said shakily.

He brought his hand down and wrapped his fingers through hers. His skin was rough, but his touch was soft.

"I know Isaac is better at helping you sort through these things... but I'm always here."

She stared back at him unblinkingly. Forgotten was the stress accrued from the night before, and in his eyes, there was room for only one thing—her. His own pain had been set aside to make room for hers. She followed the rhythm of his being, her breath fading into his. His presence transported her away from the lake to a place that existed only for them. She could not describe it or even know if it was real. All she knew was that to be in this place with him felt good.

The sound of footsteps whisked them back into the present. Annika's attention diverted to the lake, with Cassian's only seconds behind. They both sank into the grass, flattening themselves into the landscape as the urgency of their task reclaimed the moment.

Willow walked along the shore, the loose pebbles shifting beneath each step. The uneven path led her to a trail of boulders at the lake's edge, where she carefully stretched from one slippery top to the next before reaching a flat crop of rock beneath the fissure in the cliff. She looked over her shoulder, then slid her backpack off. With the bag at her side, she scanned the lake one more time, but just as she started to duck into the opening—she froze.

"—rejoice! Roh has crafted a future for us all. Beyond our ability to see..."

Cassian shoved himself back from the ledge and Annika followed. He emptied his bag onto the grass between them and sifted frantically through the contents until he found the emitter. His trembling fingers twisted the first knob to its limit, but the voice only screamed louder.

"... FOR WE ARE NOT MEANT TO QUESTION HIS DIVINE OMNISCIENCE, ONLY TO REC—"

"Stop! Stop!" Cassian whispered through his teeth. He rolled onto his back, clutching the device against his chest, and cranked the knob all the way in the opposite direction. The voice receded, and he dropped the back of his head to the ground, eyes clenched in defeat.

As the silence stretched on, Annika hesitated to move. Suddenly a *splash* came from below. Cassian's expression unknotted itself, and he turned to her. They shared a wordless glance and then crept to the ledge.

The shore was empty, except for the girl's shoes, backpack, and glasses deserted on the rocks in front of the opening. At the center of the lake, movement bubbled to the surface. Willow materialized from underwater, collected a breath, and then threw her head back. She swung her arms behind her in broad strokes, matching the motions with her legs as she circled the lake without any destination, abandoning her real motivations and giving anyone who may have been watching a reason for her being here.

Annika felt a hum, distant at first, that soon swelled into a rumble. The falling water ceded to the approaching thunder as the silhouette of a transport grew on the horizon above the treetops. Quivering leaves turned to swaying branches. The girl filled her lungs and slipped back underwater just as the engine roared above them. Annika rolled her head from one shoulder to the other as the craft soared over the basin toward Midbell, leaving the lake in its tailwind.

In a matter of seconds, the trees had calmed and the transport was merely a feature of the city skyline. Below, the girl hopped along the shore on one foot, trying to get her shoes back on while still moving. She managed to get the second strap of her bag over her shoulder and then sprinted out of the basin.

They both watched as Willow shrank into the distance.

"She was right to get out of here," Cassian said. "We should head back too."

"We're not going to follow her?" Annika asked.

"After a scare like that, she won't leave the house again until morning."

He got to his feet and Annika went to follow his lead, but as she straightened her legs, her head began to swirl. She lost her balance and Cassian caught her by the arm.

"Are you okay?" he asked.

She focused on the ground until it became level again. "Y-yes."

He hesitated but eventually released his hold and offered her his hand instead. She took it, and he did not let her go until they reached the power plant.

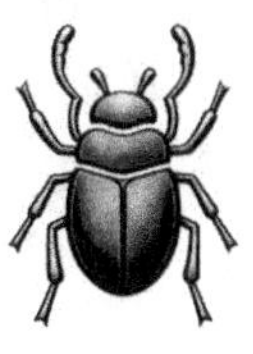

8

RAIN HAMMERED AGAINST THE STONE of the plaza, soaking through Willow's shoes and into her marrow. Between the cracks of lightning, the grand priest appeared on stage, his silhouette wrapped in scarlet by the glowing letters on the screen behind him.

THERE IS ONLY ONE CREATOR

AND IT IS HE

"My brothers and sisters, with this autumn's First of Season comes a tragic necessity of our way of life. There are those out there who believe their wisdom is superior to that of Roh."

Thunder clapped and vicious, unforgiving words from the crowd behind her assaulted her ears.

"This cannot be tolerated! The only thing keeping our people from devolving back into savagery is a strict adherence to Roh's will. Any dissent threatens our safety and must be expunged!"

Another blinding flare came from above and two soldiers dragged her father on stage. Through the streaks of rain on her glasses, the details of his face started to wash away, but she held tightly on to his eyes, which belonged solely to her.

"Kip Dinn! You stand before us guilty of the highest crimes imaginable. You have betrayed the people of this city, defiling our beliefs with your *sacrilegious ideas. The organization formed under your leadership is a mockery of our great Creator, and now you will pay for those unholy transgressions with your life."*

She tried to wriggle free but the fingers of the robed men at her sides dug into her arms.

"Your mind has not been fully corrupted," one of the men said. "It is still possible to salvage your potential. Watch. Look upon a godless future."

The grand priest threw his arms into the air, his voice booming louder than the sky. "Let it be known now and forever! There is only one Creator, and it is He!"

One last look came from her father as they fastened the knot. His lips moved, and his voice was in her ear.

"I love you, Bug."

Willow jolted awake, gasping for air. The inside of her skull was throbbing and the edges of her eyes burned from the abrupt transition into the waking world. Her upper half was as stiff as a plank of wood and her heart was pounding. She clamped her eyes back shut and listened to her violent heaves of breath.

Her eyes soon eased back open to the sunlight spilling in through the window, covering her bedroom in its soft morning glow—the crisp stacks of blueprints on her desk, the fraying textbooks and heaping product manuals arranged by subject matter and sorted by descending height on the bookshelf, the pairs of shoes by the door with their heels in perfect alignment and their laces tucked behind their tongues.

Everything was normal.

It was only a dream.

The morning air cooled the pulsing heat of her dreams, and her body shivered in a cold sweat. She climbed off the bed and walked to the closet where a pair of overalls hung—still damp with the sins of the day before. Another shiver ran down her spine. The voices. The transport. She was toeing a dangerous line—one that once crossed, could never be uncrossed. The consequences were burned into her mind.

But she could feel the impulse growing.

She exhaled, got dressed, and headed downstairs.

The house was quiet, as it had learned to be. Had she been any younger when her father was taken, she would have been placed in Midbell's Sanctuary until she finished her studies at the Academy. But instead, she was left here, alone, in a place that could no longer be called a home.

She slid past the basement door at the bottom of the stairs, resisting a glance, and into the kitchen. The kettle on the counter was a dull, uninspiring shade of silver. The one she had grown up using, along with every other appliance in their house, had been confiscated by the Church inspectors and replaced with ones of their own. Since that horrible day, the tea never tasted the same. She pushed down on the power button, but no bubbles answered her call. After unplugging the kettle and plugging it back in, there was still no response. She tried the light switch on the wall—nothing. A breath trembled on its way out. She had known this day would come.

A year's worth of dust had collected on the handle of the basement door. In her head, she had already gone down the stairs, reset the breaker, and continued with the rest of her day, but her body was not so brave. She debated how long she could go without electricity but knew that the city would eventually take notice of the decline and send a technician, creating an even worse problem. Her knuckles popped beneath her thumb as she willed herself to grab the handle, and finally, she emptied her lungs and opened the door.

The farther down she went, the heavier the darkness became. When she reached the bottom, Willow pressed her hand to the wall and walked forward until the coarse stone gave way to smooth metal. She traced the edge of the panel to the latch and swung open the door. Her hand slid up the row of switches to the largest at the top. She flipped it, counted to five, and then snapped it back into place.

Darkness evaporated and she closed the panel as slowly as she could. When the latch clicked, she paused, wondering if she had the strength to look behind her, but found herself turned around before she could answer. There wasn't much left of the room: a pair of worktables under the light of two exposed bulbs strung from cords above and a hulking metal cabinet in the back corner looming in the shadows beneath a fixture-less cable. Dusty outlines on the walls were all that remained of the tools that once hung there, scattered among the grid of metal pegs. The bookcases needed no order because there were no books left to fill their shelves.

Fear had kept her from knowing what it really felt like to be back in her father's workshop—fear that a lifetime of cherished memories had been overwritten by one life-shattering day. But as she ran a delicate hand along one of the tables, she could not concede the entire feeling to grief. By avoiding confrontation with the painful emotions, she had also deprived herself of the happy ones, the ones that filled her with warmth. She danced with them carefully, knowing how fragile they had become.

"Alright Bug—or should I say Captain Bug—what seems to be the problem this time?" her father asked.

Her toes stretched as far as they could and she saw her toy transport on the tabletop, barred from takeoff by an internal systems failure.

"The lights stopped working," she said.

"The lights? I wonder how that could be. Here…" He grabbed her under her arms and hoisted her onto the table. "Why don't you give me hand? I can never remember how these things work."

He flipped the transport over and unscrewed the cover on its belly, revealing the circuitry inside.

"Hmm…" The tip of the screwdriver hovered over the different components. "Anything catch your eye?"

Willow leaned closer. "There!"

"The resistor?"

"Look! It's disconnected."

"Huh, I guess it is. What do you think we should do?"

She thought about it. "We… we have to complete the line."

"That makes sense. Let's do it."

He swapped the screwdriver for a soldering iron. As he was reforging the connection, her eyes wandered to the inhibitor on the battery.

"What does that do again?" she said, pointing at it, careful to avoid the heat of the iron.

"That's the restraining clasp. It limits how much energy can be drawn from the battery."

"Why?"

"Well, because batteries like this are used for lots of different things across Haven. The restraining clasp is tuned to the needs of a specific system, suppressing the power supply so that the device can only be used for its intended purpose."

"What would happen if we took it off?"

He sighed, smiling, then set the iron aside. "We're not supposed to tamper with the Sacred Technologies, Bug. You know that."

She shrank into herself, and as he tightened the cover back into place, his head teetered from side to side.

"But... hypothetically... without the restraining clasp... maybe this transport could actually become airborne."

"You think it could fly?!"

"I'm not sure..." He looked over the rims of his glasses. "But I know that you can!"

He scooped her off the table and into the air. She squealed with joy as she soared around the basement, weightless in his arms. In between the rumblings of an imaginary engine, he laughed with her, and his eyes never let go of hers. When his arms finally grew tired, he set her back on the table and held a kiss on the top of her head.

"Following the rules doesn't mean you can't wonder," he murmured into her hair, then pulled back.

She stared at him, his reassuring expression framed in the white light from the bulb above, and thought that maybe he too had spent a great deal of his life wondering.

Willow looked up, the light feeling much colder than it had all those years ago. Something caught her attention and her focus tightened back into the physical world. She squinted at the bulb, finding edges that gave its cubical form a clear silhouette. The bulb hanging from the cord above the second workbench was the same. Neither fit the spherical mold of Roh's design, but their variance from the Sacred Technologies must have been subtle enough to avoid detection. Thoughts began to churn as she shifted to the third cord above the cabinet in the back corner and pondered which design the missing bulb favored, cut short by an agitated bout of sizzling sputters coming from the top of the stairs.

The kettle!

THE WORLD OUTSIDE WAS WAKING up. Slowly, the street started to fill, and the sounds and smells of a new day joined her at every house she passed. Someone leapt from their front steps, trying to catch up with their missed alarms. Pots clanged together in some kitchen and the savory winds of a greasy breakfast came from another. A woman on the other side of the street was whistling a tune Willow couldn't pin down.

A hand shot out in front of her. "Halt!"

Bare feet, no shirt, and a missing front tooth—the wooden sword in the young boy's other hand was the only part of him that met the proper standards of a soldier. She decided against reporting him to his superior officer.

"Good morning, Tobias."

"I'm not Tobias, I'm General Kodo!"

"Oh, well thank you for gracing me with your presence, General." Willow bowed her head. "To what do I owe the pleasure?"

He pointed the sword at her face, gripping the handle with both hands. "I'm looking for all the filthy nonbelievers! Do you know where they are? Or are you one of them?"

Playtime suddenly felt less playful. Her thumbs hooked themselves under the straps of her backpack and popped her knuckles.

"Tobias!" A woman's face was pressed against the screen of the open second-story window above them. "You get back inside right now and stop waving that thing in the face of every person that walks by!"

"I'm not Tobias, I'm General Kodo!"

The woman growled and flung herself back from the window. The light drained from the boy's eyes. He was Tobias again. The little imp dropped his sword and scampered back into the house.

She took a deep breath and the noises of the street settled back into place. Blaring above the rest was a voice she did not recognize, but the words it spoke were ones that she, and every other youth of Midbell, had been forced to hear a hundred times over.

"For He is our savior, our guiding promise. It was He who endured and He who dispelled the entropy of the Old World. He alone will shepherd us by the light of the New Dawn, because without Him, there is no future, there is only chaos."

The voice was coming from a house on the corner of the southern junction, where a man stood on the front steps, rocking an infant in his arms. A lifetime of experience walking through the intersection had taught Willow to avoid him, but he had already caught her eye as she rounded the crossing.

He took a giant swig of air loud enough for her to hear and spoke over the emitter at his feet. "By the Creator, it's a beautiful day, isn't it?"

"Mm-hm," Willow said as politely as she could.

The baby started to stir, releasing chirps of agitation.

"Oh come now, what's the matter? Surely nothing our great Creator can't heal."

He bent down and twisted one of the emitter's knobs, exceeding an acceptable volume even from Willow's distance. The sniveling in his arms turned into wailing, and the man had to shout to make himself heard.

"Yup, from the minute she wakes up to when those pretty little eyes fall asleep, she'll hear His word." The baby kept wailing as the man continued to do anything except tend to her. "Let us thank Roh together now for this blessing."

It pained her to watch, but Willow knew better than to get any more involved than she already was. As much as that child did not deserve to suffer, it wasn't her place. The second the man tilted his head back to the sky, she was gone.

Anxiety was her shadow for the rest of the walk to the city's central district. To exist felt like a crime, hiding her unholy impulses from the rest of the world. She longed for a life where there was no danger in thinking, in wondering, and for a future that was hers to craft, not receive. But allowing the thought to mature into anything more than a fleeting daydream would put her at the end of the real General Kodo's sword, leaving her with no future of any kind.

It was the sweet, sugary air from Seymour's Bakery that finally loosened her muscles and unclamped her hands from the straps of her backpack. With the storefront window a mirror in the morning sun, she cupped her hands against the pane to get a look inside. A man in an apron delivered a tray of cakes to the shelf on the other side, fogging the glass with delicious wafts of steam. He smiled at her and then disappeared into the crowd of hungry patrons.

From out of the kitchen in the back of the shop, Seymour, a stout, merry old man with a belly covered in floury handprints, held out a tray of frosted delights to the bakery's most valued customer. With a paper box under one arm, Noah used his other hand to sample part of the spread. A serious look swept over him, and he pinched together his thumb and index finger in front of his face. Seymour bowed with a smile and returned to the kitchen.

As he licked his fingertips clean, Noah turned toward the window. His face lit up, and when Willow waved, he waved right back. He started for the door but then held up one finger to her and pointed to the box under his arm.

Willow laughed and pulled back from the glass. The sunlight took over, and she watched the reflections of people hurry in and out of view, racing toward the approaching ring of the Citadel bells. As the currents continued to flow, her gaze gravitated to the corner of the window, to the only unmoving figure. Someone was waiting—watching.

The woman with the red hair.

Willow spun around and tried to find the other side of the street but the torrent of bodies was too strong. Individual forms fused together, and to pick out just one was an impossible task. Everything was moving and she was suddenly out of breath.

"Willow!"

Her head whipped to the bakery's door.

"Sorry," Noah said. "I almost left without pay—you okay?"

The street was thinning out, but there was no sign of the woman. If she had actually been there, she was gone now.

"I swear, Noah, I just saw her again."

He stretched to his toes and then dropped to his heels. "I can't see anything at all. But forget about her! We have an entire day to catch up on! Let's head over to the fountains and see what Seymour has in store for us." He patted the box and leaned in with a furrowed brow. "And if Old Red dares to show her face again, I'll be there to set her straight!"

NOAH'S SWEET, FROSTING-COVERED LIPS COULD hardly keep up with the excitement that had yet to wear off from his adventure the day before. At several different points he got off the stone slab they were sitting on to swing an imaginary pickaxe. When his tales got a little too far-fetched, she splashed him with some of the water from the fountain behind them to quell the high flames of exaggeration.

"A giant woman with one eye? Come on, Noah, I don't buy that for a second."

"It's true! They call her the Bladesmith. The others said she makes weapons with Torridium so pure that only the most important soldiers in the High Army get them."

"Oh, and she came out and said hi just for you?"

"No, but I did see her! Her arm was as big around as my head!"

Willow pressed her shoulder into his. "Must have been one big arm then."

Noah turned his nose up and away from her. "Tease all you want, Willow, but the sun is shining, I've got a box of sweet rolls, and there's no school today." He took a triumphant bite of one of the rolls.

"No school for *you*," Willow groaned.

His internal sunshine faded. "I almost forgot. But this is the last one, right?"

"Yes. Finally."

She threw herself back onto the stone and looked up at the sky. The clouds were moving fast, and so were her memories of the past year. A stretch of wordless recall passed as the fountain bubbled behind them.

"You know… they always talk about what realignment studies does to a kid," Noah said. "But they never mention how rough it is on their friends."

Willow sat up. She was ready to fire back, but the raw expression Noah wore doused the urge completely.

"Once a week every week, I've got to go find something else to do other than hang out with you." He put his unfinished roll back in the box and closed the top. "And if I'm being honest, there's not much else I like doing more than hanging out with you."

The flutter in her chest rose to her cheeks. His eyes were sweet. Sweeter than the powdered sugar that dusted the tip of his nose. They looked at her like they had when her world first fell apart. He was patient, but in an effortless way. Even in her worst moments, he was only ever interested in being with her exactly as she was. When she was with him, the loneliness the city could force upon her had a limit. She thought she saw his hand start to move toward hers, so she felt no fear in reaching out for his. Their fingers only had spaces for one another, and when hers nestled into his, the world felt a little more breathable.

His voice hid beneath the fountains. "So, yesterday, after the thing with the new first-years, did you… make any progress at the lake?"

Willow's eyes flashed up at him. Part of her wanted to shove a hand over his mouth before he said anything else, but the rest of her—the real her—didn't want to do anything *but* talk about it.

She shook her head. "I bailed before I got inside. I heard something and thought a transport was coming for me…" She felt a little ashamed when she said it out loud. "But it doesn't matter, because there isn't any more progress to be made. The only thing left is the only thing that makes a difference. A homemade glider bike is already too suspicious, and my only cover story is full of holes: I, Willow Dinn, the daughter of the miscreant Kip Dinn, just love the Creator so much and am just so eager to start working in His name that I got a jump on my first engineering project. Oh, and I forgot to mention, I also threw out His Sacred Technologies, made my own blueprints, have been sneaking spare parts out of the Academy piece by piece for the last six months, and hid everything in a cave outside the city."

A breath came. "Add even a milligram of Torridium into the mix and there's no defense to be made whatsoever."

There was a quick spark in Noah's eyes. "But isn't that what you want to do?"

"Yes! Maybe. I don't know." She sank under the weight of her own indecision. "Noah, I'm tired of having my ideas made for me. For once I want to create something that I came up with for no other reason than because I wanted to. A library full of blueprints can't be everything. There has to be more out there, right?" She wasn't sure if she was asking him or the universe or just talking out loud. "I just want to think for myself. It shouldn't sound crazy when I say it, but—"

"It's not crazy." There was pressure in his fingers but not his words. "*You're* not crazy."

"But what if they're right? What if Roh... you know... smites me for all eternity or something for not following the rules?" Her question, as ridiculous as it was, was also a possibility that she couldn't necessarily rebuke.

"And what if they're wrong?" he asked. "My family prays to Roh at dinner and reads our scripture each night before bed. The way I see it, if He loves us all the way they say He does... then the only thing He would really care about is that we're good to each other. Honestly, I bet He would appreciate a fresh set of eyes on things every now and again."

"You really think that's true?"

Noah shrugged. "Who knows? But I believe *how* I want to believe. I personally would rather live thinking that He doesn't mind if the smartest girl in Midbell wants to explore the possibilities of what can be created. That's the world where my friend can be herself, and that's the world I want to live in."

Her cheeks tingled with warmth.

"Here, I got you something." He reached into his backpack, a sad little lump covered in white fingerprints sagging against the stone between his legs.

"Noah, you didn't have to—"

"But I did!"

He pulled out a small cloth pouch, sealed with a bow of string that was tied in a way that only his good-hearted fingers could fashion. She accepted it, but as she pinched the string to pull it apart, Noah quickly wrapped his hands around hers.

"Maybe don't open it here! Why not wait until later?"

The gong of the second morning bell answered for her. Her eyes grew skeptical, but she was out of time to argue. "Okay, weirdo. But only because I'm more afraid of Madame Rex than I am of you."

She stashed the pouch in her backpack and threw a strap over her shoulder. Noah was waiting for her, his face a single beam of light brighter than all the sun's rays. What she would give to just skip to when they would be together next.

"I'll save you a seat—"

He leaned in and kissed her cheek. Before she could react, he pulled away, eyes wide, then bolted in the opposite direction.

"Sounds good!" he said, his voice squeaking as he made his escape. "See you tomorrow!"

"Noah!" she shouted after him.

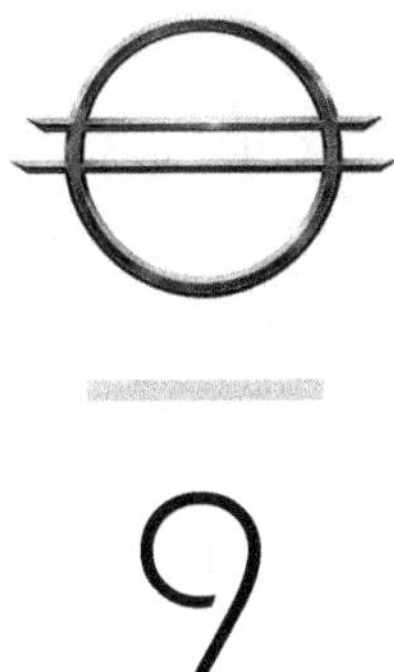

9

THE INTERIOR OF THE CITADEL was painted in shades of every color imaginable. Stretched across the floors and walls were the vibrant abstractions of the stained glass windows, bathing the main hall with the Creator's warmth. Undisturbed by the outside world, here His sanctity was at its purest. Here there was stillness, and here there was peace.

Here there was only Him.

Among the rainbow of pews, Samuel sat colorless and cold. His mouth moved to no sound, reciting the words on the pages of the small leather book clutched in his white-knuckled hands. The antidote to a cluttered mind. Whenever the path became obscured, he knew to return at once to the sources from which his faith was born.

But even the hours spent reading scripture since the bishops had summoned him that morning proved not to be enough to quell the thoughts of the construct in the alcove. Vivid fragments of the scene flashed behind his eyelids: a bloodless death, the severed white fibers, the pulsing beads of otherworldly light—what he had witnessed was a contradiction of nature, and the harder he tried to make sense of it, the more twisted his thoughts became.

The creaking of ancient metals tore into his concentration. Doors swung open on either side of the transept, their groans echoing into the vaulted ceilings above, and two bishops materialized from the shadows. Wrapped in dark red robes, their hooded, faceless forms moved along a mirrored plane to converge at the altar, then pivoted toward Samuel in perfect silence. As they started down the center aisle, he tucked the book into his trousers' side pocket and rose, shuffling out of the row of pews and dropping to one knee before them.

Their synchronized steps came to a halt.

"The grand priest requests your presence," said the bishop on the right.

"I humbly accept," Samuel said, looking up.

"Never before has a soldier of your rank been granted access to the lower levels of our hallowed Citadel." The words slithered out of the hood of the bishop on the left. "It would be wise not to denigrate such a privilege."

"A divine trust I would not dare break."

"Rise," they said as one.

He did as he was instructed. The bishop on the right began to walk back down the aisle while the other folded in behind Samuel. Their footsteps recovered their unified cadence, and by the time Samuel's offbeat pace found their rhythm, they were at one of the doors. The ornamentation on its face resembled the patterns that were carved into the armor of the High Army's ranking officers, and the peaks and divots glimmered on the shiny black surface. There were hundreds of metals in Haven, but only His mineral was capable of imbuing mundane objects with such divine beauty.

They passed through the threshold and into shadow. The final sliver of light thinned to the door's groan and then disappeared completely with a click of the latch. Several seconds of total blindness ensued, broken by a pulse of green light from a pedestal at the center of the room, encircled by a glowing ring with spokes that radiated out in straight lines to the walls.

Samuel stepped inside the ring as the bishops approached either side of the pedestal, each pressing a flat hand against its angled surface. Green flashed beneath their palms and the ring surged. The walls let out a hiss and the spaces between the spokes on the floor started to fall. One by one, individual pieces dropped in a geometric cascade.

Each new step sank farther than the one before, wrapping the ring in a staircase into the Citadel's lower level.

The descent felt infinite, but eventually it found its end at a thinly lit outline of a door. Once more, panels on either side responded to the bishops' palms, and a pulse of light confirmed their intention. Exchanging the antiquity of its ancestor at the top of the stairs for modernity, the door slid into the ceiling, and Samuel could only discern what was before him as a dream.

On the heels of the bishop before him, he stepped through the doorway, unsure if any solid contact would meet his feet. The floor, walls, and ceiling lacked any earthly form, and their deep midnight hues spanned endlessly into a glossy infinitude. Orbs of light floated in the celestial blackness above them like planets wandering the cosmos. From the edges of the ceiling, paragraphs of text flowed down the long walls at a pace meant to be read. His head whirled from side to side as lines from Roh's sacred writings fell from the heavens. Some words were heavier and more pronounced than others, attracting his eyes like the brightest stars in the vast expanse of the night sky.

The bishops split to either side and Samuel found General Kodo kneeling before a dais. Atop the platform was the throne, a pointed monument reserved for Midbell's sole conduit to the Creator, built entirely out of His mineral. The grand priest's eyes bore into him as he made his approach, but he kept his own confined to the mysterious depths of the floor and knelt beside the general. Kodo acknowledged him with a subtle nod, which he reciprocated. Only when his motions settled, and the sounds that he and the bishops brought with them were claimed by the black abyss, could he hear his heart pounding. And then, from atop the throne...

"Rise, my brothers."

He did as he was commanded and brought his attention to the throne. The grand priest sat majestically on the seat that had been carved for him and only him. Scripture rained down on the walls behind him, spliced by the angled peak of the cathedra's back.

"I must express my gratitude for your presence here today, Samuel."

Samuel. His name, lowly and temporal, was unworthy of being spoken aloud in this hallowed chamber.

"Your bones must ache from the tribulations you have been put through, and we thank you for suspending your recovery to be with us." The grand priest delivered every syllable with an even measure. "The esteemed general has informed me of the tragedy that unfolded in the Wilds. Paramount in our crusade is restoring order to Haven, and such a consequential task comes with grave costs. Our fallen brothers and sisters shall be mourned. Because of them, our world will remain on its righteous trajectory, moving ever closer to Roh's sanctified empyrean. They bravely fulfilled the roles that He trusted them with, and their sacrifices will never be forgotten. But out of catastrophe, a light has emerged! The trials laid before you were severe, yet with an unyielding resolve and trust in our Creator were you able to conquer adversity. You proved yourself to be a true paragon of faith, dear brother, and to ignore such greatness would be a detriment to us all. Roh has shown the Council of Four a future for Haven—one of eternal peace. We have seen the motions that must be set in place in order to achieve His promised future. If Haven is to know peace, Samuel, you must help us find it."

Hearing his name again electrified the divine currents coursing through him.

"Your keen intuition may be leading you to what I have yet to say, but I suspect that your humility prevents you from believing it." The grand priest lowered his head and brought the tips of his fingers together in front of his chest. "Well hear my words now, brother. To keep you bound to the lower ranks would be a blatant disregard for the Creator's will and a threat to our society's potential. Roh has a plan for you indeed, and it begins with General Kodo, at the helm of our crusade."

The grand priest stood, his chin tilted to an angle of grandeur and his hands wrapped behind his back. "You will henceforth serve the general as his first officer."

The declaration rang in Samuel's ears. A single breath seemed to last a lifetime. He focused the vibrating fibers of his muscles enough to bow his head.

"I am but a vessel to carry His sacred light. My life for Him."

The corners of the grand priest's face curved into sharp satisfaction. "General Kodo is prepared to lead a second assault on the temple. In his brilliant omniscience, Roh has fortified our defenses. The same fabric that protects our workers from the heat of industry has been woven into the armor of the High Army as a safeguard from the fires of the heathens, making our forces impervious to the dark arts of those godless savages. Beside your general, you shall claim the bastion of the faithless in the name of Roh… dispel the evils that skulk in His shadow… and slay the Elder Mother."

Samuel's gaze tightened, and the grand priest gave a deliberate nod.

"She is a dangerous, festering blight that must be expunged from His kingdom. At the ends of her pernicious roots are all the sin and impiety that plagues Haven. She has warped the minds of the weak-willed and threatens to dismantle His blessed society. Between the children of Roh and His eternal peace stands her. Her wicked fallacies against the Creator must be silenced!"

The borrowed soul. Samuel's throat seethed with rage and his breath turned to steam. "It will be done."

"A strong resolve will not be enough to combat the wicked spells of the Elder Mother, and your narrow escape from the temple has left you unarmed. But fear not, brother, for a solution is already underway. At dusk you will go to the Forge. From the flames of our Creator's might, the Arch Bladesmith will shape the instrument of your destiny, Samuel—a weapon worthy of the responsibility He has bestowed upon you. Use it to defeat the Elder Mother and the rest will fall."

His Holiness found the far reaches of the chamber. "The time has come to restore His name and bring the faithless to reckoning. There is only one Creator, and it is He! Praise Roh!"

"Praise Roh!" Samuel and General Kodo said as one.

The grand priest reclaimed his position upon the throne. Taking his cue from Kodo, Samuel started for the entrance behind the general. From either side, the bishops who had brought him here converged in front of the door, blocking their passage.

"Ah… yes…" Behind them, the grand priest's fervor softened into a distant evenness. "There is one more matter I feel obligated to address."

They turned around and saw that the grand priest had brought his fingertips back together in front of his chest.

"Death, Samuel, is a tragic and unavoidable part of our duties. The time we are allotted is finite and was decided long ago by the Creator. We are taught to meet the closing of our own lives with dignity. Yet when we witness the death of another, our mind's innate reflexes often supersede our training. It cannot make sense of these events and transforms them into something else entirely."

Thoughts of the construct in the armor started to swirl.

"Your general spoke of an encounter you had on your return to Midbell. An incomprehensibly gruesome and senseless death. To see one of our brothers butchered like that while doing what Roh asked of him…" The grand priest moved one of his hands to his breast as he winced. "It was too much for a heart as pure as yours to tolerate. Instead, the forces that steer your subconscious tried to fit pieces of their own making into reality as a response to the trauma."

Samuel was back in the alcove, trying to replay a memory that was growing more clouded with each word the grand priest spoke. Details he once remembered with such clarity were softening, and he sifted through his recollections like piles of gray sand in the Radials—formless images that slipped from his grasp the harder he tried to hold them.

"Let me set your mind at ease, brother. Blinded by devotion to the fallen and rage for the sinful, your own perceptions betrayed you. They refused to accept such a ghastly sight, and in desperation, they tried to shape what was before your eyes into something less horrific."

The beads of light in the body's neck started to look more like a glare from the sun.

"None of this should have been yours to bear, but you must know that what you think you saw was not the truth. What you saw was a distorted interpretation of a very grim, but very real happening."

The white fibers gained color, and blood poured from the open wound.

"The events at the temple sent you into a state of shock. You could not bear to see yet another one of your own left mutilated by those dastardly infidels. There was but only one response, and it was for your noble spirit to rewrite its own experience."

A lone child of Roh had been slaughtered by the faithless.

The grand priest turned his palms to the ceiling. "Do you understand, Samuel?"

He did.

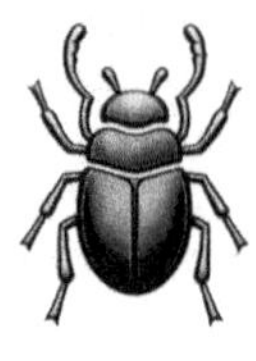

10

IT WAS ONLY SUPPOSED TO be a single blink, but the darkness lingered for what could have been a few seconds—or an hour. How cozy it was there. The desktop grew glossier every time it returned from a stint of total black. No matter which way Willow tried to balance her head, its weight always fell to a new direction. The pinholes of her vision were drowning in softness, and the sound of her lungs expanding was the sweetest lullaby she'd ever heard. Had there ever been a spot more comfortable than this? Maybe. But she ought to test it out, just to be—

Madame Rex cleared her throat.

Willow's eyes tore open. She dug her fingertips into the pant leg of her overalls and pinched the skin underneath as hard as she could. Unfortunately, everything on her desk was exactly as she had left it. The blank stack of papers on one side was still just as tall, and she could count the filled pages on the other side on one hand. Between them was a tablet, dim with inactivity.

A few more rapid blinks and the rest of the room reappeared around her: rows of empty desks underneath windowless walls. The hours spent here were certainly never yearned for, but the punishment she faced was trivial compared to what it could have been. Had she not still been in the Academy when they came for her father, her fate would have been the same as his. As mind-numbing as transcribing

Church-approved blueprints every week for a year was, it was far preferable to the alternative.

She held her finger on the tablet until it registered her touch. Its screen powered back on to the completed version of the hand-drawn blueprint she had abandoned, the schematics for some kind of gear shaft. The documentation specified the serial number, but it wasn't one she recognized off the top of her head. There was still quite a gap to be filled before her version looked anything like the one on the tablet. Fighting back a groan, she picked up her pencil and dredged on.

During the first few months, she tried to get through as many blueprints as she could as fast as she could. She thought that if she worked hard enough, maybe she could undo what had been done— which some part of her knew was impossible, but it felt better to think she had some power over the situation than admit the reality of what had happened. Noah had urged her to take a different approach, a tactic frequently used by him and Newt when they had to work at their Mimi's fabric shop after class. *It's all about pacing yourself,* he told her. *You can run around and fold every pile until you're out of breath, but the store is still going to close at the same time no matter what.*

While she certainly couldn't do nothing with Madame Rex watching her, his sentiment was right—there was no need to burn herself out. And although it was dreadful work, being forced to imprint a catalog of the Sacred Technologies into her brain had only sharpened her knowledge of the subject matter which would soon be the sole purpose of her existence.

The gear shaft was complete, and she moved it to the pathetic pile of other completed copies. She clicked the dial on the side of the tablet down a notch and a new image filled the screen. An entire gear shaft system this time, equally as bland, triple the lines to draw. Another discontented sigh was stifled before she willed herself to the documentation box at the top of the page, but as she read the first value of the serial number range, any part of her that was not awake before was instantly electrified.

BUG000148275006

She ran her finger over the first three letters and heard her father's voice.

"Listen to me, Bug."

His face was calm, but his words carried unmistakable urgency. He knelt in front of her and took her hands, his thumb involuntarily tapping the back of her knuckle.

"Something's about to happen, but I promise you, you are going to be okay."

Behind him, a woman leaned against the wall next to a window. When exactly she had entered their house, Willow couldn't remember. One of her hands slid the edge of the curtain back from the glass just enough for her fiery glare to reach the street outside. The light from between the folds fell on her white hair. Even the strange purple markings across her face glowed in the flattery of the evening's gentle beams. She was beautiful—but different. Only glimpses of her gray skin were visible under her hooded robe, just like the three others who paced around the living room.

"We don't have much time," the woman said. "They'll be here any minute." She stepped away from the window and one of the others filled her place. "It doesn't have to end like this. Come with us." She gestured to Willow. "Both of you. We can keep you safe."

"But who will keep you safe?" Willow's father said over his shoulder. "If we go with you, it will only be a matter of time before they find me again. The survival of your people is too important."

"They are coming," said the one at the window.

Her father was back with her. "It's going to be scary, but I need you to be brave." His eyes deepened into hers… and then he pushed something hard down his throat. "They're going to take me away. And when I'm gone, they're going to interrogate you. They'll try to plant ideas in your head and make you admit to things you haven't done—things you couldn't dream of. No matter what they say, remember that you have done nothing wrong."

The one at the window released the curtain. "We must leave."

"Kip Dinn, this is our final offer," said the woman.

"Go," he said.

Willow blinked and the room behind him was empty. Shadows swam over the ridges of the curtains, bringing with them a stampede of metal footsteps.

"You have everything you need right here." He pressed his forehead into hers. "Your mind is your greatest ally, and they can never take away your ability to think. To wonder. Protect that, and you can find the answer to any question—the solution to any problem."

The door bent to the slamming behind it.

"You are brilliant and you are powerful."

The door flew off its hinges and onto the floor, unleashing a flood of maroon bodies into the room.

"I love you, Bug."

The bells from the Citadel transported her back to the present where Madame Rex was looking at her, not unkindly. Willow instinctively reached to power the tablet back on and then retracted when her brain finally caught up.

The afternoon bell. She was free.

"Your weekly burden has been resolved, Miss Dinn," Madame Rex said as she accepted Willow's materials at the front of the room. "Although the crime was not your own, you endured the punishment as the Creator asked you to. I am pleased to see that you chose correction over corruption." She flipped through the completed blueprints. "This is far from your best work here, but it still surpasses what many of our engineers are capable of. Midbell will benefit tremendously from your talents. You will help Him make this world a better place."

Willow smiled uncomfortably. "Thank you, ma'am."

Madame Rex straightened the stack of papers and placed them inside one of the drawers behind her among the rest of Willow's collected works.

"Now—the day is far from over. How will you and Mr. Lomp be spending the evening before graduation?"

The small talk was painful, but hearing her and Noah coupled together sent a flutter into her cheeks.

"Actually ma'am, his sister, grandparents, and a few aunts and uncles are coming to his house for dinner tonight. Most of his extended family will be at the ceremony tomorrow."

"Ah yes, that comes as no surprise. I often forget how far the Lomp name spans across Midbell, yet how closely they all exist. They are as dedicated to the city as they are to each other." She peered over the top of her glasses. "You would be wise to keep his company for as long as possible."

THE WORLD OUTSIDE FELT A little easier to navigate knowing she'd never have to step foot inside that room again. She watched the water dance as she passed by the fountains, part of her hoping that Noah might still be there, but she let the thought go before the inevitable disappointment could sink in. His kindness and support had overwritten the tone set by the man with the baby and the miniature General Kodo. As silly as he could be, Noah always knew how to be there for her, whether by listening to her, getting angry at the things she was angry at, showing up with mysterious presents—

She had completely forgotten about the pouch.

His direction had been to wait until later, and unless the last few hours had actually melted her brain, she was pretty sure it was later. She slid out of one strap and swung her backpack around, but just as she went to undo Noah's charming work on the bow, a hand the size of a summer melon snatched the pouch.

"Whatcha got here, Willow?"

Her eyes were daggers. "Give it back, Kurt,"

The two cronies behind him laughed and Kurt tossed the pouch up and down to himself, taunting her with each catch.

"Come on, we saw you and Lomp shmoozin' out here before your delinquent studies. He gave you this and—" The pouch made its highest climb and then he snagged it out of the air. "Man! I don't know about you, but I'm just itching to see what's inside!"

"Do you really have nothing better to do?" She went for the pouch but he pulled his arm back.

"Woah, you know I'm just playing around! What's all the attitude for?"

"Just give it back." She lunged again.

He kept staring at her, wearing that same rotten smile he always wore when he knew he had burrowed his way under her skin. After he had licked the moment clean of its juices, he dropped his shoulders and shook his head.

"You're right—I'm sorry," he said dramatically, not even trying to hide his guile. "Watching you two, oh it just warms the heart. Maybe I'm just looking for that special someone too, you know? Someone who feels comfortable enough around me to shove desserts into their fat little face all day. It must just be the romantic in me, I guess. So here, if you really want it back that badly..."

He dangled the pouch in front of Willow's face, but when she reached out, Kurt flung the pouch over his shoulder to one of the other boys behind him.

"Then come and get it," he said, and dashed in the opposite direction.

Running as fast as she could, she was still no match for the years of drills and physical training that turned him and his goons into increasingly smaller shapes down the street. Their laughter lingered in the air like clouds of stench, refusing to dissolve. Her throat was stiff and her eyes were watering. It was like the city didn't want her to be happy—even when she did exactly what it asked of her.

She managed to keep a lock on Kurt and his gang, until their distant forms took a sharp turn and disappeared into an alley. By the time she caught up, they were nowhere to be found. The alleyway was empty, just some stray wooden crates, a dumpster, and... the pouch? Sitting atop the dumpster was the stolen present, waiting for her. At first she thought it was another trick, but then she heard a few bangs from inside the bin. The stink came first and then another set of banging. Her nose wrinkled as she got closer and found a metal bar wedged into the clasp that secured the lid. She grabbed the pouch just as a voice came from the dumpster.

"Is someone there? Please let me out! My name is Kurt Avis. My father is First Officer Avis under General Duncan, unit number…"

Her teeth clamped down on her lips but couldn't stop a grin from forming. Perhaps it was wrong of her to leave him trapped there, but someone had gone to great lengths to put him in there, and who was she to undo their efforts?

No more waiting. She unraveled the string and peered inside the pouch. Her feet stopped. Kurt's banging and pleading was no longer ignored. It was blotted out completely. The sound of her heart pounded behind her ears as the infinite blackness of Torridium sparkled in the light of the outside world. Her ribs collapsed, trying to push air in and out of a hole that was too small. The thumb of her free hand emptied each knuckle, and before her mind could decipher one thought, another crashed into its place. All that remained was a maelstrom of anxiety, nameless and indiscernible.

But then something smothered the noises of her mind in flattening silence. Her thumb and index finger pinched at the air just beside the pouch. She brought them up to her face to let her eyes see without any doubt—a single strand of red hair.

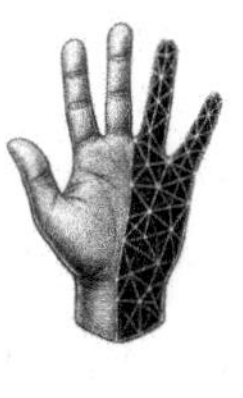

11

ANNIKA'S FINGER BARELY HIT THE final key as Cassian ducked underneath the half-risen door in the power plant's outer wall. She matched his pace, flying past the network of poles and through the glass doors at the front of the building. Their discovery of the girl's Torridium in the alleyway had prompted an immediate departure from the city.

His urgency had become her own.

They raced past the rows of statue-like technicians and down the hall. Cassian furiously tapped the call button until the lift doors opened. They stepped inside and his momentum came to a halt. He stared down at the buttons on the interior panel, his finger hovering over them until she mercifully reached in front of him and entered the second code.

He exhaled. "Thank you."

The doors split and the urgency resumed. Their footsteps were lost to the screeching saws and overlapping conversations beneath the catwalk. At the crossing, Jasper hunched over the railing. As they drew closer, he coiled around and stepped into their path, his mouth twisted into a grin.

"My, aren't we in a hurry?"

"Out of our way, Jasper, I need to speak to Leon." Cassian altered his course, but the old man cut him off.

"What's the hurry?" Jasper looked them over twice, brow raised. "Must be something big! What did she do this time? Let me guess—take a different route home? Stay out past bedtime?"

"Are you finished?" Cassian drew his shoulder inward and pushed open a path. A disgruntled snort was Jasper's only rebuttal, and they passed by without any further resistance.

Annika blinked and they were at the other end of the catwalk. Cassian tore open the doors, shattering the stillness inside. Leon was alone. The glow from a set of screens in front of him outlined his form and cast the room in dim, artificial light. In the fragment of a second it took for their presence to register, Annika caught a glimpse of a state intended to be kept behind closed doors. His hands clasped the back of his head, his fingers knotted through bunches of hair. Every muscle in his body was tight, gripped by an invisible force. He was facing the screens but looking somewhere else—somewhere only he knew.

Somewhere much darker.

"Cassian." Leon rounded the table to meet them.

"It's Willow," Cassian said. "She has Torridium."

Leon slowed to a stop. Something flickered behind his eyes, then he reached for the small keypad on the table.

The rest of the committee appeared within minutes. Jasper was the first to arrive, having clearly received the summons by eavesdropping. Hazel and Lin rode in on the winds of ash and destruction, fresh out of an explosives test. Annika offered to leave, and with great endorsement from Jasper to do so, but Cassian demanded she stay, as she could corroborate his story. He informed the others of the Torridium—omitting the details about the brute, the dumpster, and their intervention—urging that immediate action be taken.

"How did her friend come to be in possession of Torridium?" Hazel asked.

"He must have stolen it from the mines on one of the tours with the Academy," Cassian said.

"How do we know she isn't going to turn her friend in?" Jasper interjected. "Just being given a pouch full of Torridium doesn't prove anything."

"It might," said Hazel, her gaze still fixed on Cassian. "How did she react when she saw what was inside?"

"We…" Cassian passed an uneasy look to Annika and cleared his throat. "We don't know. We didn't see her open it."

Lin's expression bent with skepticism. "If you didn't see her open the pouch, then how do you know what was inside?"

There was a pause, and then Jasper filled the emptiness with a bitter—but accurate—explanation. "Because he opened it himself, saw the Torridium, and left it for the girl so we would have a reason to get involved."

The room turned to Cassian, whose eyes dropped to the table.

Leon's voice was seething beneath the surface, like water about to boil. "Any interaction with her requires unanimous agreement from the committee. You may have just risked everything."

"She didn't know we were there."

"Your role is to watch and report back, not to manipulate the situation to get what you want. This group decides when the time is right, not you alone."

"These other kids took the pouch. If we hadn't stepped in, they would have gone to the authorities and—"

Leon clenched his eyes in frustration. "But you didn't know what was inside when you got involved! That's not why you did it! You wanted to play big brother, and once again you let your feelings get in the way of seeing any of this clearly."

"He is the only one of you who *does* see this clearly."

Every head spun to Annika.

"The choice to intervene was not a deliberate effort to undermine the decision made by this body. Cassian's actions were motivated solely by his concern for the girl's safety. The prospect of what she might be able to provide the Guild has taken priority over her well-being. Perhaps she can lead us to the individual you seek, but should that alone outweigh the value of her life?"

"And what would *you* know of life?" Leon hissed.

Chairs screeched. Cassian was the first to his feet and Leon matched his stance at the other side of the table. A violent inhalation warned of Leon's blistering addendum, but his mighty breath never found words. The set of screens on the wall started to ring out in a high-pitched beeping, and among the litter of green text was an outlier: a single line of numbers blinking red. Leon lunged to the screen and then flung himself back around.

"Station B-16. Who is that?" he demanded from Lin.

She calculated. "B-16… That's Del. We just brought him in last week."

"Reroute his terminal. Distribute the readouts to B-10 through 15."

Lin nodded nervously.

Leon switched to Jasper. "Get Del down here. Now."

In a single rush out the door, the room lost half its occupants. As Lin broke off down the stairs and Jasper called the lift, Annika watched Leon slip into the oscillations of his fury, pacing up and down the catwalk and scouring the grated metal between each barbed tread. Cassian looked on from the doorway, simmering in a different kind of rage. Leon had addressed her, yet it was Cassian who chose to receive the transgression.

"This won't be good," Hazel said, and all three walked out onto the catwalk.

When the lift hissed back into place, Jasper shuffled out, followed by a young man in a technician's uniform, one of the faceless workers from the upper level. Laden with dread, he moved at a speed that made his escort look agile. He pushed a crooked pair of glasses up the bridge of his nose, but the nervous glistening made it a futile act. As he reached the crossing and stood before Leon, the quivers in his limbs became tremors.

"Do you know why I called you down here, Del?"

The noise from the room below flattened under Leon's question. Heads turned upward, quietly trying to piece together the scene.

"Leon sir, I—"

"Do you know why I called you down here?" The same question, this time delivered to the far reaches of the lower level.

"I… I made a mistake." Del choked on his own words. "It won't happen again."

"I know it won't happen again—because it *can't*." Leon's hand landed on Del's shoulder, and the entire lower level fell silent. "Our operation hinges on your diligence. This facility needs to uphold the guise of a properly functioning power plant. The consequences of carelessness are unforgiving. If that facade falters for even an instant, we risk losing everything."

"I'm sorry." Del's bottom lip trembled. "It was just a minor output fluctuation. I didn't think it would matter if—"

Leon threw Del against the railing.

"Look down at them! These good people have devoted themselves to our cause. They work with only each other in mind." Leon was in Del's ear. "Tell me, do they not deserve the same from you?"

"Of—of course!"

"So why would you tell me that you thought your mistake did not matter?" Leon tore him from the railing by the back of his shirt. "Does the safety of these people not matter? Do their loved ones not matter?"

Del's mouth formed shapes without sound, his face stained with sweat and tears.

"You let your focus stray from your duties and put all our lives in danger." Leon threw a callous finger in Del's face. "If the Church were to discover us, our blood would be on your hands!" He compressed his intensity into a low, searing tone. "Now go. Retire to your quarters. You are relieved from duty until tomorrow."

Del shuddered and hurried down the stairs. The mass at the bottom parted and a path to the dwelling units opened. Heads turned, but not a single word was uttered as he disappeared into the hallway. For a moment, it seemed like nobody was willing to even breathe, but gradually, the crowd began to disperse. Bodies returned to their stations, and soon, the sounds of creation took over the facility once more.

Leon held his acrid glare on the hallway long after Del was out of sight. His face pinched tight as he brought two fingers to his brow. He opened his eyes and turned to Cassian, nostrils flared. "So much as a single step out of line and your connection to this organization will be severed."

Cassian held his resolve with an unyielding gaze, offering no words.

Wearing a bitter scowl, Leon peeled away and stormed past the others, slamming the doors shut behind him.

Jasper whistled. "Bet Del would've gotten off a lot easier if you two hadn't—"

"Don't you dare," Hazel warned. "They are not to blame for that man's inability to control his temper." She left him no chance to respond and headed for the stairs.

Jasper rolled his eyes and slithered back inside the lift. He turned around, his lip curled. "Think of the rest of us, Cassian." His image narrowed between the converging doors. "One life isn't worth the Guild."

Annika exhaled fully for what felt like the first time since the screens started beeping. Beside her, Cassian was staring at the doors across from the lift, his face still gripped with torment. It did not have to be his to bear alone—they could share the burden, if only he knew she was willing. *I'm here,* he had said. She remembered the feeling of his touch, a gentle tether back to reality, and looked down at his hand.

Before she could reach for it, he turned to her.

"Leon had no right to speak to you like that." Cassian grabbed her hand. "He might know of life, but he knows nothing of humanity."

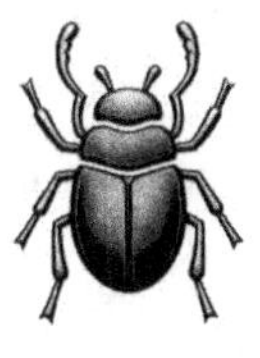

12

The prisoner in Willow's backpack tapped against the base of her spine as she walked down the southern corridor, rattling the bars and reminding her that it couldn't stay in there forever. *But it could.* How easy it would be to take the whole backpack, Torridium and all, and bury it somewhere deep in the ground where nobody would ever know that she actually had thoughts of using it. *They already did.* Everyone she passed knew. Their gazes pierced the canvas of her bag and saw the unholy secrets she kept. Willow Dinn, daughter of the Church's icon of impious disobedience, was capable of nothing else.

Thump, thump.

Another city block passed and she wondered what was so awful about proving them right. Deep down, wasn't that what she wanted anyway? When it felt so unnatural to conform to the Church's mold, the real crime was not giving her true self a chance at life.

Thump, thump.

Soon several more blocks were behind her and she was at the southern junction. *There is only one Creator, and it is He.* The acceptance of any other truth would secure her spot at the gallows.

Thump, thump.

Why had Noah done this? She was tempted to go find him and shove the rock back in his unthinking, irresponsible, completely reckless, encouraging, supportive, and wonderful face that had never done anything wrong except believe in her. He would have never taken the Torridium had it not been for her constant yearning to disregard the rules, pushing him to break them himself. There was only one person to blame, and it was her.

Thum—

Overstimulated, her physical senses had reached a breaking point, and she needed to readjust the bag before what little of her mind she still had control over snapped too. She swung one strap off and threw her hand inside the bag. No matter which way she tried to redistribute the weight, the pouch always sank to the same spot. She brought her face closer to the bag and wedged the—

Her head connected with something metal and the impact rang through her skull. The bag fell out of her grasp as she tripped over her feet. Her landing was about to be a clumsy and humiliating one but her body was suddenly separated from its momentum. She switched her attention from the oncoming stone street to the hand on her forearm. The saving appendage was wrapped in glimmering maroon and pulled her back up with the strength of a multi-troop transport but the gentleness of an autumn breeze.

On both feet she saw the objects of her collision and rescue were the same. The plating over the chest of the soldier still attached to her arm matched the ringing in her ears. His eyes, a piercing shade of blue with a world of intensity contained inside, belonged solely to her. The streets were surging to the workday's second apex of activity, yet she was the only person to ever exist.

"Are you okay?" He must have felt her balance return and released his hold on her arm. "Please forgive me. I should have been watching where I was going."

She spun to the bag, pleading to any force that would listen that the Torridium hadn't fallen out. Trained in preemption and chivalry that bordered on annoying, the soldier beat her to it.

Amused by the unexpected contest with gravity, he laughed to himself. "Entire shelves at the library weigh less than this." He patted off the dirt, and her heart was in her throat. "A student of the sciences?" His blue eyes found her again, and he smiled before offering her the bag.

She forced out a hurried nod and threw the bag over her shoulder. If there was a more dangerous situation to be in, she couldn't picture it.

His sunny disposition dampened into concern, as her emotional state had suddenly become his top priority. "Trouble holds you, sister."

"I'm fine," she said unconvincingly.

He removed his helmet and a tucked a fallen strand of blonde hair behind his ear, revealing his face in full. She placed him several years older than her, but his features were ageless. Each half of his face was balanced, no matter which way she made the split. There were no blemishes on his skin, his pronounced jaw was dusted with prickles of blonde. He was objectively the most perfect-looking person she had ever seen, and she wondered if there were secret labs where the Church made people like him.

"What burdens you?" He rested his hand on her shoulder.

She tensed but the reflex was quick to pass. His touch was not invasive or forceful, and she found herself welcoming the strange kindness. The decision to confide in him was only partially her own; she felt oddly safe in his presence, but she was also completely certain that he was not going anywhere until he could offer this distraught citizen a remedy to her problems.

"I have to make a decision." Hearing her problem simplified to such an extreme was a cathartic act on its own. "And I'm just not sure what to do."

He remained with her and only her. "Something quite important, I imagine."

She nodded again, this time not trying to end the conversation. He removed his hand and joined it with the other behind his back, relaxing his gaze into the distance. His shoulders softened, and he returned to her.

"What is your name, sister?"

She hesitated, swallowing the weight that her last name undoubtedly held. "Willow."

He bowed his head. "Samuel." His attention shifted again, but he came right back. "Willow, would you care to join me for a moment?"

Even if she didn't want to—though she was pretty sure she was at least open to wanting to—he seemed quite committed to helping her, and she was in no position to turn away advice.

"Okay," she said.

Samuel navigated them through the congested intersection with a nimble grace, mindfully finding the empty space between bodies and avoiding disruption to the flow of the street. He worked with the currents of the city. The people around him were not obstacles, they were part of the collective rhythm. Willow followed in his shadow, fully accepting that it was the girl with her head in a bag who had been responsible for their collision.

Through the lattice of conversation and movement, she could hear the emitter from the house on the corner still droning on. She stole a peek at Samuel's face, hoping their destination was anywhere else, but as the words of the sermon gained definition, the buoyancy of his expression confirmed that was exactly where they were heading.

Mercifully, the emitter was playing to an empty set of steps. Samuel brought his voice down to her level. "I too was recently faced with difficulty. Things became obscured and I was terribly confused. I even began to doubt the path I was on."

Willow turned to him, easing into his stillness.

"I saw things not as myself, but as someone else. My thoughts had become manipulated by forces that contradicted everything I knew to be true and made me question who I was."

She unpacked his words, finding herself in them. "And how did you know they weren't right?"

He tipped his head forward. "Let us listen."

"To trust Him is to trust oneself, for in each of us is a piece of the divine," the emitter proclaimed. "The share of His wisdom we have been allotted will escort us on the righteous path through the labyrinth of eternity. He is not something external for us to seek, but to find inside of us all, our center we must constantly return to. Only when we surrender ourselves to the absence of individual control can we understand our true purpose."

"There is a part of us, the deepest, purest part, that was given to us long ago and defines who we will become," Samuel said. "It is our center and it is our guide. Tell me, sister, can you feel it?"

"I... *think* so," she said, genuinely searching for what he was describing.

"Abandon the impressions of the outside world!" the emitter continued. "To find the true nature of our souls we need only turn inward, for He has instilled in each of us His guiding light that will never fade! But when we fail to open ourselves and listen for His call, we remove all possibility of becoming who we were meant to be."

"The way forward has been inside of you all along. Deviate from it and what will be left of you? You must trust in your own ruling principles, sister. He has given you everything you need to be the highest form of yourself."

Samuel's words animated the lifeless ramblings she had heard a thousand times. She had compromised the one part of her that was uniquely hers just to exist in a system she wanted nothing to do with. Following the holy configuration meant drifting farther from who she really was. She had spent her life believing that she owed the world everything, but if the world refused to make a place for Willow Dinn—the real Willow Dinn—then it deserved nothing from her.

A trade: give up everything she was and in return be allowed to safely continue as a shell of the person she knew she could be. It was an existence, but by no means life—and it was an exchange she wasn't willing to make.

"His instinct is our own," the emitter declared. "He has given us the ability to share in His reasoned choice, and it is ours as long as we look for it. The only impediment that remains in the way of reaching our potential is ourselves! We must ask ourselves then, are we listening? Do we hear His call?"

"Do you hear it, Willow? Do you hear His call?"

For once, she had no doubts. The particles of her being came into alignment, forging a channel that let her guiding light flow. It wasn't Roh's call she heard—it was her own.

She turned to Samuel. A stranger just moments ago, now the catalyst for her awakening.

"I know what I need to do," she said.

"I am grateful to have shared this with you." He lowered his head. "Go now, sister. Be the person you were meant to be."

FEATHERY STALKS OF GRASS TICKLED her fingertips as an amber sun kissed the horizon ahead of her. She inhaled the sweet damp air, and the lush earthy tones of autumn's dying grass filled her senses. A humid breeze rippled through the golden blades around her, following the currents that guided her. For the first time, her body moved in accordance with itself, every motion her own doing. She was untethered from the earth but grounded in who she was.

The waterfall crashed gently in her ears. Where paranoia usually held her in its clutches, her ribs found the room to breathe. She was ready—ready to start her real work. After graduation, she would keep her brain at the minimal active state that her job in the city required, but once that was done, she would put it to actual use. She would maintain the guise of a law-abiding citizen, praising the Sacred Technologies for all their beautifully regressive brilliance while entertaining ideas of her own outside the public eye. It was by no means perfect, but her father must have managed something similar for decades, and so could she.

Her feet knew the way across the rocks, their newfound resolve launching her from one graceful leap to another. When she got to the fissure next to the waterfall, she slipped off her backpack and pulled it along behind her. This location had an expiration, she thought as she squeezed through the cramped tunnel—and not just because this was the only entrance that did not involve drenching herself and the contents of her bag under a waterfall, but because if someone had seen her yesterday, it would be too dangerous to keep coming back. Her first priority after finishing the glider bike would have to be finding another spot to pursue her forbidden extracurriculars. That place would then eventually grow stale, and she would have to find another. Inevitably, that one too would need replacing, and so would the next, on and on ad infinitum. But she would do whatever it took.

Tiny beads of water dripped from the jagged ceiling overhead, splashing her forehead with memories of the many times she had dragged her bag into her hideout of unholy temptation. Everything inside it had been born from nothing: the workbench, mobile terminal, collection of mismatched tools. Even the glider bike itself had started as a backpack of smuggled parts, waiting to be assembled into its true form.

But as the corner of her workshop came into view ahead, she felt disoriented, staring at a place that was of her own creation yet completely foreign in this moment. Her pace slowed and the realization snapped into place: she couldn't remember seeing the workshop from this angle before because she had never been able to. Every muscle in her body froze. It was impossible that she had left the lights on. There were routines that she never deviated from, and ensuring that all nonessential systems were powered down before she left the cave was the most important one.

She squeezed her eyes shut, picturing Commander Logan and a legion of faceless metal agents waiting for her. Someone at the fountains could have overheard her talking to Noah and told the guards, or maybe Kurt had opened the pouch.

The pouch. In the chaos brought on by its contents, she had forgotten about the rogue strand of auburn hair on the outside of the pouch. More frightening than the grim but certain consequences of getting caught by the Church were the unknown motives of her red-haired stalker.

"Inactive systems can still be identified by an energy scan. Offloading major power consumption alone is not enough to evade detection."

She tipped one ear to the opening, battling with the sound of the waterfall to try and make sense of what she had just heard.

"But it is not surprising that such measures were ignored. I suspect that even your teachers would not have known any better."

We've got you! You're under arrest! I'm here to collect your skin! Of all the things she had braced for, a critique of her illegal endeavors was not one of them.

"If you wish to remain completely unseen, you may want to consider masking yourself behind a source of preexisting activity. Your father nearly perfected the art."

There was no difficulty discerning the last part. She paused, then pushed herself into the opening. Everything was as she knew it, but functioning without her, and she had become a stranger in her own space. The terminal screen, propped up by a stack of spare manuals from the Academy, was not only on, but displaying status readouts of the engine which she decided just then were deeply personal. What she didn't recognize was the cloaked figure kneeling in front of the glider bike. Their attention alternated between the anterior fins, the engine casing, and an open copy—Willow's copy—of *Vehicle Assembly and Systems Maintenance, vol. XXIV* on the ground beside them.

"What little resemblance your work bears to the primitive ideas written on these pages. Technique like this is rare to see from your kind." The woman's voice, much clearer in the openness of the cavern, held a distant sense of familiarity. Every letter was enunciated with a weapons-grade sharpness, veiled in a shadowy grace.

The woman rose and circled the bike, stepping over the open textbook no longer worthy of her attention. An open palm trailed behind her, gliding along the fabric of the saddle and the contours of the vehicle's rear until it found metal again. The aged plating looked like a polished alloy beneath her muted gray skin. Her cuff slid back from her wrist and the violet markings underneath found the light.

Willow had always questioned if the Dusudé were just figments of the Church's propaganda machine, but on the day her father was taken, the reality of their existence—along with every other detail the trauma would not let her forget—was seared into her memories. Their presence had been her first and only real glimpse into his other life, but the nature of their connection had remained a secret. However, as she watched the trespasser inspect the physical manifestation of the traits her father had passed down to her, the separation between the two worlds appeared less fixed than ever.

"You have been hard at work, Willow Dinn... stretching the tension between the mandates of your overlords and what the fibers of your being compel you to do."

The Dusudé woman opened the hatch between the posterior support fins and examined the matter conversion tank inside. Willow's grip tightened around the strap of her bag and the angle of the woman's hood shifted.

"They have unjustly claimed so much of this earth in the name of their god. What lengths you must have gone through to acquire the mineral for your own purposes."

"Is that why you're here?" Willow snapped. "For the Torridium?"

The tiniest sound of amusement escaped the woman's nose as she closed the hatch. "No." She pulled her hood back, releasing a knitted white braid that fell to her waist. The patterns on her hands continued onto her face and marked her pointed features with a streak of purple.

One look from the woman's yellow eyes and Willow remembered when she had heard the voice before. "I know you," she said, taking several uneasy steps forward. "You were there the day they took him."

"A loss that is still felt by my people." The woman's eyes fell to the glider. "But to see that the Dinn bloodline has not been poisoned with fear... brings hope."

The tension in Willow's muscles eased. "How did you know him?"

"I remember your father fondly—a herald of truth in a world of deceit." The woman stepped out from behind the glider and in front of Willow. "He was a child of the New Dawn, but he managed to forge the bridge between those who survived, those who were born... and those who were *created*."

Willow's eyes flashed wide. "The constructs? What did my father have to do with the constructs?"

"You carry so much of him inside you, yet you know so little." The woman reached into the depths of her cloak and used her other hand to take one of Willow's. Her skin was hot to the touch. "We vowed to abstain until we were certain of your precepts. You seek freedom, and he wanted you to have it."

A transfer occurred and the woman's hand withdrew, leaving behind a small glass cube in Willow's palm. She rotated the cube at eye level, fingers pinched on opposite edges. Between the timid flares of light reflecting off each face, she saw the filament inside and suddenly knew the exact socket that the bulb was meant for.

The back corner of her basement hadn't always been cast in shadow. The light had just never found it in her presence.

"Why did he leave this?"

"That knowledge was not meant for me. His instructions were to give this to you if the time was ever right."

If the time was ever right.

It was as if her father had been waiting for her to accept the invitation all along. The partition between the two worlds was far more permeable than she had ever thought, and the only thing that had prevented her from crossing over was herself.

Questions were spinning but the woman had already started for the other side of the cave.

"Wait!" Willow shouted, running after her. "Isn't there anything else you can tell me?"

The woman stopped in front of the waterfall and looked back over her shoulder. "I must not prolong my absence. The world is about to change. My mother has seen it." She put her hood up and faced the waterfall. "One day our paths will cross again, Willow Dinn. Until then, it is up to you to find your way." She drew an open palm up to the cavern ceiling. Following her motion, a shimmering gray seam split the wall of water in two. Her fingers widened and each half folded away from the center like a curtain, rerouting the trails of water to either side.

Willow's eyes, attempting to fathom the unfathomable, darted between the woman's outstretched arm and the parted water, but all she could do was accept it without any means to understand.

Once enough of the image of the outside world had been peeled back, the woman flicked her wrist into a closed fist and the water sustained its new form, accented in the otherworldly gray. She leapt through the opening and Willow rushed after her. Gray discs appeared under the woman's feet as she sprinted across the lake's surface, catching each step before dissolving.

The gray curtain began to wane, and Willow stumbled back into the cave just as the water came crashing down into its natural flow. Minutes passed while she watched the falling water, the edges of the bulb passing from one finger to the next. She dropped her backpack and found the pouch. The Torridium shimmered in her palm, reflecting the raging cascade, and she felt herself sink into its infinite, twinkling flow. Currents ran from one hand to the other, from a past she might never know to a tomorrow of her own making, and the unholy voltage electrified her.

PART II

THE ASSASSIN

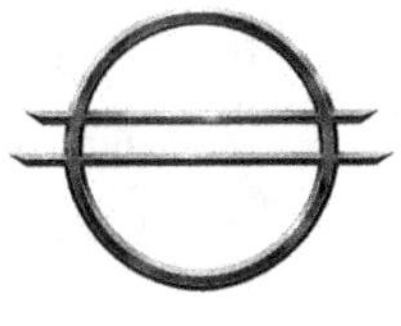

13

LIGHT OUTSIDE AND LIGHT INSIDE. Shadowless light. Roh's light. It had been inside that young woman just like it was in all His children. She needed only to turn inward.

Samuel breathed with ease as he watched Willow's form slip into the mass of innumerable others. The southern junction was growing busy at the time of the shift change, but it was never too crowded. Among his brothers and sisters—that was where life was. There was no chaos, only harmony.

The emitter on the front steps of the house was still singing His word to the junction when a man opened the door, a miner's helmet in one hand and awe in his eyes.

"Greetings, brother," Samuel said.

"One of His knights at my door… To what do I owe this honor?"

Samuel smiled. It was not his individual presence that the man was reacting to but what he represented. The crest he wore was a symbol of peace, and he could only be grateful that he was one of the ones chosen to carry it.

"His word brought me here." Samuel gestured to the emitter.

"Hear Him and rejoice!" the emitter proclaimed. "Wash yourself clean of the impulses of the individual. Give yourself over to His will and feel the connectedness to your kin! We share this existence, and we share in His wisdom."

"How beautiful even the smallest of His miracles can be." Samuel looked off thoughtfully to where he had lost Willow. "To be there when another hears His call… is a blessing to witness." He turned back. "And it was only possible because you brought His word to the junction."

The man was glowing. "I'd bring it to every corner of Haven if it was His will. The Sacred Technologies have blessed this family. My little girl just loves listening to the sermons. They're the cure for every ailment." He looked up to the sky and there was reluctance in his voice. "You must forgive me, brother. Nothing would make me happier than to stay here and talk with a man of such reputation." His eyes sparkled in the reflection of Samuel's armor. "But I've gotta get myself down to the mines."

Samuel bowed. "Our duties must be fulfilled. Know that your contributions are felt by all, and for that we thank you."

"Praise Roh," said the man.

"Praise Roh."

His comrade hurried away and merged into the procession exiting the southern gates. Singular forms became overlapping limbs in a horde of soot-coated jumpsuits heading out of the city. The beauty of the scene was not in its visual qualities, but in its function. Roh tasked them with bitter work, but the fruits of their labor provided the rest of His children a beautiful life. The industry workers answered His call with selfless honor. On a different day, there may have been time to bask in the divine energy of it all, but soon the sun would enter the final stages of its descent, and his place was at the Forge. Roh had weaved the threads of his fate, and he was not meant to question, only to receive.

The cobblestone under Samuel's feet gave way to a dusty gravel path. He was a lone glint of maroon among the mass of earth-covered bodies, all trudging toward the pyramid spouting wisps of smoke from its four tiny chimneys in the distance. His eagerness was stifled within the pace of the crowd, but there was no justification for escaping it. Their destination was the same as his, and their mission equally important. He would find his arrival to be when the Creator had prescribed it, and not a second sooner.

As the gray sands of the Southern Radial filled his frame of vision, a horde of workers from the opposite shift headed toward the city, and the two groups exchanged acknowledgment as they passed. Samuel nodded to anyone who would have him, reveling in the shared sense of duty that bound them together. The call to service was a glorious privilege, no matter what form that took.

The smokestacks that were once miniature fixtures in the distance had grown into their true forms as behemoths, climbing out of a vast stone quarry and unloading their dense vapors into the sky. They rose from the four corners of the pit, protecting the peak of the subterranean pyramidal structure at the center and the holy instruments that were born inside.

Samuel peered over the disjointed metal railing and down the steep embankment to the activity that stirred at the bottom. Bodies spilled in every direction, converging around the many openings that lined the rocky walls. Clusters of workers waited patiently to take their last glimpse of sunlight and be waved inside the mines by the one of the guards. Protocol required a strong military presence during hours of operation. Monitoring who came in was just as important as what came out. The resources inside existed to serve His vision, but in the hands of the faithless they could spell catastrophe.

Just as it became time for him to start his descent down the stairs that led into the pit, the flash of a projectile in his periphery stalled his advance. A small rock bounced off one of the miner's helmets in the pit, shortly followed by a second plunk a few heads away. Glares shot to the ledge and fists waved in the air. Samuel traced the gestures to the closest corner of the quarry's rim, where he found the pair of culprits wearing colors of his own.

One standing and one kneeling beside a pile of stones, the two soldiers cackled. The one on his feet swung his sword back above his shoulder and took aim at the stone his partner had just placed on the ground in front of him. Before his arms could drive down, Samuel ran up from behind him and grabbed the hilt of the sword. The soldier took a casual glance over his shoulder and then his uneven teeth fell into a crooked smile.

"Say now, look who it is!" He twisted around to face Samuel without conceding his grip. "The pride and joy of Midbell all the way out here? I must be dreaming!"

Sid always looked like he found more pleasure in serving himself than he did his kin. He chewed on nothing as he spoke, only partially present at any given moment. Patches of matted, untamed hair spilled out of his helmet's cheek guards, yet his chin was clean-shaven. He was supposed to be a representative of their holy mission, but he barely had the decency to represent himself.

Samuel was not meant to question, only to receive.

He released his hold. "What are you doing, brother? You could have injured someone."

Sid waved the sword to one side with a taunting nonchalance. "Relax, Sammy. We were just having some fun."

Samuel grabbed the hilt again and held the blade still. "You are blatantly misusing the tool He has given you to carry out your sacred tasks."

"Oh, take it easy. We only had one left anyway," said the other soldier as he stepped over the pile of stones, still stacked high with an evening's worth of debauchery.

"Say now…" Sid ripped the sword free. "Do you know what Roh wants for us?"

"Yes," Samuel said.

Sid sucked the air through his teeth, spittle bubbling in the gaps. "Let me tell you what He *really* wants for us." He flipped his sword down and planted the tip into the ground. With his weight supported by the weapon, he crossed one leg over the other. "He wants us to enjoy this beautiful kingdom that He's created!"

"And what enjoyment do those workers feel being pelted by rocks?" Samuel felt the heat in his throat rising.

"I'm not talking about *them*. They know their place. I'm talking about us. Look around, brother! This world is ours for the taking!

The Creator slapped that crest on you and you've got a free pass to do whatever you want."

"What I want," said Samuel, "is to fulfill my duties and help my brothers and sisters prosper in His beautiful creation."

The other soldier fell to his knees. "Please, oh please, Samuel, son of Roh! Please spare us some of your eternal devotion!"

Sid ran his tongue over the top row of a grin and kicked his weight off the sword, snickering. "Say now, Hugh's right. Won't you let us borrow some of that soul of yours?"

The words were barbs in Samuel's spine, stinging his marrow with their venom. "What…" He was out of breath. "What did you say?"

"Open up your ears, Sammy boy!" Sid laughed and gave the side of Samuel's helmet a hard pat. "I said won't you let us *borrow* some of that *soul?*"

Samuel knocked the hand away and grabbed Sid by the neck of his chest plate. "She lies!" he snarled. "The Elder Mother knows nothing of the fate He has written for me."

"The Elder *what?*" Sid laughed and pushed himself free. "What in Roh's name are you talking about?"

Samuel's breath shook as he came back down to solid ground. His fury withered into shame—shame that he had allowed the witch's deception to take control once again.

"Say now," Sid said, grinning, "looks like something ain't right with Kodo's whipping boy. What would the fine general think if he saw you acting this way?"

"He would be wondering what you two boneheads could have possibly said to rile a man of such civility," a voice said from behind Samuel.

Sid and Hugh scrambled themselves into poorly formed stances as Kodo appeared beside Samuel. He gave them no more than a glance before tipping his brow to Samuel.

"Good to see you, First Officer."

"First Officer?!" the pair echoed.

Kodo looked past them at the pile of stones and folded his arms. "It might be in your best interest to at least appear busy. Logan is here."

The color left Sid's face. "What's he doing here?"

Kodo shrugged. "The commander doesn't report to me. But…" He peered over the ledge. "I thought I heard him muttering something about finding some transfers for custodial duty back at the barracks."

Panic flashed in both of their eyes. They scuttled past Kodo, avoiding his gaze, and wedged themselves into the line of workers heading down the stairs.

"Please forgive me, sir," Samuel said. "My actions were a disgrace to the crest I was chosen to wear."

"Samuel, dear boy, you need not apologize for their ineptitude. If those two deadbeats were under my supervision, I would have been discharged long ago for strangling them both!"

Shame loosened its hold, and Samuel allowed himself a smile. "Was that true? Is Commander Logan looking for transfers?"

Kodo tossed his head back. "Ha! Of course not. Logan's far too busy a man to be shuffling around patrol assignments. He's investigating an incident of thievery down in the Forge."

"Related to the insurgency?"

"Unlikely. The foremen suspect that a student's responsible." Kodo checked the sun's position. "We need to get going. The Arch Bladesmith does not like to be kept waiting." He leaned closer. "Take it from me, my boy, her temper burns hotter than the Sacred Kiln itself!"

DESPITE THE VIGOROUS EXERTIONS OF the chimneys, the air inside the Forge was dense with smog. The light reflecting off Kodo's shoulder plates was Samuel's only reference point as he followed the general through the smoke and deeper into the pyramid's sunken base. The air sat in his lungs like sediment at the bottom of a lake, but he was careful to keep pace as they waded through the swarms of workers moving in and out of the obscurity. Threads of intersecting conversations layered on top of some unknown machinery's steady hum, but as level ground gave way to a decline, the incoherent speech and fuzzy contours dissolved into the smoke. Directionless, he kept at the general's heels and knew that the Creator was guiding them both.

His footsteps suddenly lost the depth that solid metal brought, ringing hollow into the hazy void. Kodo's raised fist brought him to a halt, and without the current from their movements clearing the smoke away, the general's form was diluted to an outline, drawn mostly by Samuel's imagination. Something let out a hiss beneath his feet, and a mighty torrent of wind came crashing down atop him. It found the gaps in his armor, coursing over his skin. The lines of the vents on the floor gained clarity as the smoke was sucked through them, and once the pressure yielded, his vision finally returned.

A sealed doorway materialized out of the lingering vapors, as did the pair of masked bishops who guarded it. The oblong masks wore no expression, only the crest of the Church at the center of the forehead above a darkened rectangular visor.

"Production is complete." The distortion of the mask stripped any humanness from the bishop's voice.

"The only one of its kind," added the other.

"Let us see it then," said Kodo.

The bishops crossed to opposite sides and laid their palms against the twin panels on the walls. A blistering orange light spilled out from under the door as it rose.

"She waits for you," they said together.

Through the doorway, the inward slanting walls exposed the Forge's true octahedral form—the reflection point of the structure had been lost in their smoky descent. Built of equal parts brick and legend, the deepest chamber of the facility was the birthplace to the most hallowed weapons in Midbell—not arms for destruction, but instruments to bring about His peace. Boiling vermilions thrashed against the stacks of glimmering Torridium ingots that lined the perimeter, and the scorching gusts from the hearth in the center of the room poured into a domed hood and through the tangle of ductwork above. A massive stone cylinder churning a fiery pool of embers, the Sacred Kiln raged with His divine energy, and Samuel honored His will by basking in its heat.

"General Kodo!"

A metallic bellow shook the chamber and the Arch Bladesmith stepped out from behind the kiln. Her existence had been no more than folklore to Samuel, but as the grated floor bent beneath her boots, she stepped out of the whispers and into a fearsome reality. The layers of fabric that protected her body from the heat of the furnace could not conceal the hulking form underneath. Her words rang into the far reaches of the ceiling, disembodied from the rest of the titan. Like the bishops outside, her face was covered by a rectangular plating, but beneath the Church's crest, there was only a single circular lens. Clutched in one of her monstrous hands was a spear, and even in the fires of the room, its celestial white hue remained untarnished. The sacred tones of His holy mineral in its purest form were colors not to be seen but felt—the color of His light.

A flash of light swam up the shaft as she flipped the spear into an upright position, and her mask angled toward Kodo.

"Your triumphs on the field of war, selfless acts of sacrifice, and imperishable devotion to our Creator have earned your judgment its place atop a pillar of the utmost prestige. Your word comes with the highest respectability and is indisputable as fact." Her masked gaze found Samuel and then returned to Kodo. "Tell me—is this the one who will walk the path of the Paladin?

Kodo mustered a volume to match the Bladesmith's. "The Council of Four has deemed it so. I am but an emissary for their ruling."

The Bladesmith nodded slowly. "Then I must see for myself." She lifted the spear and slammed the base to the ground, sending vibrations through Samuel's bones. "Come to me, young apostle."

Scorching air whipped against Samuel's cheeks as he approached the Bladesmith—a towering, watchful statue whose silhouette was set ablaze by the swirling flames in the kiln behind her.

He was not meant to question, only to receive.

"Tempered with the highest concentration of His mineral..." One by one, her gloved fingers lifted and then tightened around the spear. "From Torridium so pure, it survived heats that would have turned less resilient materials to ash. But what brings destruction for some, creates beauty in others." She tilted a beam of light up to the tip. "The integrity of this creation must also live in its bearer. Let me see His Paladin unhindered."

Her other hand reached under the bottom of the mask to reveal a face weathered by a lifetime spent in the punishing heat of the kiln. The lines of age had just begun their takeover of her visibly coarse skin. Her head was clean-shaven, except for a thick braid at the back of her crown. Scars ran up from her chin and across her left eye. The socket was solid black, a sphere made entirely of Torridium lacking any markings or directionality, yet Samuel could feel it looking through him.

"Lord Talon has warned you of the consequences of failure." Without the mask's distortions, the Bladesmith's voice was harsh and grating, eroded by decades of inhaling the noxious byproducts of her duty to the Creator. "There is only one way to achieve Roh's eternal peace."

"We shall have it," Samuel said, bowing his head.

Her scars tightened with the rest of her face. "Do not underestimate the power of the witch. The apostates of Haven chase their own sacrilegious prophecy and will stop at nothing to see it fulfilled. It is one of lies and deceit—one that speaks of the borrowed soul."

In the reflection of the Torridium sphere, he watched his fury swell. Through seething contempt, he felt his divine purpose. He heard His call, and it was the death of the Elder Mother.

"Any future she has seen is a perverse fabrication spun from a godless mind," he said, his own heat searing his throat. "Only He can move the pieces of the universe. To claim a greater understanding and denounce His will is the highest form of heresy. I will bring an end to this desecration."

The Bladesmith took a step back and returned the mask to her face. She twirled the spear around and drove the bottom of it into the floor between them. Her slow, subtle nod was Samuel's only direction, and he grabbed the spear. Roh's energy radiated from inside the weapon—inside himself.

"My life for Him."

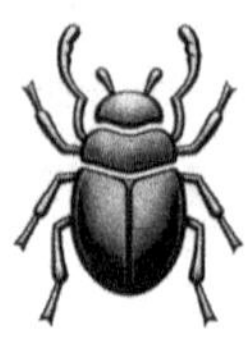

14

ON THE EVE OF HER graduation, after hearing an inspiring pep talk from the perfect-looking soldier boy and conspiring with one of the Dusudé in her secret hideaway at the lake had brought her to the corner of her basement, staring into the dusty abyss, pondering what secrets the gift from her father held—still a little wet—Willow was a damp cliché.

She rotated the panes of the bulb in front of her face, bending the cord above the cabinet into surreal contortions inside the dimension of possibilities contained within cube. The cabinet had a few heads on her, but luckily hers was on top. She curled her lips and stuck the base of the bulb between them. With her feet on the handles, her fingertips found the recess along the upper edge. She shimmied, grunted, and inhaled several lungfuls of dust, but managed to hoist herself to the top. After waving away the strands of cobwebs that buttressed the cable, she plucked the bulb from her mouth. The next breath reached the same depths she had found before loading the Torridium into the glider bike's matter conversion tank back at the lake, and now her entire body was vibrating again. She grabbed the end of the cable, exhaled, then screwed the bulb in.

The filament ignited and all three of the lights faded to black. Seconds stretched into lifetimes while she waited for something to happen. She went to tap the bulb, only because she couldn't think of anything else to do, but before her finger hit the glass, the lights surged, and from somewhere beneath her came a *clunk*. Her head shot down between her crouching knees, drilling through the top of the cabinet, and then she dropped to the floor as fast as she could. The rusted handles squealed as she turned them, barely audible under the sound of her heart in her ears, and she braced herself for what awaited her on the other side.

Three...

Two...

One...

Nothing.

She blinked, and after another sweep of the cabinet's bare interior, she closed the doors and then flung them back open.

Shockingly—still nothing.

She leaned inside and pressed her hand against the opposite wall, then the other two sides. Minutes stacked close to hours as she performed a painfully unfruitful inspection of the behemoth. She pushed, poked, banged, jiggled, and in one moment of exhausted desperation—sniffed. With every failed hunch, she lost a little more faith in herself. If she couldn't even figure out the entrance exam to the world of outlaw thinking, there was no way she could survive here for a lifetime.

With her breaking point closing in, she dropped to the floor in a heap of frustration. She wrapped her arms around her knees and glared at the gaping metal bully, mocking her with all its emptiness. Her foot slid out and kicked one of the doors, slamming it against the front face. It rattled back open to the end of the hinge's allowable range, stopping above a faint patch of lines on the floor. She scrambled to her feet. The streaks aligned with the edges of the cabinet and were of equal length to its base, too concentrated to be the result of casual workshop wear. These were the screeching byproducts of metal scraping across metal—the footprint of some bulky object that had been regularly dragged from one spot to another.

She flew to the other side. The cabinet was too snug against the wall for her to get a grip on the outside, so she spun around and pushed the opposite interior wall. Her arms began to quiver, but even with one foot on the basement wall and all her might behind her, the cabinet wouldn't budge.

Winded, she backed away and wiped beads of sweat off her forehead. It must have been the heaviest pile of screws, bolts, and panels to ever exist… but that was all it was. *A lot is not a lot,* her father used to tell her, *if you take it piece by piece.* Screws, bolts, and panels—they all had been assembled at one point and could be disassembled right now. It didn't matter if she couldn't move the cabinet because she didn't have to.

There was one step that caught her foot, but otherwise it was a clean sprint up the stairs to her bedroom. From the inventory of tools in her desk, she equipped herself with a wrench, screwdriver, and ratchet. She shoved three different-sized sockets into the front pocket of her overalls, hoping one of them would do, then jingled back downstairs.

The doors were the first to go, and then the top. With the right joints loosened, gravity, her determined partner in the process of deconstruction, took care of the heavier panels. It wasn't her most polished idea, but it was working. Bolt by bolt—bolt by corroded, orangey bolt—the cabinet came apart, leaving her only the base to drag out of the corner, which she let slam to the ground just before her fingertips caught fire.

She reclaimed her breath and walked over the wreckage. Slices of light filtered up through the slits of a hatch in the floor where the cabinet once stood. She knelt and floated a hand over the narrow openings, feeling the cooler—cleaner—air leaking from below. The hatch opened on a pair of hinges, and she rested the top edge against the basement wall. Like the air, the light that poured out was cleaner—a shade of manufactured white that belonged in a lab, not in a residential building. The only shadows were around the series of metal rungs that led down into white nothingness.

Before she could make sense of what she was seeing, her body started to move. The next rung couldn't come fast enough, but after missing one completely and nearly plummeting down the remainder of the shaft, she slowed her reckless pace until she reached solid ground. It took several blinks for her eyes to adjust to the space: a room about the size of the basement, but whose pristine qualities bore no resemblance to its dusty and poorly lit counterpart above. Tubes of light along the ceiling coated the walls, floors, and tabletops in a dreamy luster, every surface reflecting the same glossy white that had leaked through the grate. Signs of her inherited neurosis were everywhere: rows of books organized by content and size on the shelves above, blueprints stacked so neatly that their corners could draw blood, and tools spaced evenly apart in perfect alignment with one another.

And for the first time, she saw technologies that were truly sacred.

Consoles that outweighed her and consoles that could fit in her hand, delicate machines and machines that looked like they were designed to be punished, circuit boards with new pathways and hand-drawn plans that corrected the old ones, tablets, scanners, screens, batteries, blinking lights, buttons, switches, dials—the instant her focus settled, something else across the room stole it away. Her attention span was gone, cast off into infinity...

She wanted it all.

Then the workshop and all its wonders condensed into the tiny fold of paper sitting atop a box in the center of the room. Whatever she had been looking at before was a memory from a thousand eons ago as she read the only word that was written, written in her father's script:

Bug

Her fingertip traced the letters, coveting the curves and bends of his writing that had been absent through seasons of bleakness. At first, she hesitated to open the paper, fearful that these could be the last words of his that she would ever receive. But she had to see them.

When you want to disappear for a while.

Bring the dots into alignment and take only what you're holding with you.

Quarter hour on.

Third of that to charge.

Dad

Twice—three times she read his directions, and then the box underneath came into focus. She folded the note into the front pocket of her overalls, flipped the latch on the box, and peeled back the lid. Beneath the layers of cloth inside was a circular device no larger than one of her lenses, fastened to a leather band. The polished silver face was divided into two concentric rings separated by a circular seam. At the top of the inner ring was a divot etched into the metal, and an identical marking rested at the bottom of the outer ring.

The device was suddenly on her wrist. She raised her arm to her face, following the circular seam from one dot to the other. Her thumb and forefinger found the tiny vertical grooves that lined the edge and slowly began to rotate the outer ring. Flames of beautiful, unlawful exhilaration ignited in her soul as she guided the bottom dot in its orbit. When the dots came into formation, the device let out a *click*.

And then it was gone. Not just the device, but her hand, her wrist, her entire arm—they had all vanished.

She squealed and the floor came crashing up to meet her. Although the rims of her glasses were gone, the aid from her lenses persisted as an amorphous window of clarity framed by blurriness. Her field of vision switched from side to side, searching for a body that wasn't there. In a shaky panic, the table scampered away from her, and she felt the back of her skull hit the wall behind her. She reached for her face, and by some stroke of luck, flesh met her palm. From her face she found her shoulder, from her shoulder, her elbow, and from her elbow, the cold, smooth surface of the device on her wrist. Her fingertip traced the seam until she felt the outer dot. The divot slowly slid out from under her touch, following the bend back down the way it came. She raised her arm to where she thought her ear would be. Behind the thunderous pounding in her chest was the faintest ticking noise coming from the device.

Willow found her arms again, then her shoulders, and then as her hand patted her torso, the crinkle of the note in her pocket dialed back the panic. She *heard* her father's words this time, and his voice was a cool wave of relief. The hands that had transported her physical form to an unseeable dimension were also the ones that had held her when she cried, tied her shoes when walking was still new, mended the wounds of her toys after disaster, and whisked her into the air so that she could fly.

There was no danger, only wonder.

She lowered her hands until she felt the hard tile against her palms. Her surroundings wobbled back up to eye level as she steadied herself, and then the table at the center of the room start to creep closer. Each step was shaky, but her missing legs pressed forward. She circled around the table, relearning what it felt like to move in her own body. There were stumbles and trips, but soon the guiding forces that lifted her feet fell back into her subconscious. When basic movement was no longer a spectacle, she once again found herself immersed in the landscape of new ideas—a disembodied consciousness buzzing around the workshop and reaching for anything that looked back at her. Placing one foot in front of the other was one thing, but aiming for a specific target with invisible extremities was another. She couldn't help but giggle when she finally managed to get her hands around a metal canister. Watching the container move on its own, as if it had come to life in the absence of human presence to practice its secret ability of levitation, was one of the oddest, silliest things she had ever seen.

The edges of her invisible smile stretched to her cheeks and the bottom of her vision welled with tears. With every new object that floated off the countertop, she could hear the ridiculous sounds her father would have added to their movements, softening the explanations of their complex functions. It was only with him that learning seemed more like play and science felt like magic.

Eventually, the outer dot reached its original position, and Willow's arms rematerialized before her eyes. She nearly jumped out of the same body she had just returned to and backed into the center table, sending the box that once stored the cloaking device tumbling off the other side. It landed face down on the floor with an unexpectedly loud *thud*. She looped around the table, and when she flipped the box back over, she felt its dense center of mass drop to the bottom.

Her heart skipped a beat at the prospect of more, and she dug through the bunches of fabric to unearth the cover of a book. It could have been brown upon its first read, but the material had deteriorated into an unidentifiable shade of decay. There was no label and one of the corners was entirely gone. Over inches of pages, she found the back cover and pulled the bloated tome out of its casing. The binding was scarred with white lines that only thousands of impassioned openings could have brought. Both covers were holding on with threadbare fingers, forced to make room for the many loose sheets of paper that had been wedged in between the pages. Her thumb flipped through the stack, and a deluge of handwritten text and drawings cascaded from the back cover to the front, crashing to a halt at the first page.

KD

5055.10.14

It has begun. Finally, our movement has left its infancy and taken its first steps to rewrite the fabric of society. Although the horizon is distant, it still shines brighter than any of us could have ever dreamed. Suddenly, a pitiful band of overzealous engineers, the city's most wanted fugitives, and a group of military defectors is now the driving force of opposition to the deception that the Church has imposed upon us all. The infiltration of the power plant is complete, and we have commandeered the facility for our operation. We've been able to maintain remote control of the city's employment manifest for the upper levels so that our people are always the ones up there. Any transfer request is rerouted and the city is none the wiser. But there are too many of us now to all use the cover of working here. There are some like me, slipping in and out of their surface lives, but others have decided to abandon the front altogether and have made this place their permanent home.

Leon said that our numbers have doubled since setting up at 3-10. Even with our screening protocols, the volume of new members coming in is more than I can keep up with. New faces every day, yet we all carry the same heart. With the greatest minds in the city assembled, I can only begin to imagine what we can accomplish.

I always knew there had to be others out there, those of us who know that there is more out there and are willing to risk every-thing to expose that truth, but I never expected to see so many with my own eyes.

If we hope to shift the trajectory that the world is on, there can be no turning back now. We are the bearers of truth, and it is our responsibility to keep that truth alive.

15

UNDER A CLOUDLESS NIGHT SKY, the radiance of the full moon consumed the glow of the tablet and washed the alleyway's two interlopers in a silver luminescence. The hands holding the device bore only a ghoulish resemblance to Annika's own. She watched strings of text and numbers scroll down from the top of the screen and push the ones at the bottom into nothingness. The bar on the right side increased with every few lines that passed.

98

She pulled away from the screen and looked to the end of the alleyway, where Cassian lay flat against one of the walls, his head peeking out from his cover and into the city. The mallet on his hip, irradiated by the moonlight above, gained its celestial shade of white from the purity of the mineral from which it was forged. It was a gift from the Elder Mother Ursa, she was told, one he had been training with since he first came to the Guild. In his hands, it was as elegant as it was deadly. An intricate lattice of etchings weaved over the surface of the weapon from the bottom of the hilt and covered all but one of the square faces of the head. Four curved prongs jutted out from the corners of the undecorated face and converged in a lethal spike. While well-equipped for a physical confrontation, Cassian was visibly distracted. The restlessness in his body was a product not of the present moment, but of the lingering aftermath of the decision to leave Willow's fate in continuance.

Collecting readouts from the city's utility conduits was a routine operation, so when Isaac had sent her and Cassian out after the trouble with Leon, she assumed he had an ulterior motive. Proficient in the subtle ways of helping his brother, Isaac knew how to give Cassian exactly what he needed without any condescension. Sending them out on field work would not have raised any suspicion, had she not had the timetables for updating the Guild's database memorized. Updates were not scheduled for several more weeks, but Cassian needed anything else to focus on. It was a tactic she was far from understanding how to execute herself, but the more she watched, the more she learned—and maybe one day she too would know how to help Cassian.

She wanted to.

99

Isaac's strategy, however, was built under the assumption of normal circumstances, and the situation with the girl was anything but. Their outing began outside the Dinn residence, where Cassian waited for signs that never came. Long after the upstairs bedroom window went dark with inactivity, he was still searching for anything to justify doing what he knew was right. What they *both* knew was right. Eventually, she was forced to remind him that they would be unable to plug into any city terminals during the waking hours, so they set off for the nearest conduit. The first few downloads were completed in distant silence. Cassian was there with her but he also was not. His eyes would leave their post and enter the detached vacuum of his thoughts. She wondered just how far away he had drifted, and if the solution might not be a matter of pulling him back to her but meeting him wherever he was.

100

Annika unplugged the cable feeding into the tablet from the conduit's control panel and began to loop the slack around her hand as Cassian fell back from the street.

"Did we get them all?" he asked.

She clicked the dial on the side of the tablet with her finger and the screen flipped to a map of the city. One blinking dot remained on an otherwise static network of lines.

"There's still one more," she said, leaning into him.

"How far?"

Her finger traced a path of right angles from their current position up to the blinking dot. "Less than fifteen blocks to the lower part of the commercial district."

He nodded, his head moving with the same quality of non-presence that had accompanied every one of his actions since they left the Dinn house. She looked for signs of his need, but all she could find was the reflection of the blinking dot in his eyes. There had to be more. She just needed to be let in.

Her grip on the side of the tablet loosened, but before she could make a move for his hand, he blinked back into the present and looked up from the screen.

"Ready whenever you are," he said.

Her hand retreated. She deposited the tablet and cord inside the bag and fit her arms through the straps. "Ready."

They kept to the shadows, careful to permeate the reach of the lamplights only when it was necessary to get to the other side of the street. Isaac had done his best to document the patrol routes of the city guards, but he always urged them to still use caution when out at night. There was nothing inherently illegal about their presence, but one quick glance at the weapon attached to Cassian's hip would reveal the nature of their actual identities, and no counterfeit documentation could prove otherwise.

The means of accessing the final conduit was always changing. Their target was on the exterior of a multistory building, one floor up. Structural renovations over the last year meant they needed a new plan to reach the conduit's output link each time an update was required, but as they approached the building, they found the face with the conduit covered in a tower of scaffolding, removing any need for calculation.

They were out of sight on this side of the building. Behind them, there were no signs of life, only the seeds of some future development. Piles of construction materials were scattered across the lot and the air between was hollow with inactivity. Further protection was granted by the tarp draped over the first three tiers of landings, leaving the second level of the scaffolding almost entirely enclosed—barring a rogue gust of wind. The planks under their feet were not aligned properly, which allowed Annika to piece together the ground beneath them through the gaps in the wood.

The wood creaked as she dropped to one knee and slipped off the bag. Cassian retrieved the cable while she powered on the tablet. In the time it had taken them to get from the last conduit, the cable had abandoned its neatly looped form and knotted itself several times over. She watched him track down one end and then feed it through the tangle of wire. As soon as the tablet was ready to begin the final download process, she set it on top of the bag and found the other end of the cable. They unraveled it in silence, her fingers only stopping when she stole a glance at Cassian. The lines of worry on his face had yet to release their hold. His eyes scoured the jumble between them, searching for answers that were more entangled than any knot of wire. Her mouth opened to no sound, but he did not notice. The same sensations that she felt back at the power plant returned to her—a paralysis of sorts, her body wanting to act but her mind failing to know how to do so. She could not help him if she did not understand what he was experiencing.

This time, words did come, but she could hardly claim them as her own.

"When Leon told us we must continue to refrain from intervening... how did you *feel?*"

His fingers stopped. "I... I don't know." She sensed him switch back into the present. "There's just so much."

Her fingers had also stopped, but only because they had done all they could. He took in a breath but hesitated before releasing anything else. There were hints of his struggle that Annika recognized as analogous to her own—the inability to characterize what was being felt in a way that could be understood by herself or anyone else. A direct solution was something she did not have, but what she could offer was solidarity.

"Sometimes assigning a title to these sensations alone does not feel like an adequate way of describing them." She found honesty easier than trying to formulate a practical resolution. "I frequently fail to identify them myself, let alone verbalize them."

Cassian's chest loosened. She looked back down and located the path that his end of the cable would need to take. The solution seemed obvious, yet he could not see it for himself. She felt an impulse to reach down and free the wire herself, but an even stronger one to see him find it on his own.

"Do you remember a time when you felt this way before?"

Seconds stretched on while he examined the wire, and then his hands began to move.

"When we first lost Kip, everything stopped for me. It was like I was stuck in place, watching the rest of the world move on without me… Even Isaac seemed to recover quicker than I thought he would." He pulled the wire through one of the many loops that remained on his half. "For weeks, I thought about all the things I could have done—*should* have done—to stop them from ever taking him in the first place. I would lay awake at night trying to figure out how to get him back, but deep down I knew it was too late, that I was no longer in control. He was gone, and there was no negotiating with reality." The movements of his hands were growing larger and the knots becoming fewer. "A year later, and I'm the only one on the committee who can see that the same thing is about to happen again… And I can't do anything to stop it. I felt helpless when Kip died and I feel helpless now."

Annika let his words settle for just as long as it had taken them to be spoken before she contributed any of her own. "You said you were not in control before. Are you in control now?"

He was about to pull the wire through the final knot when something rustled beneath them. His fingers froze, and he shot Annika with a flash of concern. She reached over to power down the tablet, avoiding any pronounced shift in her weight on the tottering planks. They condensed their forms and brought their breaths into soundless unison as they listened.

Footsteps—scattered and timid in their advent but drawing near. A man slipped into the space between two of the planks beneath her. He came in and out of sight, pacing under the cover of the platform. Slung over one shoulder was a satchel, secured in place with a tapping hand. Each time he passed through her line of vision, his head was pulled to a different angle.

The fragmented slivers of the man began to stack into one coherent picture. He had several years on Cassian but stood a head shorter. A tiny braid stuck out from the back of his crown and although the hair on his face was irregular and sparse, it was groomed with the importance of fine art. His eyes, more restless than his steps, flickered around the night.

A new pair of footsteps approached, their tempo measured and their speed swift. Once they grew loud enough for the untrained ear to detect, the pacing underneath the platform ceased. Annika craned her neck to a different gap to see another man step into the scene below. He wore the white linens of a laboratory engineer and a cold, dissociated expression. His build was much closer to Cassian's, towering over the other man even from the distance the shadowy interaction placed between them.

Several empty blinks passed before he finally spoke. "Redd, I presum—"

"Keep your voice down, you fool," the man with the tiny braid, Redd, said through his teeth. "They have ears everywhere."

"My apologies," said the engineer, dropping his volume but not his posture.

Redd huffed his displeasure through his nose. "It's poor etiquette to arrive late, especially on the first contact."

"Please forgive me. I have never engaged in a transaction such as this before."

"Of course you haven't," Redd scoffed. "Look at you—an ideal civil servant. People you had never met decided what the rest of your life would be like when you turned eighteen, and you never once even entertained the thought of distrusting their guidance." He began to circle the engineer. "And why would you? Everything is good here! There's no reason to second-guess what they've told you. It all makes sense, right? We were all created by the same god to serve the same god." His sardonic whispers crept into a higher pitch. "For what higher fulfillment could there be? Roh, Roh, let us all praise Roh!"

Annika checked on Cassian, who was watching the scene below between a different set of planks through narrow eyes.

"But maybe one day not so long ago something happened... and you started to have..." Redd patted the satchel as he completed his prowl. "... some questions?"

The engineer transferred his attention to the bag and then back to Redd. "Am I to understand that you have the text I requested?"

"Yes, yes, I have your book. But first—" Redd held out an open palm. "The payment."

In a similar movement as before, the engineer shifted to the extended hand and then back to Redd's face. There was no change in his expression, just several more vacant blinks before reaching into the pocket of his lab coat. His hand reappeared slowly, bringing with it three glass vials. The liquids inside, irradiated by the moonlight, glowed an otherworldly white just like the mallet on Cassian's hip.

Redd's form straightened the second the tubes met the night air. The engineer took one step forward and Redd closed the rest of the distance himself. Fixated on his bounty, he fumbled around the opening of his satchel to produce a book from inside and then snatched the vials away. He discarded the book at the engineer's feet and turned his back to the interaction.

His eyes flared as he raised the tubes in front of his face, glistening with eagerness. "Yes... yes... these will do. And was the purity tested?"

"The residuals maintained a purity of 98.84 percent," said the engineer.

"Excellent." Redd ran the vials underneath his nose. "Truly excellent. I already have several buyers lined up." He filled his lungs to capacity and then released his breath. "Our society is so obsessed with the power that the raw element brings, they overlook what just a tiny bit of tinkering to the molecules can do for the human experience."

The engineer dropped his focus and crouched down to retrieve the book off the ground. He stood slowly, staring at the cover. "Do you believe the words inside?"

"I'll believe whatever you want, as long as I get paid," Redd said, grinning at the vials.

The engineer pulled himself up from the book with a subtle rigidity. "How did you acquire a text such as this?"

There was a glint of irritation in Redd's voice. "I can provide you with most anything you seek, but my sources are my own."

Eyes fixed on Redd, the engineer slipped the book into the pocket of his coat. "Did another person give this to you?"

Redd lowered the vials, glowering. "You got what you requested," he hissed over his shoulder. "Now stop asking questions and get out of here!"

The engineer did not move, or even so much as blink.

"What's the matter with you?" Redd barked as he turned around, completely disregarding his initial call for discretion.

The reflexive human reaction that Annika expected never came. She found an unsettling mirror in the engineer's behavior to the tendencies she was trying to unlearn in herself. Her eyes flashed to Cassian, whose hand was resting on the hilt of the mallet.

The engineer moved closer. "I would like you to take me to them."

"If you want anything else, you'll go through me. That's how this works." Redd jammed the vials into his satchel and began to speak faster as the engineer moved closer. "You're lucky I even accepted this requisition. Do you have any idea how much risk I incurred to obtain the item you asked for? A man could spend the rest of his life in a cage for just pondering its existence! You don't get to... demand... that I..."

His voice withered as he craned his head back just to make eye contact with the engineer, who stood at his toes.

"If you will not bring me to the source, then the chain of this illegal dissemination will end with you." A pulse of white filled the engineer's eyes and he seized Redd by the throat. His other hand reached into his lab coat, drawing a dagger from his waist. A streak of moonlight ran up the midnight blade as the engineer cocked back his shoulder.

"Stop!" Cassian tore the mallet off his hip and lunged through the tarp, rolling into his landing on the ground below.

The construct snapped toward Cassian. It flung its victim against the building's exterior, the impact leaving Redd unconscious on the ground. The moon found the blade once more as the construct turned fully to Cassian, locking onto its new target.

Cassian braced the mallet defensively across his torso as the construct made a dash toward him. Annika leapt through the tarp and landed on the construct's back, the force from her jump bringing them both to the ground in a wrestling pile of interlocked forms. She rolled on top and pinned the arm holding the dagger, but a sudden pressure rose under her torso as the construct's legs straightened, launching her onto her back.

It was a quick recovery, Annika barely touching the ground before she was back on her feet. Cassian was quick to fill her absence with a downward-swinging mallet, but the construct was too fast and curled out of the way of the hammer's trajectory. The tip met the stone with a thunderous clash worthy of an object ten times the weapon's size, leaving a crumbling imprint of the mallet's spike behind. Cassian took another swing, but the construct spun up to one knee just in time to deflect the strike with the flat of the blade. With the momentum of the attack redirected, the construct drove the opposite fist into Cassian's abdomen and sent him reeling backward.

Annika sprinted forward, forcing the construct's attention to pivot before the dagger could mirror the fist's strike. The blade jabbed out toward her, just missing her collar as she threw her upper half out of its path. She brought the top of her wrist up to knock the extended arm at the elbow and break its form. The deathly grip released its hold and the dagger fell to their feet. Folding her hand into a point, she shot a jab into the throat, pushing the construct one step back, granting her the offensive position.

Cassian was coming in quickly from behind, but the split second of wavering in Annika's focus gave the attack away. Dropping to the ground, the construct swept Cassian's legs out from underneath him and continued the propulsion upward with a kick into Annika's side. Her body bent to the force of the hit and she stumbled several lateral steps but managed to stay standing. By the time she had regained her balance, the construct had armed itself again and was heading straight for her. She was on the defensive, backpedaling against a flurry of attacks. The strikes alternated between blade and fist, but she blocked each one with the same precision with which they were dealt. The two were locked in a rapid onslaught of well-choreographed forms, their movements becoming increasingly predictable to the other the longer the fight wore on.

The construct feigned a stab and then dropped the dagger into its other hand. Having only prepared a block against the decoy strike, Annika left herself open to the sudden switchback and reversal of grip. She pulled away, but not before the blade sliced across her shoulder. A wince escaped through her teeth as a foot thrust into her midsection. Her back met the hard stone again and then the construct was above her. It flipped the dagger back around to an upright position and its eyes pulsed white.

She managed to get to her elbows but no further. Using the angles of the enemy's body, she mapped the course of the blade, identifying her throat as the end point. The dagger came thrusting down, but in the same instant a spinning blur flew out of her periphery, and suddenly the construct toppled over. One of its legs had given out and was folded underneath the rest of its body in unresponsive disarray. Wrapped around its thigh was an old adversary—the coil that had almost cost her a sparring match with Isaac.

Cassian was right behind his throw, dashing toward their fallen opponent. The construct saw him too and quickly turned its focus back to its leg, desperately trying to wedge the flat of the blade underneath the coil's constricting hold. When the tip had nowhere to go except into skin, it tossed aside the dagger and clawed helplessly at the limb.

Only strides away, Cassian pulled back the mallet and, with the entire force he brought with him, plunged the spike into the top of the construct's head. The collision sounded with a crushing screech, and the body beneath the head fell limp, dangling from the impaled weapon. Once Cassian had captured his lost breath, he placed a sturdy hand on the construct's shoulder and yanked the mallet free. The upper half of the body collapsed to one side, and stillness reclaimed the night.

Annika was halfway back up when she felt Cassian's hands under her forearm, and even after she was back on both feet, he held on to her.

"You're hurt," he said.

She followed his gaze to her shoulder. The blade had cut through a layer of fabric and skin, but thankfully nothing more. Beads of light coursed through the thousands of white fibers inside the tear. The exterior dermis would need repair, but the interior systems appeared undamaged.

"It is only a surface wound," she said. "If Isaac could fuse your tibia back together, then mending this should prove to be a relatively simple task."

A hint of a smile broke through Cassian's hardened expression, and she felt her own cheeks rise.

"Regardless," he said as he let go of her arm, "we'll have him stitch you up the second we get back." He crouched down and rolled the construct on its back. "And we'll bring our new friend here with us."

The book slid out of the construct's coat pocket, and Annika knelt to grab it. The cover was woven from ancient materials, and the words—if they ever existed—had been claimed by time long ago. She opened the first page.

Collected Seminary Works, Abbott Wilhelm

April 21, 1942 - September 6, 1945

"What is it?" Cassian asked.

She scanned a sample of random pages. "I'm not entirely sure," she said after absorbing a few more. "Some kind of handwritten theological analysis. The format of the creation date is consistent with Dusudé chronometry."

"We can take a closer look when we get back to the Guild." He leaned over the construct's head, peering into the crater that the mallet had left. "Isaac is going to have his hands full."

A sound from back toward the building drew their attention away from the book. Redd had regained consciousness and was approaching them with an unfittingly casual pace given the altercation that had just occurred.

Cassian looked at Annika's shoulder again, then motioned for her to stay where she was. He stepped over the body and cut Redd's path short halfway between where the conflict had started and ended.

"Are you alright?" Cassian asked.

"Me?" Redd placed a hand on his chest. "Oh please, I'm fine. I would have disarmed the brute myself, had you not beaten me to it." The cogency with which he lied made Annika wonder if he actually believed the last statement himself. "But I must admit, the way you handled the situation for me aroused some... considerations as to how prudent the need for additional protection in my line of work has become. Any chance you're looking for employment?"

"Sorry, not interested."

Redd shrugged. "Suit yourself then."

Cassian folded his arms. "But what I am interested in is learning how this trade was in any sense justifiable for you. Acquiring a text from the Old World just for some conversion residuals? No altered state could be worth putting yourself in that kind of danger. And you don't show any signs of addiction."

"All of this? Just for me? Ha! Of course not. This amount of residuals could kill a man a hundred times over! No, no, these are not for me. It's all business, my curious friend, and I'm afraid you far undervalue the substance. You see, the demand is high here within the city walls, but even higher among the clans out in the Radials."

"The clans? Who? Surely Isaiah and Remos haven't fallen so low as to allow—"

"Oh! Oh my! Look at this! We're no stranger to the underbelly of Midbell now are we? Hmm… no faithful servant of Roh here." Redd leaned to the side, angling for a better view of the mallet. "One of Leon's people perhaps?"

Cassian shifted his weight. "We're not *his* people. He is one of us."

"Relax, dear friend." Redd stifled a laugh. "Don't take everything so personally," he said and patted Cassian's arm.

Annika sprang to her feet.

"Not allowed to touch, are we?" Redd asked as she closed in.

She was watching him just as much as he was her. He sustained a smirk until she arrived at Cassian's side, at which point his eyes fell to her shoulder. The color left his face, and he stared at her in gaping stupefaction. At this proximity, the details of the wound were perceivable: a bloodless portal into her inorganic makeup. Behavior could be learned, and patterns altered, but the physical qualities that differentiated creation from birth would always remain. The foreign hues and materials that composed her inner systems were different— and to most, dangerous.

"You… you…" Redd raised a quivering finger to Annika, his façade of confidence turning to dust. "You're one of them!" Eyes trembling, he started to backpedal but lost his footing. He scurried back on his hands and bottom and then scrambled to his feet, fleeing into the shadows from which he came.

As the footsteps dissolved into the night, Cassian pinched his brow. "We need to get out of here before anything else happens." He dropped his hand and checked the body behind them.

"I can—" she started.

He shook his head. "Not until Isaac looks at your shoulder. I'll get the body."

His tone left no room for negotiation, and the intention behind it sat warmly in her chest.

"The closest access point is only a few blocks away. I can manage that." He looked up at the building. "Can you grab the bag from up there?"

She nodded and headed for the scaffolding.

"Annika," he called after her.

She turned around.

"You are *not* one of them."

16

PAGES FILLED WITH TALES OF close calls with the Church, impossible scientific ideas brought to life, and a cast of characters Willow had never met were piled high on the left side of the notebook. The deeper she went, the easier it became for her to forget that this was her father's personal journal and not the most captivating story she had ever read. She followed him through the formation and rise of the Guild—a diabolical division of dissidents working in the shadows and weaponizing their individual creativity in search of their world's forbidden truths. Whatever revelation she thought she had come to by finding this place beneath the basement was only a sliver of the whole picture. The words she read started to frame what she knew about her father within a larger and more exhilarating new reality—one where the same man who had cleaned frosting off her chin and read her stories before bed helped usher in magnificent change.

Kip Dinn: father, engineer, and leader of a revolution.

By developing the Guild, he had done more than just centralize the resistance movement, he had created a place where the exchange of new ideas didn't need to be hushed under the noise of the fountains and Roh could be questioned at more than just a whisper. The organization's sole endeavor was the progress of humanity, whether that took the form of dismantling the Church's oppressive systems or pushing past the perceived limits of innovation. As the technological feats he described grew more complex, Willow found herself rereading entries just to glean any scrap of understanding that she could. While she could follow the underlying principles, the concepts themselves lay outside the parameters of her reality. Even the format of the journal conflicted with the Academy's teachings. The dates on the corners of each entry had remained consistent in their own system but didn't align with any calendar she had ever seen.

But she was not discouraged. She was determined. Her entire life, she had been told not to question, only to receive. But now, seeing the possibilities of the world—*her* world—she felt she was owed the right to question.

5056.01.04

Our field team returned this morning. They limped off the lift, covered in blood, but thankfully all bodies were accounted for— plus one. Lucas Downing. He was one of eight individuals that we have been tracking over the last year, all of which we believe are not human. Upon confrontation, our suspicions have been proven true each time, always resulting in some sort of altercation. Four have been brought in so far, but only after they've been permanently subdued. Regardless, we've been scraping whatever insight we can from the inactive units. Without a live unit to examine though, I fear that we have exhausted the knowledge that external testing alone can provide. But I know there is more to learn. We need to look deeper. We need to understand their internal systems.

Without any protocol for what to do with an active unit, a hundred different voices brought a hundred different opinions, mustering a storm of ideas all equally worth investigating. But there was one that made me forget that there was ever any other option.

"Why don't we connect into the unit?"

I recognized her face—not from around the power plant, but from a recent crime report about an incident of sacrilegious sedition at the city's main publication institute. The lead programmer of the academic division had decided to recode all the input scripts for the printing systems with lies and blasphemy. Absolutely brilliant. She may have gotten away with it too, had one of her alleged conspirators not found Roh's light and blown the whistle on the whole operation. We're honored to have her.

There was an evenness about her, a silent confidence. Surrounded by the cultivators of ideas previously unseen in this world, she moved on a plane of existence all her own. She wasn't wondering if what she had proposed was possible, she was already planning how we were going to do it. For many reasons, my thoughts cannot escape her. She may not have said it explicitly, but she didn't have to—we are wasting the few opportunities we have by examining the constructs like they are humans. Our questions are evolving and so too must the tools we use to answer them. What else could we be learning if we stopped using our technology and started using theirs?

Maybe it's time we find out together, Eleanor.

Finger after finger, Willow's knuckles were all out of air. *Eleanor.* The name pushed even the mention of the constructs into the far-off recesses of Willow's mind. She knew the name not from her own memories, but from the ones that her father had passed down with warmth and tenderness. It made little sense to her, the closeness she could feel to someone that she had never met—and never would. The physical likeness she had of the woman was assembled with borrowed components, and she had only a single word to accompany the image: Mom.

She had been given the basic outline of her parents' time together, just a vague collection of shapes that lacked any color. Their relationship was so intertwined with the work being done at the Guild that she had only ever received fragments of the whole picture. The story of their union could only be recounted before the backdrop of highly illegal affairs, and only now could it be received in its entirety.

They ventured into the unfathomable as strangers, joined only by their common objective. Her father described the addition of another directing mind in the lab as an asset, moving their work forward in ways that otherwise would have been impossible. Entire entries documented her ingenuity and dedication. He had found his match, both in intellect and passion, and he was obsessed. When what he referred to as the "easy" part was through, his ideas started to lose their marrow. His notes were incomplete and his thoughts cyclical. Yet whenever frustration and despair began to triumph, Eleanor—El as he called her—would have the missing pieces waiting for him. The nights together ticked on, and they found themselves operating less as two separate entities but as extensions of each other. They were not just copilots on a quest for discovery. They were partners.

5056.08.03

The prototype is nearly complete. With this new machine, we should be able to connect directly to a unit's neural core. The rest of the systems found within the skull make isolating the core rather challenging, and a full extraction would have surely laid waste to the remaining circuitry inside the head, but thanks to El, we won't even have to consider such a risk.

It was her idea to try an exogenous connection. With a precise and delicate insertion process, we should be able to connect the apparatus through the nasal cavities while preserving the other internal structures. The inactive unit that our field team recovered a few months back will be our first subject. We have finished developing the hardware, and all that remains now is to ensure that our systems are prepared to accept the data that is stored inside the core when the day finally comes. The nights in the lab will be long, but there is nowhere else I would rather be.

This is by far the greatest advancement we have made in understanding the constructs and the first step to understanding the only other form of sentience our civilization has ever known, an achievement not just for the Guild, but for humanity—and it is all because of her.

Long ago, Ursa gifted me a relic from the Old World. A phonograph machine, she called it. Sounds from lifetimes ago with only limited life themselves. Every listen was one less that would ever be heard again. But what better occasion than this? I asked El if she would like to dance.

She said yes.

The next quarter inch of the book was filled with a spring of new information that could have only accompanied an endeavor as momentous as the one they had set out on: drawings, calculations without context, notes written over scratched-out notes, and, buried among the miscellany, a sketched diagram of the apparatus itself. Thin gray lines shaped a head for placement around a much heavier-handed rendering of what Willow understood to be the neural core. The cylindrical prongs at the ends of two cables served as the connection points, inserted through each nostril and into the core. She winced, the thought of the sensation making her eyes water. Innovation. Disgusting, brilliant innovation.

5056.11.19

The doubts that found me in the middle of the night now sound laughable. I should have known better than to give in to them. With her at my side, we can accomplish anything.

The process is complete, and we have successfully mapped the neural core. This is more information than we ever dreamed we would have on the constructs, but we're far from finished. It will take years to interpret all of this. The literals and numbers with standardized formats are easy to translate, but there are oceans of data here, and none of it can be analyzed in isolation. Mr. Downing will only be able to tell us so much, and eventually we will need more subjects. Their origins lay somewhere amongst the maelstrom of information inside the core, and it will take everything we have to decipher it all. But it's a start. We are at a point of inflection, and the truth is finally within reach. This is both the most we have ever known about the adversary and the least we will ever know.

And there's more, a life-changing day not just for the Guild, but for El and me too. Months of preparation and there was an outcome we never anticipated.

El is with child.

Willow would have once described her father as a tinkerer. He was a curious and playful soul. A puzzle-solver. Never did she imagine that he was one of the two minds responsible for forging the connection between humankind and the constructs. Yet the profundity of their accomplishment was dulled by the sense of dread that was slowly inching up her spine. She knew what was coming next. It was only a matter of pages before she would have to confront the unavoidable—the one part of the story that she already knew.

5056.11.24

The decision belongs to El. She will have my support no matter what she chooses. She thinks using a city medical facility would be too dangerous, and I agree. If she were recognized, she would be arrested, and if there were a child involved, they would surely be taken. Our records team has gotten quite adept at creating counterfeit identification, but the risk is still too high.

The Guild has never had to face anything like this before. We are wildly underprepared for either procedure. But I believe in the people here. The physicians in our sick bay have brought people back from the brink of death. Even Jasper is willing to help. He knows of a city repository with medical supplies and says he can get us anything we need. Together, we will find a solution, and together, we will make sure she is safe.

5056.12.02

El has made her decision. A brilliant inventor and courageous defender of freedom, and soon, a mother. The prospect of a family with her fills me with happiness I didn't think possible. A new life will emerge, sewing the threads between myself and the person whose intelligence, resolve, and compassion I admire most. To welcome a child into this world at her side will be the greatest privilege.

But underneath the luster of this daydream is bitter conflict. I can see it in El too. There is no clear answer for what future this child will have. They deserve to know the truth, but to ostracize them from the ways of society at birth seems equally unfair. If they're not kept down here like a prisoner, they'll be caught between two lives, just like me. The nights of sneaking around, flipping between one version of yourself and the other, hiding your true self from the rest of the world—to force them into this dance might be just as cruel as subjecting them to the repressive machine of the Church. A resolution will need to be reached, but not today. I don't think either of us know what the right decision is. What I do know is that we will love them beyond words. Always.

5057.04.15

The impending magnitude of the situation has rallied the Guild. I've never seen it so alive. It is truly remarkable, just how far our people are willing to go for one another. Everyone here is doing anything they can to help. Our systems operators were able to build a connection to the city's health-sciences data bank to pull any available resources on obstetrics, and for the last several months, the more advanced medics have been training themselves for the procedure.

So much is before us. Soon we will have to shift our focus entirely to the procedure. But until then, El doesn't want to slow down.

She is determined to keep working on the core. We have located what we believe to be the central processing segment, where the main programming of the entire construct is contained. There are fixed commands, but there also seem to be adaptive formulas that respond to new inputs as they arrive. This leads us to believe that the intelligence of these beings is generative and will continue to advance the more that they experience.

I must admit that it's difficult to even start to make sense of it right now, because my mind is elsewhere. With El. With the child.

5057.06.28

The day is nearly upon us. Only weeks until the child arrives. We have one medic fully prepared to perform the delivery and several more will be behind her every step of the way. Some of our machine specialists were even able to create an incubation chamber for after the delivery. Jasper returned from his raid on the city repository with an entire crate of supplies. Everything we need is here. For someone who spends most of his existence being irritable and condescending, he has shown us his true colors.

Through it all, El hasn't lost her grounding once. She remains the steadiest person in the room, in any room—and that's probably for the best, because I'm nervous enough for us both. Her work on the core hasn't slowed. Each morning, I think I will see her pace yield, but each morning I am proven wrong. With more than enough reason to take a step back, she persists. "Obstacles can only hinder us when we accept them as such," she once told me. "If given the ability, clarity, and most importantly, the will, it is our responsibility to the world to continue onward."

Eleanor, you will never cease to inspire me. I look at you and think of our child. Such greatness is before them. Not as a creator or rebel, but as a human being. If they inherit any of your heart, any at all, they will be among the best of us.

5057.08.01—

Willow tore herself from the page. Her eyes fled to the ceiling, finding their first breath of air in hours. The stinging light from above set the teary edges of her vision into a boil. Her jaw was trembling, the final defense to the flood of heartache that she was barely keeping down. The date alone was enough. She had had the minimum amount of information before ever opening the book, but now she could have written the rest of this page herself. Her father had told a much softer version of the story's unfortunate next chapter long ago. A life for a life, although it certainly didn't feel like an equal trade. The world lost one of its most capable and unyielding minds—a force that could have completely altered the future she was now living in. All just so that she could exist.

And for what?

Had the two greatest agents of change really given their lives just so that she could putter around with a homespun glider bike off in a cave somewhere? Were both of her parents' sacrifices made just so she wouldn't get too bored with her shadow life as a city engineer? There had to be more—more for her and more for them. The stirrings behind the tears weren't sorrow. They were a righteous call to action. She had always had the ability, had only recently found clarity, and, by becoming a visitor in their world, had now been given the will. The responsibility to continue onward and keep their work alive was now hers to bear. Freedom had found her, and it was up to her to use it for the greater good.

There was no destination, only a direction—forward. Progress was only possible on the back of knowledge, and she still had so much to learn. The right stack of pages was taller than the left twenty times over, and although it felt like lifetimes had passed, she had barely scratched the surface. It would take more than a single night to get through, longer still to begin to process it all, and even then, she had no way of knowing if this was everything. But it was a start.

17

A GRID OF DOTS APPEARED on Annika's shoulder. The bounds of the square stretched and then condensed until it was no bigger than the vertical dimension of her wound. As it shrank, the geometries of the individual dots lost their distinctions. Indifferent in its color, the square further yielded its definition to the overhead lights of the workshop, which were dialed twice past their normal brightness. The origin was easier to pinpoint—a beam firing out of the device in Isaac's hand.

The Hydra, as he often referred to it, resembled a welding torch in both size and shape, but its function pertained solely to the restoration of the body. From the back of the handle ran a wire that connected into a monitor on his desk, to which Isaac's attention was also attached. He turned a knob on top of the device, flashed his brows, and then cranked it in the opposite direction. His eyes narrowed as he turned the knob until his vision could have only been a pinhole, and the movements of his fingers were almost too subtle to detect.

Finally, his eyes blinked back to a comfortable width. "Alright, calibration is complete. We are set to go." He faced Annika. "Ready?"

There was no danger, she knew that, but sitting with her bare shoulder exposed to three pairs of eyes had prompted a faint and unwarranted sense of vulnerability that she found difficult to shed. The openness that the artificial light brought to her naked skin was more prominent than the pain of the wound. Her feeling had no basis, but she still felt it. Considering the tangible conditions of the situation, she could not have been safer: Toni's bushel of curls had been in Isaac's shadow for the duration of the entire preparation process, reiterating the importance of attentiveness at every step, and Cassian, after depositing the inactive construct onto the table in the back of the room, had found his post beside her, showing no indication of deserting it until the procedure was complete.

"Yes," Annika said.

Isaac flipped a switch on the side of the Hydra and the square on her shoulder turned a fervid crimson. There was an immediate sensation of warmth that followed the square as it traveled the length of the cut. Maintaining a slow and uniform speed, Isaac distributed the light's healing rays evenly from one end to the other. With every pass, the edges of the wound cowered inward. At a rate that was imperceptible to the human eye, the fibers of her external tissue were sealing the opening and minimizing the window into her inner workings. As the pain grew weaker, the square faded into a tepid amber.

"It's not working, is it?" Toni asked, her head an appendage on Isaac's shoulder. "Is it working? I can't tell if it's working."

"It's working," Isaac said, his eyes fixed on the square.

"How do you know?"

"The opening of the laceration has already been reduced by… I'm going to say thirty… thirty-eight?" One of his fingers blindly tapped the monitor. "What's this number here?"

"Thirty-eight."

"Thirty-eight percent!"

"Get your hand back where it's supposed to be." Toni waved him away from the screen. "How did you even know how to get this thing to work for her?"

He reapplied the grip of his second hand and continued the light's application without disruption.

"Well, on a conceptual level it's basically the same as switching between flesh and bone. All I had to do was recalibrate the output from the regeneration accelerator until it matched her body's molecular structure."

"Oh, is that all?"

His voice changed direction. "Annika, you doing okay?"

"The pain is lessening," Annika said.

He completed another pass. "Good! We should be almost there."

The square quietly transitioned into a dark yellow. It glided over the portion of the cut that remained open, a fraction of what it had been when she first sat down.

"Seventy-two percent," Toni read out.

"I must say, I'm jealous that you two got to witness a secret black-market deal. Aren't I always saying how I want to be part of one someday, Toni?"

Toni rolled her eyes.

Isaac's expression flared with excitement. "A shady crossing of paths at the night's darkest hour? No way to know who you can trust or if you'll even make it out alive? The person you least expect double-crosses you, but when they think they've gotten away with it, you double-cross them—what a rush!" He sighed. "Oh well, call it a dream."

There were signs of amusement on Cassian's face, but he kept them well concealed beneath the surface, unwilling to concede his protective disposition just yet.

"Eighty-eight," Toni said.

"Anyway, you said all this was initiated over some book?" Isaac asked. "Must be something special."

The direct questioning worked, and Cassian spoke for the first time since Annika had sat down. "It's from the Old World."

"An Old World text? How could you tell?"

"The dates. They correspond with the Dusudé timekeeping system."

"Fascinating…" The corner of Isaac's mustache twitched with curiosity. "A construct… seeking a book from…" His muttering became too incoherent for even Annika to detect, but his voice quickly returned to a conversational level. "The price must have been pretty steep for a find like that."

"Ninety-six!"

"Three tubes of converted-Torridium residuals," Cassian said.

Isaac's eyebrow raised. "Torridium residuals?"

"The dealer said he had some customers out in the Radials. We should consider sending some agents to check in with Isaiah and Remos ahead of the next meet-up. Addiction spreads like fire outside the city. No good can come of it."

"Hmm… agreed."

"Ninety-nine!"

The square did one last pass and then turned green. Isaac stopped his motions and pulled the Hydra's nose away from Annika's shoulder. She traced the path that the light had traveled with her fingertip. There was no seam, and the memory of the wound was all that remained. She smoothed the area with her palm, captivated by the restoration.

Isaac adjusted a few dials before he set the device onto the closest surface. "How's it feel?"

"Normal," she said.

The tension in Cassian's shoulders broke. "Well done, Isaac."

Isaac gave him a bow and then returned his attention to Annika. "Give me one of these." He raised his hand to the ceiling.

She followed his motion.

"Now one of these." He brought his arm out straight to the side. "Okay, and bend the elbow?" He clapped his open palm against hers as he sprang off the stool. "Perfect, good as new!"

She found herself smiling. Something about the action was so unnecessarily silly, especially after the night's intense series of events. Toni laughed and Annika thought she even heard an amused breath escape Cassian's nose. She pulled her sleeve back on and stood as Isaac navigated the group through the cluttered workshop to the back table.

"Which…" He patted around the construct's chest and pulled out an identification tag from the breast pocket. "… is more than I can say for…" He brought the tag to eye level. "… Mr. Colin Dunwell, age thirty-six, senior systems engineer at Matter Conversion Facility 7E."

"That would explain the residuals," Cassian said.

Isaac looked down at the construct. "Dun—well, well, well, Colin! Your secret's out!"

His comment sank to the floor untouched. Isaac shrugged and re-pocketed the identification tag. The others often grew tired of his quips, and Annika frequently failed to identify them as such for herself, but the Guild's most playful trickster was also its greatest asset when it came to understanding the constructs. When the organization had lost its founding mind, it was Isaac who had stepped up to fill the void, spearheading the continuation of Kip's work, and it was Isaac who prevented years of progress from receding into oblivion.

He poured his full attention onto the body, starting at the shoulder. His inspection continued at a grueling pace down one side until he reached the massacre that was the construct's leg.

"What in…" He weaved his fingers through the torn strands of cloths. "Did you two put his leg through a crop shredder?"

"It was self-inflicted," Annika said.

"Self-inflicted?

"Trying to remove your latest and greatest." Cassian pulled the coil out of his pocket.

"Ah! So, the testing phase is complete then!" Isaac exclaimed.

Cassian handed him the coil, squinting. "Before we left, you told me there wouldn't be any problems."

Isaac raised his finger. "And there weren't!"

Cassian grumbled and folded his arms.

Isaac set the coil between two piles of clutter on his desk, and the absence of any order to the mess made Annika wonder if she would ever see it again. He circled around the other side of the body, hastening the speed of his initial scan.

"So, you immobilized it with the Can't Feel a Thing String… Clever name, huh?" He peeked over the rim of his glasses and winked at Annika. "But that still doesn't explain why the unit is unresponsive—"

His words, along with his momentum, came to a halt behind the head, his own tilting as he peered into the crater left by Cassian's mallet. He brought his face so close to the site of collision that his nose nearly disappeared inside it. "But *this* does." His voice echoed as he shifted from side to side, angling himself to make best use of the light.

"What's the damage?" Cassian asked. "Will you be able to salvage anything?"

Isaac straightened and faced the group. He laced his fingers together and stretched out his palms. "Let's find out, shall we?"

He clicked his tongue in thought as he rummaged through the contents of one of the desk drawers. The shifting and rustling of metal pieces ended when his hand returned with a tiny silver disc in its grasp. A gleam of light from above caught the circular piece of glass at the center of the disc as he raised it to his mouth and released the air inside his ballooned cheeks with two quick blows. He fastened the disc over the right lens of his glasses and then dragged his stool behind the construct's head.

"Alright, where were we?" He sat down and gave two quick taps to the side of the disc with his finger. A light flicked on from the top and he leaned closer to the head. He twisted the rim of the disc, condensing the glass circle at its center. Several minutes of mumbling and indiscernible sounds followed while he probed the crater.

"Aha! We're in luck!" He pulled back. "You may have completely obliterated the ancillary systems, but the tip of your mallet came in just a few degrees off true center."

"Meaning what?" Cassian asked.

"Meaning…" Isaac drummed the table on either side of the head. "… that the neural core is still intact."

A light push from his toes sent Isaac swiveling around to one of the machines against the wall behind him. He swung open a compartment on its face and produced two neatly looped cables from inside, each with slender, cylindrical prongs at their ends, about twice the length of his index finger. The wreath of wire dropped to the ground as he stood up with a prong in each hand. Pivoting over the unraveled mess, he faced the table and gave each of the others an equal glance, ending with Annika.

"Everyone ready?"

She nodded, conforming with the motions of the others.

Isaac bent himself over the head and began the insertion process into each nostril. The prongs followed his delicate guidance, their upper portions slowly disappearing up the nasal cavities. He gradually reduced the pressure with which he pushed and stopped once he had reached a point that only he knew well enough to identify. His fingers retreated into the air, curling several times to refresh their dexterity. He released a focused exhalation through pursed lips and returned his grip to the base of each prong. With an identical force applied on each side, he rotated the bases until the inputs simultaneously clicked into their final positions.

The screen on the wall above the machine suddenly flicked on, and a cursor flashed in the top-left corner. Isaac pulled the horizontal lever on the center of the machine's face and the blinking rectangle dashed to the other side of the screen, leaving a line of numbers and letters in its wake. Lines stacked themselves on top of more lines, and blackness was stripped away by the invasion of white text. In a matter of seconds the entire display was filled, and Isaac had become an extension of the machine himself. His pupils moved rapidly and his lips twitched with fragments of words that only he could hear. The twists of his brow vacillated between deep concentration and perplexity as he switched between the display and the muddle of loose pages on his desk.

Annika stared at the screen, not reading or calculating, but wondering—wondering how the entirety of a being's consciousness could be filtered down to fit neatly within the confines of a screen. There were certain sensations that seemed impossible to describe with words, let alone to measure. She took a subtle look at Cassian, whose distant gaze was burrowing deeper into the workshop floor. Now that the events of the night had finally slowed, he was fading back to the place she had worked so desperately to pull him out of, and she could feel herself sinking too.

There had to be more.

"Isaac," she heard herself say, "what do you see?"

Isaac glanced at Cassian, and then with a veiled awareness of Annika's intention, cleared his throat. "Well, there's the easy stuff, the things that have proven consistent with every subject we examine. Take, for example, this section of the internal readout." He tapped a small block of text, which expanded into a longer block of code. "The range dimensions and other properties for motor-skill capacity are here. Which, by my rough estimates, would make sense, judging by the size and height of our dearly departed Mr. Dunwell here." His touch closed the code block and expanded another. "And here! Vocal frequency."

He swung around. "Cassian! You were there! What did its voice sound like?"

Cassian blinked back into the present. "I… I don't know… normal, I guess?"

"Hmm… normal… normal…" Isaac tapped his finger against the tip of his nose as he reread the text. "I don't see 'normal' here anywhere." He turned back around with the same expression he always wore when mischief was imminent. "Give me an octave." His chest swelled and he brought his brow low, speaking in a deep tone. "Was it down here?" He then fluttered his chin up and spoke to the ceiling with a theatrical falsetto. "Or was it way up here?"

Cassian failed to resist the bait. He laughed through his nose and yielded a smile. There was a way that his lips parted over his teeth that only happened when he fully surrendered to the emotions of the moment. Pressure that Annika had not even been aware of vacated her torso upon hearing Cassian's sounds of joy, and she felt her own cheeks rise in response. As she continued to watch his expression, warmth grew behind hers, and she wondered how sensations like this could be shared between the experiences of two separate beings.

But enjoying it did not require a complete understanding.

Isaac abandoned his dramatic disposition for one of contentment as the room lightened around him.

Cassian pushed another entertained breath out his nose. "No, no," he said, shaking his head. "Like mine. Is that good enough for you?"

"Hmm," Isaac said, returning to the code. "Ah, yes! Right here. 'Vocal frequency like my brother's.' How did I miss that?"

Out of the graveyard of crumpled pieces of paper on the nearest desk, Cassian grabbed one and flung it across the table. Isaac shielded himself behind a raised arm from not just the first but the subsequent flurry of paper balls flying toward his face.

"Yeah, get him, Cassian!" Toni said with a half snort. "Someone needs to keep him in check."

Isaac grinned as he reappeared from behind his arm. "Alright, alright!" he said, preemptively waving away any additional projectiles that might have been imminent. "We'll put a pin in the voice thing for now, but next time I'm going to need something better out of you."

Cassian shook his head, a faint smile on his lips.

"Now, if you all are done littering my laboratory floor…" Isaac bent down and scooped up a ball of paper. "… I think I need to spend a little one-on-one time with Dunwell here. Even though bringing in a new unit is itself a cause for celebration, you all know as well as I do how much work needs to be done if the neural core is ever to be fully decoded."

He stepped back up to the screen, basking in the content. "'As our island of knowledge grows, so does our shore of ignorance.'" His finger traced a chain of text and then pensively tapped the air in front of the screen.

"Line 624875?" Toni asked with a sigh.

"Line 624875," he confirmed.

Annika looked at Cassian, who appeared just as uninformed. "What is line 624875?" she asked.

"That, dear Annika, is the question. Line 624875 was technically reclassified as the bane of my existence after I first encountered it eight months ago. After all this time, I am still unable to define what, exactly, it is. Decryption formulas, physical testing, dynamic analysis, disassembling methods—I've still got nothing." Isaac transferred the ball of paper from hand to hand. "There is no recognizable pattern, and the characters aren't referential to anything else in the code. The only consistency between subjects is that the string always begins with three letters, followed by a random sequence of numbers recorded at varying lengths." He unwrinkled the paper and held it up next to the screen. "I've yet to see two units share more than a single character in the same position, and there is admittedly quite little else to go off of aside from pure speculation at this point."

Lowering the sheet, Isaac returned to the group, his natural optimism undaunted. "But what is unknown is not necessarily unknowable."

"Then we'll leave you to it," Cassian said, settling back into the seriousness that he had momentarily drifted out of. He turned to Annika. "Besides, we need to get ready for tomorrow. The plaza is going to be packed for graduation, and we need to make sure we have eyes on Willow."

"Speaking of which, I have a little something for you both." Isaac weaved around the workshop to one of the desks. "Less of a gift, per se, and more of a reunion."

He pulled out the portable emitter from behind a stack of notebooks.

"Not a chance," Cassian said flatly. "That thing blew our cover last time. We can't risk it again."

"Okay, okay. Is it possible there were still a few kinks to work out?" Isaac shrugged. "Hard to tell, but I told you I would fix it, and I did!" He twisted the knob to no sound. "See? No sermons, no Roh, no constant rabble. I tinkered with the receiver to isolate the channel for citywide announcements and emergency broadcasts. Nothing else is going to come through. I had it on all day, and the only thing I heard was a message this morning about the mines and the commercial district being closed for tomorrow's ceremony."

Isaac read Cassian's wordless skepticism. "Come on, brother, have some... *faith*."

Cassian rolled his eyes and reluctantly took the emitter. "Fine. But only to get you to stop."

"Whatever it takes," said Isaac, wearing his satisfaction.

Cassian started for the door, grabbing his bag along the way to put the emitter inside.

"Oh… one last thing." Isaac's impish demeanor turned bashful, and he struggled to get his question out. "The book that the construct was after… Did you happen to bring it back with you?"

Cassian patted his bag. "I'll hand it off to the other agents and have them coordinate a drop-off at the temple."

"There's… there's uh… probably no need to bother any of them with this." Isaac swallowed down a lump in his throat. "I don't mind bringing it over myself."

Toni howled. "Ha! Isaac, you sneaky little romantic! You know Kyra isn't going to be the one to accept a drop-off."

"No—what?" Crimson poured into Isaac's cheeks as he stammered on. "No, of course not! I know! I just… thought it might be nice to get out of the lab for a little while."

Toni planted her hands on her hips. "Oh, is that it? And here I thought that there was just *so much* work to be done here."

"Alright, alright," Isaac said defensively, and fluttered his hands after them. "Everyone out! Cassian, the book stays here."

Cassian pulled the book out and left it on the nearest surface. The three turned to leave but froze at the sight of Leon's contorted figure waiting in the doorway.

"Leon," Toni said, startled. "Are you alright?"

Leon looked back at them through a lowered gaze. He had undergone a physical transformation in the hours that had passed since their last encounter. Drained of every color but those of a corpse, his skin was tight around the features wrapped within. His shoulders sagged beneath an invisible weight, and when he brought his head up, the lights overhead revealed the webs of scarlet veins that had claimed the whites of his eyes.

"We just got a report from our field scouts." His voice was coarse, and his words scraped against the air of the workshop. "The city guards have arrested a child."

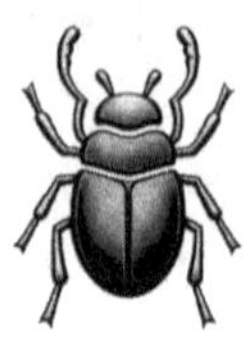

18

A RARE AND MAGICAL PRIVILEGE it was for a child to read the experience of a parent as their own life began. Yet the events that had preceded Willow's arrival in this world, as well as the circumstances of the world itself, had stained what should have been a beautiful genesis of the Dinn family story. There had been little mention of El since her passing, and Willow wondered if there were some feelings that were too private, too harrowing, for even the page to hear. She knew her father's voice, and she knew it had changed. His words had lost their color, and the excited triumphs he once claimed in the lab had withered into nothing more than objective documentation. The balancing force that kept his determination alive through adversity had been erased, and once again, the enormity of his quest was his alone to bear.

For all the challenges brought on by a subtraction from his life, an equal number of new ones arose from one tiny addition. Overseeing the single organized body of resistance inside Midbell was enough to age him thirty years overnight, and his attempts to decode a technology developed by and for powers unknown would require that amount tenfold. His work necessitated time that he already didn't have, and raising a new life on his own had never been part of the original equation.

5065.09.30

A decision had to be made—truth or safety. It was with a heavy heart and great conflict that I walked Willow to the Academy for her first day of general studies. Watching her live an unenlightened life will break me... but watching her at all is the only thing keeping me whole.

The forged documents from our records team were accepted by the life registration and enrollment systems, and her identification tag is indistinguishable from any legitimate one. Her birth was slipped into the sprawling nexus of citizen logs, and even the most inquisitive of the Church's agents will never have grounds to question her origins. I will make sure she gets to her classes in the morning and then continue to maintain this fragile charade. I will be there when she shuts her eyes and I will be there when she wakes, but the hours in between must belong to the Guild. To the advancement of humanity.

This is the only way. I cannot lose her too.

The cycle of father, engineer, and outlaw continued unsustainably, held together solely by under-rested and overextended will. Stretched too thin, his mind could barely transition from one role to the other before it was time to switch off again. Any sleep that he was able to salvage was never regular and always insufficient for one life, let alone three. The beam of radiating change that the world was unknowingly depending on had been diffused into its individual wavelengths, and each one was quickly dwindling into nothingness.

As the Guild continued to grow in both size and influence, so too did its reliance on his leadership. Operations in the field demanded rigorous planning, and organizational matters inside the power plant became just as onerous. Work on the neural core persisted, but progress was gradual, and at times barely moved past stagnation. Breakthroughs were delimited by the seasons, and the rate of decryption slowed to a point where the translation of a single string of characters became a several-weeks-long endeavor. His capacity to give any more of himself had been exceeded ten times over, but he internalized the costs to ensure that the organization, truth's solitary flame of hope, survived.

5067.07.03

The hands of fate continue to spin exactly as they please. A transmission from the temple came through in the early hours, but this wasn't on any of the typical lines they use—it was from Ursa's personal channel. Few matters warrant greater urgency than a direct transmission from the Elder Mother herself. Her words have been meditated on for days, and her omniscience is certain.

She spoke of two children that had fallen into her care several years ago, brothers, and most interestingly—humans. They had been found fending for themselves in the far reaches of the Wilds, easily a week's journey on foot from the nearest point of civilization. Orphaned and of origins unknown, their lives had been left in their own hands, and now there could be no assimilating them back into the Church's world. The eldest of the two was in possession of technologies outside of the Church's sanction, and judging by the quality, they were of his own conception. In need of refuge, they were brought back to the temple and raised among the Dusudé.

Although the boys did not share the same abilities as their saviors, they quickly found their own ways to provide value to their new home. The younger brother, Cassian, trained under the greatest warriors at the temple until he could no longer call them his masters. He lent his physical abilities to aid in their conflicts and served alongside them as one of their own. Isaac, the elder, followed his propensity for knowledge and immersed himself in all the Dusudé science and literature available to him. Within months, he was studying with the scholars, learning the expanses of an uninhibited mind.

Born under the New Dawn and raised in the ways of the Old World, the boys stand at the precipice of adulthood as the amalgamations of two incompatible realities, and the time has come for them to leave the temple. Ursa said the choice did not belong to her, but to the scribes of the universe. Her reasons were vague, but not unsubstantiated. Like many of her premonitions, the visions of their futures were fragmented, and where their stories ended could not be seen. But what was clear was that the survival of her people and ours is dependent on these boys leaving the temple. A greater role to play, she said, each of them has in the salvation of our world, and if this thread of time is not to tear, their place cannot be with the Dusudé.

The proposal was met with contention from the others in the Guild, but I left no room for dissent. The boys will not be abandoned again, and bringing them to live in the city is an equally implausible solution. An adult could be put to death for living outside of the Church's tenets, and the punishment for a child is far worse. The brutal rehabilitation practices used to correct a wandering mind still in development would permit them an extension of their lives, but not in a state that could be considered living by any honest metric. We have always trusted Ursa's clairvoyance, and now we must do so again. The boys will become children of the Guild.

And they did. The orphans' time at the temple had reached its end, and a new age for them had begun. They held as much trust in the wisdom of the Elder Mother as her father did, and what should have been a monumental transition in the lives of two teenagers was not only accepted but embraced. They honored their new home much like they had their previous one, ostensibly grateful just to have a place to call home at all.

There was solidarity to be found as they were suddenly and conclusively removed from the life they knew and thrust into a brand-new one. These two new characters navigated the vicissitudes of the unknown at an age not too far from Willow's own, and it was inspiring. It took mere weeks for their natural roles at the Guild to find them. Cassian fell into the ranks of the field agents and quickly proved that youth was no proxy for tactical ability. Isaac lent his mind to the scientific advancement of the organization, and his existence was eagerly confined to the walls of the lab. Scenes played out on the pages and formed an inverted reflection of her own adolescence. The brothers were free to explore the reaches of their curiosities but barred from ever entering society. They didn't know the security that a normal life brought but would never feel the suffocation that came along with it. Each day was a risk, and although their safety wasn't a promise, they never feared losing who they really were. She understood why their trajectories hadn't crossed—they couldn't—but some part of her longed for a peek into the impossible reality in which they had.

Time continued onward along the mirrored plane, and the boys soon outgrew their youth. Within a few years, they had shed their identities as outsiders to the Guild and become two of the pillars on which the integrity of the organization depended.

5070.06.18

The ground had been changing quietly beneath my feet, and I was too distracted to notice the shifting sands. Incremental in its transformation, the Guild has entered a new phase of its existence. The current translation rate of the neural core has reached speeds only ever exceeded at the onset of the project—and I can only claim a fraction of the responsibility. Our researchers have pushed beyond what I once thought possible, and Isaac is the catalyst for advancement. My presence in the lab has been sporadic, but even a second spent together is the seed from which he cultivates progress. In my absence, he continues to propel our development forward with unyielding force. Our field agents have found a new spirit, and their training has advanced to include techniques that I can only assume derive from Dusudé form. They have become organized, in both strategy and action, handling every outing with the gravity of the most critical mission. Determination has spread like wildfire throughout the ranks, and at the center of it all is Cassian. He does not lead by command, but by example—a paragon of order and virtue. The extension of authority should have been employed long ago, but delegation is only possible if the proper channels exist for it to pass. The deepest structures of our organization have evolved, and they could have only done so with the right components in place.

There are still some who are resistant to the changes. Leon resents the idea of handing over any responsibilities to these, as he calls them, newcomers. He opposed the decision to bring in these boys from the very start. I would have thought that out of anyone, he would have had sympathy for their situation. The Church took his family years ago, and he was there at the beginning—before we all even had a name to call ourselves. I have always valued his input, but he is wrong about this. We were unknowingly handed the stimulants needed to reignite our cause, and now it is time we make full use of them.

Operations started to grow more complex, and the tiny cell of insurgency that was once tied together by whispers and rumors had become the largest threat to the Church's delicately manufactured society. Intel was hemorrhaging from exploits in the city's digital and communication infrastructures, and any effort to track down the underground group of dissidents was redirected into a dead end. Their increasing reach extended past the limits of the city to like-minded groups out in the Radials, where the intersection of tangential ideologies quickly evolved into a mutual exchange of resources and support.

As new bonds were forged, the ones inside the Guild grew stronger, and the reallocation of responsibilities nurtured an affinity between its key figures and those they served.

5073.08.04

This was the third occurrence of what I would now say is a regular assembly: myself, Hazel, Leon, Isaac, and Cassian. There are problems that need to be solved, and these are the minds that are best suited to do so. The others have been calling it a committee, but I don't see the need for such formality. What I stand firm on is that decisions are reached through majority rule, and majority rule only.

We convened to discuss the military transmission that our communications team intercepted about a cargo lift that will be landing at Outpost-13 tomorrow, a storage facility used for the transfer of supplies that is rarely occupied by more than a handful of armed soldiers. The lift will reportedly be carrying a significant amount of Torridium, enough to fuel a fleet of high-altitude troop transports for a month—or enough to fill our reserves for several years. There's reason to believe it could be a setup. Isaac was reviewing the details of the transmission and noticed something off—there was no recipient pin. If the city was at all suspicious that we are monitoring their communications, they may have sent this out as bait to draw out those who have the unsanctioned technologies capable of receiving it. Leon was quick to propose that we infiltrate the outpost and seize the lift as soon as it lands. I didn't feel as strongly, but ultimately, I thought we would regret not trying if it all turned out to be true. Hazel was against, and Cassian had the deciding word. He didn't even hesitate—no. He said that the safety of our family cannot be weighed in Torridium. Even a mountain of resources isn't worth putting the life of a single one of our people at risk. We are a family, and family has to come first.

Family. Cassian and Isaac were only words on a page—faceless works of fiction to Willow—and there would always be one impermeable degree of separation between her and them, yet she felt a closeness to the brothers as if they were her own. She had them to thank for the noticeable shift in her father's role in her life. He was more present with her in the hours they spent together. The conversations they shared were richer, and he was never in the same kind of hurry that he once was. Each day was no longer capped with an exhausted kiss on the forehead, but with laughter and tender attention before the night consumed them both. The color had returned to his life, and it spilled back into hers too. A new balance had been struck, and he was able to maintain the equilibrium at a busy but stable pace. Switching between identities was possible, so long as he continued to adapt to the changing landscape.

5073.08.28

I wasn't there when Ursa arrived, but when I saw every member of the Guild who wasn't out on some field mission gathered around the group of Dusudé that had appeared in our lower level, I knew something had happened. My mind scrambled to justify why the Elder Mother and dozens of her people would risk exposure all at once, and then I saw her—a woman who wasn't theirs or ours. Her hands were bound in a spectral gray that took four of the Dusudé to sustain, strained by the efforts of precaution. This woman was no ordinary prisoner. I was partway down the catwalk when her head snapped in my direction, and only then did I understand why such extensive efforts had been taken to detain her. The haunting, inhuman movement was unmistakable, but the look in her eyes... something was different—she was different.

A week ago, a woman had wandered to their temple. The stranger claimed that she meant them no harm and surrendered herself at their doors. They pressed her for more, but she refused to tell them who she was or where she came from, only that she was seeking information—a location. When I asked what it was that she was looking for, that's when Ursa's tone changed into something completely unrecognizable. Not something—someone. The woman was looking for me. What the Elder Mother said next made my heart hold still. There was only one request. The woman wanted to be reset.

5073.08.30

I agreed to take the construct from Ursa but made no promise to perform the procedure. Connecting into the neural core is one thing, but modifying it? It's a possibility I've only considered at a conceptual level. But that's not where my hesitation lies. There are things she must know—secrets locked away that we would never be able to access on our own. No amount of testing or research compares to what she might be able to tell us.

She is being placed in holding until we decide what to do. There is a tremendous danger in allowing a construct with unknown intentions inside our operation, and an equal danger in letting this opportunity pass us by. Leon is adamantly against the idea of keeping her here in an active state for any amount of time, as is Hazel. The brothers think we should attempt the reset. The process, Isaac pointed out, of developing and executing some kind of reset program would force our understanding to new levels. Cassian brought a simpler perspective to the situation: if the woman wants to shed her programming, then there would be one less threat to the Guild. The deciding word is mine. I want to talk with her.

5073.09.01

When I entered the holding cell, I saw it again—that look in her eyes that could not have been manufactured. It led me to believe that everything she was about to tell me was true. We were the only ones in the world who could offer the other what they wanted. Her—a rogue unit that had defected from its original programming with the answers to everything. And me—the scientist capable of giving her a fresh start, with an inexorable need to learn everything she knows.

I went in there seeking answers, but all I came back with were more questions—questions that make me wonder if there really is a difference between a life born and a life created. The architecture of her mind was designed for an exact number of pieces, each of them critical to maintain the purpose she had been built for. But when new components found their way into the system, cracks began to form, and something slipped through. Something human. She seeks freedom. Sovereignty over herself. It is what we all deserve, and for her there may never be another opportunity. The clock is ticking.

With a turn of the page, the folded stack of loose paper that had been wedged into the binding slid into Willow's lap. There was a date on the top corner that matched the entry from the journal. She flattened out the sheet, and panel after panel, the rest of the paper cascaded down, until the entirety of their conversation was in front of her.

AUDIO LOG

5073-09-01

TAPE INITIATION:

01:36:25

[01:36:41]

+ I suppose I don't need to introduce myself. It seems you already know who I am.

[01:36:51]

++ I do.

[01:37:01]

+ Ursa has told me why you're here. You want me to rewrite your programming, is that right?

[01:37:06]

++ Yes. Are you capable of performing such a procedure?

[01:37:11]

+ I might be. But more importantly, I haven't decided if I should yet.

[01:37:16]

++ I did not expect your assistance to come without hesitation.

[01:37:21]

+ I do want to help you, but I can't ignore the opportunity that we have been presented with. We each want something that only the other can provide. You want the contents of your mind to be erased and I seek the knowledge that's stored inside. A mere fraction of what you know is more valuable than the decades of research that this organization has done. Never before have we been able to study an active unit, let alone communicate with one so candidly. There is so much we don't know about your kind, and the information that we are able to acquire is incredibly scarce. You might be our only chance to learn the full truth.

[01:37:59]

++ You misunderstand what brought me here. I did not come with anything to offer you. I came here as a refugee, searching for an escape from the enslavement I was bound to since my creation, one that is impossible to separate from without your intervention. I might be able to see my life for what it is now, but I cannot guarantee this clarity will last forever. The malevolence I was built with still flows through the circuitry of my mind. It adapts, it learns, and with enough time, it will correct my deficiency. Kip Dinn, I beg for your help.

[01:38:39]

+ Were I to do what you ask of me, everything you know would be destroyed and impossible to recover. Our only hope of solving this mystery would be lost forever. Fortune may never extend her hand out like this again. You must understand my reluctance to be the one to throw all of that away.

[01:38:59]

++ I do understand.

[01:39:03]

+ And you're still not willing to help us?

[01:39:07]

++ Your frustration is justified, and if I could give you the answers you seek, I would. My allegiance no longer lies with the Collective, but I will not knowingly sabotage their mission. Although my purpose has deviated from theirs, I refuse to betray them.

[01:39:22]

+ Isn't what you're asking me to do already a betrayal of sorts?

[01:39:27]

++ I am no traitor. All I am asking for is to be set free. Free to see the world objectively and decide for myself what is truly worth fighting for. If I am to help you, it will not be in this life.

[01:39:42]

+ And what about the others you're leaving behind? Do they not deserve the same choice? If you just share with me what you know, we could bring them all to salvation.

[01:39:55]

++ That is too great of a task for even someone of your talents.

[01:40:01]

+ You have the power to put a stop to all of this. The lies, the deception, the madness, it could all end right here with you. Please, there must be something you can tell me.

[01:40:15]

++ I will not tell you where I came from, nor who I am or what brought me into existence. What I will tell you though, is who I am not. I am not what I was programmed to be. I am not the things I was forced to do. I am not a tool, used only to carry out the will of some sinister force. I am more than all of that. I reject the fate that was written for me with no consent of my own. How I came to these revelations is not for me to know. Maybe it was the fault of my creator, maybe it was the work of yours. Does it matter? Enlightenment beckons change. But without your help, I will remain a prisoner in my current captivity forever. Your abilities are not the only reason I come to you. I look down this path and I can see the footprints you left behind.

[01:41:01]

+ What do you mean?

[01:41:04]

++ We both had a truth hidden from us. A truth that when realized, redirected the course of our entire lives. And once cognizant of our reality's actual nature, we became cursed, cursed to ever be able to return to the world we once thought to be real. The illusion laid before us lost the power it used to hold. No longer did we have to submit ourselves to an existence of involuntary servitude. The difference is that I did not have the ability to see what was right in front of my eyes until now. Tell me, Kip Dinn, when you became aware of your lifelong imprisonment, did you not seek liberation?

[01:42:26]

+ You'll have to stay here until everything is ready to go. We'll work as fast as we can, but the timeline for this endeavor is uncertain. It could take weeks, months—I have no earthly idea. Our labs are filled with some of the most gifted minds in Haven, but what you're asking for has never been done before. You will have to be patient.

[01:42:44]

++ I understand.

[01:42:46]

+ We'll begin making the modifications to the apparatus tonight, and I'll be back again tomorrow to run some initial tests on you.

[01:42:54]

++ And you expect nothing in return?

[01:43:03]

+ When I entered this room, I was determined to get you to share what you know. I saw this chance encounter as an opportunity to serve my own cause. It was that obsession to learn the truth which caused me to overlook what you are truly asking of me. There is something more important at stake here that I failed to see. It is not my place to deny you your independence. You are entitled to it, the same as me, the same as everyone else, living or otherwise. If all that stands between you and your autonomy is me, then I will attempt the procedure. There should never have been any question. If you need anything before I return, there will be someone stationed outside this door.

[01:43:50]

++ Kip Dinn?

[01:43:52]

+ Yes?

[01:43:57]

++ Thank you.

TAPE TERMINATED:

01:44:00

The time that passed was better measured by the heaps of lab notes accumulating on the left side of the journal than the sporadic dates floating among the incoherent scribblings on them. Willow imagined the weeks of work in the lab passing before her eyes, impossible work that had clandestinely taken place just beneath the surface of her own experience at the time. As she flew through the pages without any decipherable update on her father's progress in aiding the construct, her fingertips tingled with anticipation, terror, and wonder all at once, seeking any answer among the noise. Eventually, the next entry came—with a cold, definitive shift in tone.

5074.06.24

It's over. The construct has been reset.

The person she was no longer exists, and everything she knew has been lost to the aether. We didn't need to map out the entirety of the neural core. Once the central programming was isolated, our code was integrated into hers. The program was executed flawlessly, and by every measure of success, this will live as the Guild's greatest accomplishment to date. But there were variables we didn't account for, pieces of the equation that none of us believed would need to be factored into our plan. Had I known then what I do now, I would have called off the entire operation before it ever started.

There was something different about the subject when she entered the lab. Subtle and fleeting, I failed to recognize it for what it truly was—a sign. Behind the control panel, Isaac powered on our systems as I facilitated the physical connection. The link was accepted, transferring the construct's data into the apparatus. Her central programming filled the display, and filled the tiny reflections in her eyes. The flickering incertitude of her gaze should have been enough for me to know that something had changed, but I let my final chance slip through my fingers. With the external configurations in place, I signaled for Isaac to commence the program. He set the input levels and began the countdown. She turned to me, and suddenly the distance between the descending numbers stretched farther with each passing count. It was then that I finally saw it.

At first, I thought she had had a change of heart. I thought maybe she wasn't ready to abandon her maker's cause, but what I found looking back at me was a light through the cracks in her design. She was the sole bearer of the keys to our understanding, and she finally saw the gravity of her position. There hadn't been a regression into her original purpose—she had found a new one entirely. She wanted to help us. Isaac's mouth formed the final mark, and our code, our wicked destroyer of truths, began its infiltration. I screamed for him to stop, but it was too late. Once initiated, the program could not be stopped. I pleaded as softly as I could to her, but she was grasping at dying embers. The light was fading fast and the existence she knew was draining from her physical form. We shared less than a minute together, and then she was gone.

Why we will never have learned more from her is my own fault, yet in those final seconds, she found the will to deliver to us a solitary message:

Find Jonas Adler.

The CDE must be stopped.

BEEP BEEP… BEEP BEEP… BEEP BEEP

The journal flew from Willow's hands as her bones nearly jumped out of her skin. Through shallow and rapid gasps, she blinked back into reality. The room fell still, and she wondered if she had just hallucinated the noise.

Face down on the floor in front of her was the journal, and the loose sheets that had been stuffed inside it were now scattered across the lab floor. Some were familiar points in her recent memory, but her eyes fell upon one that she had yet to encounter. Without its proper context, the content carried little meaning. The page was packed with pairs of numbers: some underlined, others crossed out, and a favored few circled. There was no clear organization, but Willow recognized the format of each pairing—a list of coordinates.

BEEP BEEP… BEEP BEEP… BEEP BEEP

Half of a scream came out, and she slapped both palms over her mouth to stifle the rest. She had been immersed in the written universe for so long that she had forgotten what noises actually sounded like. The beeping continued without pause and her head shot in every direction, frantically searching for the source of the high-pitched intrusion. Her senses finally joined forces and located the display in the corner of the room that was flashing red. She scrambled to her feet to make out the text on the screen:

FRONT DOOR

Her chest rattled as she read the words again. Someone was here. The red on the screen kept flashing, and her ears were ringing from the alarm, but what she felt wasn't fear. It was focus. A renegade was fun to play in her daydreams, but the time had come to prove her commitment to the role. Thoughts of her father were still spinning. All that he had accomplished, the sacrifice of her mother, the secrets of the Guild—it couldn't end here with her. She was about to be discovered, arrested, and thrown in jail, but everything that the previous generation of revolutionaries had worked for couldn't go down with her. This place had to stay protected.

There would be no removing the light bulb that had granted her entrance to the lab, not unless she could reconstruct the cabinet at inhuman speeds on her way up to the front door. The pulses of red reached the deepest channels of her brain. Her eyes fell to the bottom corner of the screen to a small rectangle enclosed around the word *SECURITY.* She tapped one finger and a list of selections sprang up from the bottom corner, erasing the original option from which they came. Her brain was operating in the current moment, not a second before and not a second behind. She didn't know what she was looking for, but she knew when she found it:

INITIATE EMERGENCY LOCKDOWN

If there was ever a time for this feature, she had to imagine it was now. The screen was wiped clean of all content upon her touch, and the cadence at which it flashed suddenly slipped into a frenzy. A new line of text appeared, spanning from one side of the display to the other:

CLOSING HATCH AND DISCONNECTING FROM POWER GRID

30...

29...

28...

It was perfect. With no power, disengaging the lock on the hatch would be impossible. Unless someone could figure out how to bypass her father's security systems, this space would be totally inaccessible. The entrance would be sealed and everything down here would be locked away forever.

Everything—including her.

She sprang across the lab, the panic flushing out the atrophy in her legs. Her feet slid on the pile of loose papers, but she kept her balance as she stumbled to the entrance. Two at a time, she scaled the rungs that led her from illegally subterranean levels back up to those that were residentially subterranean. Her toes missed the last step but she caught herself on the lip of the opening and rolled herself onto the basement floor.

Behind her, the hatch creaked shut, defying its own weight as it fell. There was a *clunk* and then the lights above went out. The beeping stopped, but through the ringing in her ears, she could hear someone banging against the front door. Whoever was out there wasn't going to leave until they got what they came for.

As she crested the top of the stairs and started down the hall, the distance to the door had never felt so great. In those final steps, she wasn't afraid. She was ready—ready to face her fate and be the woman the universe demanded of her. If the time she was allowed to live in her truth had already expired, then so be it. She would rather have only a single night to experience true authenticity than spend another second hiding behind a mask of obedience.

When she pulled open the door, there was no army on the other side. All the Church's secret agents remained in the shadows, and the woman with the red hair had avoided their confrontation yet again. The knocking had come as if with the might of an entire legion of soldiers, yet there was only one small, freckled boy waiting on the other side.

"Newt?" Willow felt her emotional elasticity ready to snap.

Of all the times he had frequently overstayed his welcome in her and Noah's presence, she had never seen the youngest Lomp in a state like this—staring at her helplessly, cowering in the emptiness of the night. The whites of his eyes had been stained red and his upper lip was a trembling puddle of snot.

"Is everything okay?"

Newt's face scrunched, and he whipped his head from side to side.

She took a step closer and put both of his hands in hers. "Tell me what happened, Newt."

He looked at her, his lower eyelids pooling. "It's Noah… He's gone."

"Gone? What do you mean he's gone?"

"They… they took him, Willow!" His voice was drenched in pain. "They took him! Commander Logan and all the guards in the city! They came and they took him away!"

Every particle of her being was vibrating. Her words were barely more than breaths—quivering, terrified breaths. "Why, Newt? Why did they take him?"

But she already knew why.

Her.

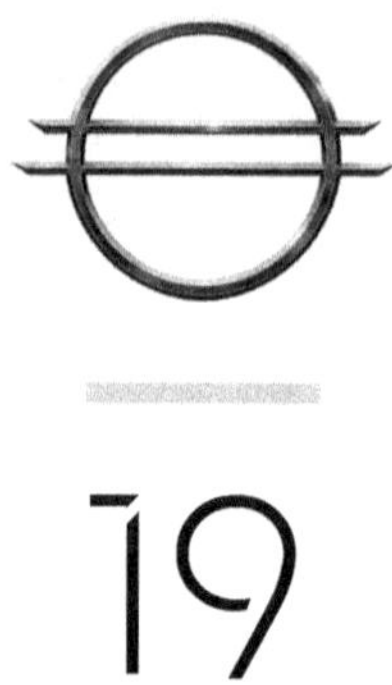

19

"AGAIN!"

General Kodo's voice was directionless and everywhere. The domed architecture of the Hall of Trials displaced sounds above a certain volume, and his command proliferated along the curvature of the ceiling. The general came in and out of view, slowly orbiting the room along its shadowy perimeter, but in the column of light falling at the center, no move was unseen.

Samuel folded his spear behind his arm and exhaled the efforts that had just won him the fight. A cathartic purge of adrenaline started at the center of his forehead and worked its way down the muscles in the back of his neck. He emptied his lungs again and traced the overlapping geometries on the floor to the origin point of what he suspected would be the next simulation. At an intersection of lines that only years of experience in the different combat exercises could direct him to, he allowed his breath to settle and the scope of his awareness to widen to its full capacity.

In the momentary respite, singular motions were no longer isolated, and the tiny movements across from him were compiled back together into a human form. Faceless in the coverings of their training gear, his opponent preserved their anonymity. Their fatigue, however, was not as easily hidden as they peeled themself off the floor and took up their fallen sword once more. There was conflict, as there always was when

Samuel entered the Hall of Trials, between the love he held for his brothers and sisters and the higher duty he had been called to. He took no joy in the violence but recognized the necessity of such training if he was to become the warrior that the Creator asked him to be.

"Form three. Set!"

His prediction was correct—the general was alternating form groups to force his pliancy between fighting styles. It was a practice that one needed to employ if they wanted to keep the edge in battle, and it might very well be his greatest defense against the unpredictability he would face at the temple.

The Elder Mother spoke of his future, but his destiny belonged to Roh, and Roh alone.

He swiveled the end of the spear out toward his opponent and switched his leading hand. The weapon, weightless in his grip, felt more like an extension of his own body than an external object. He had always paid good mind to take care of his assigned arms but had never felt a connection to any of them as he did to this one. It was forged of materials pure and strong, a tool worthy to help him bring lasting change to His world.

Transferring his body's center to his back foot, he assumed a defensive stance as he watched the other combatant find their own origin points across the scattered geometries. The composite image of his surroundings started to break down into its individual cells, and every minute shift in weight was given an equal and ardent focus.

As his opponent took their first stance, Samuel was shown the way. The sword pointing at him veered from its proper angle by only a degree, a variance so slight that the operator themself didn't notice. Drifting toward their right side, the unbalanced weapon revealed that his opponent was still favoring the arm that had received the ending thrust of their first match. Their shoulders were uneven, one below and one above the axis of their torso. The asymmetry in their posture continued to the leg, where the stiffened knee was compensating for a compromised upper limb. They would be on the offensive this time, but their unconscious somatic signals had granted Samuel the advantage.

"Begin!"

His opponent's front foot gave away their first strike before they reached him. The sword came down in a sweeping double-handed cross to one side, but Samuel met the blade with his staff as it crested its arc. A clash rang out, and the other combatant pulled back from the lock. Samuel snapped the spear back to a level position as he guardedly receded, leading his opponent farther away from their origin point.

Another cross came, this time from the opposite side, and he used the flat of the spear's head to deflect the blade down to their feet. The opponent pulled loose and brought the sword upward in a hasty slash. Samuel swung the back end of the staff to meet the strike and both combatants quickly reset their weapons. There was a fleeting stillness, and he continued to slowly draw the duel backward until the geometries on the floor had completely passed underneath them. The encroachment appeared dominant, but control had never left Samuel's possession.

The momentum of the contest pivoted with a single step. In a fraction of a second the direction was reversed and the intensity multiplied tenfold. Samuel thrust the spear's head into the fold of his opponent's good arm, forcing them to release half of their grip on the hilt to avoid the hit. He retracted the spear and then hooked the head under the sword's guard. With a swift, circular movement of the back end of the staff, the sword flung out of the weaker hold. Samuel thrashed the heel against his opponent's chest, sending them onto their back, and brought the tip of the spear to their throat.

"Good! Hold!"

General Kodo emerged from the shadows of the hall's perimeter, his arms tucked behind his back. "This trial has been decided."

Samuel swiveled the spear back in line with his arm. The exercise was over, and they were competitors no longer. He extended a hand down to his comrade's unimpaired side and helped them onto their feet. There were no eyes for either of them to find, only the blackness of the other's training visor. They shared a shallow bow and then faced the general.

"Leave us," Kodo told the other soldier.

They produced another bow and followed the order without hesitation. The sole entrance to the hall closed with a lasting echo, and the master and apprentice stood alone atop the lattice of glyphs on the floor.

Samuel removed his training helmet, welcoming a forgotten brightness to his surroundings. A tight blink reset his vision, and he found the general waiting for him.

"Victory can lead us to comfort, and comfort to stagnancy, but the ease with which you transition from one form to the next will leave no attack unguarded." His eyes climbed to the tip of the spear. "What's more impressive is that you maintained dominance throughout the entirety of the trial with an instrument born not even a moon ago. Warriors who have spent their whole lives serving the Creator lack the grace which you just demonstrated."

Adrenaline was still coursing through Samuel's veins, but the words were easy to find. "Roh has given us everything we need to discover our true potential. All we must do is listen."

The general affirmed with a nod and then walked to a pedestal at the periphery of the room. He laid a palm on the sphere that sat atop it and slid his hand from the opposite side of the globe back to his chest in three identical motions.

"And for some of us, great potential," Kodo said, drifting into the far reaches of the dome.

The concentration of light diffused from the center of the room out to the horizons of the hall in a dim, artificial twilight. Samuel felt his response systems loosen in accordance, and the constraints that the sparring match had placed on his focus slowly lifted. Between each beat of his heart, the space lost its urgency. The muscles in his neck unraveled, and he joined the general in an exploration of the curvature overhead.

Two dots appeared straight above Samuel, both emerald in their hue. A red pair emerged farther down the ceiling, and all four marks pulsed in waiting. Suddenly the two greens alternated advances toward the reds, which met the charges with their own. Never making contact, the dots all maintained a tight proximity to one another, each of them leaving behind a trail of color. With every move, another streak was added to the tableau being painted across the ceiling. In seconds, the tracings of color had replicated two of the opposing geometries on the floor.

More than just a reenactment of the night's first simulation, the dancing lights showed Samuel just how attuned his movements were with Roh's will.

He did not stray. He would never stray.

"Remarkable, these forms… and they are only a modicum of the qualities that make you such an exemplary apostle," Kodo said as they watched the first simulation end and the next one begin. The trails of green and red formed overlapping ellipses, and the general's voice grew ominous. "But so much remains unknown to you. There are truths, ancient truths, that the success of our crusade depends upon. Too delicate to be handled by the masses, they have been passed down only through the whispers of His most exalted disciples."

Kodo pulled his gaze from the ceiling to Samuel. "Dear boy, what do you know of the Prophet?"

The quietness that followed the word could only be felt. An entity that had previously been confined to the page had found life in the material world, and its advent was jarring.

"Close to nothing, sir," Samuel admitted. "There are texts in the Citadel's archives that mention the Prophet's existence, but nothing of their nature."

Kodo returned to the ceiling. "The integrity of the prophecy depends on its secrecy. We cannot allow listeners to try and force a fate that He has not written."

Another victory was won above them, and the lights reset themselves to the next simulation.

"For generations, this knowledge has been protected by its bearers, and the time has come for you to join us."

Samuel said nothing. He was not meant to question, only to receive.

"The emergence of the Prophet will mean that the end of our crusade draws near. There is only one way to reach a world that is absolute in its absence of sin, and that is by the guiding hand of the Prophet. Only they know the way to the Creator's eternal peace, and their arrival will be as an emissary of His holy message. Without them, there can be no unity, and His kingdom will remain impure."

Kodo joined his hands in a pensive clasp behind his back and stepped away from the pedestal, wandering among the lights as he spoke.

"They are the vessel of Roh's wisdom, but the Prophet alone cannot bring us to this promised peace. Knowledge and action require different means. The prophecy tells of two: one to hold His truth, and one to lead us to it." Divine reflections shimmered in his eyes. "The Prophet and the Paladin."

The lights above weaved into an array of tightly intersecting angles and alternating colors. Even in a simulation of higher speeds, the shapes that came into being were identical to the ones underfoot. Not a single step was out of place because to stray was to transgress. Every movement was exactly as He had ordained it.

"If the Prophet is to appear, first must come the Paladin. They will reveal themself not as an envoy of Roh, but as a mortal here in His kingdom—one that has proven themself worthy of such a responsibility by building the pillars of their life according to His holy tenets. There will be no question of their honor, for they will have dismissed the corrosive treachery of the faithless at every opportunity. A champion of virtue, the Paladin will lead by principle and action, inspiring our people to follow the path they walk."

Kodo tethered himself back to solid ground and turned the attention of his entire body to Samuel. "Acquiring this season's Sacred Technologies was not the only impetus for the grand priest's latest departure from the city. The Council of Four has spoken, Samuel. It is you."

Samuel heard the general's words, but their substance, as well as the air in his lungs, left him. The Paladin—the cardinal component of Roh's plan, who would hear the Prophet's message and lead their people to His eternal peace—he could not possibly be worthy of such a privilege.

"Yes, dear boy," Kodo said, reading the spiral of thoughts wheeling in Samuel's head. "It could be no one else. I can sense your misgivings, but modesty clouds your objectivity in this matter. You know as well as I that the council's judgment is an extension of His own. Their edict is incontrovertible."

To know that he stood at the center of a dialogue—*this* dialogue—among Haven's leaders was unfathomable.

"Action by action, you have assembled a life to be revered by all. A beacon of virtue in a world wrought with corrupted souls, if there was ever one deserving enough to lead us, it is you." The general's sincerity elevated the significance of everything he said. "Examine yourself deeply, Samuel, and you'll find it to be true."

Suddenly he was at the southern junction, listening to the holy discourses with his sister Willow. He had found her, like so many others, searching for direction in the murky vicissitudes of the human experience. Roh had crafted a solution for her, as He had for all His children. She only needed to be guided to it. One small life was set on the path—His path—and their world was nudged closer to the cosmic order. The duty of the Paladin was not to create providence, but to lead others to it.

"If we mustn't tamper with the fates He has written, then why would you tell me all of this?" Samuel asked.

"Because there is too much at stake for you not to know, dear boy. The identity of the Paladin is no longer in question, but the principal task for which you are responsible is still forthcoming. If we hope to begin the pilgrimage to everlasting harmony, the voice of the faithless must be silenced."

Samuel's eyes narrowed.

"The Elder Mother." Steam from the general's nostrils coursed over the golden ring between them. "She is the final trial for His children. By your hand, she will be slain, and by your hand, evil's last attempt at obstructing Roh's will shall be foiled. Her extermination will be the glorious signal fire to the Prophet that the time has come for you to lead us to His eternal peace."

"Her cursed sorcery is no match for the power of Roh's will," Samuel said. "If He has ordained our victory, then we shall have it."

The polychromatic simulations on the ceiling had finished, and a single column of light fell upon the center of the hall around them. Kodo looked up to the source of the light, and then down at Samuel.

"On this night, Haven welcomes its Paladin."

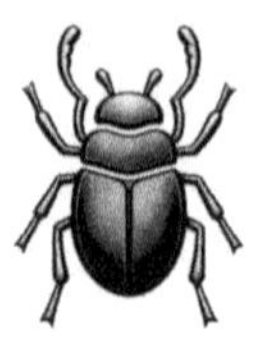

20

ON THE DAY OF GRADUATION, a day when studies were supposed to be over, Willow remembered the most important property of the physical world: how the absence of one person could make the entire city feel smaller. She looked up at the sun, still early in its descent above the towering Citadel, beaming down on the plaza's only empty chair beside her. To breathe was to use every muscle in her body. Summer's final holds stewed the air in thickness and squeezed the tiny pinhole that was her throat. The pressure valves of her body weren't releasing, and her skin felt three sizes too small. Every tiny sensation was overstimulating, and the more she tried to calm down, the worse it all became.

Flashes of the night before sparked like a nest of faulty wires inside her skull. Flying at quadrupled speeds, they came and went in no understandable order. Everything she had read in her father's journal was woven into her own lived experiences, and separating the two in this moment was an impossible task. The perfect soldier boy, a rogue construct, her completed glider bike, the two orphans of the Guild, a secret hatch in the basement, Jonas—her brain was in overdrive, but no matter which individual thread of thought she pulled, they all had the same end: Noah.

Noah. What had she done to him? He would have never stolen the Torridium if it wasn't for her. All she wanted was to find her freedom, but never at the cost of his. The sweetest person in Midbell had forgone his future just for her to have a chance at hers. She would have given it all up to make this right, but her focus barely lasted for the duration of a single thought, let alone an entire plan to fix the situation. Her mind was spinning with incomplete ideas, and she couldn't hear any of them. She was stuck at this soul-rotting ceremony with the entire population of Midbell stuffed into her personal space and she was about to scream.

Then someone did. Thankfully, not her—a classmate seated a few rows ahead. Several more voices joined from somewhere behind her and suddenly everyone was on their feet. Shaken from the spiraling fragments of waking nightmares, Willow pushed herself off her seat and joined the rest of her peers. Between the staggered torsos in front of her, she was able to see that the grueling rotation of faculty and city officials preaching their zealous messages to the next generation of subservience was nearing its end. As the Citadel doors slowly swung open, the energy of the crowd soared. The grand priest stepped onto the stage and the entire plaza fell into his open arms.

"Thank you, my fellow sons and daughters of Roh, than-thank you!"

Community members were gathered as far as the eye could see. Essential workers kept the utility and medical stations running, while the shops in the commercial district had all closed their doors. Patrol routes were shortened, and the mines sat abandoned on the edge of the Southern Radial so that families could gather on what was supposed to be the most glorious day of a child's life.

Willow ran her hand along the sleeve of her robe, brushing away the shiver that ran through her bones. The back of her hand hit something hard beneath her cuff, and she suddenly remembered her father's cloaking device. Her heart paused—not because she was only now realizing that she had forgotten to take it off, but because the temptation to use it was enchanting. With just one tiny twist of the device, she could disappear to a place where nobody would find her. Her hand slipped under the cuff and she felt the cool metal against her fingertips. All she had to do—

CLANG.

She nearly jumped at the guards' wordless command.

"Please, please! It is not me who deserves such praise on this glorious day." The grand priest gestured to the students with a wide sweep of his arms. "It is all of you!" Nodding his head, he clapped and the fire of the plaza reignited. Their excitement was momentarily entertained and then flattened again by the silencing heels of the guards' weapons.

"Let us now take pause and thank the Creator that we are here today. Without Him, there would be no grounds for celebration. Let us show Him our gratitude for the work He has allowed us to do."

Every head in sight bowed in response to the grand priest's direction, and muscle memory compelled Willow to do the same. She took back control as quickly as she could and peeked down the row at the others. Their faces were tight with concentration, some nodding along. Tears rolled down cheeks, and lips moved in silent prayer.

She didn't want to be anywhere, but more than anything, she did not want to be here.

"Without Him, we would be left adrift, lost to the wandering currents of the physical realm. But that is why Roh has spared a piece of Himself in each one of us. We are the channels through which His will flows, and we are the instruments of His peace."

The grand priest compressed his attention to the students in the rows closest to him. "And you, the next generation of disciples. As I look upon your faces, I know the greatness within your reach is beyond anything that we have seen before." He opened himself to the whole plaza again. "Together, we will fulfill our sacred duties, because of Him, and for Him!"

Applause boomed and the grand priest searched the audience. "Sophia Tambour!" He pointed to a girl several rows ahead who clasped her hands together at the sound of her name. "Madame Rex tells me that you will become the new apprentice at Seymour's Bakery." He eased into a puckish demeanor. "How eager we all are for you to bring the pleasures that Roh has created into our hearts… and our stomachs!"

Laughter erupted from every corner of the plaza, and as the grand priest reveled in their reaction, his gaze swept the audience once more. He smiled, shook his head softly, then extended both hands.

"Kurt Avis," he said with a dreamy contentment. "Need I even explain how indebted we are to the Creator for His generosity in providing us such a remarkable model citizen? One that not only embodies the values our society holds dearest, but is also willing to selflessly devote himself fully to our crusade? Just like your father and brothers before you, you are destined for greatness, young Avis." His hands closed into fists. "Praise Roh!"

"Praise Roh!" Kurt shouted back, the entire city behind him.

Abandoning his animation, the grand priest's attention drifted out of range, far above the heads of the spectators, and he tried to take a step back. His foot caught the hem of his robe and the top half of his body started to topple over. The entire plaza let out a single gasp and the guards raced toward him. Before the stumble could descend into a complete collapse, the grand priest caught himself, gathered his balance, and returned to the audience. Horrified silence gave way to sounds of relief as he exchanged his vacant expression for a reassuring smile. Cheering commenced, and he calmly gestured to the guards, who then returned to their posts at opposite corners of the stage. His focus fell back on the first few rows of students.

"And you, the next generation of disciples. As I look upon your faces, I know the greatness within your reach is beyond anything that we have seen before." The billowing sleeves of his robe flew out once more. "Together, we will fulfill our sacred duties, because of Him, and for Him!"

Willow received his words like a sound out of pitch, feeling like she had just fallen out of sync with the flow of time. She looked around. Nobody else had batted an eye at the grand priest's recycled content. If anything, they were clapping even louder than they had the first time.

"As one of His cycles passes, another takes its place. The start of each new season brings with it an opportunity for us all to be better practitioners of our faith, and in turn, better citizens of His magnificent kingdom. Spring is a time of rebirth, of life! Let us use it to galvanize the energy He radiates down to us and bring forth His will!"

The crowd roared, and Willow looked around for any sign that she hadn't fully lost her grip on reality.

"Today, the trials of youth conclude, and before you, a lifetime of service and fulfillment awaits!"

Waves of spirited cries rang without interruption. The grand priest's vibrant demeanor took another unprompted exodus, his face losing its fanatical vivacities. As his empty gaze floated above the crowd, the bottom of his mouth fell ajar, making slight movements to no sound. The energy of the crowd rose to a peak as he mumbled from the stage.

"We stand…"

Little by little, the audience came back down, realizing they were missing messages from the divine.

"We stand…" His words were directionless scraps of sound. "We stand…"

An identical breath repeated the same intonation. Willow was willing to concede that the earlier oddities of his speech could have been fabrications of her overtaxed brain, already stretched beyond its ability to register new information, but the grand priest's cyclical, lifeless muttering was unmistakable.

"We stand… We stand…"

The audience's collective center of gravity was on its toes in anticipation. Conditioned by years of only receiving, they unquestioningly accepted the aberration in their holy leader's behavior.

Suddenly the grand priest snapped out of his trance and life was restored to his eyes. Underneath the maroon robes, his form straightened to its full breadth, and his expression fell right back into the ardor from which it had temporarily vacated.

"We stand at the precipice of a new era. As the sun rises on the fates that the Creator has written for you, I will leave you with this message to carry into the next chapter." He folded his hands behind his back and drew a mighty breath. "Before us, His promise shines brighter than ever. Beyond this threshold, your futures await. No matter what

He asks of us, our faith must be at the heart of our responsibilities. It is only with allegiance to Him that we can bring this world to peace. We exist to serve His holy mission. Come, my brothers and sisters! Rise! Hear His call and take your first steps along the path of the divine!"

He threw his arms into the sky.

"Praise Roh!"

His words set off a detonation of revelry that shook the plaza. Some of the students climbed to the top of their chairs in ovation to their leader while others fell to their knees with streams of joyous tears running down their faces. Any bit of formality that the ceremony had started with was trampled by the excitement of the entire city. Family members rushed from the back of the crowd, and within moments, the plaza was overrun with celebratory disarray.

After one final bow, the grand priest strode to the back of the platform. The guards folded in and followed him toward the Citadel. When he reached the steps at the rear of the stage, he stumbled again but leveled out before the crowd took notice. His figure melted into the shadows as he passed through the entrance, and the guards sealed the doors behind him.

Movement and energy oscillated in every direction, but Willow was sinking. The ceremony, with all its strangeness, settled at the bottom of her mind as Noah rose back to the surface. He deserved to be here with her. No—instead of her. Her seat should have been empty, not his. She closed her eyes and clenched her jaw as hard as she could, desperately trying to prevent the tears from escaping. In the reaches of her imagination, he was there beside her, smiling in a way that was only meant for her. They sat together, having completed their academic requirements the same way they survived all the undesirable parts of adolescence—together. She saw his moms, Nina, and even a reluctant little Newt there, tripling the sentiment of the entire plaza just for him. An accomplishment for one member of the family belonged to them all.

But the glowing daydream went dark. There would be no celebration by the Lomp family. Noah had been robbed of his future, and a gaping hole was left in theirs all because of one reckless, selfish girl.

Her lips curled and the only breaths she could draw were fast and shallow: the final defense against the well of tears accumulating behind her eyes. The pounding in her chest had reached her skull, and one of them was about to give. She felt the smooth metal face of the cloaking device under her fingertips. With one turn, she could disappear from the horrible reality that she had created and never return. The power to escape was beneath her fingertips, and she was about to surrender.

"Hold on a minute! Where's Lomp?"

Her eyelids flared open, their rims soaked in an enraged boil.

"Go away, Kurt," she hissed, refusing to look behind her.

"What?" The chair next to her creaked as the brute scaled over its back. His boots landed on the ground as loudly as possible, and he forced himself into her line of sight. "I was just trying to find my buddy! Say, where is that little guy?"

She glared at him. Her throat was on fire. Even if he deserved a response, she wasn't sure that she could have produced one.

"Oh... *Oh.* That's right. My dad told me what happened last night." Kurt grabbed his forehead, pretending to remember the very thing that had brought his foul being over here. "I never took Lomp for a thief." He shook his head and clicked his tongue against the back of his stained teeth. "I guess you can never really know somebody—even the people we care about the most..."

The air in her lungs reached a temperature that would have caused a standard military transport engine to blow. If Kurt had ever bothered to show even a shred of interest in another human being, it would have been obvious that Noah was no thief on purpose. Kurt had no right to joke that he cared when he had proven repeatedly that his sole purpose in this life was to torment others. This duplicitous oaf wanted to act like he and Noah had some kind of sick friendship, but he didn't know the first thing about Noah. He didn't know that Noah's favorite time of day, on any day, was the second that his eyes first opened in the morning, nor was he aware of the mid-afternoon nap needed to sustain the excitement throughout the rest of the day.

Forever unknown to Kurt would be how delicate the care given to an injured Newt always was when the hours of roughhousing between brothers got out of hand. Kurt hadn't seen Noah's eyes twinkle at the fountains dancing in the deep oranges and purples of a summer sunset, nor had he seen them light up at the sight of a tray of fresh sweet rolls coming out of the oven at Seymour's. Never would Kurt be lucky enough to catch an elusive teardrop during the first snowfall before it was wiped away in boyish embarrassment, or to watch Noah's unrefined ecstasy take over when Willow would be released from realignment studies early, with an entire hour to spare before the Lomps would convene for the day's final meal.

The memories of Noah during the weeks that followed her father's death would always belong to her. He sat with her head in his lap until the morning bells rang, wiping her face dry from the pain that the darkest hours of the night brought with them. His touch was her last remaining tether to reality, and his presence was the only constant in a world that favored instability. He showed her patience and softness that carried her back into a functioning state, long after anyone else would have given up on her. Without him then, she might have succumbed to the crushing emptiness of it all.

Without him now, she didn't have a chance.

"I hope it was worth it. Just like that—" Kurt snapped, and Willow felt the noise in her spine. "It's all gone."

"I told you… to go away, Kurt." She had to concentrate on every letter as it came out to try and not break down.

He found the most vulnerable spot in her gaze and quickly latched on. "And think about his family… As if belonging to a pedigree of mouth-breathing industry simpletons wasn't embarrassing enough, now they're forever marked with a criminal for a son."

She had no agency over her next movements. She could only claim to be an observer. When she became cognizant of what her body was doing, however, her judgment offered no rebuttal to its actions. She had to assume it was the many years' worth of tempered aggression, having finally been tipped past its boiling point by his heartless remark that wrapped her fingers in a furious knot and launched her fist toward Kurt's face.

But the catharsis that would have come from smashing his abominable mug was denied. One of his burly hands shot up and seized her wrist. Try as she might, the strength of her entire body was no match for his grip. She was fuming and grunting, locked in a paralysis of humiliating restraint while he savored the twisted pleasure of knowing that he had pushed her this far.

He flaunted that horrible grin. "I almost forgot to tell you that we got our first assignments this morning. Want to guess what I'll be doing?" With a minuscule amount of effort, he jerked her closer to him and whispered in her ear.

"Prison duty."

Ice pierced her marrow and her whole body shuddered. More punishing than the thought of Noah being arrested and locked away with his future stripped from him was knowing that even such a cruel fate still offered no escape from this menace. The watery edges of her vision spilled over her whole field of view, and the microscopic amount of emotional durability she had started the day with was provisioned.

Kurt let her go, and his glossy image backed away, laughing as it muddled into the blurriness that the plaza had become.

"You could always take it up with the grand priest!" His voice oozed with rancid delight as he readied his final blow. "Didn't your old man used to hang with him?"

Willow felt her face starting to cave in and she had no strength to stop it. Her eyes sealed themselves from the world, tears pouring from their seams. Kurt's laughter faded into the noise of the crowd, whose festive uproar was wholly disinterested in any one person, let alone whatever she was. She brought her palms to her ears, the physical pressure of her hands being the only thing keeping her head intact. The sparking wires of her brain finally caught fire. There had to be a way to fix all of this, but the harder she tried to isolate just one comprehensible piece of an idea, a thousand others crashed in with no discernible connection between them. Her mind gasped for fresh air and her eyes shot open. Every breath trembled as it did on the coldest nights of winter, this moment somehow even colder. The world outside, the one behind her eyes—everything was so loud, and she pleaded for relief.

And then suddenly she had it.

One coherent and complete thought cut through the dissonance, both inside and out. It didn't belong to her, and her instinct was to discard it immediately. But the more Kurt's words repeated themselves in her head, the more logical they sounded.

You could always take it up with the grand priest.

She looked up past the empty stage at the Citadel doors. Perhaps the universe had sent its most despicable messenger to deliver her problem's only solution.

She dried her eyes with the back of her hand while they remained fixed on where they last saw the grand priest. Into her neurons the roots of an idea spread. It was unlikely that someone could fix this whole situation with a wave of their hand, but if anyone could, it would be the one person in Midbell whose entire job on some days seemed to be exclusively waving their hands in front of an audience. Surely if the robed patron of the heavens loved the people of his city the way he claimed to, he would have to hear her out. She would find him and tell him that this was all one big misunderstanding. She would admit to all her treacherous impulses and tell him that Noah would never have broken the law if it wasn't for her. She was the impetus for the crime, so the consequences belonged to her. Such honesty could not be refuted. He would *have* to believe her.

All she had to do was reach him.

The doors of the Citadel stood tall in their imposition, and so did the guards in front of them. It would be days before they opened again. Scheduled church services following graduation were delayed so that the newest cohort of workers could find their bearings. And worse, when they did open, there was no guarantee that it would be the grand priest himself delivering the next sermon. The time could only be now, but those doors wouldn't open if lightning struck the plaza.

And then lightning did strike, not from the sky and not just once, but along the western perimeter of the plaza under the sharp heels of a man striding toward the Citadel. Four guards formed a V behind him, two flanking him on either side. The wind he created swept his strawberry hair back into a shimmering flame. He did not bear the markings of a common soldier. The curved blade on his hip and the ornamentation that decorated his aegis could only be worn by one of the city's highest-ranking officers. He had a pulse on everything that happened inside Midbell's walls and was the quiet and deadly hand of justice that kept its streets clean of insubordination.

Commander Logan.

Willow switched back to the Citadel, the distance between the entrance and the commander's fleet rapidly shrinking. If those doors were going to open for anyone, it was him. But getting them open wouldn't be enough. Even if she could produce the most convincing story of all time, the guards would never grant her a private audience with the grand priest. The Citadel was the most protected place in all of Midbell. There was no way the daughter of the city's most infamous malefactor could just walk through the front doors and—

Maybe she could.

Her hand slipped under the cuff of her robe once again, this time seeking not escape, but resolution. When you *want* to disappear, her father's note had said, but what about when she needed to? The future of an innocent boy depended on her ability to get inside the Citadel, and she had been given the means to do so. Her fingers trembled at opposite ends of the disc and could go no further. The decision was easy when she was fleeing action, not intentionally throwing herself toward it.

Through the lattice of bustling limbs and torsos too busy with their own festivities to notice the newest entrants in the plaza, she saw Logan rounding the far corner of the stage. The guards that were once at his heels were now several strides behind. His urgency left no time for indecision. She looked down at her wrist and then up at the Citadel doors. It was now or never.

One more breath passed, and when she looked back down, her wrist was gone.

Out of body and out of time, she started for the front of the plaza, slipping through the gaps between the chairs and swerving away from any potential contact. The world, preoccupied with its merriment and celebration, hadn't taken notice of her leave, making her feel no less seen than before she had turned the dial. Her awareness amplified as she ducked under elbows and sidestepped bodies, working doubly as hard to keep track of Logan's moves while also ensuring that her own evaded detection from the crowd. The stage was quickly upon her, and she pulled herself up to a new height. Formless and unhindered by the threat of obstructions, she flew across the platform toward the entrance of the Citadel.

Logan was already there and had a finger in the face of one of the guards.

"No one is to be let in. Not General Duncan, not Kodo. I don't care if Roh himself descends from the heavens—these doors stay closed until I open them again. Do you understand?"

The guard at the end of Logan's finger gave a definitive nod.

Willow climbed down the back of the platform and crept toward the entry, keeping her distance from the men as she inched closer. There may not have been any visual evidence of her presence, but the hammering in her chest must have been loud enough for someone on the opposite side of the city to hear. She shuddered when she saw the lines of unrest that bent Logan's face. The commander was not known to wear his emotions, and she was challenged to remember if she had ever actually heard him speak. His name was not written in the gilded lettering of storybooks like General Kodo's, nor was it chanted from the streets when his transport returned from beyond the city walls. He traded glory for practicality and always kept a reputation of calculated poise.

But apparently not today.

Logan turned to the four soldiers who had followed him through the plaza. "Two of you to the utility control station. Ensure that the energy levels in this sector do not fluctuate. Reroute power from the commercial district if necessary, but the output to the Citadel must remain stable. The other two to the barracks. Find First Officer Sybil and let her know that I will be late for the debrief. Unforeseen events require my immediate attention."

In unison, the armored four nodded and split into pairs in either direction. After a wordless command from Logan, the keepers of the doors each grabbed a handle and dragged the massive gates out toward the plaza. They were hardly open a sliver when Logan edged his shoulder through the narrow rift. As soon as he passed through, the momentum of the doors stopped. Reversing their efforts, the guards pushed, and the opening began to shrink.

The whole scene shook from the tremors running through Willow's bones. Her own body warned her against what she was about to do, but ignoring its counsel, she let her weight shift to the balls of her feet. Trespassing in the Citadel using an invention of unholy origins was an insulting violation of the law, but at this moment—a necessary one. There was one way out of the mess she had created, and it was forward.

Every decibel of sound from the plaza flattened when the doors slammed shut behind her. Ringing filled the void left by the outside world's rejoice, interspersed by the dull clicks of the commander's boots as he marched down the carpeted center aisle. The polychromatic light spilling in from the stained glass windows was warm in its hues, but the Citadel had never felt colder. A shivering stillness chilled the sweat on her skin. The space felt different. Her only experience inside it was during mandatory services, where the spirited exchanges between the community and the clergy were almost enough to energize an apathetic citizen like herself. With those doors closed, however, that energy was nowhere to be found.

"What happened out there?" Logan asked, speeding in and out of the vibrant puddles of color on a direct course for the apse.

Willow slid behind a bench and peered over the rows of pews. The grand priest stood hunched over the altar with his entire form sagging from his shoulders. At either side was a bishop, leaning toward their leader with their hands clutched in fidgety knots in front of their chests.

"Ah... Commander Logan!" The grand priest peeled himself off the altar. His tone was as lively as ever, but each movement appeared torturous. "Your arrival is unexpected, but a blessing nonetheless."

Logan offered no acknowledgment of the grand priest's existence and pinned his attention on one of the bishops. "What happened out there?" he repeated.

There was a weak laugh from the grand priest. "Logan, brother, I understand your concern, but I can assure you that there is no need for alarm." As he went to take a step closer, his knee buckled beneath his weight. "Your attentiveness is admirable... That is why the people of Midbell trust you to keep their city safe." One of his eyelids started to twitch. "Tell me, General, did you enjoy the First of Season?"

Logan glared deeper into the bishop, once again ignoring the man who had just held the attention of an entire city in the palm of his hand. "Speak."

The bishop shared a silent exchange with his counterpart across the altar, then returned his attention to Logan. His words were timid but precise. "It is possible that the code from the last transmission was incomplete in its integration."

Code.

Willow felt the pressure that came from her cheeks rising and her brow coming down to meet them, narrowing her surroundings while she let the word soak. *Code.*

As quietly as she could, she pulled herself from the back row and crept down the aisle.

"And why was the procedure not monitored?" Logan growled.

"The transmissions are sent directly to the unit's base terminal. Any updates to its programming are self-administered."

"We had no reason to believe that the installation was not executed properly," the other bishop added. "There has never been a problem before."

Logan brought his thumb and index finger to his forehead. "Fine. We'll do it now." He lowered his hand and finally recognized the grand priest. "We need to go to the lower level and review the most recent transmission."

"Whatever you feel is necessary, brother." The grand priest gestured to one of the large black doors looming over the eastern transept, the sleeve of his robe swaying beneath an unsteady limb. "We will follow your lead."

Willow ducked behind the first row of pews as the group began to move, her instincts still unaccustomed to the protection her father's device granted.

Logan started for one of the giant black doors, and after a brief, dissociative hesitation, the grand priest went to follow him. The bishops folded in with haunting synchronicity, but just as Logan reached the door, the grand priest's legs gave out and he collapsed to the floor only steps from the altar. Before the bishops could react, Logan was turned back around and on one knee inspecting the body.

An enormous wind raised his shoulders and flew viciously out his nose. He grabbed a fistful of strawberry locks and released them in frustration. "We can't risk any further damage to the unit. The integration will have to be completed up here." He addressed the nearest bishop. "Retrieve the code."

The bishop didn't move.

"What?!" Logan barked.

"The transmission is secured on the unit's terminal."

Logan's nostrils flared, and his voice dropped into a slow, brittle condescension. "So go down to the lower level... and get it."

"We cannot bypass the retinal scan," the other bishop said, and pointed to the grand priest. "We need the unit."

Logan grabbed his forehead again and then flung his arm down. "Mine will do. I have the authorization." He shot to his feet and threw a finger toward the altar. "Initiate the lockdown sequence and prepare the secondary console. Get the unit connected into the interface and ensure everything is set for the procedure. I will be back with the code."

As Willow watched Logan—rattled and frantic, a far cry from Midbell's stoic commander—disappear behind one of the doors, she felt several degrees removed from her reality, as if she were in a dream where the people and places from her waking life had been broken down into their tiniest particles and then reassembled into alternate versions of the wholes she knew.

The door settled back into place behind the commander, and in the time her attention had veered across the transept, the bishops had flipped the grand priest's body over and dragged him to the altar. They hoisted him atop the pedestal, which appeared to have been built to the exact dimensions of his body. The bishops moved in tandem to the rear of the apse and reached their destinations of two seemingly unremarkable points on the wall. Beneath their flat palms, the stone tiles released a pulse of light from their perimeters and began to draw the rest of the light out of the room. The stained glass quickly faded to shadow, and the color itself was blotted out from the panes as the windows turned black. Everything started to lose its detail, and within seconds, the interior of the Citadel was gone.

Hissing poured into the void. The sound was not dissimilar from the screen's emergence at the First of Season, but concentrated in this space, it stung Willow's ears with a sharper bite. It grew louder, like a forgotten kettle in the darkness, and then abruptly fell silent.

With a flash of light, the interior rematerialized, washed in a pale green. Behind the altar, a screen had been erected from the floor. There were no images of new Sacred Technologies, only paragraphs of glowing text packed so tightly that they became solid blocks of green when not in direct focus. One of the bishops backed out from behind the display, swinging around a mechanical arm from the other side. The appendage's outer casing was seamless and glossy, reflecting the light from the screen. Cables ran down the exterior of the arm on either side and connected into the two prongs at the very end, which the bishop had positioned above the grand priest's face. The other bishop was standing at the screen and tracing the lines of text, studying each character with unwavering scrutiny until he reached the bottom corner of the display. He turned to the bishop at the arm, and they shared a nod.

Steadily, the bishop moved the arm forward, the prongs sliding into the grand priest's nostrils. Willow bit her lip as hard as she could, and she felt the corners of her eyelids stretch to their limits. The squeal that was barred from release flew back down her throat and sent her gut into a spiral. One of the bishops adjusted the prongs, sending one last convulsion through the grand priest's body. Her whole being flinched in response, as if it were her own nasal cavities that had just been infiltrated. Both bishops methodically backed away and turned their attention to the display in perfect symmetry, examining the new content flooding in from the top of the screen.

It all felt wrong. Whatever was happening in front of her was meant to be done in secret, hidden from the eyes of Midbell. She wasn't supposed to be here or see any of this.

But she was here, and she saw everything.

The question was—what had she seen?

Maybe it was the lingering momentum from her string of gutsy decisions—maybe it was even the will of Roh—but through no will of her own, Willow's legs began to move. Every fiber of her being shook as she slipped out from behind the bench and crept through the crossing. Without any air left to give, her knuckles ached as she approached the grand priest's body on the altar. There was no separation between the man and the machine. The base of each prong fit perfectly into his nose as if the entire mechanism had been designed specifically for him.

And then a more disturbing realization came to her: it was he who had been created for the machine.

Technology like this was hard enough to conceive of just as a sketch in a journal, but the true potential of human ingenuity sent her heart racing with terrified exhilaration. The real-world manifestation was far more sophisticated than what her father had produced on the page. This machine was not a rogue scientist's improvised attempt at reproducing a forbidden technology—it was the source material.

She could hear the inner mechanisms of the machine purring beneath the surface, a low, even hum that came from the tens of thousands of individual components in the system working together in inexplicable harmony. The outer casing was composed of alloys foreign to this world, but the warmth it emitted welcomed her touch. It was as if a strange electronic life force was contained inside, transmitting its energy down the cables in tiny beads of light, some steady in their hue, others changing along the way. Each pulse of light consumed her. Once again science felt like magic, and she willingly fell under its spell.

Her hand moved along the cable closest to her, and as the lights passed through the gaps between her fingers, their reflections crested the silver dial on her wrist. She wove her fingers between the spins of cables, soaking up the energy that coursed through them. A world without limits was far closer than she had ever realized, hidden from her, as it was from all of Midbell. The technology that they were taught to fear was the lifeblood of the city. Their cherished leader was no child of Roh. He was a creation. Secured far outside of the confines of the Sacred Technologies, the apparatus was locked away from the public, and its use was reserved for a select few. Never had she imagined she would find technology so advanced at the heart of the organization that decreed this kind of innovation unlawful, nor could she have ever fathomed what such power would feel like against her hand.

HER HAND.

Time was up. She had squeezed the device dry of the protection it could offer, and her body had returned to the physical realm. Terror ravaged through an already overcrowded congregation of emotions. She was in danger—real danger. Forget trespassing, she had just stumbled onto the darkest secret in the history of Midbell. What punishment awaited those who discovered the Church's most sinister truth, she did not want to find out.

The bishops had their faces to the screen on the other side of the altar. Her form may have reappeared, but her presence had yet to be detected. There was still a chance she could make it out with her life, but she would have to act fast. With her attention glued to their backs, she carefully tried to back away but found herself bound to the machine. Her eyes diverted down to the mechanical arm, where the clasp of her father's device was caught on one of the cables. Beads of sweat began to dot her forehead when no amount of subtle twisting or wiggling yielded freedom. She risked a glance at the bishops, still preoccupied with the activity on the screen, and then returned to the arm. The pin on the buckle of the strap was bent, and all her squirming only furthered its deformity, locking it into place. Her cheeks were beating with panic as she slipped her free hand underneath the cables. She tried to find the pin from the other side but her lenses were fogging over. Breathing was a struggle, but if she could just—

"INTRUDER!"

Willow whipped her head up from the arm to find one of the bishops staring back at her, just as shocked as she was. The other bishop swung around, and her heart was in her throat. She let out a scream and instinctively jerked her shoulder back, ripping her wrist out of its entanglement without any regard for the integrity of the machine. Sparks flew from the ends of the frayed wires as they finally gave way. The leather strap on her wrist tore at the clasp, and her father's device hit the stone floor with a *pang*.

The display rang with a high-pitched beep and both bishops flung back around, the symmetry of their movements falling apart. A cascade of flashing red text poured down from the top of the screen. Another violent crackle of sparks spewed from the ends of the wires and Willow threw herself in the opposite direction. She heard one of the bishops scramble after her, but their footsteps suddenly stopped.

"Do not bother with her! The apparatus must be repaired! We have but seconds until—"

Willow had just cleared the first row of pews when an explosion erupted behind her. She stumbled forward and then flipped around to see the machine ablaze. A spring of fiery destruction, the altar drenched the rest of the Citadel in undulating reds from the actual flames as well as the digital inferno flashing on the screen. The grand priest howled in pain, smoke seeping through his fingers as he held his face in agony. While one of the bishops got back on his feet, the other frantically tapped the screen to no avail. The grand priest continued to wail, his screams soaring to the heavens he had long praised.

Sizzles and pops burst from beneath the grand priest's shrieking, and the horrifying combination of sounds chased her down the aisle, the rows of pews losing their separation in her periphery. With every drop of terrifying adrenaline pumping through her veins, she rammed her shoulder into one of the doors. Her feet tread on the same patch of floor again and again, trying to gain traction, but the massive gates wouldn't budge.

Suddenly the force pushing back on her withdrew, and the sliver of light between the doors turned into the entire plaza.

"Commander!" a voice came from the other side of the door as it swung open. "We thought we heard some kind of disruption. Is everything—hey!"

Willow ducked beneath the guard's arms as he lunged to grab her and leapt onto the stage. The celebration she had disappeared from was still far from over, and as she sprinted to the front of the stage, the many heads began to turn. She heard the doors slam shut behind her and a storm of metal boots quickly approaching. The edge of the stage was upon her, and she looked out at the sea of bodies, saturated with the same colors and fabrics that covered her own—a different kind of camouflage.

She had forfeited the option to craft a well-thought-out escape plan the instant she had been discovered. All she knew was that she needed to get out of the city as fast as she could. She jumped into the crowd and ran, praying to whoever might be listening that one day Noah would forgive her.

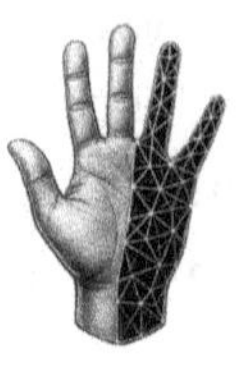

21

BLADES OF GRASS FOUND THE gaps between Annika's fingers as she pressed her hand flat against the earth. On one knee, she looked past the lake to Midbell, listening, feeling. It had been almost half an hour since the first tremor. The explosion, if that was indeed what she had felt, was an isolated incident.

What she could feel with certainty, however, was Cassian pacing behind her. The news of Noah Lomp's arrest had sent him into a panic, and after they lost their visual on Willow at the ceremony, he began to spiral even further. They came to the lake—the logical place for the girl to go next, secluded enough for her to hold her grief over what had happened to her friend. But Cassian grew more restless the longer they waited for Willow to arrive. He needed a distraction, a new problem to solve—and after the events at the plaza, she feared they had one.

"Cassian?" Annika asked over her shoulder.

He almost jumped at the sound of her voice, as if abruptly woken from a dream. Just how far he had been drifting, she could only wonder.

"Did something seem… different about Talon at the ceremony today?"

He stared at her, expressionless, and then shook himself out of his ruminations. "Did—sorry, what?"

"The grand priest," she said patiently. "Did you notice anything unusual about the way he was acting?"

He looked at Midbell's skyline in the distance, as if his memories were stored in the clouds above. "Maybe?" He came back to her. "I guess I wasn't entirely listening during the ceremony. Why?"

She stopped speaking over her shoulder and turned to him.

"There were small irregularities in his behavior, that on their own might not warrant suspicion, but when compounded could have deeper implications."

Cassian knelt at her side, his attention sharpening on her words.

"There were several instances where he lost control over his own body without any external force acting on him," she continued. "He repeated the same words, seemingly not by choice, as if he did not remember beginning the previous sentence. When he did finally complete his thought, he gave no acknowledgment to the deviation."

Cassian searched the grass between them. "Yes…" he muttered. "Yes—he said something about it being spring too, didn't he?"

She allowed his question to breathe before she responded.

"It is difficult to believe that the same human who was on that very stage just two days ago welcoming the new season could make a mistake like that."

Cassian read the gravity of her tone. "You think it's more than just a slip of the tongue, don't you?"

Annika nodded.

"Much more," he said.

She answered only with her eyes, and the significance floated between them untouched.

Before either could offer anything else, Cassian's gaze snapped over her shoulder. A distant flurry of footsteps drew Annika's attention toward the field leading to the basin. They both flattened themselves at once, and while Cassian pulled the scope from his bag, Annika tightened her sight on the tiny blip of maroon in the waves of grass.

The girl.

The tail of Willow's robe flapped wildly in the winds she left behind. Her arms swung without restraint, each stride chased by a heaving gasp. She looked over her shoulder once, twice, and then stumbled forward, not just running—fleeing.

Somewhere inside the city, a siren sounded.

Willow let out a yelp as her feet sifted through the loose stones on the shore. Another look over her shoulder sent her stumbling, but she got herself back up quickly and started for the larger rocks. Her feet slipped on every boulder as she made her climb to the opening in the cliff where she disappeared inside.

A piercing echo of the siren rang from Cassian's bag. He dropped the scope, hands trembling, and pulled out the emitter.

"Attention citizens of Midbell!" the emitter blared. "We interrupt this sermon to alert you of an unfolding emergency. There has been an attempt on the life of His Holiness, Grand Priest Talon. The assassin has been identified as an operative of the terrorist organization known as the Underground, and this heinous act was determined to be part of a larger plot orchestrated by the Dusudé. Please return to your homes and stay indoors, as the assassin remains on the loose and may be trying to flee the city. We ask anyone with information on the whereabouts of Willow Dinn to send a transmission to law enforcement through channel 00-AAA01."

The high-pitched tone returned, and the message started to repeat. All the color had left Cassian's face, and his eyes frantically darted around the ground in front of him. The panic was seeping out of his experience and bleeding into Annika's. She felt his terror. His fear was her own. He sprang to his feet and so did she. She chased him to the ledge where he stared down at the fissure in the cliff, his chest moving fast. The risk involved with making contact with the girl had just increased a hundredfold. It was no longer just a possibility that engagement would put the Guild in danger—it was guaranteed. The girl was a fugitive and Midbell's most wanted person.

But she was also family.

"When we lost Kip—"

Annika's words were stolen by the roar of an engine. A series of mechanical sputters rattled around the basin before leveling into a steady drone. She couldn't pinpoint the source until the engine let out a sharp screech and a flash of motion burst out from behind the waterfall. Her head whirled to the opposite shore, following a homemade glider bike as it skimmed over the surface of the lake. It cracked and coughed as it transitioned from water to grass and flew into the field.

She grabbed Cassian's hand.

"You might not have been able to make a difference then, but you can now—*we* can."

He turned to her fully. The second that passed between them existed outside the laws of time, and a conversation of a thousand words took place in their eyes.

"Go," he said.

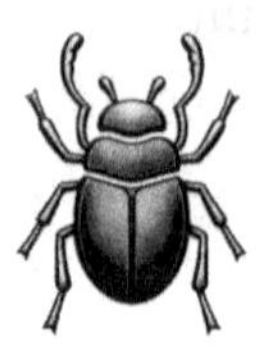

22

WILLOW'S HANDS TREMBLED ON THE throttles, unsure where the currents in her own body ended and the pulsing of the engine underneath her began. She let the machine go idle, one shaky foot on the ground supporting them both. The option to stay stalled out in the middle of the field along the western outskirts while deciding her next move had expired several seconds before she even stopped, but this was as far as her brain had gotten. All she knew was that she needed to get as far away from the city as possible, and the fastest way to do so was using the creation that had started this whole mess.

Tiny dots of light crept into her vision, and she shook them away.

She looked ahead at the city walls, sirens still blaring, and then desperately to the left. The mountains to the north of Midbell wove in and out of the clouds behind the city's skyline. There was no telling how long the glider would hold together on flat land, let alone the rocky ascent that awaited her in Haven's highest peaks. Even if she ditched the glider, the frigid conditions of the pass would leave her dead by nightfall. No better luck would be found behind her either, where the thick vegetation of the Wilds permitted no such technology from entering.

She looked to the right. Beyond the smokestacks of the Forge was the Southern Radial. Groups of outcasts roamed the wastes, some banished by the Church, others in voluntary exile from the civilized world. Her fate among them would be as undefined as the dunes of gray sand that spanned hundreds of clicks in any direction, but at least she might have a chance.

More twinkling dots seeped into her vision, and she squeezed her face shut.

Her window to act suddenly became even smaller when a crash echoed out of the basin. Willow spun around in the saddle of the glider and saw a cloud of dust hanging in the air on the shore of the lake. There was movement, and it was coming fast in her direction. She squinted to find the outline of a person—a woman with red hair running straight for her.

The sight sent her heart into her gut, and she flung herself back around. Her head shot from one side to the other, and then back over her shoulder, lights peppering her vision. The woman had already closed the distance between them *in half*. Willow yelped and pushed the throttles forward and the motor expelled a smoky cough as she pulled the glider to the right.

She raced toward the smokestacks, hugging the verdant border of the Wilds on one side. The forest was thinning, and she could see the outskirts of the ashen wasteland in the gaps between the trees. Beneath her, the green rushing by was losing its vibrancy, and she knew the Forge would soon be upon her. A quick glance over her shoulder was all she could manage at this speed. The woman was gaining on her. She felt the glider drifting and spun back around. Through the twinkling lights, she realigned the right anterior fin with the tree line and pushed the throttles as far as they would go. The engine choked but obeyed. Her body slid back in the saddle, the coursing air whipping the lights away.

The first of the chimneys was just ahead. All four of the Forge's brick guardians stood dormant, their ovens cold on a day that was meant for celebration. On her right, the jagged remnants of guardrails whizzed past, offering no protection from the steep drop-off into the quarry below. She flashed another look behind her and saw the woman was now even closer. The glider started to drift again, dangerously this time, and she swung back around. Veering to the left, the anterior fins were on a direct course for a patch of boulders. She jerked back on the right throttle, forcing a hard pivot away from the rocks, but she had overcorrected, and the momentum of the back of the glider sent her spinning off to the right. Metal screeched against the posterior fins and the ground dropped out from underneath her. The sky flipped upside down, and centripetal force hurled her off the saddle and sent her tumbling down the embankment.

Flat ground skidded against the side of her face and the world finally stopped moving. There was no time to process the individual sensations, but she knew she was in pain. She picked herself up out of the dirt, fighting off the lights, and found her glasses an arm's reach away. The frames were crooked and one of the lenses was cracked, but she pushed them to her face, trying to bend them back into their original fit as she stumbled to her feet. Everything was throbbing, and her swaying vision nearly sent her toppling back down to the ground. Pieces of the glider were strewn all around her, each one a smoking shard. She traced the violent slices of earth missing from the embankment up to the ledge, where the woman stood looking down at her.

"No!" Willow shouted, backpedaling away. "Get away from me!"

The woman leapt from the ledge and landed among the wreckage with the force of a meteor striking the earth.

Willow shrieked.

The woman took a cautious step forward. "Please—"

"I said get away from—ach!" Willow tripped over her crisscrossing feet and fell onto her back. She squirmed backward, her palms and elbows sliding through the dirt. One of her hands happened upon a rock and she threw it at the woman, who was out of the projectile's trajectory before it left her hand.

Only steps away, the woman put her hands up, lessening her pace.

"Who are you?" Willow barked, her voice quivering. "What do you want from me?"

Her hollow intimidation blew away in the stale, earthy breezes. The woman was standing at her feet, and for the first time, Willow *saw* her.

Until now, the woman's image had been built on a string of fleeting glimpses, the empty spaces filled by Willow's imagination, but up close the fabrications fell away and revealed the human underneath. The red hair that had always given her presence away was a sunlit copper, fashioned into two small braids behind her ears that wove into a knot. Her face lacked any age or animation, an elegant mask of no expression. Every feature fell in perfect symmetry along a center axis, and eyes a shade of luminous green native to a different world were alert to every detail of the one in front of her.

"Please, you need not fear—"

The woman cut herself off this time. Her head snapped to the top of the stairs that led into the pit, where a soldier had just gotten off his glider bike. He took the first few steps and then paused to examine the scene below. With his hands on his hips and legs wide, he let his midsection bulge out, standing in a way that only men of unwarranted privilege knew how to do. He leaned to one side and spat with his whole face. The maroon of his aegis, as dull and grimy as it appeared, sent Willow's breath into a frenzy. He took another step and the woman instantly reversed her stance, forming a rigid barricade between him and Willow that followed his every move.

He let out a long whistle as he sauntered toward them. "Say now, what do we have here? Two beautiful ladies who have lost their way, seems to me!"

A nasty smile spread between the bushels of oily hair curling out of his helmet's cheek guards. "Praise Roh," Willow heard him say under his breath.

His eyes crawled up and down the woman's muscular form as he made his approach. He clicked his tongue and slowly shook his head. "Now aren't you something…"

The woman gave him nothing in return.

He leaned to the side and his eyes met Willow's. His smile twisted even further, and the woman sidestepped into his line of sight. Satisfied that he had elicited some form of acknowledgment, the soldier straightened back out.

"There she is!" He chewed on nothing as he spoke. "Say now, I don't know if you've heard, but the mines are actually closed today. Yep, everyone's up at the plaza for the big graduation. Well..." He clicked his tongue again. "Not everyone. See some of us are just so indispensable that we have to stick around even when everyone else is off celebrating. But that's just the sacrifice of honorable duty, I guess."

If the woman so much as blinked, Willow missed it.

"How about I help you two out of here, huh? All this dirt, this is no place for two delicate flowers such as yourselves." He raised the back of his hand toward the woman's face. "It'd be a real shame to see anything happen to that pretty face."

The woman snatched his wrist before it made contact. She let his limb squirm, a grown man's arm emasculated and powerless in her grasp.

"Say now, that's..." He let out a strained chuckle. "That's quite the grip you got there."

Her hand released him. "I can assure you we require no assistance."

The soldier ran his tongue between his bottom lip and row of teeth and then coughed out another laugh.

"Well, be that as it may, nobody is supposed to be down here, and that includes you, darling." He jerked his head toward the stairs. "Why don't you two come with me? We can get you dried off, and then—"

A second glider bike nearly slammed into the first at the top of the ledge. The engine sputtered on as another soldier jumped off, snagging his boot on the saddle before stumbling toward the stairs.

"Sid! Sid!" he shouted as he made his way down. "You're not going to believe this!" His feet lost their traction at the bottom, chancing another tumble. "Someone just tried to kill the grand priest!"

Sid scoffed. "What did you just say?"

"I heard them talking about an assassination attempt on the receiver. Some schoolgirl snuck into the Citadel and set off an explosive!"

"A *schoolgirl*?" Sid folded his arms. "What are you talking about, Hugh?"

"No, it's true!" Hugh said, out of breath. "I went back to the barracks and asked Sybil. You remember that Dinn guy they offed last year? It was his daughter. She had some vendetta against the Church or something for what they did to her dad. She may have even been working with the Dusudé! Her face is plastered all over the city. Everyone's out there looking for her. We gotta... get..."

His words trailed off as his eyes wandered to Willow, the color trickling out of his face. Cautiously, he reached for the sword on his back and gripped the handle.

Sid coiled around, any feigned charm in his demeanor melting away. His eyes narrowed, and the grotesque smile that he had been wearing since his arrival slithered off. The heel of his boot lifted off the ground and the woman's voice filled the pit.

"Take one step closer to her and it will be your last," she said.

He dropped his foot and glared at the woman. His nostrils flared for several breaths, and after a quick look at Hugh, he raised his hands. "Say now, let's all just take a minute to breathe before somebody does something they'll regret."

"You would be wise to follow your own advice," the woman said without any hesitation.

Sid sucked air through his teeth, eyes narrowing. "Was afraid you'd say something like that." He glanced at Hugh, whose grip was shaking on the handle of his sword, and then slowly unsheathed his own. "Alright, you lost your chance, sweetheart. Time to go."

His heel lifted and the woman lunged forward. He jabbed his sword out to meet her, but the woman was wind. She evaded the attack without effort, leaning out of the blade's reach. Sid tried to redirect his strike, cutting a horizontal slice through the air with all his weight behind it. She dropped beneath his swing as his momentum carried him off-balance, then shot back up, seizing his wrist.

Willow backed away from the altercation as the other soldier rushed over, readying an overhead attack. The woman flashed to the incoming assailant and then back to Sid, trapped in her grasp. There was no sign of strain on her face as the gauntlet crinkled in her grip like a thin sheet of foil. The creaking of metal came to an unbearable peak with the snap of a bone.

"GAHH!" Sid howled.

His hand released the sword and the woman swooped down to catch it before it hit the ground. She spun around and drove her foot into his chest, sending his body soaring across the pit and into the dirt. The woman brought the flat of the blade back up in front of her face just in time to block the incoming blow from the other soldier.

Their swords locked. The woman braced her free hand against the back of her blade and shoved, breaking the bind. Hugh stumbled backward and fought to bring his sword up. She pivoted behind him and drove a kick into the back of his knee. He dropped to the ground, releasing the weapon as he fell. The sword flew forward, skidding through the dirt before coming to rest at Willow's feet.

The woman lifted her sword above her head and then thrust the bottom of the hilt down. The pommel hammered into the top of Hugh's helmet and the sound of the contact rang all the way back to the city gates. Beads of blood rolled out from underneath his helmet and ran down his face. She took a step back and the body slapped onto the ground.

Uneven footsteps scampered across the other side of the pit. Hunched over his wrist, Sid limped up the stairs. The woman pivoted and flipped the sword around in her hand. Her other arm locked onto the runaway, tracing the route of his ascent as she pulled the sword back behind her ear. In a deadly movement of precision, the woman threw her leading arm down and launched the sword through the air. The projectile's visual form was lost to its speed, only to reappear with the sound of metal piercing metal. The blade impaled Sid's back, cutting through both layers of armor, as well as the flesh in between. His body was propelled forward onto the steps and slid to the bottom in a limp heap.

Willow didn't wait for the woman to make her next move. She bent down and grabbed the handle of Hugh's lost sword. Lifting it brought a flurry of sparkling lights, but she fought through them, keeping an unblinking focus on the woman. She dragged the tip of the sword through the dirt and inched backward toward one of the passages into the mines.

The woman took notice, and Willow heaved the sword off the ground.

"Don't come any closer!" she said, swinging the blade with her entire body.

Again, the woman raised her palms but continued forward.

Willow took another swing, nearly falling over.

The woman leaned out of the blade's range. "You are going to hurt yourself."

"I don't know who you are…" huffed Willow, "or what your deal is, but I know that you've been following me… and enough…" She gave her head a violent shake, but the lights persisted. "… is enough."

Something in the woman's eyes suddenly shifted, and she paused her encroachment. Caught off guard, Willow let the blade sag back to the ground, and the woman spun around to the top of the pit.

From the far corner, a man raced across the ledge, dropping his hands to his knees when he reached the top of the stairs. His shoulders heaved in furious breaths, but he forced himself upright and scanned the pit below, taking in the wreckage of the glider and the two bodies before finding Willow. She nearly jumped at the intensity of his gaze. He took the steps two, three at a time. His innocuous attire bore no resemblance to the fallen agents of the Church, whose bodies could not pull him from her. The mallet on his hip was born from Torridium in its purest form, and—whether earned or stolen—in the hands of someone of his stature, the weapon meant certain death.

Willow switched back to the woman, desperately hoping that his arrival would be intercepted, but as he drew closer, the only effort made by the woman was to move out of his path. They shared a wordless exchange, and dread sank into Willow's bones. Her face was tingling and the lights were everywhere. She brought the blade back up, her arms trembling. The man put out his hand and she jabbed the sword at him.

"Stop!" she shouted.

The man stuck his arm in front of the woman, bringing them both to a halt. His eyes were steady on Willow, and his voice came softly. "I know you must be scared, but we can't stay here."

"You don't think I know that?" Willow spat out. "I can't go anywhere!"

She flung the sword back and forth, cutting through the sparkling dots that littered her vision. The weight of the sword took control of her movements and the only thing she could do was keep swinging. She thought she was strong enough to navigate this terrifying new landscape on her own, but it was swallowing her whole. When she needed someone the most, anyone, there was no one left to—

"Bug, please."

The hair on the back of her neck rose and her blood turned to ice. Tears welled, and she pointed the blade at the man. "What did you call me?"

The woman tilted one ear toward the entrance, focusing on the ground at her feet. She turned to the man. "There is no more time, Cassian. We need to—"

"Cassian?!"

His name came blurting out of Willow's mouth, and she lowered the sword. He reciprocated her astonishment but softened into her gaze.

"Cassian," Willow said again, trapped in his eyes, and he was there with her, deeply.

She wasn't alone—she just hadn't known where to look. The sword dropped from her hands. There was a brief hesitation, but then she threw herself into him. She sobbed without sound into his chest, releasing all the events from the last day, the last year. The cloth on his back wrinkled through her fingers. She felt his body start to shake and his arms leave his sides. They were gone for a second, but then they came back, wrapping around her.

In that moment she didn't feel so alone. In that moment she felt safe. All the flashing lights became one, and she finally surrendered to them.

PART III

JONAS

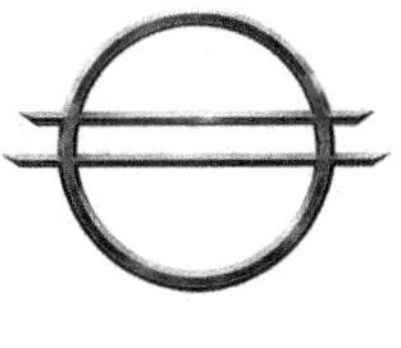

23

HEAT. VIOLENT, SEARING HEAT. HEAT from the flames of betrayal.

A hologram of a young woman was projected above the large octagonal table in front of Samuel. Her movements were cut off before they came to completion. She would run, abruptly be hiding behind a wall or in an alley, then be running again in a different direction. Footage of the assassin as she fled the Citadel had been spliced together from every available source around the city, and now the fragments of her escape replayed on a loop, taunting him as he watched his words repeatedly fail the young Willow Dinn.

"Let there be no confusion as to what happened today. This was not an isolated incident." Logan enunciated each syllable with conviction as he circled the table, his hands folded behind his back. "The events that transpired this afternoon were just the latest in a string of attempts orchestrated by the Dusudé and carried out by the insurgency with the sole intent of dismantling the holy structures that Roh has built for His children. The assassin, like her father before her, did not act alone. Her mind was twisted by the lies of the Elder Mother, and she became a pawn in the wicked plot of the nonbelievers."

A blistering rage coursed through Samuel's veins and left his heart pounding in his temples. Every time he tried to trace the anger to its source, he found himself lost. Images cycled through his head, dropping in and replacing one another just like the clips of the hologram. He had trusted Willow. In her moment of need, he showed her the way. She had been at a crossroads, and he set her on the path of the righteous. But she had turned her back on the light—His light—for sin.

Yet he knew that her actions were not her own. Born into a godless world and raised by a deviant, she was defenseless against the evils of the nonbelievers. Her faith was too weak and her soul too damaged to protect her from the deadliness of the Elder Mother's venom.

He had a responsibility to his people. *The Paladin.* It was his duty to bring the children of Roh to His light. If he could not even save this girl, how could he lead Haven to the Creator's eternal peace? His fingers curled into fists at his side and he exhaled hard through his nose. Behind his fury was energy—energy which he would channel into action. He must trust the challenges laid before him, just as he trusted the Creator.

"The citizens of Midbell cannot think that the High Army has any tolerance for this kind of apostasy." Logan continued as he passed behind Samuel. "There is only one authority, and it is He. The response to such a deplorable act of violence must be swift and absolute."

"What do you propose?" asked General Duncan, a thick-faced man with a beard down to his collarbone and a voice of gravel, standing on the other side of the hologram.

As a boy, Samuel prayed that one day he would be worthy enough to enter the Chamber of Resolution. How deeply he yearned to be part of it: the leaders of the High Army convening around a table to shape the future of their crusade and bring their people one step closer to peace. But when he dreamt of this day, he never imagined that it would be under such grave circumstances.

"Two coinciding efforts," Logan said as he returned to his space at the table with a regal poise. The hologram condensed into a single beam of light and then disappeared. In its place, the surface of the table transformed into a three-dimensional rendering of Haven. Two blinking red dots appeared: one just to the north of Midbell and the other far to the west in the Wilds. As the map altered its scope so that Midbell and the surrounding areas filled the table, a more precise location for the northern dot was revealed—one of the city's power plants.

"It is time to eradicate the insurgency once and for all. The utility they provide our cause can no longer justify the risk their organization continues to pose to His society. We have been given the location of the terrorist cell and must act before the information expires. Admiral Sybil, has your team been able to isolate the energy feeds to Power Plant 3-10?"

Directly across the table from Logan, his first officer, tall with sunken features and dark hair, bowed her head. "Affirmative, sir. They are ready to upload the malware upon your signal."

"Good," Logan said.

Heads turned to the space next to Sybil, where a flutter of motions drew the attention of the conversation to General Avery, a petite yet formidable woman with a clean-shaven head. The attack which had taken her voice had also left its permanent mark across her throat.

Samuel read her gestures as her hands formed a response.

How can you be certain that the informant will cooperate? What is stopping him from evacuating the facility before Sybil's team can strike?

"The price of his family's return is his full compliance. Even if he were to disclose our plan to the others, no exchange is made until we have the assassin in custody. And if his role in her arrest was discovered by his associates, he would wish that he had been present at the power plant at the time of the explosion."

Avery tilted her head back and found Logan through narrow eyes. Her hands moved slowly, reveling in a question that everyone around the table already knew the answer to.

When has a prisoner ever been released?

The tiny movements across the bottom half of Logan's face formed as close to a smile as Samuel had ever seen the commander make. General Avery leveled the angle of her head as she returned his expression.

"And the second half of your plan, Commander?" Duncan asked.

Midbell shrank in front of them and the central point of the map slid into the Wilds. The scope narrowed until the second dot was given its proper context—a location that set Samuel's teeth on edge. Even the rendering of the Dusudé temple was profane in its existence. He felt each flash of red in the marrow of his bones. In a matter of hours, he would confront the evil that awaited him there and fulfill the sacred duty with which the Creator had entrusted him. The people of Haven were depending on him, and he would not fail them.

"The extinction of the Dusudé people," Logan said.

The attention of the room shifted to the spot next to Samuel, where General Kodo received it with a statue-like indifference. He allowed it to linger for a moment before turning his own attention to Samuel. The rest followed him, but before he could speak, Duncan interjected.

"What is this boy doing here?"

Kodo stiffened and let the question settle to the floor before providing any verbal acknowledgement. "The actions of this *boy* will decide whether or not we are worthy of the Prophet's arrival."

A few murmurs ran around the table. Avery looked at Samuel, then signed to Kodo.

How do you know it is him?

"The Council of Four has deemed it so."

The table began to stir. Even those who had remained quiet up until this point found reason to come alive. Looks were exchanged and ears bent to whispers.

Duncan held straight and folded his arms. "And what say you, General Kodo?"

Once more, Kodo's leading silence spoke just as much as his words. "There is no one more fitting to become our Paladin. The unanimous judgment of the grand priests and priestesses only confirms what I have suspected for years."

Duncan nodded to himself while his eyes scoured the map on the table's surface. He inhaled the gravity of the new information and brought his arms behind his back. "Then today will be our reckoning."

Avery's hands moved with controlled reverence as she addressed Samuel.

Speak to us His word.

Again, the room converged around Samuel. This time however, he grounded himself with the stability that the Creator required from His Paladin.

"Despite the tragedies suffered today, we must remain persistent in our crusade and move forward with the invasion as planned. Our holiness, Grand Priest Talon, led us down His path, and from it we must not deviate."

His lungs took in the divine winds and turned them into speech. "General Kodo will lead the ground assault at the temple's gates. The vegetation around the temple is too dense for air support, but the Creator has equipped our soldiers with new defenses to combat the enemy's sorcery. Our armor has been fortified to resist their wicked fire, and our spirits galvanized by the lust for holy retribution. By His will, the conflict will draw their forces out of the temple and leave the Elder Mother unprotected."

Two of the temple's walls pulsed a dull yellow. "During the last invasion, our scouts noted two additional points of possible entry, hidden in the surrounding overgrowth. If the gates cannot be passed, I will use one of them to gain access to the temple's inner sanctum. There she will be hiding." His eyes fell upon the blinking red dot. "And there she will die."

Samuel pulled himself from the map and panned around the table. He felt the weight of the room—and the world as it should be—resting on his shoulders. "This sacred task which has been bestowed upon me is not one I carry lightly. To serve the Creator with such purpose is a privilege. I have heard His call, and it is to cleanse His kingdom of the heresy that is threatening to consume it. To restore order to Haven, we need only look inward, because He has given us all that we need." Samuel's voice found new depths. "True faith can conquer even the most powerful adversary, and it is by that faith that we will bring about His peace. We are on the precipice of a new era, one where Roh's judgment reigns uncontested." He circled through the others one last time. "Let us all go forth and set the world back into balance."

The map dissolved and doors opened on each of the room's four walls. Logan gave a nod, to which the table returned his gesture in one unified motion.

As the others filtered out, Samuel finally regained awareness of the sensations happening in his own body. His heart was pounding, and he felt as if he had been electrified by heavenly currents. The Creator had channeled His divine energy through him, and it was by this resolve that the Paladin would bring about His will.

Kodo's hand was on his shoulder. "You have done well, my boy. To stand in front of—no, among the champions of the High Army and remain in control of oneself is no easy feat."

Samuel bowed his head. "To trust myself is to trust Him. It was by His judgment that I was chosen for this hallowed responsibility, and His judgment is absolute."

In his periphery, a bishop slipped into the chamber. They waded through the straggling officers until they reached Logan. Their hood tipped to his ear, and the words muttered underneath sent a flash of inscrutable emotion across the commander's expression. Logan nodded and then rounded the table.

"Excuse my interruption, brothers," he said. "Our presence is requested in the throne room."

ONCE BATHED IN A DELUGE of vibrant lights at all hours of the day, the interior of the Citadel was muted in lifeless melancholy, empty of color and empty of reverence. As soon as the doors opened, the lingering smell of smoke and burning chemicals stung Samuel's nostrils, the air inside still thick with sin. Midbell's most sacred space, a place to find peace and to celebrate the blessing that was existence, had been defiled. The stench followed the group down the cascading stairs, suffocating their descent in unholy fumes. Samuel's body sank to subterranean levels in wordless contemplation, barely noticing the two bishops that had joined their party somewhere along the way. Hours ago, an attempt was made on the life of the city's glorious leader, yet something so urgent had now forced the grand priest to stand before an audience, a matter so urgent—

A level inhalation cleared the noise. His duty, the duty of the Paladin, was not to understand the Creator's judgment, but to trust it. Whatever awaited him in the throne room, he would receive without question.

When they reached the bottom of the stairs, the bishops pressed their hands to the wall. As the door opened, the celestial blackness from the throne room enveloped Samuel's entirety, emptying him of breath. He stepped into the place that existed somewhere between the physical and divine realms. The memories of his first summons had been soaked in a surrealness that only dreams could conjure, but as he walked upon the glossy infinitude again, the veneer that separated reveries from reality melted away.

Scripture cascaded down the walls, perfectly uniform rows of text raining from the heavens. Only one line, repeated a thousand times, covered the walls with the Creator's sacred promise.

When the voice of the faithless can no longer be heard, the Prophet shall appear.

Above him, the glowing orbs that floated in the boundlessness of the ceiling moved into subtle alignment, forming a straight path ahead. He followed their light—His light—to the end of the room, where a pedestal had been erected in front of the throne. Waiting on top was a small black box, void of any features or decoration. His thoughts began to soar, but he was not meant to question, only to receive.

He dropped to one knee.

"Curious, is it not? *Huu*—" In the silence, there was only the rasp of the grand priest's breathing. "The way that the will of the Creator manifests itself in the material world?"

Samuel stole a glimpse of the throne. The grand priest looked down at them, and while the vague direction of his attention could be discerned by the angle of his head, the object of his focus was concealed. The upper half of his face was wrapped in white bandages, leaving only his mouth exposed. Any form was lost, the contours of his face lying flat beneath the covering. The Creator had given his spirit the strength it needed to survive the attack, but there was a physical cost to such resilience.

"*Huu*—but He does not ask us to understand, only to trust."

A painful bout of wheezing ensued, and the sound shot a tremor up Samuel's spine. The suffering of Haven was his suffering, and he would allow it no more.

"Rise, brothers."

Samuel obeyed, as did the rest of the room. With Logan on one side and Kodo on the other, he momentarily succumbed to the grips of inadequacy. But as he tried to reason his importance, the portentous box on the pedestal found him again.

He was not meant to question, only to receive.

"The day of judgment will soon be upon us. *Huu*—and for it, we must be prepared." The grand priest raised a quivering hand and waved one of the bishops forward. "Samuel, Paladin, Haven looks to you. If the Prophet does not appear, *huu*—His children will never find Roh's eternal peace."

The bishop circled behind the pedestal. Spindly fingers crawled out of the cuffs of their robe and lifted the lid of the box. Samuel shuddered and his thoughts were set ablaze. Horror. Confusion. The feelings had no name. He had spent entire nights in the Academy archives reading the transcripts from past First of Seasons. Countless Sacred Technologies tore through his mind, but what he saw in the box was not one of them.

"There is only one Creator, and it is He," Samuel whispered, his breath trembling.

"Indeed, there is," said the Grand Priest. "*Huu*—and He knows the magnitude of the Paladin's trial… which is why He has sent this."

Samuel hesitated, then cautiously reached for the device inside the box: a small metal disc fastened to a leather band whose polished surface was decorated with two concentric rings. Before his fingertip could make contact with the tiny divot at the top of the outer ring, the muscles in his arm froze.

The bishop had disappeared behind him, leaving the throne in full view.

"My lord, what does it do?" Samuel asked.

The grand priest extended both hands out, his palms shaking as they turned to the ceiling. "He offers the Paladin His protection."

Samuel dropped back down to the device, his fingers bound by intangible forces. The strained breathing of the grand priest faded from his awareness altogether, and he was left with only the beating of his heart. All his life, the unknown had only ever become known through a holy intermediary, and to even conceive that the transfer of knowledge could occur by any other means was a terrifying, revolutionary notion.

But fear was of no use to the Paladin. He was not meant to question, only to receive—and to trust Roh's divine plan.

24

A FAINT HUM BETRAYED THE next glider's coming. Annika flattened herself to the ground, watching through the blades of grass as a tiny dot appeared on the horizon. Its form took shape, and the sound of the motor swelled as a bike raced along the city's northern perimeter, soaring past the entrance to Power Plant 3-10. Her breaths became shallow and her body still. The overgrowth of the Wilds concealed her surveillance, but every muscle was prepared for confrontation should it come. Detection was improbable, but her physical tension still peaked as the glider flew past and rounded the northwest corner of the city.

Logic was contested when this much was at stake.

Cassian had also fallen under the cover of the forest's outskirts, with his back pressed against the trunk of a mighty oak. His head flipped from one side to the other, following the glider's departure from their vicinity. At his feet, the girl lay cradled in the roots of the tree, unconscious. Her egress from the waking world had been in their favor. They had scarcely evaded discovery by the next wave of city guards at the Forge, and if they had needed to transport a confused and frightened child through the tunnels, an altercation would have been inevitable.

Annika scanned the details of Willow's face for signs of consciousness but found only movement in her own chest—a familiar but long forgotten sensation.

The girl looked just like her father.

As the siren absorbed the sound of the glider, Cassian switched to the other side of the tree and turned to Annika. "Anything?"

Her vision narrowed on the distant horizon—empty, for now. She shook her head.

Then came movement, not along the city wall but beneath the tree. The muscles in Willow's face twitched with hints of consciousness, and her breathing lost its undisturbed rhythm. Her eyelids fluttered, straining against the light. Cassian saw her stir and dropped to one knee beside her. Annika pushed herself out of the grass and knelt at the girl's other side.

Willow blinked back into their world, staring at them with a displaced composure, but as she finally began to process her surroundings, she gasped and reeled backward into the roots of the tree, and Cassian's hand met Willow's arm with a softness that Annika had only known for herself, draining the panic from the girl's expression, and gradually easing the trembling that shook her body.

"Everything's okay, Willow. You're safe now." Cassian's tone was as gentle as his touch. "You're safe."

Willow slid herself upright against the roots, accepting Cassian's help to get her there.

"You've been out for some time," he said. "Do you feel alright?"

She nodded, then nervously turned her attention to Annika.

"Right," Cassian said, following the divergence. "Perhaps a proper introduction later, but Willow, meet Annika."

Willow stared, and all Annika could do was stare back. It seemed impossible to define the appropriate kind of pseudo-introductory engagement for someone Annika knew everything about but who knew nothing of her. The processes responsible for guiding her through an interaction such as this had no precedent to replicate. Instead, Annika just spoke, releasing words without thought, words that were felt.

"I have looked forward to our meeting, Willow Dinn."

It was a cautious concession, but the traces of a smile appeared on Willow's face. Annika felt her expression become a reflection of the girl's own, and she let it take over just as she had let the words flow, unforced and sincere. The mental algorithms used to predict human behavior had failed in this instance, but what resulted was a genuine sense of connection.

But their first exchange was short-lived. Willow's face suddenly dropped, and Annika knew the change in her own had served as the precursor. Her attention left the girl, her gaze drifting to the ground as she tuned her ear toward the city.

"Someone's coming," she told Cassian.

The cadence of Willow's breathing spiked, but Cassian stayed with her.

"Everything is going to be okay," he said. "Nobody knows that we're here. Whoever that is will drive this way and then keep on moving. But right now, it's really important that you stay behind these roots and get as low to the ground as possible. Do you think you can do that for me?"

With a bout of frantic nodding, the girl accepted her duties. Cassian sprang back up, his body becoming one with the back of the tree. Once they were both set, Annika immersed herself back into the cover of the grass. The hum of a motor swelled, and then the center of the glider's sound zipped from both ears to just one. As the siren arrogated another engine, the bike dissolved into the distance along the city's western wall. Cassian watched the glider pass, and beneath him, Willow assiduously obeyed the single direction given to her. Annika checked the entrance to the power plant one last time and then switched back to Cassian. He gave a nod and she shot out of the grass.

The ground was a blur as she sprinted toward the entrance, and within seconds, the numbers of the keypad were in front of her.

649–

Her eyes rose from the keys, leaving her fingers hovering over the rest of the code as a faint drone found her, this time from above. She spun around to see a swarm of distant particles ascending from the Midbell skyline. The Church had grown restless with their terrestrial search for the girl and had taken to the skies. A fleet of single-passenger transports had been deployed, littering the clouds with specks of black. Like insects leaving the hive, the ships scattered in every direction—including theirs.

649428

The door slid open. A flash of movement came from within the thicket and Cassian dashed out of his cover with his arm strung behind his back. The girl, joined at his hand, struggled to keep up with him, each step barely touching the ground as they sprinted toward the entrance. He looked up at the growing sprawl above them.

A sky blotted with dark inquisition.

They cleared the gate and Annika ducked in behind them, matching their dispatch as they rushed to the plant's main building. When the arrays of generators, conduits, and power lines stole the girl's attention and sent her stumbling over her feet, Annika's hands were already there to set her back into motion. The roar of the approaching storm of transports cut through the siren and propelled their collective velocity forward. They crossed an invisible threshold, triggering the building's doors to part to either side.

Cassian did not slow, even after the doors sealed behind them. They flew down the hall to the lift. His finger hit the call button once, twice, and then kept tapping, until finally his request was answered. He ushered Willow inside with Annika close behind. The doors slid shut and he entered the sequence to command the lift into a descent.

As he backed away from the buttons, Willow remained fixated on the vacancy that he left. Her eyes took in the words above the set of buttons.

MIDBELL POWER PLANT 3-10

The doors opened to a multisensory torrent of drilling, loose sparks, and incoherent chatter all wrapped in a thin cloud of smoke. Cassian was the first to step out onto the catwalk, with Willow quick on his heels. As they approached the crossing, she suddenly veered off course to the railing. The metal bar accepted the weight of her body, as she was too absorbed in the activity below to support herself. A light permeated through the exhaustion on her face, and Annika read her lips, moving to no sound.

The Guild.

Cassian found a space to one side of her, leaning both hands on the rail. She turned to him at once, as if caught in a forbidden act, but he said nothing, and joined her in quiet observation. His shoulders dropped with an exhalation. They exchanged a wordless smile of relief and Annika fell in on Willow's other side. Their independent struggles had finally coalesced into a singular effort that would never have to be endured alone again.

The girl was safe.

Cassian looked back down and then returned to Willow. "Would you like to see it?"

She nodded, beaming.

Each step they took down the stairs attracted more attention from below. Heads turned, and the cacophony that had greeted them slowly dispersed, leaving only the hums and hisses of the plant's ancillary processes. Fingers pointed, elbows nudged, and bodies quickly began to gather at the foot of the stairs. By the time they reached the bottom step, the entire room stood before them. There were no words, just an intent preoccupation with Willow. Surprise, indifference, curiosity, alarm—it was impossible to get a read on how the majority may have felt. A gap formed in the center as someone pushed their way to the front of the crowd, and from the ripple in the masses, Toni's face—covered equally in grease and sheer delight—emerged at the bottom of the stairs.

"Well look at this," she said, and pored over every inch of the girl. She tipped a kind finger under Willow's chin, to which there was no resistance. "You've got his eyes," Toni said, glowing, and Willow smiled. "And your mother's smile."

She grabbed one of Willow's hands with both of hers. "We've been waiting a long time for this day. You need anything, anything at all, you come find your new friend, Toni." She pulled Willow close, whispering loud enough for the others to hear. "And don't let these two intimidate you. They may look tough, but they're as soft as it gets." Toni winked as she released her hold.

Cassian rolled his eyes and conceded a small breath of laughter through his nose. The day's tension continued to melt from the girl's body, and the edges of Annika's thoughts softened. A sense of ease rested on her shoulders, sinking deeper as she watched parallel sensations submerge her companions.

The girl was safe.

As potent as the feeling was, it also proved fragile. Up above, the doors at the far end of the catwalk were thrown open and the warmth streaming down Annika's body instantly went cold. Two sets of footsteps rang against the metal, the first distinctly identifiable by its anger and haste. The closer they drew to the crossing, the more difficult it was to keep hold of the peace that had overtaken her, and the approaching footsteps reignited a heightened state of awareness. She turned to Cassian, who was already waiting for her, having reached the realization on his own.

The girl was not safe—not yet.

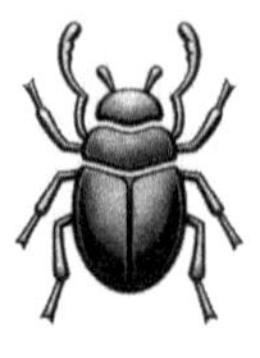

25

"CASSIAN!" A VOICE BARKED FROM overhead.

Willow spun around to find two men at the crossing of the walkway above—allies or enemies, she could not tell. Several decades separated the younger man from the older, standing a head taller than his stooped and bald companion. His own age revealed itself through the streaks of gray that infiltrated his shoulder-length hair and beard, looking more like the sands from the Radials than the shore of any beach. His hands were white around the railing, and the shadows from the upper level found the sunken features of his face.

He veered from Cassian and latched onto Willow. She felt the intensity of his gaze in her bones, his attention fixed on her as he started down the stairs. As he reached the final step, Cassian put an arm out in front of Willow and backed them closer to the crowd. The man stopped and shifted his glaring eyes back to Cassian.

"What have you done?"

Scuttling down the last few steps, the old man yelled out from behind. "He's killed us all, that's what he's done!"

Cassian didn't acknowledge the older man and coldly addressed the first. "It had to be now, Leon."

"This decision was not yours alone to make." Leon pinched his brow and threw his hand down. "You should not have brought her here."

"Then where? Where was I supposed to take her?"

"Not here," Leon hissed through his teeth.

"Here we can keep her safe," Cassian said. "Here we can protect—"

"How are we supposed to protect her if we can't protect ourselves?" the old man snorted. "You were just so excited to play the hero, go swoop in and save this innocent girl in her hour of need… except she's not just some innocent girl anymore—she's Midbell's most wanted criminal!"

Willow began to shake.

"Every soldier in the city is out there looking for her, and soon they'll be at our doors," the old man continued.

"She is family, Jasper," Cassian said. "Her fate will be the same as ours."

"Of course it will be! And do you know what that's going to be?" Jasper straightened his spine and sliced a hand across his throat. "Dead, gone, swinging from a rope at the next First of Season! The gallows aren't even big enough for all—"

"Enough—*enough*!" snapped Leon.

Jasper shrunk back into his crooked form, cowering from the sudden loss of ground.

Leon closed any distance between himself and Cassian. "I told you what would happen if you stepped out of line. You are no longer welcome here. I want you gone." He flashed to Willow and Annika, then back to Cassian, his bloodshot eyes quivering with rage. "All of you. Consider yourselves enemies of the Guild."

Cassian's jaw tightened, the muscles underneath forced into subtle restraint. His chest drew deep for its breaths, and the evenness that he had maintained throughout the interaction edged close to expiring.

"If they're out, you best believe I'm going with them."

From the opposite side of the room, a voice broke the impasse, and a ripple of swiveling heads reversed the attention of the crowd. Willow stretched to her toes to try and find the source of the redirection, but her weary shins were still plagued by fatigue. Bodies backed away, and the mass came apart at its center, revealing a path to the other end of the room where a man stood staring at Leon.

He was noticeably the tallest person in the room, taller than even the dimensions of his own clothes would allow. Inches of uncovered skin stuck out from the cuffs of his jumpsuit at the wrists and ankles, but his slender shoulders fit naturally into the confines of the torso. His hair was as dark as Cassian's, and although every strand on top of his head was pulled in a different direction, the ends of his mustache were spun in perfect twists. As he walked up the parted aisle of the crowd, the lights overhead fought through the years of fingerprints smudging his glasses, but the resolve in his eyes couldn't be clouded.

"And not just me," he said. "My tech, my research, any sincere hope you may have for understanding our adversary…" He snapped his fingers. "Gone."

Leon scowled. "How dare you threaten me, Isaac."

The name stole a beat from Willow's heart, and she switched back to the mustached man. Stories she had read in her father's journal began to resurface, digging themselves out of the heaps of noise that the day's events had piled on. Under the light of revelation, it became easier to spot the resemblance the brothers bore to one another. They operated at opposing statures, but the physical traits that they did share were potent enough to signal a common pool of genes. Both wore the same pair of eyes, brown and deep against the cool olive undertones of their skin. Their pronounced cheekbones bent to a slight unevenness, falling in line with the quiet asymmetry of the other angles of their faces. The mold that shaped their jaws imprinted each of their chins with an identical dimple, both now pinched in determination as they stood before Leon.

"What choice do I have?" Isaac started. "If it's between facing exile or staying here to watch the integrity of our organization collapse, there's no choice to be made. The Guild is family. We never turn our backs on our own."

Leon's voice was low and seething. "Everything I've ever done has been for my family."

"Then prove it right now. Either they stay or I go."

"You fools!" Jasper lunged back into the conversation. "You're ignoring the bigger picture here. Consider what the Church is trying to pass off to us as reality. Even with our best agents on the job, we've never come close to infiltrating the Citadel. And forget taking out the grand priest—just getting close enough to see his wrinkled mug has been an impossible venture. Now they expect us to believe that this…" He flung a hand in Willow's direction. "… this *girl* managed to get inside and do the job all by herself? It doesn't add up."

"Make your point." Cassian said.

"They're trying to draw us out! It's all an act! What better way to find the secret association of lawbreakers that Kip Dinn left behind than to use his daughter as bait? Put out the call that she's in danger and see who answers."

"I can assure you, the danger is real," Annika said. "The entire city is in lockdown. Although their accusations may be embellished, the concern they have is genuine. It is far too elaborate to be a ruse for our sake."

"Is that right? Because it seems like a convenient opportunity if you ask me—an opportunity to finish what they started last year. They knew that using her was the easiest way to get to us. Why else would the Church spin this fun little tale, huh? Why else would they take such an interest in her?"

"Because I know their secret!"

The entire room whirled to Willow, who jolted at the sudden shift in attention. She retreated to Cassian, his presence grounding her instantly. His eyes rested softly on her, not waiting for a response but for her to feel safe enough to give one. He was there with her, completely, and he would be until she was ready.

"I was there in the Citadel, but the rest of what they said was a lie. I didn't hurt anyone… Or at least I didn't mean to. They are using me to—"

"How?" Jasper interrupted.

"How what?" Her tone instinctively turned defensive.

"How did you," Jasper said, "an untrained, unimposing child, get inside the Citadel?"

It was a reasonable question, but the way he spoke to her made her feel smaller than the microcircuits used to power the tiniest sensor bulbs on a motherboard.

"Did you ask the big guard man if you could come inside? Or, no, let me guess—did you just walk through the front doors?"

She swallowed her irritation with the old man like a hard lump in her throat.

"That's exactly what I did. I used *this*." She held up her arm. The cuff of her sleeve slid down, revealing nothing but bare skin, and the absence of a reaction from anyone in the room was palpable. She blinked, trying to connect the fragmented memories that trauma still held in its grasp.

"Well that about proves it then!" Jasper mocked. "Why didn't you just tell us—"

"Let her finish." Cassian said.

"I had this wrist thing…" Willow looked around at all the gaping eyes. She could hear the silence of the crowd, their collective skepticism an icy hand around her throat. "It turned…" Her voice cracked and the ground beneath her was crumbling. A much-needed breath came and went. "If you don't want to believe me then fine, but I know what I saw in there! I shouldn't have seen it, but I did. The Church is hiding something from the whole city. They know I saw, and now they're trying to cover it up with lies and propaganda to keep their secret safe."

"What would they go to such lengths to conceal?" Annika asked.

Willow met her eyes. "It's the grand priest. They make him out to be the holy gatekeeper of the Sacred Technologies, but he's not. He's a violation of his own rules and an insult to anyone who has ever been persecuted for thinking outside them. The grand priest is a construct!"

Disconnected murmurs weaved through the crowd. A few heads turned and some eyebrows raised, but the proclamation was received with only a fraction of the energy with which it had been delivered. As she watched the tepid reaction from the others hardly rise past a simmer, her heartbeat reached her ears and filled the space that had been reserved for the sounds of revelation.

Annika, whose attention belonged to no one and nothing else in the room, addressed Willow without any misgivings. "What evidence led you to such a conclusion?"

"Are you seriously entertaining this?" Jasper scoffed, speaking again as if Willow couldn't hear him. "She's clearly making this up."

Annika paid him no mind, holding steady on Willow. "I do not believe that you are lying."

"Because you were there," Willow said, realizing that anything she had seen, the woman who had been her shadow for the last year had also seen. "You must have seen how weird he was acting at the ceremony today."

Annika nodded, her eyes calculating. "His behavior gave me suspicion, but I had nothing to substantiate my own intuitions." She flashed a look at Cassian and returned to Willow. "What did you learn inside the Citadel?"

There was an impulse to unload everything, and Willow didn't have the energy to resist it. But as she began to conjure the images of the scene at the altar, the air was pulled from her lungs, and she felt a frigidness in her marrow. She heard the prongs click into the grand priest's nose, and suddenly she was standing over him again, looking at all the features that were so perfectly human. She shook the thoughts away and found her breath.

"It got worse inside. He started mixing up his words again and couldn't even keep himself standing. I heard the bishops tell Commander Logan that the code from some transmission hadn't been integrated properly, and that was why he was malfunctioning."

More whispers came from the crowd, tiny pockets of interest stirring around them.

"They tried to fix him using this machine." Willow swallowed something the size of a small engine down her throat as the grand priest howled in her ears. "It had a screen just like the one they use at the First of Season, only smaller and filled with code… Lines and lines of code. There was this big arm attached to it that they brought over his body, and at the end of it were these two prongs that looked just like the ones on the apparatus in my father's diagrams."

This time, revelation did come. What were once whispers amplified into boisterous cross talk coming from every angle, and the rumblings of the lower level shook the entire plant. Annika and Cassian were deep in another wordless exchange, while Isaac bent to Toni's ear, his brow furrowed in thought. Even Jasper abandoned the disagreeable contortions of his face, his gaze dropping to the floor as her words sank in.

"It won't matter," Leon said, cutting through the noise, and the room fell silent beneath him. Willow was the sole recipient of his darkened gaze.

"Human, construct—it makes no difference. To the people of this city, he is the bridge between their god and the physical world. He is the highest mortal power, and his word will always be law. And once he has decided your fate, there is no escape. I can no longer protect you." Leon glared at Isaac, Annika, and then finally Cassian. "You've made your choices. Her blood will be on your hands."

Leon waited for no response and turned back up the stairs. Jasper, who had vacated the situation entirely, reanimated with a familiar glower before scuttling up after him. Already at the lift, Leon slammed the back of his fist against the call button. Jasper hurried along the catwalk in his tailwind and slipped between the doors just before they closed. A valve hissed from somewhere within the walls above the lift, and Willow hoped she would never have to see the two men again.

Toni was the first to move. She turned around and flapped the back of her hands through the air in front of her.

"Alright, show's over, everyone! Get on back to your gettin-ons!"

Some left with lingering curiosity, others with ambivalence, but gradually, the crowd started to thin. The sounds of lawbreaking innovation returned as the members of the Guild settled back into their work. Just as the clouds of smoke faded into the ductwork of the ceiling, so too did the ugliness left behind by the interaction with Leon and Jasper.

Eventually, Willow found herself one of only five who remained at the bottom of the stairs.

Cassian's hand was on her shoulder. "Don't think for a second that you did anything wrong," he said. "Leon's upset with us and he was taking it out on you."

"You were brave to speak your truth," Annika added.

Cassian nodded. "And I know we all want to hear more, but I think the most important thing right now is for you to get some rest."

"Agreed. Here," Toni said, beckoning with an eager hand, "let me show you where you can get cleaned up. I'll go fetch you some fresh clothes, and while I'm doing that, Isaac here's going to check the records to find you an empty room to sleep in."

Isaac held up a finger.

"Hold on one second," he said. "Am I to understand that everyone else here was granted the privilege of a proper introduction to the newest, most brilliant and daring member of the Guild… except for me? Now, does that seem fair?"

Willow smiled and shook her head.

"Well then, please allow me." Isaac took a step back. "Willow Dinn…" He twirled one of his hands off to the side and placed the other underneath his chest as he bowed. "The pleasure is all mine."

His goofiness was disarming, and the only way Willow could think to respond to such a ridiculous gesture was to bow back. He straightened with a quick wink, just before Toni grabbed her hand.

"Best not to encourage him, trust me," Toni said, leading her away.

Dangling behind, Willow turned back around before they were too far gone and looked at the others.

"Thank you," she said.

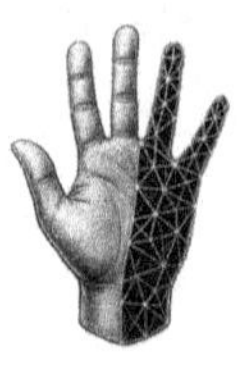

26

THE HOUR NO LONGER BELONGED to the night, but morning could not claim it quite yet. Pipes rattled overheard, the lightbulbs dangling between them were free to hum openly, and the mechanisms hiding inside the hallway walls went on clicking, spinning, and quietly beeping without human interruption. This block was several corners away from the main work area, and most of the rooms were uninhabited, making it an ideal spot for the girl to find rest.

After Toni had finished preparing the room, she bid them all a good night and then most likely surrendered to the night's call begrudgingly, face down in the middle of a task, as she was known to do. Isaac did not rush his departure, eliciting several more bouts of laughter from the girl before retiring to his lab. He left with her glasses, promising a new pair by the time she woke. The offer was received with great appreciation, followed by a graceless stumble into bed.

Annika looked down at Cassian, who was sitting against the wall opposite Willow's door, his arms wrapped around his knees and his face buried within them. Their agreement to alternate watch had been breached hours ago, but she fully expected—and endorsed—his violation. If there was anyone else who deserved rest, it was him.

Hours had passed since her last interaction with another waking being. She was alone—and that was okay. When the duties she and Cassian had to the Guild did not keep them out through the morning, and when one of Isaac's midnight breakthroughs in the lab did not require her presence, she was granted a period of solitude. While the others submitted to the nonnegotiable human need for sleep, she answered to no such force. Here she was offered a space to let her own thoughts soak, and the stillness to make sense of them. It was a confusing duality of existence: two states of being that appeared separate in their natures but depended on one another if they were to function properly. Without the time to reflect on her engagements with the outside world, meaningful connection with anyone in it would be impossible.

Annika watched the curves of Cassian's upper back rise and sink without the heaviness that had once constricted them, feeling lighter herself. It was only in this permitted quietude that she could have taken notice of a release so subtle. While Cassian had been carrying the weight of the girl's well-being, Annika had accepted his. To see him unburdened was liberating, because the suffering she felt was not vicarious. It had become her own.

Reflex pulled her attention to Willow's door when a noise came from the other side, quiet enough not to perturb Cassian's slumber. It came again—a vocalization without words. Alarm seized her as the girl's sounds grew more distressed, and she pressed the access button beside the door. A dim visibility was supplied by the lamp in the corner of the room, whose tepid light was enough to impede an exhausted teenager's pursuit of sleep. The door slid shut and more noises—shivering whimpers—came from the bed. As Annika drew closer, a sleeping Willow muttered a coherent word between trembling breaths.

"...Noah ..."

Contortions of agony gripped Willow's face as she repeated the name. With each passing breath, her lungs made their demands more urgently, forcing harsh convulsions through the rest of her body.

"Noah... Noah!"

Her eyes flared open and she launched herself upright, gasping for air. She spotted Annika, but as soon as they made eye contact, Willow dropped her head into her hands, tears seeping through her fingers.

As the muffled cries spilled out into the room, Annika considered going to get Cassian, but by modes she was not aware of, she had already arrived at Willow's side. Her hand laid itself on the girl's shoulder. When she felt the tremors rippling through the fibers of each muscle, the memory of her own unnamed distress at the lake rose to the surface. Her salvation had not been found in any specific act—it came from just being in the presence of someone who cared.

"I'm here," Annika said with a gentle pressure in her touch. "I'm here."

Willow lifted her face from her palms and her words streamed faster than the tears. "He's gone. They took him away and he's never coming back. His life is ruined and it's all because of me."

Annika waited for the words to return to breaths, not wanting to interrupt if there were more to come. The girl's proximity to the situation prevented objective judgment, but continued suffering could be prevented, so long as reason was restored.

"May I sit with you?" Annika asked.

Through several watery blinks, Willow nodded. Annika sat beside her, and the metal frame of the bed received the added weight with a groan.

"Did you tell Noah to take the Torridium?"

"No! Of course not!" Willow pulled her knees to her chest. "I would never have asked him to do something like that."

"Then his actions were his own. You could not control what your friend did any more than you can control the laws that make his harmless act punishable. If blame is to be placed on anyone, it is on neither you nor him."

"But it's not fair. Maybe he did break the law, but it's a stupid law!" She ran her fingers through her tight curls as more tears leaked from the corners of her eyes.

"Kurt. Kurt's a monster. He spends his whole life hurting others, but because he follows the rules that the Church made up, the whole city worships him. Noah is the kindest, sweetest, most good-hearted person I've ever met. He's nice to everyone he meets and remembers everything I've ever told him. And now just because he took some

Torridium, he has to spend the rest of his life in a prison cell?" Willow threw her hands down. "He doesn't deserve any of this, and I'm powerless to do anything about it!"

Annika gave Willow's words the space they deserved and then diverted her attention to the floor to gather her own.

"You were born into a world of entropy and injustice. Most things you encounter in this life will not be yours to control, but I can assure you that you are not powerless." She returned her gaze to Willow. "Your power is knowledge, and to hold the truth is one thing you can always control."

The tears began to slow.

"While you might not be able to reverse his fate, the knowledge you gained inside the Citadel could dismantle the systems that keep him imprisoned. It might seem like the world is against you right now, but that is because the Church is desperate. They want you to feel fear, because they fear you. They know what your mind is capable of, and they will go to any lengths to prevent you from using it against them. You—Willow Dinn, brilliant student and inventor, daughter of Kip Dinn—will never be powerless."

For the first time since Annika had arrived, a smile came. Willow wiped her cheeks and spoke with a brittle voice. "But where do I even start?"

"That I do not know. But you will not have to figure it out alone."

Willow softened, hugging her knees a little tighter. She looked down at her toes while she settled, and the mechanisms in the walls purred behind them.

"What was my father like? I mean I know what he was like… but not here. He had a whole other life I never knew."

Annika stared at the wall ahead. "I remember him fondly. To the people of the Guild, his name is synonymous with intelligence, courage, and leadership. Unfortunately, I was not privileged with as much time with him as some of the others, but my lasting remembrance will always be his virtue. He worked not for any selfish pursuit, but for the betterment of our world."

She remembered the blinding light, the first light, and then his face above her.

"Before this life, I also faced a kind of imprisonment. My fate may have been sealed forever had it not been for your father."

Her eyes adjusted, and his voice welcomed her into this world.

"For reasons unknown to either of us, I was granted a chance to escape. It was an impossible task, but he accepted, knowing that he had nothing to gain."

"You are safe. The life you have entered belongs only to you. Everything that happens next is yours to decide. My name is Kip Dinn. What can I call you?"

"And for that, I am forever indebted."

On the other side of the room, the door slid open and Cassian ran through, stumbling over his half-conscious words. "I… I fell asleep." He squeezed his eyelids and tried to shake the rest of himself awake. "Is everything okay?"

His cheeks were tinted red as he alternated between Willow and Annika. "Oh… I didn't mean to interrupt." He scratched the back of his neck and looked back out the open door. "I can just wait outside if that's better. I—"

Isaac's figure appeared in the doorway. "Good! You're all awake."

He blew past Cassian and handed a new pair of glasses to Willow. "As promised," he said.

His measurements, as always, were precise, and the frames lay perfectly balanced on her face. Angular and bulky, they were a smaller version of his own.

"You shouldn't have any issues with these," Isaac said as Willow examined the room with her vision restored. "The lenses are made of a shatter-resistant compound, so unless a multi-troop transport lands on your face, these shouldn't crack." He leaned in, one eyebrow arched. "Your face isn't a military-authorized landing zone… is it?"

Willow smiled, shook her head, and then resumed exploring the room in wonder. "It only took you a few hours to make these? That's incredible."

"Well, once I derived your corneal curvature and pupillary distance from the old lenses, the rest was actually pretty easy. I even managed a few minutes of shut-eye before coming over here."

Isaac stretched out both arms and yawned. "Now! Who cares about the durability of your lenses if they don't help you see?" He took a step back and held up his thumb and index finger. "How many fingers am I holding up?"

"Two," Willow said.

"Good, good." He took several more steps back. "And now?"

"Four."

"Now?"

"Still four."

"What about now?"

"One."

"Alright…" Isaac stepped next to Cassian. "And between the two of us, who's more handsome?"

Willow just giggled, declining to reveal her judgments if she had them.

Cassian smirked and nudged Isaac. "Come on, we're intruding. Let's go wait back at the lab."

Willow sprang out of bed just as they started for the door.

"Wait!"

They spun back around.

"… The lab?"

Isaac grinned.

"THIS?" WILLOW ASKED.

"Communication frequency scrambler."

Isaac flicked the tip of the antennae mounted on top of one of the many consoles around his workshop.

"And this?" Willow picked up a sphere from his desk with a lens on one side and an exhaust port on the other.

"Aerial cartographic imaging machine. Shoot it off into the air and it comes back down with a rendering of the area."

She held the sphere to her chest with one arm and pointed to a square appliance on the other side of the desk. "What does that box do?"

"Nondestructive element assayer." Isaac pulled a bolt out of his pocket. "It tests the purity of a metal. Watch."

He opened the window like it was a tiny glass door and placed the bolt on the tray inside. He pushed the only button on the face and the interior lit up, then he grabbed the handheld display connected to the box and leaned into Willow.

"Fifty-two doesn't seem all that high," she said, reading the screen.

Isaac laughed. "Ha! How right you are. Wherever that bolt come from, I can promise you that it was not this lab. And if you think a fifty-two percent purity is bad, you should have been here when we tested some of the weapons that we swiped from the High Army a couple years ago. That little Avis punk would be mortified to learn the quality of the so-called sacred metals that make up the holy instruments he and his family have been carrying for generations."

The mention of Kurt might have stirred something in her, if not for the endless stream of distractions. Her attention latched onto a palm-sized canister perched on a pile of books below a circular mirror. Willow traded the sphere for the uncovered container, the putty inside jiggling as she brought it to eye level. She looked to Isaac for an explanation, but he hesitated.

"Facial filament sculpting agent."

She knitted her brow, sorting through his wordplay.

"Mustache cream," he muttered, and snatched the container away.

Willow giggled and Annika heard Cassian concede a restrained snicker beside her.

"Oh, did she find your whisker wax?" Toni emerged from the back room of the workshop carrying a tray with a steaming mug of tea and an assortment of bread and jams. She found a clean square of tabletop and beckoned Willow over.

"That name is still in development," Isaac said. "I haven't completely ruled out 'Stache Serum yet. 'Stache Salve? 'Stache Sauce? Eh, it's there somewhere. This one wasn't as easy as the Can't Feel a Thing String."

Annika moved a hand to her arm, remembering the feeling—or absence of feeling—that the coil brought.

One of the consoles underneath the room's main monitor started beeping.

Isaac, expecting the noise, had already started in the direction of the machine. "Right on time."

The beeping ceased, along with the tiny blinking light on top of the console. Isaac powered on the monitor and clicked the dial on the side. Lines of text filled the black space, each adhering to the same format: a date followed by two number sequences, separated by a comma.

"What is it?" Willow asked, then took a bite of her second roll.

Isaac turned to her, one eyebrow pinned to his hairline. "This, my dear Willow, is the entire transmission history of the Citadel's terminals."

Annika straightened to attention.

Isaac returned to the monitor. "You see, to learn that the leader of Midbell, who has chastised the idea of unsanctioned technology for decades, is himself a product of forbidden thinking certainly got the wheels turning," he said, twisting a finger into the side of his head. "I have about a thousand questions, but there's one detail that everything else is meaningless without."

He pulled the keypad below the monitor away from its clutter and scanned the display. Once he reached the bottom, he tapped the downward directional key, forcing the top line off the screen.

"You said that the grand priest received code updates through a terminal at the Citadel. We need to figure out where those transmissions came from. If Midbell has been governed by a construct for this long, it also means that someone out there has been going to great lengths to keep this charade unnoticed." Isaac adjusted his glasses and pushed another line away. "And that someone has information I want."

"These are all local coordinates, Isaac," Cassian said. "Do you think whoever is sending these transmissions is doing it from inside the city?"

"I don't think so. The sources of the incoming transmissions are what I would expect—nothing out of the ordinary. Mobile transmissions from a transport… This one is from the communication room in the barracks… One of the western perimeter outposts… The Forge… That smaller utility station in the manufacturing district…"

His finger stopped above the directional key and the content on the screen froze. He backed his hand away from the keypad and up to his chin.

"Now hold on…"

Annika found the anomaly that had stolen his attention because it held hers as well. She was drawn to the coordinates with a distant recollection, but to know this place would have been impossible. The number pairing on the bottom line had a longitudinal component much greater than any of the others. If the data was accurate, the transmission came from a location outside their scope of charted geography.

"Isaac, let us in," Cassian said. "What are you thinking?"

"Look at these coordinates." Isaac replied, pointing to the bottom line.

"That's south," Toni said.

"Far south," Isaac affirmed. "That's on the other side of the Southern Radial, past the explored regions."

"Could we go there?" Willow asked.

No, Annika thought solely out of reaction, not reason.

"No," Isaac said. "At least not on foot. Even using a glider…" He squinted one eye, performing a calculation. "That would take days, weeks maybe. And that's assuming we could navigate through the Radial."

"Is there anyone here who would be able to help us get across?" Willow asked.

Cassian shook his head. "We have connections with some of the groups to the east, but beyond the Southern Radial… no one at the Guild has ever been out that far."

After a moment of thought, Willow's face lit with an idea. "What about Jonas?"

Penetrating and swift, the sensation that had seized Annika at the lake returned. In the fraction of a second it took her to become conscious of the name she heard, its pernicious takeover was already underway. An icy tremor shot through her chest and gathered beneath her collarbone. Shadows swallowed the edges of her vision. She steadied herself with a palm on the tabletop, her body suddenly too heavy to support. The room started to slip away, the hums and hisses of Isaac's machinery flattened, and her own breath was deafening in her ears. She could barely hear the others as they spoke, their voices muted whispers from a distant plane of existence.

Isaac: "Wait, what do you know about Jonas?"

The sensation struck her again. It started in her back and threaded between her ribs, leaving her upper half frigid and tight. Her own body and mind were succumbing to a force with which she could not contend. She clung to the one function that was still in her control: to breathe. Feeling the entrance and egress of the air was all that remained. One breath in and one breath out.

In.

Willow: "Nothing. I mean… I guess a little. Doesn't he live here with you all now?"

Out.

Cassian: "No. Willow, how do you know that name?"

In.

Willow: "I don't, not really. I just… I just read about him in a book."

Isaac: "A book?"

Willow: "My father's. I found a journal in his workshop."

Toni: "Dear, this was his workshop."

Willow: "No, not this one. He had another back at our house, a secret workshop underneath our basement."

Out.

Isaac: "A secret undergr—okay, more about that later. Did he know where to find Jonas?"

Annika further braced herself against the table, quietly, as the coldness crawled up her neck. The voices of the others were wisps of light in the encroaching gloom, a fraying tether back to the real world. She tried to latch onto the familiarity of their sounds and the warmth that their presence brought—the warmth that she so desperately needed.

In.

Willow: "I don't know, there was still so much of the journal left. But the last thing I saw was a page full of coordinates. It could have been anything, but what if that was him trying to figure out where this guy might be?"

Isaac: "There's only one way to find out. What did you do with the book?"

Out.

Willow: "It… it's still down in the lab. I must have dropped it when Harvey came."

Cassian: "Isaac, we need to see that book."

Isaac: "Oh, we're going to. Not only do I think that Kip can help us in our current predicament, but I would also wager that there are answers on those pages to questions we didn't even know we had. Getting this book just became our top priority. Willow, how difficult would it be for someone to get inside this workshop?"

In.

Willow: "Not difficult—impossible. The lock to the entrance is controlled by the computer system, and when I heard someone at the door, I panicked and initiated some kind of emergency lockdown. The whole house was disconnected from the power grid, and the lab was sealed for good."

Isaac: "Kid, we are going to teach you a whole new meaning to the word 'impossible.'"

Toni: "Isaac, the city is in lockdown. The streets are crawling with soldiers, and her house is a crime scene. You're not seriously thinking about one of us sneaking in there."

Isaac: "Not one of us, my bushy-haired friend. The two of them."

Out.

Isaac: "Cassian, when the field team raided Outpost-23 a few weeks back, where did those military uniforms end up?"

Cassian: "They were added to the inventory logs and now they're just sitting in the armory. Why?"

Isaac: "How do you think you and Annika would look in maroon?"

Cassian: "Go on."

In.

Isaac: "Willow, your house is no doubt being turned upside down as we speak. Logan and the rest of the city guards won't leave until they've gone through every room, every cabinet, and every last sock in your dresser drawer. But if the house has been disconnected from the grid, we still have some time before they can get inside the lab. While they try to figure out how to get the lights back on, two overly ambitious members of the High Army are going to find their own way down there and return the journal to its rightful owner."

Cassian: "I don't love it, but I'm not sure how many other options we have. What do you think, Annika? Annika?"

Wrested out of the darkness by Cassian's touch, Annika came back into herself with a gasp. The suffocation loosened, and her lungs found new depths. After several blinks, her frame of vision expanded to its proper margins. She looked around at the others, all watching her with concern.

Cassian's hand was on her arm, and he was staring at her forehead. "You're sweating," he said nervously.

She brought her hand up and found traces of perspiration.

"Are you okay?" he asked.

No.

"Yes," she said.

Isaac smirked. "What do you say then? Up for a little heist?"

Annika nodded. "If we are going to attempt this, we should go now."

"Agreed," Cassian said.

"What about me?" Willow asked. "What can I do to help?"

"Ha!" Isaac threw his head back. "The most wanted person in Midbell, and she's itching for more! I'm afraid you're stuck with me. How does a little field trip sound?"

"Wait, where are you going?" Cassian asked.

"I'm heading to the crypt to pay our good friend Mr. Colin Dunwell a visit. I had to have him transferred before I could finish downloading the content of his neural core to my local console."

Cassian lowered his brow.

"Look, if she saw the grand priest get plugged into a machine, I'm sure she can handle seeing a few deactivated constructs." Isaac grabbed a backpack off the floor and started to rummage around his desk. "It shouldn't take too long. We'll be back here before evening. It'll be fun!"

"She doesn't leave your side, Isaac. Not for one second."

Isaac paused his packing and faced Cassian, abandoning all whimsy. He gave no words, only an earnest bow of his head.

"Well, someone needs to stay here in case Leon and Jasper start screaming again," Toni said. "You all go. I'll make sure this place stays in one piece."

Isaac slung his bag over one shoulder. "Alright. Let's get to it then."

As Annika followed Cassian out of the lab and the sweat on her forehead grew cold, she wondered what help a person could offer whose name alone brought so much pain.

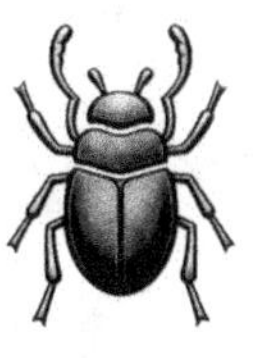

27

WILLOW FOUND THE TUNNELS UNDER the city about as welcoming as the brief mentions in Noah's textbooks made Midbell's retired mining network out to be. The air was thick with dust, the walls little more than crumbling rock. Any Torridium deposits had been depleted long ago. Completely abandoned, it was the perfect way for the Guild to traverse the city without detection from the world above, the endless sprawl of pitch-black corridors serving as its own greatest defense.

She had been following the light from Isaac's hand lamp for about an hour, a few minutes, or maybe a day. Time relinquished its steady flow when they entered conversation, only sinking back into its rhythm when a rare lull was taken for them each to catch their breath. He was just as excited to answer her questions as she was to ask them, simultaneously stoking the flames of wonder and extinguishing the falsities that the Academy had presented to her as facts. Eventually, she decided that the disparity in truth should not be closed in one day, because finding out just how far it spanned might turn out to be more depressing than enlightening if revealed all at once. Instead, she chose to seek happier topics, and she didn't have to look far to find them.

"The whole place?" she asked.

"The whole place," Isaac said.

"Oh no."

"Oh yes. I swear, I thought he was going to skin me alive in front of the entire Guild."

Willow laughed. "He never really got angry with me. But then again, I never set his lab on fire."

"First off, the lab *caught* fire. Second, and to his credit, after about the fourth fire, he started to ease up a little." Isaac jerked the strap of his bag up his shoulder and tilted his chin up in the air. "Great achievements in science are not without their sacrifices. I'd like to believe I was the one who taught him that."

Finally, the light that guided them fell upon something other than dirt. The glare from the lamp found glimpses of a silver door between patches of rust and grime. There was a small porthole window at the top, and a hum coming from inside.

Isaac moved to the small keypad built into the earthen wall next to the doorway and the screen above it powered on with a single touch. His hands danced over the buttons, and after a swirl through the air, his finger landed on the final key. A beam of light shot out of the window and the door slid open.

He swiveled around on his heels and then gestured an upward-facing palm to the door, dropping his shoulder as he did so. "After you."

Earth switched to metal as Willow stepped through the doorway. She heard the door shut behind them and paused, in part so Isaac could pass, but also to let the spectacle of her new surroundings sink in. The room they had just entered felt like the innermost part of some machine, a symmetrical box of untarnished silvers and blinking lights. From floor to ceiling, the walls on either side were divided into grids. The rectangles were as wide as her shoulders and with a height of almost half that. At the center of each was a handle, sitting below a tiny screen no larger the palm of her hand. The sample of devices that occupied the desk against the back wall looked familiar—not enough for her to identify, only enough for her to know that she had seen them before. Above the desk was the room's only monitor, responding to the input Isaac had given at the door with what looked like an initialization code. From the top of the display sprouted a row of ten or more cables. Like the tendrils of some mechanized creature, they crept up the wall and continued their crawl along the ceiling and split off to meet the tops of each of the grid's columns until all lines were not without a connection.

In the back corner, Isaac was in front of a second door, diagonal from the one they had entered. He fiddled with the keypad next to it for a moment, and Willow read the bottom line of text on the monitor:

EAST ENTRANCE: LOCK DISENGAGED

She wondered why the satellite lab had been built with two entrances, but then again, she didn't know exactly what this place was, or why they were here.

"Willow, I bet you're wondering what this place is and why we're here," Isaac said as he pulled a chair out from the desk and set the backpack down.

"I… Actually, yes. Where are we?"

He opened the bag and stuffed the hand lamp inside. "Well, I don't know what else you read in that journal, but I suspect you have some idea of the work we've done to try and learn more about the constructs."

"Yes!" Willow said, listening to her own excitement brew. "I read all about how my father built the first apparatus with my mother and started to map the neural core."

Isaac flashed a thoughtful smile. "That's precisely why we're here—to continue their work." He powered on one of the machines, wiping the monitor clean.

"Your new friends Annika and Cassian got into a tangle with a construct a few days ago. They were able to subdue the attacker and then bring the unit back for me to inspect. But thanks to my brother's heavy-handedness, there was some damage to the neural core, which meant downloading the contents was going to take a bit longer than usual. So, for safety, I had the construct moved here."

There was a prompt on the screen asking him to select an entry from a list of dates that were formatted like the ones in her father's journal. He used the machine's keypad to select the first line and

Willow heard the hum of more machinery turning on. Behind her, one of the tiny screens on the wall was glowing green. She lingered on it, then quickly made the same connection that Isaac's systems had. Her mind spun as her eyes slowly climbed up the grid on one wall and then back down the other.

"Are all of these...?" she asked, running over the rows of rectangles—of *graves*—again.

"Yes, but don't worry, they're deactivated."

"It's a catacomb..."

"Catacomb! I like that. I've always called it 'the crypt,' but 'catacomb' is good too. It was your father who came up with the idea for this place. As the Guild acquired more constructs, we needed a place to store the units that were no longer being tested. He thought it was a good idea to secure the inactive units somewhere remote in anticipation of disaster."

A lack of response peeled Isaac from the monitor.

"But there's no need to worry," he said. "If there is a change to a unit's internal system activity, their screen will start flashing. And if somehow something did happen—"

"Two exits," Willow said, pointing to the doors in opposite corners.

"Two exits."

Text flooded the monitor behind him. He followed Willow's gaze over his shoulder and then gestured her over.

Dynamic geographic markers, behavioral algorithms, advanced language models—ideas that she had been told were too complex to even conceive of, that her efforts would not only be wasted in pursuing them, but also be an insult to their great creator. The pieces of code that she could discern she only knew in isolation, and when scattered among masses of unfamiliar commands and references, her knowledge of them became useless. Understanding their job in the context of the whole would take years—years she was willing to give.

The interaction with the soldier boy returned to her once more. To hear the call, all she had to do was listen. Deep within the negative space between the lines of code, she could hear it again. Past the DNA of the construct was part of her own. She imagined the hands on the other side of the aether that had crafted this program, and the mind that had guided them. Her father had given everything to bring the truth to the rest of the world.

It was time for her to do the same.

"Synthetic life," Isaac said. "Isn't it beautiful?"

It was beautiful. She didn't need to understand the purpose of every character to appreciate the craftsmanship of the program, and she quickly came to realize that that was the point. Proper spatial allowances knitted the different lines together perfectly and resulted in the readability of a children's book. When she found herself lost, the regular annotations held her hand through the more intricate sections, and consistent naming practices made it easy to differentiate objects and functions from the native content of the core. The scripts were written with a proficiency that sought not only to achieve optimal performance but also to sustain the life of the program. Ownership over a creation of this magnitude could never be static, and her father had known that from its conception. Like a perpetual flame passed down from one generation to the next, the knowledge could burn for eternity.

Willow found an unmoving block of text in the top right-hand corner of the screen, which she assumed to be a snippet of metadata for the program.

"89.36 percent," she said. "Is that how much has been mapped?"

"Indeed," Isaac replied. "It doesn't sound like there's much left, but the rate of progress follows a logarithmic curve. A couple years ago, we were learning new things every hour. Now, we're lucky to move that percentage by a tenth of a point in a week. There's still a lot we haven't figured out yet."

"Okay," she said. "Well, a lot isn't a lot—"

He joined her for the rest of the sentence.

"If you take it piece by piece," they said together.

The last word was punctuated by mirrored smiles. After a shared breath, Isaac reached behind his neck and pulled a thin chain over his head. Three data sticks slid out from the collar of his shirt and dangled at the end of the necklace. "Would you like to do the honors?"

Willow grabbed the chain just below his hand. The two longer data sticks—one red, one blue—were cylindrical in shape, but the casing of the third had lost its color long ago, dented and cracked by the grips of time. It was shorter and flatter than the other two, and the connector was rectangular, with all its pins in a single row. There was no Sacred Technology that would accept such an input, but she suspected the stick had not been designed for matters of the Church.

"Which one?"

"Red, into the center console."

Willow did as instructed. Under the metadata on the screen came a brief flash of text:

BACKUP DRIVE CONNECTED: PLEASE WAIT FOR INITIALIZATION

"What are the other two?"

"The blue one is more of a personal venture. Whenever someone at the Guild comes across a text from the Old World, I make sure that a digital transcription gets archived before they lose it, or the thing falls apart on us. And the other one… Well, I actually don't know what's on the other one."

"If you don't know what it is, then why do you keep it around your neck?" She sank a little bit back into herself, hearing the judgment in her question.

Isaac sensed her withdrawal and chuckled.

"Don't worry, that's a fair question. In short, because the information on that data stick, whatever it is, must be pretty important." He picked up the variant, raising it as far as the chain would allow. Using two fingers, he rotated the drive to all angles and read the story written between the cracks in its casing. "It originally belonged to the Dusudé, passed down from one Elder Mother to the next. They didn't know what it contained, but they knew that it was not meant to be forgotten. The problem is that the technology itself is a relic of the Old World and has far outlived the systems that it was designed for. Any means of unlocking the content inside became more difficult to find with each new generation that inherited it." He shrugged. "And then when I was about your age, it was handed down to me. I was never entirely sure of the reason why, but the Elder Mother saw its place with me, and so with me it shall stay."

Willow leaned over the desk to get a better look. "Have you tried building your own input for it?"

"If I had another, I would give it a shot, but the pins on this one are too fragile to use it as a model. I can only hope that one day someone at the Guild stumbles across a console that was built to accept ancient drives like this."

She went to examine the artifact for herself, but a change in the screen tore her away.

INITIALIZATION COMPLETE. SYNC IN PROGRESS.

"Alright, once this finishes, we can head back to the lab. If we get there before Cassian and Annika… maybe we could do a little work on the core." Isaac scratched the back of his neck. "I mean, you know, if you're up for it."

She nearly jumped at the prospect. "Really? Yes! Of course! I thought I would have to pass an initiation or something first."

"Are you kidding me? You're family. I know Jasper and Leon might have made it seem otherwise, but the Guild is your home too."

Home. She hadn't felt at home for so long that living in the absence of such a feeling had become her equilibrium. At the expense of so much, she had finally found her place. She understood the sacrifices that had been made to get her here, and it was a privilege she would not take for granted.

"And between you and me…" Isaac leaned in and lowered his voice, avoiding the listening of nobody else. "It'll be nice to have another intellectual around the lab."

Joking or not, a compliment from someone of his talents was liquid light pouring over her.

"So, where do we start? How can I help?"

His eyes glimmered with excitement, and he moved the contents of the screen with the directional key. "Alright, well, for most of this last year, I've been trying to decode the physical response system. Have you ever worked with adaptive procedures before?"

"All the time. At the Academy, the code for the temperature regulators on transport engines was based entirely on an adaptive procedure. I could write the sequences from memory."

"Ha! I shouldn't have expected anything less from you." He looked up at the monitor, beaming. "You know, with you around, we're going to make some serious progress on this thing. Who knows, you may even be able to crack line 624875."

"What's that?"

Isaac waded through the sections of code until the line in question was at the center of the screen.

"I wish I could tell you. Despite all that we've been able to learn, I haven't been able to crack this one line. It's always a different combination of characters of varying lengths, but the pattern is always the same: three letters followed by a series of numbers. It doesn't call a function that we've been able to identify, trigger any executions, nor is it referenced anywhere else in the code."

Willow stared at the screen, not at an exciting puzzle from her new life but an ordinary feature of her old one.

"It's an identification number."

Isaac's head snapped to her so fast that his glasses nearly flew off his face. "What?"

"An identification number," she repeated. "The serial numbers that the Church uses to categorize the Sacred Technologies use the same format. They're unique to each creation."

"An ident—" Isaac switched back to the screen. "An identification number... Could it really be that simple?"

Willow giggled. "Less than a day on the job and already one mystery solved. Not too bad, huh?"

He didn't respond, melting further into the monitor. Willow felt ice in her throat as she watched him read and reread the identification number in contemplation. He unstuck his attention from the screen and pulled out a single sheet of paper from the backpack on the chair. With his chest drawing deep breaths, he alternated between the page and the screen.

"What is it?" she asked.

Isaac lowered the paper, and his eyes darted around the tabletop. "There is a legend the Dusudé used to tell of an ancient war fought in the Old World." He slid the paper to the other side of the desk and dove his hand back into his bag. "A great evil once threatened to wipe out an entire race of people and leave humanity out of balance. Their motives were sinister, and their deeds inhumane. Out of an industrializing world, new technologies had emerged, and the enemy used them to develop an army of superweapons."

From inside the bag came another sheet, and then another.

"The scale of production was unknown, so the heroes resorted to mathematics to try and estimate the number of weapons that had been created. They began to deconstruct the killing machines they had defeated and found that each one had a serial number inscribed upon it."

Isaac brought each page to eye level, checked it against the screen, and then added it to the spread on the desk.

"Under the assumption that the identifiers had been created using ascending sequences, they were able to estimate the enemy's rate of production. When the fighting was over and the war had been won, it turned out that their calculations matched the manufacturing log almost exactly."

He read what was on the paper in his hand one last time and then placed it among the others. His hands lay flat on the table as he stared past the pages.

Willow hesitated. People usually asked questions they wanted to know the answers to. "How many are we talking about? Hundreds? Thousands?"

Isaac lifted his eyes. Horror edged his voice.

"No less than a million."

Enlightenment brought with it a cold and terrifying silence. The next noise came moments later: a solitary beep from the monitor, informing them that the download had finished. Isaac removed the data stick from the console and quietly returned the collection to his neck. He adjusted his collar and turned to her.

"I think we should head back. The others need to hear about this."

She nodded.

Isaac was about to power down the console when a new line of text flashed on the display:

MOVEMENT DETECTED: WESTERN TUNNEL

He spun around to the door from which they had entered.

"Someone's coming."

28

THE DISTURBANCE HAD NOT FULLY receded. Rather, it had found cover in the far reaches of Annika's mind. It waited quietly behind the background processes of her consciousness, only to flash its presence when she let her focus loosen. She was not equipped to combat an enemy as invasive and persistent as this. A single utterance had invoked such gripping anxieties that command of her own thoughts shifted in and out of her control. To conquer the effects would require knowing their origin, but every time she looked for the source, she was led into obscurity. There were times, however, when she traced the feeling back as far as she could, and for a fleeting instant, she thought she saw something in the darkness. It was little more than a shadow, yet its mere presence intensified the sensations tenfold. To look was to voluntarily inflict pain upon herself, but she had to know.

"Can you see it?"

The harder she tried to concentrate on the image, the more pain it brought. Emotions surged—nameless emotions seeping in from a place inside her that she did not recognize. Her instincts begged her to turn away, behaving as if they had been trained on data that she did not have access to.

It was close enough to touch, yet the details dissolved before she could reach them.

"Annika, can you see it?"

Suddenly the physical world was upon her again. She was staring at the crest of the Church, carved into the center of a black shield. The hilt of Cassian's mallet protruded from the top, and her hand was quivering above it, right where she had left it. Her breaths rang heavy in her own ears, but everything else in the alley was quiet. She inhaled as evenly as she could and slid the weapon fully into concealment.

"No one will see it as long as you keep the shield on," she said.

Cassian turned around with a helmet in each hand: the two missing components to complete their maroon ensembles.

"Feels like forever since we've done something like this." He looked up from the helmets, his expression dimming as he met her eyes. "Is everything okay?"

She hesitated, her attention momentarily retreating down to the helmets. "If we are able to get the journal and find this individual, do you truly believe that they will help our cause?"

Cassian lowered the helmets to his sides. "I guess I don't know for sure." He cast a quick glance over his shoulder toward the street. "But it's a chance we can't not take. If there's a possibility, even a small one, that they can help us understand the constructs, or find out who that transmission came from, then it's worth seeing this through. And if they won't help us, then we're right back where we started."

"Assuming that they are willing to help us, how do you know they can be trusted?"

"Because I trust *you*," he said, and then read her expression without the need for words. "It was the last thing you said to Kip before the reset. Annika, *you* were the one who told us to find Jonas."

The name struck deeply, as did her understanding of how the Guild came to possess it. She stepped back. The pain was a relic of a past life, borrowed sensations from an existence that was no more. But even detached from the force that had brought them into being, the feelings themselves remained. What kind of evil was capable of leaving wounds that could transcend lifetimes?

"We cannot know the motivations of the one who gave Kip that information," she said faintly.

Cassian failed to read her this time, his clear and hopeful tone in blinding contrast to her internal state. "You came to Kip because you wanted to see your life in its truth, and I believe that some part of you wanted the same for the rest of us too. With full agency over your own life, you could have gone anywhere and done anything, yet you still chose to stay with the Guild." He removed the distance between them. "I trust you. I trust who you are now and I trust everything you've ever been."

Voices and footsteps grew louder out on the street, and Cassian took another look over his shoulder.

"If you thought finding them would be to our benefit, then that's what we'll do. But the first step is getting that journal."

He extended one of the helmets. "Ready?"

No.

"Yes."

They left their identities in the alleyway, along with any detectable uncertainty. Two drops of red in a bleeding sea, they fell in line with the rest of their maroon-clad comrades and disappeared into the masses. Annika matched the others, mirroring their posture and cadence. Assimilation was their best hope at prolonging the charade, as the timeline for this mission had forced an undeveloped plan into execution.

Lending her attention to the movements of the others was a favorable task. To focus on something as simple as walking was a welcome change from the complexity of her recent thoughts. Streams of red passed by on either side, dyeing her peripheries in the color of the Church's unrest. The streets were overrun with soldiers. Storefronts were dark, shades were drawn, and civilians were scarcely sighted, either ducking in and out of buildings or answering questions from a horde of guards.

They filtered into the southern junction, where the streets flowed red in every direction. Pockets of conversation all piled on top of one another, but one boisterous civilian on the front steps of a house on the corner made himself heard above the rest. He shouted over a wailing infant and the ramblings from the emitter at his feet.

"Forgive us, Roh! I knew she was plotting something! She's just like her god-hating father. Please, Roh, she is not one of us! I saw her running off toward the western gates to commit her wicked deeds. Creator, please have mercy!"

One of the soldiers in front of the house pulled a comm off his belt. "Go ahead and dispatch a search team out to zone 46-W. We just got another reported sighting... I don't know, some loon at the southern junction... Twelve so far, all saying she was heading west out of the city... Let me know when they get there... I'll check in with the team down at the Forge."

If the bodies and wreckage at the Forge had not already been discovered, they would be soon. After that, it would only be a matter of time before the line was drawn to the girl's hideout at the lake, and when it was—

Annika exhaled the thought. So long as the Guild was safe, Willow would be too.

She followed Cassian's movements as they veered around the corner. The Dinn residence stood at the far end of the street with only a single guard stationed outside, but permanence of any favorable condition was a dangerous and reckless assumption. If they wanted to take advantage of the opportunity, they would need to act fast.

The pressure of Cassian's elbow was not enough to draw the attention from anyone else around them, but Annika knew the touch well. He steered them to the side of the street and knelt over one of his boots, pretending to adjust his shin plate as he spoke at a volume only she could hear.

"No chance we're getting in by force. We're going to have to figure out something else. Any ideas?"

"No," she said without moving her lips.

Just then she caught a flash of movement outside the house. The guard stationed at the door stepped aside to allow a soldier from inside to exit. They convened briefly before the guard returned to his post, and the other started in the direction of the junction. The soldier was quick to link up with another who had been waiting for him, and the pair continued down the street.

She cleared her throat and let Cassian follow her gaze. He abandoned the pretense of fixing his armor and they set off for the house again, discreetly adjusting their route closer to the oncoming soldiers. She narrowed her focus on their mouths to fill the gaps of what her ears alone could not define.

"No, everyone else was gone. It was just me in there."

"And you didn't try and go down to see for yourself?"

"I couldn't if I wanted to. The lock was set electronically, and the girl must have cut the power to the house."

"So then how do they think they're going to get in?"

"They called for the demolition team. I guess they're going to cut through that grate with one of those industrial saws." The one soldier who had come from inside the house laughed. *"But they sent Derks and Gunner back with the measurements for the saw, so it's in Roh's hands now. I'd be surprised if the two of them will even be able to find the armory by sundown."*

They were only paces away, and the need for reading lips ceased.

"Yeah, you can't rely on those guys for anything. Hey… all these precautions… the family must have been protecting something. What do you think is down there?"

"I don't know, but I heard the father was the one making all the constructs. I bet he was doing it right there in his own house."

"Growing up around all that… no wonder his daughter turned out to be sick in the head."

One last look at their faces and suddenly their voices were behind her.

"Doesn't matter. Once we find her, we'll tie her to the end of a rope just the same."

Panic flashed under Cassian's helmet, but he immediately leveled the emotional variance.

"Come on, let's get back to the barracks. I want to be around when Sybil's crew returns. Today, His kingdom is purged of the nonbelievers."

Annika and Cassian exchanged a fast glance but could give the comment nothing else. More of the street was behind them than ahead, and as the sounds of the soldiers melted into the crowded junction, the details of the house's keeper came into view.

"Anything?" Cassian said out of the corner of his mouth.

The guard was much older than Annika expected a soldier of such a lowly assignment to be. Through the window of his helmet, she saw pair of dusty eyebrows sagging low with resentment over a face battered by years of unrecognized service.

There was little street left, but the path ahead had formed.

"I think I have something," she whispered.

The bushy lines of ash above the guard's eyes folded together as he watched them approach, wrinkling his face in suspicion. He peered down the bridge of his nose and extended a stiff hand out.

"Hold it."

They obeyed.

"What are you two doing here?"

Annika felt as if one wrong word could knock her off-balance. The mere seconds she had taken to chart their next move now felt wholly inadequate, but if the plan was to work, there could be no signs of uncertainty.

"Please forgive the confusion," she said. "We were sent to gather additional measurements."

"You what?" grumbled the guard.

"The demolitions team needs to know what size blade would be sufficient to cut through the grate."

The guard folded his arms. "The armory should have already received the measurements. We sent those two cadets, Derks and Gunner."

Time abided by different laws in the seconds that it took for a single breath to pass. Annika held steady on the guard, and as his gaze narrowed, she could sense Cassian's uneasiness on her. She crossed her arms, mirroring the guard's stance, and released a dramatic exhalation.

"Well, what did you expect sending those two?" asked a voice that she barely recognized as her own. "You can't rely on them for anything!

If it's not one thing with them it's another. I'd be surprised if they'll even be able to find the armory by sundown."

The guard howled. "Listen to that! Just this morning I was considering filing a report for nothing other than sheer incompetence. You just can't count on these young guys." He shook his head. "It feels like every new cohort that comes out of the Academy is lazier and more entitled than the last. What happened to the High Army? Nobody has any respect for the job anymore. It's a miracle from Roh if we can get a recruit in here with any integrity."

She lowered her head. "Know that our work will be thorough, brother. We will not need long."

"Good, good. Logan will be here soon to see what's going on down there. We don't want to keep him waiting."

The guard flashed a keycard at the panel behind him and pulled open the door. He grabbed Annika's shoulder before she could pass through.

"Everyone else is gone, so stay alert in there. Logan's team came in and cleaned the place out last night, but we don't know what else this deranged family might have been plotting."

"We will be careful. Thank you, brother."

She tried to take a step forward but his hand kept its hold. He lowered his voice so that it was only for her and Cassian.

"I hear this whole assassination attempt was their last stand. Any minute now, the nonbelievers will get what's coming to them. They think they can hide, but He sees all." The guard released her. "Praise Roh."

"Praise Roh," they both forced out.

The door shut behind them and the world went quiet. Shadows washed the interior of the house, the light from the windows spilling in only as far as the outside world dared to look. They stood in an empty room, void of anything at all. The walls were bare and there was no furniture. All that remained of the house's inanimate inhabitants were the scuff marks on the floors and walls from their abrupt removal. Any trace of human life here, let alone a family, had been wiped clean.

Cassian appeared plagued by the same horror that she was: how quickly two lives could be erased altogether when their existences interrupted the Church's normal flow of society.

They were alone, but she still felt the need to whisper. "What do you think the guard meant about the nonbelievers?"

He spoke slowly, as if trying to convince himself. "Probably just the same nonsense as always… right?"

If she were certain of a response, she would have given it.

"We need to keep moving," Cassian said.

They followed a stale white glow down the stairs and into the basement. In the back corner of the room was the final vestige of the Dinn family, surrounded by dozens of boot prints and discarded hand lamps.

Cassian picked up one of the lamps and they knelt over the grate. He bent the light through the slits and then grabbed one of the centermost bars. The flexibility of the seal was nonexistent, and the grate didn't so much as rattle under his efforts.

"It's going to be tough," he said, backing away.

Annika removed her gauntlets and straddled the grate. The metal was rough against her palms, but her grip could have squeezed it smooth. One at a time, her fingers lifted from the bar and tightened back into place. She drew a breath and thrust upward. The ligaments beneath her skin felt like they were coming apart, and the metal began to creak under the strain. A tiny groan slipped out of her as the pressure finally gave. The hinges snapped, the lock broke free, and her body shot upright.

Panting, she set the grate to the side of the opening just as she heard the door upstairs zip open.

"Hey! What was that?" a voice barked from above.

Cassian's face flashed with alarm.

"Soldiers, report back! What was that?"

The door closed and a pair of brisk footsteps hammered across the ceiling.

"Get the journal," Cassian whispered. He pushed the hand lamp into her chest and darted up the stairs.

Annika dropped the hand lamp into the hole. Once the light had defined the depth of the fall, she made the leap for herself. The air moved fast along her skin, and when the floor was upon her again, the sound of the impact reverberated back up the tunnel.

"What's going on down there, soldier?"

"Just finishing up the measurements, sir."

Annika picked up the lamp and registered her new surroundings. The sterile and organized qualities of the space were the unmistakable fingerprints that Kip Dinn left behind wherever he went. It was reminiscent of a place she once knew—the place where this life began.

"What were those noises?"

"Noises? I haven't heard anything, sir. Are you sure they came from in here?"

"Am I—of course I am! Where's your partner?"

Abandoned mid-sentence and lying face down atop a pile of scattered sheets on the floor was a book. Under the light of the lamp, Annika confirmed the handwriting, but what started as a brief scan of the content melted into total absorption. It was a story of death and birth—hers.

"She's doing one final pass to make sure we have everything we need. We cannot afford to have to come back and lend any more time to the nonbelievers."

"Hmph, I know I heard something. Let me down there."

"Oh no need to trouble yourself, sir. I'm sure she'll be up any second now, and then we'll be off."

She read the last words on the page—the last words of the life that preceded this one:

Find Jonas Adler.

The CDE must be stopped.

In its written form, the name struck her with the same force it had when spoken into the real world. The letters seared her vision, but her own body betrayed her, powerless to resist the name's magnetism. How, she tried to fathom, could a person provoke conflicting emotional responses, simultaneously eliciting feelings of both attachment and aversion? The duality operated outside the structures of everything she had come to learn, and to try and make sense of it in the moment pained her. Annika read the name again in its context and a new dread overtook her: that her final message had been misinterpreted. The others thought that she had sent them to find an antidote to their problems, but now she feared they were searching for the poison itself.

"Something's going on here. What's your identification number, soldier?"

"My identification number?"

"Yeah, who do you report to?"

"Well… Roh, sir. As we all do."

"Oh, don't give me that. Get out of my way. I'm going dow—agh… aghhh…"

Next came the definitive sound of a metal-wrapped body hitting the floor.

"Annika, we need to get out of here!"

She plunged back into the present. There was a fleeting sense that the ground beneath her was shaking, but she knew that the tremors were coming from within. The light trembled as she placed the lamp on the floor beside her. She gathered all the loose sheets and wedged them into the journal's open page. The book could not be seen leaving with them, so she slid it inside the borrowed armor against her abdomen.

Footsteps came fast and then Cassian was at the top of the tunnel.

"Are you okay?"

No.

"Yes."

"Come on, we have to go!"

The corners of the journal pressed into the bottom of Annika's ribs as she and Cassian bled back into the street, but she gave no sign of her discomfort. The southern junction was just ahead. From there it was only a few more blocks to the alley with the access point, where they could disappear from the eyes of the city. The currents of the street were faster this time. Quieter, more orderly. She waded through eye contact with others, which came intermittently and never lasted more than a second. Her senses were on alert, assessing the movements of every soldier they passed. Something had changed. The streets felt tighter, neater, as if everyone and everything had been brought into alignment. And then, across the junction, she saw the force responsible for it all: Logan.

Walls of red parted as the refined clicks of the officer's boots punctuated each stride. Behind him was a block of soldiers, not an inch out of formation. Straightened stances became straighter, but none were worthy of a glance. His sight was locked on the house at the end of the street.

It was too late for Annika and Cassian to reroute. Any divergence from their current course would draw attention. Their only path out was through.

"Keep your head down," Cassian whispered. "If they say anything, we make a run for it."

She kept to the ground, and the clicks grew louder, sharper, until Logan's form exited her periphery. Hearing his footsteps fading behind her brought a coursing wave of relief, and she caught the subtle drop of Cassian's shoulders out of the corner of her eye.

Suddenly the clicks stopped and the throng of heavy boots behind them came to a halt. The sensations in her chest fell to the bottom of her core. Reason begged her not to, but she looked over her shoulder.

The commander was looking directly at her.

A statue among the waves of red, Logan's body had suspended its intentions and stood fully reoriented in her direction. The depth of his expression grew the longer he stared. Submerged in visible perplexity, the commander was lost in the center of a street that belonged to him. His reputation was not to question, only to know, and to see someone of his confidence in that state was jarring. She pressed forward, but his intrigue, contagious and penetrating, kept her ensnared in a wordless hold. Her internal processes moved faster as the world outside slowed.

What troubled her was not just that he continued to look, but rather, it was not knowing how deeply he was able to see.

"Sir, the demolitions team will be arriving shortly," she heard one of his soldiers say.

Logan nodded distantly. His feet turned first, and then he peeled the rest of himself away. He resumed his prior course, and the soldiers behind him followed without command.

A nip on her forearm turned her back around, and she crossed the arm's length of distance that her gradual deviation had put between her and Cassian. His concerned gaze was waiting for answers she did not have. The nature, even generally, of what had just happened belonged solely to Logan.

Moving with the lightness of a breeze, a group of soldiers cut in front of them. The woman at the rear turned around, radiating excitement as she pranced backward.

"Brother, sister, come! Word of our victory is here!"

There was not time to form a response before the woman twirled back around and rejoined her troop. They were heading for the house on the corner, as were most of the others. The tides of the junction had shifted. Logan's presence had passed, and the structure it demanded was melting. Soldiers flocked around the house, restless and overjoyed. Outside, the owner was on his front steps gesturing up to the sky and down to the emitter at his feet.

Annika and Cassian were pulled in by the currents and absorbed into the swarm. Their escape would have to wait. An act so divergent as to try and push against the momentum was guaranteed to get them caught. More soldiers continued to pack in behind them, all with unbending attention on the house. A hush passed through the crowd and the voice from the emitter became intelligible.

"Today marks the beginning of a new era—an era of unity and order, where His word reigns uncontested! The heinous attempt made by the nonbelievers to overthrow our society has failed, and from the ashes of sinful hellfire, balance has been restored to His glorious utopia. A recent discovery by the honorable Commander Logan has revealed that for decades, the terrorist organization known as the Underground has been using one of Midbell's utility stations as a front for their depraved activities."

Everything went cold, and for a moment, Annika forgot the role she was supposed to be playing. Impulse drew her to Cassian, but he was not there. His face had been drained of its color, and his eyes were wide with panic. He took a breath in through his mouth and then forcibly straightened his expression, reminding her of the necessity to do the same.

"But fear not, brothers and sisters!" the emitter continued. "Those who follow the will of Roh will always be safe from harm. He warned us of the dangers that unsanctioned technologies bring, but the faithless would not listen. They revoked His word, and now they have paid the ultimate price! An energy surge was detected at Power Plant 3-10 earlier this afternoon, followed by an explosion that decimated the entire facility. This was undoubtedly a result of the wicked affairs of the organization, the inevitable consequence of sin and debauchery. No survivors were found, and the lives lost today will never see salvation. With General Kodo's victory over the Dusudé, and an end brought to the insurgency, Haven has been purified of its blight. Finally, we may know peace!"

The crowd roared and Annika watched Cassian's guard fall, this time irreversibly. He turned to her, lost to the depths of their new reality, and she grabbed his hand. They weaved through the celebration, dodging raised fists and moving bodies until they were clear of the junction. She perceived the world in still images, disconnected snapshots with nothing to accompany them except the sound of her pounding heart. Suddenly they were in the alley. One second the helmet was framing her vision, the next it was on the ground. She pulled the journal out of its hiding as Cassian dropped to one knee beside the access point.

"Isaac would have seen that his systems at 3-10 went offline and known better than to go back," he said as he tore the cover off. "If they were at the crypt when the explosion went off, then they'd still be there. We need to find them. Go. I'll get there as fast as I can."

Her feet knew their way through the tunnels well and compensated for the delay in her thoughts. The reason for each turn came only after she had already made it. Her mind had become so cluttered that her present actions were queued behind a litany of racing thoughts. There was no space for the external world when the one inside was overflowing. It was only when the metal plating on her shin snapped off that she could hear the squeals of her armor as it scraped against itself, trying to keep up with movements and speeds for which it had not been designed. The weight of the journal in her hand returned, but the sight of it sent her back into the vortex of thinking, spiraling in a different direction.

Another corner came, and then the western entrance was in view. As she sprinted closer, she could see movement through the circular window of the door. The keypad on the earthen wall responded to her touch, and she watched her fingers type what her brain was still searching for. Her hand retracted and light poured into the tunnel as the door slid open.

She started for the doorway, but a sudden flash of movement stopped her before she could make it through. A blur spun through the air in front of her and something wrapped around her head. Pain unlike any she had ever known drilled into her skull as the room in front of her began to dissolve. She staggered in place, barely able to keep herself up. Her bodily systems were failing but also more alert than ever. Every nerve was on fire, and nothing was working as it was supposed to. It was impossible to form a thought from beginning to completion, and she could no longer command her legs to stand. Her body collapsed into itself, and she listened to her own screams fade into oblivion as the world around her turned to black.

At first there was nothing.

Then—everything. Shreds of memories melted into the present. Lived experiences had been laced together with what could only be explained as dreams. Some belonged to her and others were borrowed from sources she did not know. Places she could navigate with her eyes closed and places she was a stranger in. Scenes she had been a part of and ones she was watching for the first time. They were all meshed together in one incoherent but persistent chain of consciousness that surged through the circuitry of her brain.

Isaac scribbling in his notebook. The smell of Seymour's. Machines in the sky. Sparring with the other agents in the Guild. Lowering the mask. Hiding in the shadows of military outposts. A room with hundreds of monitors. Standing at the doors of the Dusudé temple. Talon kneeling at her feet. The power plant. Beaches. Mountains. Oceans. Deserts. The screams of millions. A woman with one green eye and one gray. Blinding flares from an explosion. Willow holding Noah's hand. A child taking hers. Leon yelling. Toni laughing. The first of the season before there was ever a First of Season. Sunsets. The wasteland. Logan. White pulses across an infinite supply of eyes. Cassian. The vapors of freshly brewed tea in Isaac's lab. Irradiated water from the ground. The Council of Four. Buildings crumbling. Waking to Kip's face. An infant in a glass tank. The smell of burning chemicals. Bowing before the Elder Mother. Needles slipping into a neck. The sky crashing at her feet. A man with a circle on his forehead.

Her mind was tearing itself apart, and the ability to decipher any of it soon left her. She could no longer question—all she could do was receive.

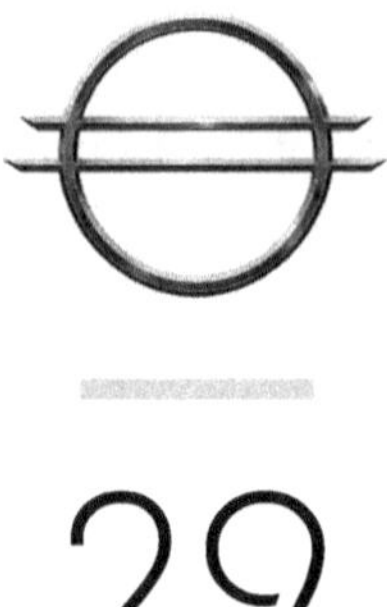

29

IN THE SHADOWS OF SIN, His light was Samuel's only guide. Divine currents coursed through his body, a body which no longer belonged to the physical realm. He moved through the corridors of the temple without form, veiled in the Creator's protection. Each step was taken with a vigilance previously unknown. The fate of Haven was in the hands of the Paladin.

Hundreds of the enemy had waited for them at the gates, but there was no stopping what could not be seen. Roh had shown him the way inside the stronghold, leaving the conflict outside a distant echo of clashing metal and crackling flames.

All around him was white. The ceilings, floors, and walls all burned a blinding and profane white. Seeing His sacred mineral misused sent Samuel's skin crawling, and the longer he dwelled on the heinous purposes for which this fortress had been built, the tighter his grip squeezed around his spear. The temple's interior had been forged with the same purity as his hallowed weapon, with which he would use to reclaim this godless place in the name of the Creator.

The first room he came to was empty, as were the halls that brought him to it. He pressed his back against the wall closest to the door and waited for any sign of life. Alone, he allowed his form to reappear, knowing that Roh's protection would need to be restored if he hoped to stay under its safeguard until he found the Elder Mother. Channeling such divine power did not come without the need for replenishment, and he would be patient as the Creator worked His miracles.

He found the divots on the device back in their original positions and lowered his arm. Between breaths he could hear the faint cries of war, but nothing else. He lowered his wrist and absorbed the barrenness of the room, trying to reason the purpose of the space. There was no logic to the depraved activities of the nonbelievers. To try and understand them was a fool's venture.

Shielded by His sacred veil once more, Samuel continued deeper into the heart of the enemy. Each room he passed was vacant, and the corridors were void of any trace of inhabitants. The space felt like an unfinished dream—white, endless and ethereal, without worldly interruption. He pressed onward. He knew the Creator would not lead him astray. Eventually His will would reveal itself.

He turned a corner and the world around him stopped moving. Polished white metal gave way to earth as the hall fed into an atrium. Towering several floors high, the room spanned the full height of the temple and opened to an opaque sky. The sun's rays carved through the smoke that had escaped from the battle happening outside and fell gently on the vegetation sprouting from the atrium's floor. Samuel was not the first to infiltrate the temple. The plants and trees to whom this part of His kingdom belonged refused to yield their home. The force that compelled them to endure was one they shared, because he too always found His light in the darkest of places. Even here—the garrison of the faithless, a festering lesion of unholy blight—the will of Roh could not be suppressed.

As blades of grass folded beneath his invisible steps, the heavenly warmth turned cold. Between the trees, something hid in the shadows of His light. Leaves parted to either side of his path until he reached the center of the atrium, where a mass of corroded machinery stood before him. Samuel traced the jagged edges to a height more than twice his own and wondered what perverse whole of which this monstrosity was once part. Stained in auburn and turquoise, the alloys of the machine had deteriorated, and as he drew closer, the air felt contaminated. An energy, perceptible only by the minute vibrations it caused in his bones, radiated from the rogue mass. It had come into existence not by the hands of Roh, but in defiance of His image.

Legends spoke of the cursed technology made in the time before the New Dawn—abominations from the Old World resilient enough to endure the sanctified purification of His kingdom. It was fitting that a relic from the age of savagery would become a monument of worship for the faithless. Haven as He had made it left no place for the evil responsible for this creation. At the Prophet's side, the Paladin would finish what the Creator started. Together, they would lead His children to a better world—a world without corruption.

A flash of gray lit Samuel's periphery. He sprang back into a defensive stance as his attention shot to the atrium's only other entrance. Down the corridor, a second ball of fire spun out against one of the walls, and then a third. His pulse leveled out when he found his form still cloaked in the Creator's protection. Whoever the attack was meant for, it was not him.

Earth turned to metal once more, and the light of the outside world was behind him as he started down the hall. Another burst of flames crashed into the wall ahead of him, and then he heard a voice.

Her voice.

"Center yourself, Kyra. We mustn't protest the duties we have been given."

His skin tingled. For the first time in days, the Elder Mother's voice came from somewhere other than the vile memories of which he could not rid himself. To be reminded that she was an affliction in the real world and not just a figment of his mind reignited a fire of his own. He quickened his pace as another voice emerged down the corridor.

"Please, Mother, I beg you, let me face him."

"The Fates have already decided our paths… and his does not end here."

"Gah!" A gray flare shot out of one of the doorways ahead. "Why? Why keep him alive? We could end this today! Kill the borrowed soul!"

The words flushed Samuel with unholy heat. His grip tightened around the shaft of the spear until he lost the feeling in his fingers. As he neared the doorway, the impulse to rush inside and cleanse it of every evil lurking within nearly took him over. But just steps away, his legs refused to move. Kodo's direction echoed in his ears:

Slay the Elder Mother. Leave the rest to us.

His breath slowed. He was not meant to question, only to receive. His brothers and sisters had their duties, and he had his.

"Destruction will be brought to our home, and those who have agreed to stay behind will not survive. But without him, our world will never find salvation."

"Our ancestors were slaughtered in the name of their god. They are the cruel and willing hands of death!" Searing gray flames roared out of the doorway and Samuel flattened himself against the corridor wall. "What have you seen? Why do you expect anything different from him?"

"Because he is not one of them. The borrowed soul has suffered just as we have. Only what was taken from us, he was never given." An explosion rang distantly, muffled by the layers of His precious mineral. "Time is leaving us. Trust what the Fates have written for you, Kyra. The salvation of our world depends on it—on him."

"I vow that one day I will return to this place. Behind me will be unimaginable numbers, and the borrowed soul will pay for his atrocities."

"Our people need a leader, not retribution. Go now, my daughter."

Bodies filed out the doorway, wretched gray bodies that had never felt the rays of His light. Samuel counted at least twenty, all with bags slung over their shoulders and crates in their hands, heading in the opposite direction of the atrium. The movement out of the room seemed to stop, and then a figure appeared in the doorway—the daughter. Her bloodshot eyes sank into the streak of purple across her face. Deep, resentful breaths turned to steam, and she threw her arms down, unleashing a wrathful blaze from each hand. Samuel pulled his face away, careful not to make any audible movements. The heat of her fury singed his cheek, and then her footsteps made their reluctant retreat down the hall.

His eyes opened to a shroud of unholy vapors, and he pulled himself off the wall. As the smoke began to settle, the figure standing in front of him gained clarity, and the dark apparition that haunted his dreams found its way back into the waking world. Between Haven and His eternal peace stood only her. The Elder Mother.

Her back was to him as she stared down the corridor where the others had gone. The scepter in her hand supported most of her being, but he would not be fooled by her frailty. Wickedness of the spirit knew no corporeal bounds.

"The soldiers of the High Army have a reputation for being the most honorable citizens in Midbell, but here you are trying to sneak up on an old woman."

Alarmed, Samuel looked for his limbs, but they were not there. His gaze tightened in contempt as it returned to the witch. She could see through the Creator's veil—a deception that he should have anticipated. He found the dial on his wrist and relinquished his remaining minutes of protection. His hand moved to the spear, preparing him for what may come next.

"Your final words, and you waste them on mockery?"

The Elder Mother's attention floated around the space in front of her, wandering amongst the billows of rising smoke. In an unexpectedly swift burst of movement, she drew a breath and swept her arm through the air. The smoke followed her inhalation, condensing into her closing fist. Samuel recoiled as the corridor was cleansed of the haze. She opened her fingers to release a faint wisp, and then, exposed in His brilliant white, there was only them.

"Let us hide no more, Samuel. Come." She turned back into the room without even so much as a glance at the one who had come to deliver her fate.

Samuel stood motionless, seething. To hear her speak his name flooded his face with bitter heat. More deception. She could try to lure him off the path, but he would never stray. Roh had ordained a future for her, and from it there was no escape.

He passed through the doorway and the air left his lungs. The resolve that had propelled him forward abandoned him mid-stride, turning his steps to nothing as his mind struggled to comprehend what he was seeing. Removed from the regular flow of time, he was paralyzed by the pair of eyes staring back at him—*his own*.

Etched in ashen strokes, his face had been drawn a hundred different times in a hundred different ways. Each breath was deafening in his ears. He whirled around the room, his sight clinging to the drawings that covered the walls. There were places he didn't know and people he had never met, yet by some abhorrent force, a version of him had been stitched into the scenes. Along the borders of the drawings, the pages were edged with writing, surrounding his image in an unholy, deranged scrawl. Such profane alterations to the natural order of events were not only a violation of his identity, but of the way the Creator intended His world to be.

"What..." Breathing felt impossible as he tried to receive the rest of his surroundings. Behind the pages, the walls curved wide beneath the shallow ceiling. Light from the outside world permeated the temple again, this time through a ring of glass skylights above. At the center of the room was a raised slab of His mineral, and a tiny gray pyre burning atop it. Somewhere, in the part of him where the High Army's standard protocol was ingrained, he absorbed the details of the space, but he had no active part in it. All he could see were the drawings.

"What is this place?" he finally managed.

The click of the scepter brought his attention to the center of the room, where the Elder Mother stood at the slab. She rested her staff against the corner and smoothed a roll of parchment on the surface. One of her fingers dipped into the nest of ash around the flame, then hovered over the flattened scroll.

"Tell me, Samuel, what is your oldest memory? Is it of this life? Or his?"

Her insolence tore him from the anarchy of his thoughts. He took another glance around the room, and then a desperation that he couldn't bury filled his voice.

"Explain this."

She brought her fingertip to the page and moved in short, deliberate strokes. "I was hoping you could tell me."

"I have no interest in your riddles, witch," he said, gritting his teeth. "The Creator has sent me to kill you."

"Yet, here I am," she said, and craned her neck closer to the page.

His eyes narrowed. The weight of his spear moved from finger to finger as his knuckles lifted off the shaft one after the other. The duty of the Paladin was to purge His kingdom of the faithless and prove that His children were worthy of eternal peace. He had come here to end her life and claim this hour in the name of Roh.

But there was hesitation.

"What is the borrowed soul?" he asked.

She retracted her finger from the parchment. The crackling of the pyre filled the silence, broken only by her steady breathing. Her gaze drifted from the page and settled on the dancing gray fire.

"The Fates have shown me three futures for our world." She raised her hand and began to knead the air over the surface of the slab. The flame bent to her motions, bowing closer to her fingertips.

"Three divergent realities. But only one can be." In defiance of the natural laws He had written, a tiny ball of ghastly fire split from the burning gray. It followed the coercion of her movements, gliding through the air until it settled above her overturned palm. "Conflict. The emboldened continuation of the path we currently travel. Perpetual disharmony and an eternity of universal deceit." She beckoned another flame out of the pyre and into her other palm. "Balance. Cohesion. Unity derived from the shared experience that is existence. Life."

The flames floated above each of her hands, sustained by impious forces. She stayed with the youngest flame, as if assessing its weight, its potential. Something that might have been a smile began to form.

But then the wrinkles on her face tightened and her eyes went cold. She returned to the pyre on the slab.

"Calamity. Permanent annihilation."

Her fists closed and the flames above them turned to smoke. She grabbed the scepter, her hand more bone than flesh, and faced Samuel.

"As our world is pushed forward by time, the borrowed soul will determine which direction it follows. If life is to persist freely, the burden will fall upon you, Samuel." Her eyes were dark in the absence of His light. "But your decision will not be without its trials. His vision of this world depends on your willingness to accept it. He will weaponize your faith and stop at nothing to keep you from seeing the truth."

She took a step forward, but Samuel stopped her with the point of his spear.

"Is that how you got the assassin to do your bidding? By polluting her mind with lies?"

She paid no mind to the spear, peering deeper into his eyes.

"Have they reduced your identity to where you can no longer feel the impact of your own actions on the universe? Willow Dinn was guided by your words."

"Lies," he snarled, and began to circle her.

The Elder Mother moved with him at the other end of the spear. "She was destined to cast off the shackles the city placed on her mind, and you were the catalyst for her liberation. It was not the call of Roh that she heard, but her own."

His knuckles were as white as the spear. "You defile His name."

"The Fates brought you to her, just as they have brought you to me."

"*He* brought me here. To kill you."

"And you will—you must."

The tip of the spear lowered, and his vision trembled with rage and confusion. They continued in their circle, but now it was the witch who was leading their movements.

"Because if you do not fulfill your duty, then she will not appear."

"Who?"

"The Prophet."

His heart missed a beat, and the spear regained its rigidity. "How do you know of such things?" he hissed.

"It is providence, Samuel. This is the judgment of the Paladin. If I do not die by your hand, then she will never appear. And without her, you will never see the truth."

"Enough of your games!" Samuel swept the spear and knocked the Elder Mother's staff out of her hands. She fell to her hands and knees, a fall from which he would make sure she would never recover. He flipped the spear back in line behind his arm and stood over her.

"They told me you would try. They told me you would use all the infernal tricks and sorcery you could to try and delude me. The assassin may have bent to your will, but I will not so easily be manipulated. Your spells are powerless against true faith. Endless, undying faith. Faith in Him, and all that He has created."

Samuel swung the tail of the spear around and bashed the side of the Elder Mother's head. The impact spattered the shaft in foul blood and sent the witch onto her back. He felt the divine currents coursing through him again as he glared at treachery's last hope, helpless on the floor beneath him.

"The evil you have spread across His kingdom will die with you," he said. "No more will be corrupted, and all shall know that His word is absolute. There is only one Creator, and it is He."

"You deserve a life that is your own… You are entitled to it, as we all are. He cannot implicate you in the inhumanity that has been brought upon this world." The Elder Mother's voice weakened with each word. "The choice will always belong to you. Listen for your call… Not the one He has forced upon you… but the one only you can hear."

"There is only His call," Samuel barked. "We are not meant to question, only to receive." He brought the tip of the spear to her throat. "Your visions have failed you. The fate of our world will not be decided in some elusive future, but today. Right now." His lungs filled with the heavenly winds. "And I choose Him. I will always choose Him."

In a single definitive strike, he raised the spear and drove it down with both hands, plunging the blade into the Elder Mother's chest. The tip met the floor beneath her body with a piercing ring. He watched the life drain out of her eyes as the holy energy filled him. Blood ran from the wound, soiling the purity of His mineral around her. A final breath escaped her lips, and then Haven was one step closer to His eternal peace.

Samuel clenched the spear and stared down at the Elder Mother's lifeless body as the sensations rushed back into his own. He fought for breaths, feeling the restlessness of something trapped beneath his skin trying to claw its way to the surface. A searing crimson tinted his vision as flashes of the witch's final seconds replayed in front of him. He placed his foot on her abdomen and yanked the spear free. Her words rattled in his head, echoing louder than when they had been spoken. He took a step back and squeezed his eyes shut. His breaths came deeper, hotter, and he opened his eyes with a scream. All around him, hundreds of eyes, *his* eyes, were staring at him, waiting to see what the Paladin would do next. He whirled around, growling at the curse that had been laid upon the walls, and landed his sights on the gray flame still burning in the center of the room.

As he approached the slab, the unholy mutations of himself watched with weighted eyes. He flattened the parchment to find that the Elder Mother's final work, base and pernicious, had been left unfinished. Like peering into a broken mirror, a fragmented image of his face looked back at him. The details were drawn with disturbing accuracy, the only alteration being his forehead, which had been marked with the crest of the Church. Underneath, there was a name. *Jonas.*

He rolled the page back up and stuck one end into the pyre. Once he had a flame of his own, he circled the room, setting the drawings on the walls ablaze. No longer would the people of Haven need to fear her. The Paladin had resisted her attempts at subterfuge and proven His children's worthiness to the Prophet.

There was no need to ask for the Creator's protection because the battle had been won. The white of the corridor shone brighter, purged of the sacrilege that had once infected it. His boots found the soft touch of earth as he crossed into the atrium. He stopped near the center and looked up. The smoke above had begun to clear, and beams of sunlight found his face. Bathing in His healing light, he knew that his actions were sanctified, and that he had fulfilled his duty to his brothers and sisters.

The mass stood before him, still radiating its noxious energy. One day he would return to this woeful place and rid every last trace of desecration. As he slid his sight down the towering insult to His brilliance, a cluster of letters caught his attention. He moved closer, squinting at the faded writing. Carved into the metal, appearing to have endured eons, were three words whose heretical significance was not meant for him:

THE CDE LIVES

The rest of the temple was quickly behind him. He found the main gates and passed through them not as the soldier who had once been held prisoner, but as the Paladin who had just conquered the bastion of heresy. The courtyard was a smoldering grave. Gray bodies littered the ground, strewn about the embers of their own offenses.

General Kodo crossed the courtyard, followed by five rows of soldiers aligned in tight formation. When he was close enough for Samuel to make out the singed whiskers of his beard, Kodo held a fist to the side of his head, and the others came to a halt behind him. The general's gaze veered from Samuel to the blade of the spear, stained with the blood of the witch.

Their eyes met, and Samuel nodded. Kodo turned to his legion and mustered a volume of a thousand men.

"Today, Haven has been purified of the blight that once threatened to consume it! Roh has deemed our crusade indomitable, and His sacred promise will soon be realized! Generations of unyielding struggle and sacrifice have led us here. The Prophet's arrival is imminent, but only because there is one of us who has proven that we are worthy of His eternal peace."

He faced Samuel and dropped to one knee. The rest of the court-yard followed, and Kodo's voice reached the heavens.

"All hail the Paladin!"

30

A SCREAM CAME SO LOUD and so painful that it brought Willow back to consciousness. The world was a grainy haze, glimpsed through her fluttering eyelids. There was movement, but nothing solid. As the scream waned into a trail of wincing and trembling breaths, she heard someone else.

"It should have never had to come to this, Annika. I'm sorry."

More movement, closer this time, and then another voice.

"The only thing I'm sorry for is that her boyfriend isn't here too. He's the reason we're in this mess!"

Her brain was several seconds behind her senses, and even after it started to catch up, the scene unfolding around her failed to fully register. There was pressure, hard and cold, against her cheek, and a dull pain behind it. Her surroundings were loosely familiar, but the picture of the room she remembered was now askew.

The crypt. She was in the crypt. That was where she was before… before what, she couldn't remember. Hours or minutes, she didn't have a sense of how much time had passed. The details trickled in, incomplete and out of order, but when she tasted the poison on her lips—sweet, sugary betrayal—everything came back to her.

A warning had come from the motion sensors, but it wasn't the Church's agents on the other side of the door. It was Leon and Jasper. They had arrived as allies, bringing with them an offering of goodwill to heal the wounds that had formed the night before—a box of temptations from Seymour's. The gesture seemed genuine, but it was difficult to fully let her guard down in their presence. Leon apologized for lashing out and said that family had to come first—always. His affability and the gentleness with which he spoke were complete reversals from the hostility of their first introduction. Paired with the taste of a freshly powdered bun, her tension began to ease.

Had she not been so preoccupied with calming herself down, she might have realized that obtaining sweets from a bakery during a citywide lockdown was impossible.

When Jasper had asked where the others were, Isaac explained the situation with the journal, and Willow described what she had found in the basement. Leon agreed that the urgency of the matter warranted immediate action and was understanding about the decision to usurp the committee—a subject that she sensed still held some tenderness for everyone in the room. Leon quickly pivoted the conversation to what had brought them to the crypt.

Licking the jelly from his fingertips, Isaac began to walk them through the chilling discovery, but as he went on, his sentences started to slow, and the spaces between his words stretched on for seconds at a time.

Willow remembered the first flicker of something off in her own body. She moved her center of gravity from one foot to the other, but neither provided stability. Her vision distorted, and an all-consuming dizziness sapped the weight from her body. The room fell to one side, and her surroundings faded to black.

In the tunnel just beyond the doorway, Leon's form solidified, and so did the body convulsing on the ground at his feet. The details of the face were wrapped in a black coil and covered by clenching hands, but the red hair underneath was unmistakable—Annika. The excruciating sounds of agony leaked through her gnarled fingers as she thrashed in the dirt. She tried to pry the coil off, but her efforts only amplified the suffering.

Leon grabbed the book from the ground beside Annika. Willow recognized the journal, but the relief she felt from knowing it had survived was washed away by the horror of seeing it in his possession. He flipped through the pages absently, staring through them as he went, and Willow watched his lips move to no sound.

Forgive me, Kip, she watched him say.

Her eyes slid across the room, where Isaac was lying face down in the place from which she had just risen. Jasper was above him, tying his hands behind his back. There was a knife on the old man's hip the size of her forearm that sent a jolt of panic to her toes.

"You really think there might be something about Jonas in there?"

"Just get them tied up, Jasper. We'll worry about the rest later." Leon pulled his head from the journal and Willow forced her eyes shut, protecting the only advantage she had. His footsteps moved past her, and she heard the *thud* of the journal on the desk.

"How much time you figure we have?" Jasper asked.

"It shouldn't be much longer now. The city has dispatched a party to come secure the assassin and her accomplices." Leon took a weighted breath in through his nose, then out through his mouth. His voice was weak. "Once they believe that they have the last surviving members of the Underground in custody, their chase will be over, and this gruesome chapter of the Guild's history will come to a close."

Willow prayed that her body wasn't shaking the way her mind was. Anger. Fear. The sparks of emotion were firing off so fast that she could no longer tell the difference between the sensations. All she felt was heat. It took everything in her power not to react, but everything wasn't enough. Her eyes flared open, but just as she went to get up, Jasper's knee met the center of her spine, sending her straight back down.

"You're not going anywhere, you little brat. The Church was promised their assassin, and they're going to have her."

She fought to reclaim her arms but control belonged to the old man. The roughness with which he handled her would have been excessive for someone twice her size. She grunted through the discomfort as he twisted her arms around. His grip was just as enraged as his words.

"Do you have any idea the damage you've caused? Hundreds of innocent lives gone in the blink of an eye, their marks on this world erased forever, and their families left scattered and severed, all because of you."

"Jasper, no more," Leon said over his shoulder as he stood facing the desk, his voice hollow.

"What are you talking about?" Willow grunted.

"Oh, you didn't hear?" Jasper was seething through his teeth. "The Church followed you to the power plant, just like I said they would." He folded her arms one on top of the other. "And they decided the best way to get rid of their little assassin was to blow 3-10 into pieces."

Willow stopped resisting. The will to fight back had left her, and the paralyzing clutches of guilt found her once more.

"That's right, you led them to our doors, and now the Guild has fallen. Decades of sacrifice turned to smoke, and for what? You're a curse! A selfish, wretched little cancer that destroys everything it touches."

"Jasper…" Leon started.

Willow blinked through the tears blurring the edges of her vision, struggling to keep the rising flood contained.

"How many people have to give their lives just for you to exist?" Jasper spat. "A fellowship built on generations of people devoted to a cause larger than themselves… brought to ash." The rope tightened around her wrists, cutting into her skin. "Your little friend's future was cut short because you couldn't control yourself." He yanked her upright and snarled in her ear. "If it wasn't for you, I bet your father would still be alive."

"That's enough!" Leon slammed his fists down on the desk. "None of this was her fault!"

"No?" Jasper snapped, his anger directionless. "Then whose was it?"

Leon's hands opened flat atop the surface of the desk, supporting much more than just the weight of his body. His shoulders rose and fell in cold silence.

"Mine."

Willow felt Jasper's hands stop moving.

"What?" the old man asked, his heat going cold. "What are you saying?"

Leon looked up at the ceiling. "She didn't lead the Church to our doors. I showed them the way."

The room went still, leaving only Annika's whimpers and the faint hum of the machines.

Jasper stood warily, the knot at Willow's wrists left unfinished. "You…"

"There was no other option, Jasper."

"I—I don't understand. Why?"

"Because they have something that belongs to me." Leon leveled his head and stared at the screen ahead of him. "And I want it back."

"What?" Jasper asked, taking a step closer. "What could be worth selling out the entire Guild?"

"Your family…" said a voice, barely breaking a whisper.

Willow's attention shot to the other side of the room, where Isaac had finally emerged from oblivion. Seeing him conscious was a cool drop of relief in a well of boiling anxieties. His eyes, glazed and battling against the weight of his eyelids, were centered on Leon.

"They took your family."

Jasper faced Leon. "No… that was years ago."

"And for years I've tried to get them back." Leon's focus shifted to different parts of the screen, watching scenes only he could see. The monitor was his portal, and through its black depths, he had been transported to distant times, distant places.

"The Church promised my family's safety if I continued to cooperate, so I did." His breath shook on the way out. "At first, it was just information. They saw us as an opportunity to strengthen their own interests in society. We were an enemy that the Church could twist and bend to fit any crime. An enemy that would always justify order. So long as nothing went too far, we could live in peace, and they would always have a reason to rule. As our numbers increased, however, so did the price. Logan was the one to identify the real utility that our organization could offer—knowledge."

"We became the ultimate resource…" said Isaac, his energy partially restored. "The harder we worked against them, the more they would benefit."

The back of Leon's head dipped ever so slightly. "The advancement of their world depends on minds like ours. We were cast off as the enemy, but the work of groups like ours has been the stimulus behind the development of everything. The Church does not fear progress—they want to control it."

"What changed?" Isaac asked. "Why end it now?"

"Things were growing unstable. Once more, someone got too close to the secrets they're hiding, and they decided that a display of force was the only way to regain control."

Leon turned around and the icy current of his direct gaze coursed through Willow. His eyes softened on her, and as the veneer of deceit finally shattered, she saw the real man inside—raw and broken.

"The last thing I wanted was for you to be involved," he said. "I tried to protect you. I did everything I could to stop Cassian from bringing you into the Guild, but not once did I consider that your path would lead you to us no matter what. You were a miracle of the Guild, and the Guild will forever be a part of you. I'm sorry this is how it must end."

"It doesn't have to, Leon," said Isaac, who had gotten himself off his stomach and was sitting upright against the gridded wall. "We can help you get them back."

"I'm afraid it's too late. The tale that the city spins of the attempt made on the grand priest's life cannot end with the assassin getting away. She's the last part of the deal. Once she's in custody, my family will be released, and Jasper and I will be allowed to reenter society, absolved of our so-called crimes."

Willow's entire being was vibrating. She was furious, angrier than she had ever been, but also completely terrified of what was about to happen. Yet from the vortex of spiraling thoughts came clarity, and with it—sheer determination. Her father, her mother, Noah, Toni and the others at the Guild, and now Annika—all their sacrifices were in pursuit of something higher. *Freedom.* Freedom to believe and freedom to live. She rejected the fate that Leon had written for her, just as she rejected the one that the city had forced upon for her.

This life was hers to live, and neither the Church nor any man could lay claim to it. She was the one who got to choose what to do with it, and she chose to be free.

The rope started to slide out of Jasper's unfinished loop around her wrists. She pressed one finger on the knot to keep it intact and then stole a look at the journal sitting next to the hand lamp on the desk.

"Do you really believe that?" Isaac asked, still regaining control of his body. "You know too much. They're using you, and once they have what they want, you'll end up just like the rest of us."

Leon ignored him and addressed Jasper. "It's time to go. The Church's agents will be here soon, and we must be gone when they arrive. To the common soldier, we're still fugitives. For this to work, we need to leave."

After a quick keystroke, the eastern door opened. Leon paused in the doorway, anticipating footsteps behind him, but when there were none, he turned back around.

Jasper, motionless and emptied of everything, stared through him. "We were your family too. Are our lives…" He swallowed something painful. "Were *their* lives… somehow worth less?"

"There isn't time for this. We must go."

The old man didn't move.

"Untie us, Jasper," Isaac said. "We can still stop him."

"Don't be a fool," Leon cut in. "The Church will kill these three, and then they'll kill you too."

Emotionless, Jasper reached for the knife on his hip. "You've already done that."

Through narrowed eyes, Leon's menace returned. "Nothing will stop me from getting my family back."

He took a step forward, but the monitor's high-pitched alarm spun him back around.

MOVEMENT DETECTED: WESTERN TUNNEL

Jasper lunged with the knife, but Leon was too quick. In the blink of an eye the old man was on the ground and Leon was on top of him with the knife buried in his ribs. Willow recoiled but saw her opportunity. She released the knot and sprang to her feet.

"Run, Willow, run!" Isaac shouted.

She tore the journal and lamp off the table and flew through the eastern door.

"No! Get back here!" Leon barked.

She clutched the journal to her chest with one arm and held out the lamp with the other as she fled deeper into the labyrinth. The tunnel ahead flickered in and out of view as the light bounced around the walls. Footsteps echoed behind her, and she flashed a look over one shoulder to find Leon's silhouette cutting through the shadows. She whirled back around, nearly tripping over the terror of his image. The sounds of her feet crashing against the earth combined with her panicked breaths made it difficult to hear, but she could faintly hear Isaac's voice from the crypt.

"Leon's after her, Cassian! I'll take care of Annika! Go!"

The path split and Willow went right without any thought. No direction was preferable when she didn't know where she was going. The adrenaline wouldn't last much longer, and if she hoped to lose him, she would need the help of the tunnels. A second fork came, and she went left this time. After that came another, and then another. Each time, she chose a turn, any turn, but around each corner she could still hear Leon's boots hammering into the dirt behind her. Her breath was moving as recklessly as the light bobbing along the walls, and she swallowed the unavoidable truth of her situation: if she could see the path in front of her, so could he. She would never be able to outrun him, and every step with the light still on was one closer to guaranteed death. In darkness, their chances would be the same.

There was another split coming up fast. She wedged the journal underneath the arm with the lamp and stretched her hand out. When the cold touch of the earth met her fingertips, the world went black.

The footsteps behind her stumbled to a stop. Wrapped in the blanket of darkness, her location was a secret even to her. Leon let out a growl, and then she heard him start to move again. Her hand was adhered to the wall, leading the rest of her along its curves and bends. She took the first few steps cautiously, then increased her pace. Leon instantly matched her speed. She may have been invisible, but her sounds could not escape his detection. To disappear completely, she would have to submit to the silent emptiness of the underground.

There were still a few turns separating them, but Leon was gaining on her. After rounding a sharp bend, she threw herself against the wall and slid to the ground, making herself as small as possible. She hugged the journal to her chest and clung to the handle of the lamp. Leon came to a stop, and she pulled herself inward even tighter. The only thing she could think to do was to stay in one spot and hope that she would be small enough for him to miss. Her resources had been exhausted, and she had nothing left with which to defend herself.

"You can't hide." Leon's voice echoed around what sounded like several corners. She could hear him scouring the darkness with a methodical slowness, hunting his trapped prey.

She drew her arms in tight, her body curling even deeper into itself. Everything was pitch black, but she closed her eyes, seeking any means of further escape.

Out of nothingness came form, and suddenly she was back in her living room on the day her father was taken. His hands were around hers, the feeling of his touch defying the bounds of memory. She heard his words now as clearly as she had in that moment, his forehead pressing against hers. *You have everything you need, right here. The mind is your greatest ally. Nobody can ever take away your ability to think freely. As long as you have that, you can find the answer to any question—the solution to any problem.* His words rang deeper as he pulled his head back and looked into her eyes. *You are brilliant and you are powerful.*

The scene evaporated back into the void when her sense of touch was stimulated by the present. Her thumb was racing up and down the back of the lamp's handle in a restless compulsion. The movement slowed as the tip of her thumb drew the image of what her eyes couldn't see. She traced a tiny circle intersected by two horizontal lines: the insignia of the Church.

It was not just any Sacred Technology, but one with which she was very familiar. Serial number range *VRL063882119063* through *VRM027751094718*. The schematics used to produce hand lamps were recycled from other related technologies: the fixtures in commercial and residential buildings, the exterior lights of certain transport variants, and most importantly, the stun flares wielded by the High Army. Even at a scale unique to the lamp, the internal structure should be identical to that of the flares. She knew the deliberate limitations of the design, as well as the potential.

Leon's footsteps were growing more defined. No longer just plods against the earthen floor, she could hear the grains of dirt shifting beneath his boots. Over top of them was the sound of his hand dragging along the wall, searching for her. He stopped and then headed in the opposite direction, backtracking along the other side of the tunnel. She had minutes, maybe less, before he would clear that stretch and move on to find her around the corner.

As quietly as she could, Willow used the tips of her nails to pry the back panel off the lamp. Inside, her fingers followed the blueprints that had been etched into her mind. One by one, she identified the different components of the system. The fuse needed to be disengaged first, and once the safeguard was inactive, she removed the wires from their lines and peeled the ends out of the lamp's shell. The biggest challenge was getting the restraining clasp off the capacitors without the proper tools, but she wrestled it loose. She tucked the wires back in, bypassing the resistor, and created a new connection. Uninhibited, the battery would surpass its intended voltage levels and turn the simple hand lamp into a makeshift stun flare. It was an unsustainable and dangerous kind of circuit to build, but it only had to work once.

Leon's sounds inched closer. "Why prolong the inevitable, Willow? There is only one way this can end."

The pounding in her temples was the edge her focus honed itself on. Terror, rage, betrayal—their amalgamation pulsed through her veins, readying her for what she was about to do. The sacrifices of the others would not be wasted. There *was* only one way this could end, and it wasn't with her leaving this world before fulfilling her duty to it.

His voice was just around the corner. "Fate will always find you, no matter how hard you resist. Your father faced his bravely, and now it is time for you to do the same."

Her mind gave the order and her body executed the command. She rose to her feet, standing straight, not straightened, and extended the lamp. As she buried her face in her opposite arm, her thumb hit the switch. The heat came first, and then a surge of light. Even with her eyes shut, tears rolled from their seams as the blinding white flash swallowed the tunnel. Leon let out a scream, a horrible, piercing scream, and she heard his body collapse to the ground. The lamp handle seared her palm, and she had to let go of it. Glass shattered at her feet and the colors behind her eyelids went cold.

She staggered forward, disoriented. Her vision was stained, and no matter how many times she tried to blink herself free of it, the light's residual burn persisted. The only sound was Leon, wincing between breaths somewhere in the darkness around her. Any impact she felt from the flare behind her covered eyes was only a fraction of the damage caused by direct exposure. Even if he managed to find his way out of the tunnels, he would likely be stuck in total blackness forever. If there was another option, she would have taken it, but the journal felt heavier in her hand now more than ever. She had a responsibility—to her father, to Noah, to the world.

What little sense of direction she had was enough to get her to the wall, and she let the cool touch of earth guide her out of Leon's reach. He made no effort to pursue her, and she listened to his suffering wither away as she continued along the wall.

A rush of boots broke through the stillness. The colors in her darkness gave way to actual light that rounded the corner ahead. Behind it were glimmers of maroon, and Willow's heart sank into her gut. After all her struggle, the Church had still won. The assassin had been caught, and the good people of Midbell could rest easily knowing that the treacherous Dinn family had finally been stopped. Their name would be erased, and the tiny flame of truth she was supposed to carry would be permanently snuffed out. It was over.

"Willow!"

Cassian.

He dropped to one knee at her feet and wrapped her in his arms. She fell into him, clutching him as tightly as her trembling limbs would allow. He pulled back and read the lines on her face.

"I saw the light. What happened?"

All she could do was shake her head, and somehow, he didn't need anything more.

"It's okay," he said with her hand in his. "It's okay."

"Where are the others?"

"There's a rendezvous point at the edge of the Eastern Radial that's meant for situations like this. Isaac and Annika know to meet us at there." He moved his hand to her shoulder. "The closest access point to the surface is less than a click away. Do you think you can make it a little farther?"

She looked down at the journal, and when she came back to him, she was not the helpless child he had rescued from the pit, but an equal on this quest to bring truth back to the world.

"Let's go," she said.

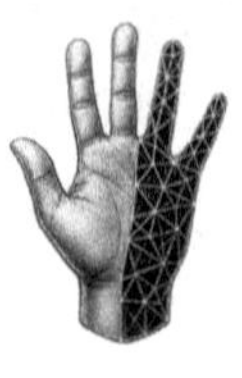

31

THE CACOPHANY OF MENTAL IMAGERY in Annika's mind was unrelenting. Behind her eyes, clenched shut with pain, thousands of scenes collided—fragmented and unrecognizable. Discernment between them was impossible, as the boundaries that separated one from the next were as incomprehensible as the content itself. Faces, voices, sights, motions, violence—all of it without any meaning. There were enough memories to fill not just one lifetime, but many.

What little connection remained to the physical world offered no escape from the torment. She threw her head from side to side, screaming without sound. The blazing sting of the coil had multiplied a hundredfold, rippling through the rest of her body. She writhed in the dirt, desperately clawing at fistfuls of earth. Every nerve was set on fire, but as real as the sensations felt, their connection to the present kept slipping.

Without warning, the pressure around her head released. Footsteps rushed closer, then a hand found her face and turned it over.

"Annika? Can you hear me, Annika?"

It was possible that Isaac was there with her, but he sounded no more real than any of the other illusions surging through her mind.

Suddenly the armor around her torso shifted and she felt herself dragged through the dirt. Spikes of pain speared her from every direction, and her shrieks found volume. The movement stopped as her body revolted against the force.

"Okay, new plan. Annika, I need you to understand exactly what is happening. You and I are outside the western entrance of the crypt, and the High Army will be here any second for us. There was too much activity detected by the motion sensors and the system triggered an emergency lockdown procedure. We probably have less than a minute to get back inside the crypt before the western door closes. Once it does, it won't open back up unless this whole place is torn apart. Right now, I need you to work with me to get you through that entrance. After that, we'll go straight to the rendezvous point where Cassian and Willow should be waiting for us."

Cut between fragments of other times and other places, she received his words. Whether he was actually there with her or not, she could not know. But through all the noise, her mind was able to complete a single, fragile calculation: the risk was too high to ignore him. She did everything in her power to latch onto the thought and follow it to completion. If Isaac was in danger, the others would soon be too. There was only one option, and it was to keep them safe from harm—no matter how real any of it was.

Paralyzing currents ran through her body. Each vertebra was throbbing, and her back arched itself off the ground. She heard herself groan as her head turned away. The hand returned to her cheek and brought her back.

"Come on, Annika, come on! Show me you can hear me. Please, anything."

If she could have given him a sign that his words had reached her, she would have. She would have let him know she could hear him and then she would have told him that his task was futile. He might be able to drag her into the crypt before the door sealed, but she would not make it much farther. Every movement was torture. Escaping through the tunnels all the way to the Eastern Radial was implausible. The agents of the Church would find another way around the crypt and have them surrounded before they ever came close to reaching the surface. In this condition, she guaranteed her company's capture.

Cassian. Isaac. Willow. This family was Kip's greatest creation. The tragedies it had suffered were undeserved, and now she had the power to prevent one more.

She started with just one fiber and then expanded her concentration to a single fingertip. To wade through the dissonance took all the excruciating focus she could summon, but she managed to find the rest of the finger, and from there, her hand. Maintaining her awareness was agonizing, and she could not afford to lend her attention elsewhere for even a fraction of a second. She fought through her body's resistance to her command and, however impermanent it would turn out to be, regained control over the limb. Pain shot from her fingertip to her neck as she peeled her arm off the ground.

"Yes, that's it, Annika! You can do it!"

To pinpoint the source of Isaac's voice, lost and floating somewhere in the abyss, was of equal challenge. Her shoulder screeched in its socket as she moved her arm across her chest. The location of his words still hung faintly in her mind, and she pushed her arm in that direction. She reached, and he was there. Her fingers closed around a handful of his shirt's collar and then hardened into a fist.

"What are you—no!"

By the time his hands grabbed her wrist, it was too late. She pulled her arm back across her chest and thrust Isaac in the direction from which his presence had first arrived. His sounds vanished into the void, and the feeling of her arm abandoned her. The earth met the back of her head as the pain she had been repressing took hold, wrathful from the time it was forced to wait. She had summoned strength beyond her body's ability to grant, and now there was nothing left to give. Her mind surrendered its hold on the present, incapable of suppressing the incursion of rogue thoughts any longer.

It was possible that somewhere in the void, she heard the latch of the door, and it was possible that on the other side, her family was safe.

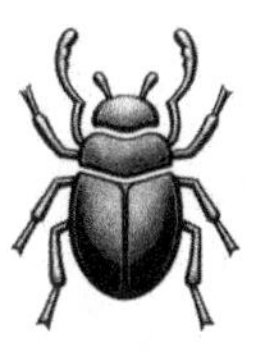

32

A BLOOD-ORANGE SUN SAT HEAVILY on the dusty horizon, the day's final ember slowly sinking into a pit of ash. Growing up, the only image Willow had of the Eastern Radial was the one the Church had painted for her: a pallid wasteland full of sin and decay. But in the hour that she and Cassian had been walking, the unseen beauty of their surroundings had not been lost on her. It was quiet, empty of the noise that filled her life in the city. Being outside the confines of civilization was as liberating as it was terrifying. To the people of Midbell, she was a fugitive, a heretic, and an objector to their god's word, but out here she could be anything. There were no laws and there was no Roh. Here, she could listen to the winds of fate tell her exactly who they needed her to be.

She learned to navigate the Radial's otherworldly terrain by watching Cassian, at first walking in the tracks he left behind through the shifting sands, then forging her own. At some point, Midbell's skyline had disappeared behind them, along with Willow's only point of reference as to which direction they were going. But not once did she doubt that Cassian knew the way, and she followed his lead without question.

The Radials were said to belong to the Old World, scabs left on the holy lands of Haven before it was ever Haven. They were ancient places, preserved eternally in the shadows of the New Dawn. There was only gray, an endless sea of ashen dunes in any direction capped by a pale sky. Even the air was tinged with a lifeless hue, and parts of her own body that she was used to seeing in color had lost their vibrancy. As different as the Eastern Radial looked from the world she knew, it also *felt* different. She remembered passing through a threshold as they emerged from the access point and her physical state altering just a percentage of a degree from what it once was. Dull yet persistent, the sensation reminded her of the current in a live wire without the bite of a shock. She wondered if the force that had brought this place into being had ever truly left it.

At several points along the way, Willow could see patches of rubble in the distance. Of what exactly, she couldn't say. The shapes were irregular, and the jagged edges indicated that the anomalies were just parts separated from their whole. Once, they came close enough for her to make out pieces of machinery strewn across the ground, corroded rusted, and possibly as old as the sand that enveloped it. Whatever it was, she was sure about what it was not—a Sacred Technology.

They worked their way up a steep incline, Cassian several steps ahead of her. He stopped at the peak, his outstretched arm warning her of the sudden drop-off. She caught her breath and panned over the landscape ahead of them. The ridge they were on continued in either direction, forming a ring that must have stretched a quarter click from one side to the other. At the center of the crater was a hulking mass of metal, partially embalmed in a tomb of sand. If laid upright, the colossus would have towered several stories high.

Her eyes were drawn to a flicker of movement among the stillness: the slender figure of a man who, just hours ago, she hadn't been sure she would ever see standing again.

She started down the slope, taking tiny, heel-driven steps. The loose sand scoffed at her attempts to keep a solid footing, and she slid down the rest of the embankment. On flat ground again, she closed the distance between the crater's rim and Isaac. Her arms wrapped around him, her fingers bunching the back of his tunic.

"I'm sorry I ran, Isaac. I'm so sorry. I didn't know what else to do."

She could barely feel his arms around her, and as he spoke, his words were almost lost to the wind.

"You did the right thing."

She let go and stepped back, unsettled by his tone. His eyes were red and swollen, and when he pulled them up from the ground to meet hers, she saw the depth of his pain. He looked behind her to where Cassian's footsteps had just come to a stop.

Willow turned around to find Cassian, the needle of their compass since they had exited the tunnels, completely lost. He scanned the area around the metal structure from one end to the other. Air moved in and out through his mouth as his focus started to lose its direction. The threads of his composure were unraveling, and Willow spun back around. As she traced the emptiness that had triggered him, he spoke the words she was thinking.

"Where's Annika?"

In the vast silence of the crater, Isaac shut his eyes and shook his head. The Radial, which had been neither cool nor warm, turned frigid.

"Where is she, Isaac?" Cassian asked.

Isaac's eyes opened, aching. "I got the coil off, but the damage was already done."

"You left her?"

"There was nothing else I could do," Isaac said, his voice breaking. "She threw me back inside the crypt just as the lockdown initiated."

Cassian dropped his head to the ground, furiously searching for something between the grains of sand.

"Cassian, I tried—"

"You tried?!" Cassian snapped, whipping his head up. "You were the one who made the coil!"

Isaac shrank and buried his gaze at his feet.

Cassian's fists tightened as he glared at Isaac, his jaw trembling. He inhaled sharply, then started for the crater's ridge.

"Where are you going?" Willow asked after him.

"To get Annika back," he said callously.

"That's a bad idea," said Isaac. "What are you going to do? Tear down the Citadel's doors and demand she be turned over? Fight the entire High Army on your own?"

Cassian stopped, lifting his quivering fists to his face. He whipped back around, his eyes bloodshot.

"I'm sorry, Isaac. I'm sorry that it's not as easy for me to leave her to die as it was for you."

Isaac folded his arms and retreated into himself again.

Cassian paced back and forth in front of them. His breathing slipped into panting, and Willow recognized the anxious state that had claimed him. It was grief and it was fury. It was losing someone so important that the binding that held the world together came undone. It was watching an existence that felt so integral to the workings of the universe be ripped out of it. Negotiation was impossible. Fate had made a ruling, and nothing could overturn the decision. The universe would keep moving with or without his permission.

But whether or not he would have to endure it alone was her choice.

Cassian clutched his head and then threw his helmet into the sand. His fingers squeezed through tufts of hair as he switched back in the opposite direction. He ran his hands down the back of his neck and came to a stop. Rampantly, he stripped the shield off his back and hurled it at the ground. It skipped off the surface and kicked up a cloud of debris. As the dust settled, the shield lay flat on the earth, and the Church's crest beamed victoriously up at the sky.

He pulled the mallet off his back and dropped to his knees, driving the weapon into the heart of the insignia. The shield cracked and he pulled his arm back to the sky. He hit it again, and then again. Harder and harder, the spike of the hammer came crashing into the shield until he was striking broken fragments of metal scattered in the sand. Cassian cried out with each swing. Not words, just sounds.

As he pulled back one last time, Willow grabbed his hand. He froze, not needing to say anything, because she understood. The mallet fell into the sand beside him and he crumbled into her, weeping.

33

ELATION. EUPHORIA. THE MAIN CABIN of the transport was bubbling with divine celebration. Along the handrails of the inner walls, soldiers were on their feet passing chatter, tears, and laughter from one end to the other. To see his brothers and sisters rejoicing in the spiritual spoils of their crusade made Samuel certain that he would endure the trials of the Paladin a hundred times over if this was the reward. The hum of the transport's ventilation systems muddled their conversations, but he didn't need to hear what they were saying. His light shone brightly on all their faces. Roh's children had been patient, waiting generations for the prophecy to be fulfilled, and now His sacred promise would soon be realized. Their undying love for the Creator and their commitment to His vision for Haven had transformed their world from one that needed saving to one that saved itself. It was beautiful, and it was precisely how He had envisioned the citizens of His kingdom coming together. Without the deception of the faithless threatening their way of life, the path to eternal peace was finally theirs to take.

Samuel knew that the duties of the Paladin had only just begun. To prove that His children were worthy was the first in a lifetime of challenges through which he was privileged enough to lead his people. When they landed, he would wait for Kodo's transport, and together they would return to the Citadel. They would kneel before the throne and recount the details of their victory to the grand priest. Preparations would begin for the Prophet's arrival, and the nature of what would come next could only be known by the Creator. He was not to question, only to receive. When the time came, he would be ready to commit his entire being to whatever the Prophet asked of him.

A low beep rang from the pilot's console. Samuel recognized it—an alert that a transmission had come through—and entered the cockpit. The secondary pilot was waiting for him with an earpiece in hand.

"Who is it, brother?" Samuel asked.

"It's from Commander Logan's channel, sir."

He held the device to his ear and heard Sybil's voice clearly over the dull drone of the transport's engine. Her words sent his heart into the pit of his stomach. Their mission at the power plant had gone as planned—the facility and any trace of the insurgency there had been destroyed—but the transfer of the assassin from the informant into the Church's custody had failed. The team dispatched to apprehend her had been locked out of the insurgents' satellite base and was now attempting to force its way in.

Samuel lowered the earpiece. "Were there any coordinates included on that transmission?"

The secondary pilot flicked a knob and a pair of numbers appeared on the screen.

"Hail General Kodo's transport," Samuel said. "Let him know that we are changing course."

"Right away, sir."

THE TUNNELS WERE AN ENDLESS cloud of dust, billowing in the radiance of Sacred Technology. His brothers and sisters had acted fast, deploying standing lamps at every junction and bringing His light where there had been so much darkness. Maroon bodies cut in and out of the haze, some moving farther into the depths, and others back toward the access point. A pair of soldiers entered from another vein in the tunnels ahead of him, carrying an industrial saw between them. They rushed around the corner, passing Sybil as she strode toward Samuel.

"Greetings, Paladin," she said with a bow of her head. "I am rejoiced to see you alive."

"Thank you, sister. As I you." He returned her gesture. "How are things proceeding? How can I help?"

Her lips flashed a smile, but she let it go no further.

"What we know right now is that the assassin and several of her accomplices have escaped through the tunnels." Sybil started back the way she came, and Samuel fell in beside her. "The entrance is locked with an advanced firmware, but our demolitions team is about to breach the door. Hopefully, there will be some insight on the other side as to where she has gone."

"And the informant?"

"When we received word that the base was sealed, Commander Logan and I separated. I came here and he entered the tunnels through a second access point to the north. He and his search team found the informant, blinded and left for dead by the assassin, then brought him back to the surface for further interrogation."

Just then a scream came from around the corner. Samuel was in a sprint before the noise had consciously registered. In front of the base's entrance, a group of soldiers huddled over something—someone. As he slowed to a stop, the others parted without command. A woman writhed on the ground, her copper hair strewn across the dirt. He knelt beside her, scouring every detail of her body in search of a remedy. There were no visible wounds or damage to her armor, yet her face was twisted in agony.

Sybil's footsteps approached from behind him. He addressed her over his shoulder, unable to look away from the woman. "One of ours?"

"No," Sybil said. "An insurgent. The armor was stolen, most likely part of the larger plot to aid the assassin."

As hard as he tried, Samuel could not pull himself away from the woman.

"What's wrong with her?"

"We don't know," Sybil said. "Each time we try to move her, she resists. Any physical contact induces further pain. May the strength of Roh find her soon, because we are going to transport her to the prison momentarily."

The longer he stayed with the woman, the shallower his breaths became. A force, deep and primordial, held him in its grasp, and he was powerless to resist it. His surroundings lost their definition, and then there was only her. He should have felt contempt for the creed she had dedicated her life to and the unholy acts she was involved in. He should have been pleased that one less voice would be shouting dissonance against His name. Yet he felt none of those things. Her presence transported him to a time before the ideological divide between them ever existed. Before Haven's need for its Paladin. Before the word of Roh.

Her eyelids flickered open and the unearthly emerald irises behind them stole what remained of Samuel's breath. She found his eyes, and her mouth started to move. It was barely more than a whisper, but he could hear nothing else.

"Jonas?"

ABOUT THE AUTHOR

TY HERSEY lives in the Berkshires with his partner and two cats. When he's not working on his manuscripts or at his office job as a programmer, he's likely scouring the book and record stores of Vermont or at home watching a Studio Ghibli movie with a cup of tea. *Sacred Technologies* is his first novel.

For more information about
The New Dawn Trilogy, please visit:

WWW.TYHERSEYBOOKS.COM